MR. BELUNCLE

V. S. PRITCHETT

Mr. Beluncle

A Novel

Introduction by Darin Strauss

THE MODERN LIBRARY

NEW YORK

V. S. Pritchett

Victor Sawden Pritchett, the extraordinarily prolific and versatile man of letters widely regarded as one of the greatest stylists in the English language, was born in Ipswich, Suffolk, on December 16, 1900. His father, whom he recalled in the enchanting memoir *A Cab at the Door* (1968), was a boundlessly optimistic but chronically unsuccessful businessman whose series of failed ventures necessitated frequent moves to elude creditors. These uprootings interrupted Pritchett's formal education, yet he was a voracious reader from an early age. Apprenticed in the London leather trade at fifteen, Pritchett alleviated the boredom of a menial clerical job by delving into the classics. At twenty he left for Paris, vowing to become a writer. He later reflected on his experiences there in *Midnight Oil* (1971), a second volume of autobiography that endures as an intimate and precise record of an artist's self-discovery.

Pritchett began his writing career as a contributor to *The Christian Science Monitor,* which, in addition to sending him on assignments in the United States and Canada, employed him as a foreign correspondent in civil-war Ireland and then Spain. *Marching Spain* (1928), his first book, recounts impressions of a country that held a lifelong fascination for Pritchett. His other travel writing includes *The Spanish Temper* (1954), *The Offensive*

Traveller (1964; published in the U.K. as *Foreign Faces*), and *At Home and Abroad* (1989). In addition, he collaborated with photographer Evelyn Hofer on three acclaimed metropolitan profiles: *London Perceived* (1962), *New York Proclaimed* (1964), and *Dublin: A Portrait* (1967).

While continuing a part-time career as a roving journalist, Pritchett increasingly focused on writing fiction, living with his Anglo-Irish first wife in Dublin, and then in the bohemian London of the mid to late 1920s. *Clare Drummer* (1929), the first of his five novels, draws on his experiences in Ireland, while *Elopement into Exile* (1932; published in the U.K. as *Shirley Sanz*) again reflects his enthrallment with Spain. He also wrote *Nothing Like Leather* (1935), a compelling saga about the rise and fall of an English businessman, and *Dead Man Leading* (1937), an allegorical tale of a journey into darkness reminiscent of Conrad. Pritchett's best-known novel, *Mr. Beluncle* (1951), is a work of Dickensian scope featuring an endearing scoundrel-hero modeled after his own father.

Yet it is widely acknowledged that Pritchett's genius as a storyteller came to full fruition in the short fictions which he began to publish in his early twenties and continued to write up to his nineties. "Pritchett's literary achievement is enormous, but his short stories are his greatest triumph," said Paul Theroux. From *The Spanish Virgin and Other Stories* (1930) right up through *Complete Collected Stories* (1991), Pritchett published fourteen volumes filled with masterful tales that chronicle the lives of ordinary people through a flood of details and humorous, kindhearted observations. His other collections, all of them published during his long second marriage to Dorothy—a working partner as well as an adored wife—include: *You Make Your Own Life* (1938), *It May Never Happen* (1945), *The Sailor, Sense of Humor, and Other Stories* (1956), *When My Girl Comes Home* (1961), *The Key to My Heart* (1964), *Blind Love* (1970), *The Camberwell Beauty* (1974), *Selected Stories* (1978), *On the Edge of the Cliff* (1980), *Collected Stories* (1982), *More Collected Stories* (1983), and *A Careless Widow* (1989).

"We read Pritchett's stories, comic or tragic, with an elation that stems from their intensity," observed Eudora Welty. "Life goes on in them without flagging. The characters that fill them—erratic, unsure, unsafe, devious, stubborn, restless and desirous, absurd and passionate, all peculiar unto themselves—hold a claim on us that is not to be denied. They demand and get our rapt attention, for in their revelation of their lives, the secrets of our own lives come into view." And Reynolds Price noted: "An extended view of his short fiction reveals a chameleonic power of invention, sympathy and selfless transformation that sends on back as far as Chekhov for a near-parallel."

The acclaim lavished on Pritchett for his short stories has been matched by that accorded his literary criticism. "Pritchett is not only our best short story writer but also our best literary critic," stated Anthony Burgess. *In My Good Books* (1942), *The Living Novel* (1946), *Books in General* (1953), and *The Working Novelist* (1965) contain essays written during his long association with the *New Statesman* and also, after the Second World War, *The New Yorker* and *The New York Times Book Review.* Pritchett continued his exploration of world literature in *George Meredith and English Comedy* (1970), *The Myth Makers* (1979), *The Tale Bearers* (1980), *A Man of Letters* (1985), and *Lasting Impressions* (1990). His magnum opus of literary criticism, *Complete Collected Essays*—which reflects, too, his central association with *The New York Review of Books,* from the journal's earliest days—was issued in 1992. In addition he produced three masterful works that artfully meld criticism with biography: *Balzac* (1974), *The Gentle Barbarian: The Life and Work of Turgenev* (1977), and *Chekhov: A Spirit Set Free* (1988).

"Pritchett is the supreme contemporary virtuoso of the short literary essay," said *The New York Times Book Review.* As Gore Vidal, who deemed him "our greatest English-language critic," put it: "At work on a text, Pritchett is rather like one of those amorphic sea-creatures who float from bright complicated shell to shell. Once at home within the shell he is able to describe for us in precise detail the secrets of the shell's interior; and he is able to show us, from the maker's own angle, the world the maker saw." "It would be very nice for literature," Vidal added, "if Sir Victor lived forever."

From the 1950s on, Pritchett was increasingly in demand as a distinguished visiting professor at American universities, from Princeton to Berkeley, Smith to Vanderbilt. But in spirit he always remained a freelance writer. "If, as they say, I am a Man of Letters I come, like my fellows, at the tail-end of a long and once esteemed tradition in English and American writing," Pritchett once said. "We have no captive audience. . . . We write to be readable and to engage the interest of what Virginia Woolf called 'the common reader.' We do not lay down the law, but we do make a stand for reflective values of a humane culture. We care for the printed word in a world that nowadays is dominated by the camera and by the scientific, technological, sociological doctrine. . . . I found myself less a critic than an imaginative traveller or explorer . . . I was travelling in literature."

Contents

Introduction

Darin Strauss

1.

V. S. Pritchett, in one of his many pleasing, unpedantic mid-century essays, wrote that "no one reads Scott now," and by the end of the first paragraph he managed, insightful critic that he was, to explain why that was so—Sir Walter Scott's language "nags and clatters," for one thing—but who could explain why no one reads Pritchett now?

"He is by such a margin the greatest English writer alive that it hardly seems worth saying"; "No one alive writes a better English sentence"; "In the variety of his powers I think he is now unrivalled"—Pritchett drew all this rowdy applause and more in 1982, with the huge success of his *Collected Stories,* the 1,926,172nd most popular book on Amazon at the time of this writing.[1] What's more, Pritchett's been dead less than eight years, and until now, you couldn't find mention of his most famous novel—the hilarious book you hold in your hands—anywhere on the Amazon website, not even with the out-of-print titles, the unvisited hardcovers deemed undeserving of graphics. It's as though one of the great comic novels of the 1950s had never been written.

And it's not just Amazon. Pritchett, knighted for services to literature in 1975, may have been a favorite of Eudora Welty, Raymond Carver, William Trevor, A. S. Byatt, John Updike, Martin Amis, Kingsley Amis, Salman Rushdie, etc., and yet I know a score of young (and not so young) American fiction writers who have never read him. And for silly reasons! One novelist told me recently: "He seems too aristocratted out, Pritchett—the stodgy name." Another said, "It's stupid, but I always get him confused with V. S. Naipaul. [So] I never bothered."

Of Pritchett's forty books of fiction, nonfiction, biography, and literary criticism, exactly one is in American print at the time of this writing (not counting the posthumously published *The Pritchett Century*. With that book, and Modern Library's publication of this novel and also Pritchett's *Essential Stories*, one hopes that Pritchett's star will again rise).

The speedy decline of Pritchett's fortunes is puzzling; he's as accessible a titan as ever lived—generous, witty, impossible to dislike: "One of great pleasure givers in our language," to quote Welty. Check out the opening of *Mr. Beluncle,* with its mischievousness, its sly reference to the devastation that awaited 1940s England; check out the music of the prose:

> Twenty-five minutes from the centre of London the trees lose their towniness, the playing fields, tennis courts, and parks are as fresh as lettuce, and the train appears to be squirting through thousands of little gardens. Here was Boystone before its churches and its High Street were burned out and before its roofs were stripped off a quarter mile at a time. It had its little eighteenth-century face—the parish church, the alms-houses, the hotel, the Hall—squeezed by the rolls and folds of suburban fat. People came out of the train and said the air was better—Mr. Beluncle always did . . .

Isn't this just what we want in a first paragraph, a fresh way of seeing the familiar? What a jolt it is to read a writer like Pritchett today, when so many books plod along efficiently but never try to take off flying.

Because of those lower-middle-class Londoners whom Pritchett so often drew, the antique dealers, morticians, and homeowners who peopled his stories, he was called a "narrowly and definably" British writer,[2] but in his prose, at least, he was pretty un-British—and by that I mean he was a stylist unlike the sort of wholly conventional, stout writer that Britain was so adept at producing in Pritchett's heyday. The devilishness, the turmoil and forward rush of his language ("As he says this he gives a lick of glee to his lips and his hands jump"[3]), the cheerful loose risky metaphors, locate Pritchett closer to a homespun maximalist like Isaac Babel than, say, to John Galsworthy, Haddon Chambers, or W. Somerset Maugham—authors who share a kind of received flatness in tone.

(I think it's relatively uncontroversial to argue that, at least until recently, most vibrant English-language prose came from outside England, from authors who brought external rhythms to the language: Joseph Conrad, who grew up in the Polish Ukraine and for whom English was a third tongue; the Irishman James Joyce; American expatriates Ernest Hemingway and Gertrude Stein, two stylized experimenters influenced by the painter Paul Cézanne and the particular cadences of American English; Saul Bellow, an American Jew, whose writing style is built of Eastern European inflections and Chicago slang; the transplanted Russian Vladimir Nabokov; and, more recently, Indo-English authors such as Salman Rushdie. There were a few exciting Anglo-Saxon English stylists who were Pritchett's contemporaries, including the strange and spirited Henry Green and, some would argue, Virginia Woolf. Moreover, contemporary English authors—Martin Amis, most notably—have picked up the vitality of these earlier writers, and today's England has its share of vibrant stylists. But enough of this; we're here to talk about Pritchett.)

An example of Pritchett's vitality, more or less picked at random:

> [London is] like the sight of a heavy sea from a rowing boat in the middle of the Atlantic. . . . One lives in it, afloat but half submerged in a heavy flood of brick, stone, asphalt, slate, steel, glass, concrete, and tarmac, seeing nothing fixable beyond a few score white spires that splash up like spits of foam above the next glum wave of dirty buildings.[4]

But if his sentences are crowded and more often than not carry a barb of surprise, a little razzle-dazzle, Pritchett was rarely a showy writer and never a lofty one, even in his literary criticism. In fact, he's probably the most unassuming great lyrical stylist you can think of. There's a casualness about his language, for all its inspired metaphoricity—an offhanded air you'll never find in, say, Nabokov, to name another notable stylist. Pritchett, for example, would often repeat words with seeming haphazard ("He sourly began to ruin the line of his poem that never progressed beyond this line"[5]) and make use of unpolished colloquialism ("Through all the towns that run into one another as you might say, we caught it"[6]). Of course, he had an enormous technical proficiency—and so what appeared to be prosaic chattiness was really a chosen element of his painstaking craftsmanship. His style never trumpets its own great stylishness, and I'd venture that this casualness is not only the core of Pritchett's famed equanimity but also a theory of aesthetics in itself, a lesson to other writers: Develop an artful style—"the distinctive voice which is indispensable to the short-story writer and the poet,"[7] as the man himself put it—but all the same, don't get too caught up in formal perfection; never torpedo a story for the sake of its prose.

2.

V. S. Pritchett was very funny. His is the comedy of ordinary lives meticulously observed, and his eye is keen in *Mr. Beluncle*.

Comedy of close surveillance is reliant on context; *Mr. Beluncle* is full of laughs that, like shadows, would die if I were to shine a light on them; also, to quote any of the best lines here would spoil your fun later.

I will tell you, though, that like most great comedy, *Mr. Beluncle* makes sport of the Stuffed Shirt, the Hypocritical Pious Gentleman, and the Tyrant, as well as the Big Spender—and all these descriptions fit a single character: Mr. Beluncle himself. A furniture manufacturer as plump as a scone, egotistical, superreligious when it suits him, despotic, a miser whose taste runs to expensive houses, childish nearly all the time, a world-class bullshitter, and one of the more haunting characters of twentieth-century fiction, Mr. Beluncle dominates the novel as he does his wife and three children. He is Pritchett's grand, comic, and heartbreaking invention, and he is derived, at least in part, from the author's own father.

Walter Pritchett, often on the threshold of financial ruin, had a habit of always relocating his family on a whim, to avoid creditors. That's true for Beluncle, too:

> The furniture van would be at the door. . . . The taxi arrived. Mrs. Beluncle would be sobbing; Mr. Beluncle would be catching two trains—one to put his family into and one for some business errand of his own. In the taxi, if Mrs. Beluncle was still crying, Mr. Beluncle would sing: "*Tell me the old story*" and go on with warmth, putting his arm around Mrs. Beluncle, to the second verse: "*Tell me the story simply, for I forget so soon.*" ("Yes, you forget, you forget. I remember," Mrs. Beluncle called out.) Or, if the removal was especially disastrous, Mr. Beluncle would sing a song to remind her of their courtship, like "*Oh dry those tears, oh calm those fears—Life will be better tomorrow.*"

Pritchett duplicated this scene almost to the letter—with his father singing the very same lyrics to calm his mother—in *A Cab at the Door,* his autobiography.

There are more similarities between Beluncle and Pritchett's father, more convergences of the author's life and his fiction. Pritchett's father tried on and discarded religions time and again, never giving thought to how this might distress his family.

Likewise, in the Beluncle family, God is always changing His mind.

> Once God had been a Congregationalist; once a Methodist. He had been a Plymouth Brother, the several kinds of Baptist, a Unitarian, an Internationalist; later, as Mr. Beluncle's business became more affluent, he had been a Steiner, a Theosophist, a New Theologian, a Christian Scientist, a Tubbite, and then had changed sex. . . . to become a follower of Mrs. Crowther. . . .

Mr. Beluncle's search for a creed that will jibe with his own feelings of omnipotence leads him to the Church of the Last Purification, Toronto—a religion "dedicated to the belief that evil and therefore pain of all kinds are illusions of the physical senses." The local chapter worships in a rented dance hall next to a run-down movie theater. But the religion flatters Mr. Beluncle. Everything he does is according to the will of God.

Although this Church of the Last Purification, Toronto, springs from Pritchett's imagination, it bears many similarities to the real-life religion the Church of Christ, Scientist, the sect the author's father eventually settled on.

Pritchett tells us that his Church of the Last Purification, Toronto, was founded by a Mrs. Parkinson; the Church of Christ, Scientist, was established by Mary Baker Eddy, who argued that given the God's perfection, He never would have created sin, disease, and death; those blights, therefore, weren't a part of God's reality. The material world was a deceptive combination of spiritual truth and material "error" that could be transcended through a more perfect spiritual understanding. "Error," not coincidentally, is the bugaboo that vexes Pritchett's Church of Last Purification, Toronto. And on it goes.

Pritchett plays screwball doctrine for laughs, but not only for laughs. Given his own past, he was hung up on unpopular religions and how they're seen by the majority. In one of *Mr. Beluncle*'s funniest and most excruciating passages, Beluncle's oldest son Henry—something of a stand-in for a young V. S. Pritchett—has to defend the Church of Last Purification to a skeptical teacher named Mr. O'Malley, in front of a full classroom.

"How dare you contradict me, Beluncle!" said Mr. O'Malley. "Do you stand there in your idiocy and tell me that if you fell out of that window, three floors into the street, and broke your neck, you would say it was a false belief and hadn't happened?"

A murmur of laughter came from the other boys. . . .

"I would, sir."

"Oh no you wouldn't, sir," said Mr. O'Malley. "Oh no you wouldn't. You couldn't, sir. You'd be dead, sir."

This scene, too, has its twin in Pritchett's oeuvre. His oft-anthologized story "The Saint" also concerns the "isolated and hated" Church of the Last Purification, Toronto. In that story, a schoolteacher—who is, like *Beluncle*'s Mr. O'Malley, an Irishman in England—condemns the church, in much the way O'Malley does, asking the narrator the very same "if you fell out a window" question, his eyes sparkling with pure pleasure.

There was a reason Pritchett wrote so often about radical religion (and the rejection of it): What better way to examine hypocrisy, self-discovery, the influence of one's parents, the price of nonconformity, and the warped vanity of the outcast?

This is Mr. Beluncle inducing his sons to join him at a lecture by a Mr. Van der Hoek, which will presumably show the superiority of spiritual life over the world of material possessions:

> "I want you boys to come . . . Mr. Van der Hoek is one of the Big Three in the movement. That man gave up a thousand pounds a year in dentistry [to join the church]. Sacrificed everything. I don't know what he makes now. Three thousand perhaps," said Mr. Beluncle.

Religion, then, as a way to better yourself spiritually, morally, socially, and financially.

Mr. Beluncle wounds nearly everybody he meets; and all of those wounded submit willingly to their hurts. *Mr. Beluncle* is a family novel, and Jeremy Treglown, in his sharp, persuasive biography of Pritchett, calls the book "a study of abusive relationships."[8] But while Treglown's modern phrase certainly fits the way that we in the twenty-first century would view Beluncle's treatment of his sons and especially his wife, you may find it useful also to see the novel as a depiction of family politics as they existed in the twilight of household autocrats like Beluncle. The novel plays out along the front edge of the social changes that would force husbands and fathers to reconsider the nature of patriarchy; twenty years after the events of this story—or, if not twenty, then fifty—Beluncle's brand of middle-class familial despotism will have gone the way of the doctor's housecall.

Beluncle's sons—unlike their father in their sensitivities, and more like the men of our generation—often find themselves crying when Beluncle speaks to them, sometimes for no reason other than the heaviness of his presence in their lives; sometimes it's merely the peculiar joy they feel in yielding to his will.

It's handy for Mr. Beluncle when people yield to his will, because he sees disagreement as his religion would have him perceive "error"—that is, he persuades himself that it isn't important.

It was a way [for Beluncle to turn] realities into unrealities and that was rather urgent. . . . A quotation from the Bible would transpose the dispute to the moral plane where it would become more congenial and more manageable.

Religion, then, is also a way to get out of any moral dilemmas that are bothersomely real.

Although Mr. Beluncle dominates the book, Pritchett is an excited connoisseur of human quirks, and the novelist's all but Tolstoyan touch gives unpredictablity, complexity, and singleness to most every character: the corybantic schoolteacher O'Malley, who gnashes his teeth if he's called Irish; the secretary Miss Vanner, whose cheeks color over "in some continual, unpeaceful, private struggle" and whose "sorrow was a way of punishing" the men she dealt with; Mr. Phibbs, the socialist churchgoer who "had the detachment of those belonging to an old culture which has reached the phase of contemplation"; Mrs. Truslove, Beluncle's business partner, who takes off her glasses when she talks of private matters—the most private being her platonic sort-of love affair with Mr. Beluncle, which is an infidelity only because it's approached in a spirit of infidelity.

V. S. Pritchett, like Henry James, is a writer on whom no detail is lost.

3.

Not that this book is perfect.

I mentioned that Pritchett gives complexity to *most* every character. Consider Mr. Beluncle's wife, Ethel, who "even in sleep seemed to be shouting out an insult." It's a surprise that despite her prominence in the novel, Ethel seems underused by Pritchett. Not that he doesn't make this woman vivid for us;

as ever, with a hunter's eye, Pritchett targets the little rifts in the sides of his character's speech or appearance or ethics. He always strikes a great note, describing his people in wonderful detail—but Ethel, for one, never gets a second note. Her sorrow is mentioned without being fully investigated. This is a shame, because that long disappointment, Ethel Beluncle's daily life, offered the author a chance to examine even further the human cost of household despotism; it was a chance Pritchett missed. (In the coming years, quite a few women novelists would, of course, write about this with famous success.)

E. M. Forster said of Charles Dickens's characters that often they're "flat but vibrating very fast." The characters are, in other words, the quintessence of their eccentricities and nothing besides. Pritchett is as good as any writer in history at depicting the surface life of his characters, but at his worst—which comes very rarely—the luminosity of those characters comes across as merely stagy. I'm thinking mainly of Beluncle's youngest son, Leslie, an irritating and falsely precocious boy, who deals out lame one-liners like a TV sitcom kid. What's more, Mr. Beluncle's sister is introduced with a flourish, but then the subplot dedicated to her languishes.

Which brings us to another criticism: At times—not often, mind you, but occasionally—*Mr. Beluncle*'s narrative lacks a sense of forward progress. Now and again one gets the feeling, even with the most inspired, distinctive characters—and there are many of them: Mrs. Truslove, Henry Beluncle, Mr. Vogg, Chilly, Mrs. Vanner, Mr. Phibbs, and of course the classic, inimitable Mr. Beluncle himself—that Pritchett isn't putting them through their paces enough, that the novel's story lines aren't as fruitful as they might have been.

Perhaps all this accounts for the one knock against Pritchett that dogged him even when he was in vogue: that the man was a better short story writer than novelist. Think of him as an English John Cheever—another writer who had an intelligence for the rigors of the concise, a lyrical gift, and a calling to observe the conventions of his own class and place. But if both men never exceeded the brilliance of their short stories, they also wrote novels that dazzled in their own right—Cheever's

Bullet Park and *Falconer* and, of course, this near masterpiece of Pritchett's. And make no mistake. For its small blemishes, *Mr. Beluncle* is still a book to be admired and loved.

That's why it kills me to have written at all critically of it. I point out what I see as the novel's few flaws just to prove that I'm not merely a witness for the defense. But you don't speak ill of one of the writers you most esteem and enjoy without feeling heavy-hearted and suspicious of your own conclusions. Kingsley Amis thought *Mr. Beluncle* proved that Pritchett was mid-century England's leading author, and I agree with him. This is an inviting and expert book, wise and beautiful, and best of all, it's heartbreaking and funny at once: It holds in view the totality of a distinctive family, in all its viciousness and affection, its sadness and comedy.

A book in which brutality is only one facet of an unhappy family's daily life—maybe that's why this novel has been undervalued by today's readers, who have come of age to the simplicity of melodrama.

Recently, I read a book that was published not too long after Pritchett wrote *Mr. Beluncle* : Richard Yates's *Revolutionary Road,* a harrowing story of desolation in the American suburbs. It's a book that, more than ten years after Yates's death, has found quite a large following among young writers and readers. *Revolutionary Road*'s revival, in fact, prompted the biographer Blake Bailey to write *A Tragic Honesty: The Life and Work of Richard Yates,* a 2003 bestseller. Yates's novel is very fine, severe, gorgeous in parts, its every scene lighted by the kind of crucial authorial compulsion you often find in the classics. All the same, Mr. Beluncle is the superior book on almost every count. I compare them because both take consumerism, the suburbs, and troubled families as their chosen topics—and yet these novels go about their business quite differently.

A story of brutal, unremitting desolation—a *Revolutionary Road*—will always be more fashionable than a story that, without melodrama, shows a troubled family's life in all its many sides.

Melodrama, being histrionic and unchanging in the bleakness of its tone, rarely achieves the complexity of real art: *Everything is awful all the time* is just the simplistic, artless *Everything is wonderful all the time* stood on its head. Pritchett understood that. As much as people called him a craftsman, an old warhorse, and a man of letters, V. S. Pritchett was a true artist. In his novels, in his hundreds of stories, there's never a hint of melodrama or sentimentality.

And so, more even than Pritchett's X-ray eye for detail, his eager and grounded intellect, the power of his prose—the very fun of it—the quality that stays with me most about *Mr. Beluncle* is that, while an author like Richard Yates has disdain for the characters in *Revolutionary Road*, V. S. Pritchett's sweetness of temperament led him to empathize even with the nastiest or most wretched of his people.

He's one of the very best writers of the twentieth century.

———

DARRIN STRAUSS is the author of the novels *Chang and Eng, The Real McCoy,* and the forthcoming *Family Love.* He teaches at New York University and lives in Brooklyn.

NOTES

1. The people who wrote these kindnesses about Pritchett were, in order: Frank Kermode, Irving Howe, and Philip Toynbee. The good news for today's readers is that the Modern Library has just published a new edition of Pritchett's revelatory *Essential Stories,* along with this re-release of *Mr. Beluncle.*
2. *The New York Review of Books,* "V.S.P.," 11/08/1990
3. V. S. Pritchett, *More Collected Stories,* "The Last Throw" (New York: Random House, 1983), page 61.
4. V. S. Pritchett, *London Perceived* (New York: Random House, 1976) pp. 1–2.
5. *Mr. Beluncle,* p. 101.
6. V. S. Pritchett, *Collected Stories,* "Sense of Humor" (New York: Random House, 1982), p. 112.
7. V. S. Pritchett, *Collected Stories* (New York: Random House, 1982), preface, p. x.
8. Jeremy Treglown, *V. S. Pritchett: A Working Life* (New York: Random House, 2005) p. 208.

To Dorothy

MR. BELUNCLE

I

Twenty-five minutes from the centre of London the trees lose their towniness, the playing fields, tennis courts and parks are as fresh as lettuce, and the train appears to be squirting through thousands of little gardens. Here was Boystone before its churches and its High Street were burned out and before its roofs were stripped off a quarter of a mile at a time. It had its little eighteenth-century face—the parish church, the alms-houses, the hotel, the Hall—squeezed by the rolls and folds of pink suburban fat. People came out of the train and said the air was better—Mr Beluncle always did—it was an old town with a dormitory encampment, and a fizz and fuss of small private vegetation.

The Beluncles were always on the look out for better air. Mr Beluncle moved them out to Boystone from the London fume of Perse Hill when Henry was fourteen and had a bad accent picked up at half a dozen elementary schools.

"Aim high," said Mr Beluncle, "and you'll hit the mark."

He wrote to six of the most expensive Public Schools in England and read the prospectuses in the evening to his family, treating them as a kind of poetry; blew up when he saw what the fees were, said, "Every week I pick up the paper and see some boy from Eton or Harrow has been sent to prison, dreadful thing when you think what it cost their fathers," and sent his boys to Boystone Grammar School.

The Beluncle boys lifted their noses appreciatively. The air was notably better than at Perse Hill Road. They were shy, reserved and modest boys who kept away from one another in school hours and who rarely came home together. When they saw one another, they exchanged deep signals out of a common code of seriousness and St Vitus's dance. "We are singular," they twitched. "No one understands us. We have a trick up our sleeves, but it is not time to play it." They separated and carried on with their shyness which took the form of talking their heads off.

The Beluncles talked with the fever of a secret society.

O'Malley was the frightening master at Boystone School. There was always silence when he came scraping one sarcastic foot into the room, showing his small teeth with the grin of one about to feast off human vanity.

He was a man of fifty with a head like an otter's on which the hair was drying and dying. He had a dry, hay-like moustache, flattened Irish nostrils. He walked with small, pedantic, waltzing steps, as though he had a hook pulling at the seat of his trousers and was being dandled along by a chain. Mr O'Malley was a terrorist. He turned to face the boys, by his silence daring them to move, speak or even breathe. When he had silenced them, he walked two more steps, and then turned suddenly to stare again. He was twisting the screw of silence tighter and tighter. After two minutes had passed and the silence was absolute, he gave a small sharp sniff of contempt, and put his hands under the remains of his rotting rusty gown and walked to his desk.

One afternoon in the spring term, after the French period, O'Malley went straight to his desk in a temper and said in an exact and mocking voice:

"I have been asked by the headmaster," he said, "to enquire into your private lives. This is deeply distasteful to me, as a matter of principle. I do not consider, as I have told the headmaster, it is desirable to encroach on anyone's private affairs; nevertheless I am obliged to do so. Eh?" he suddenly asked.

The silence, beginning to slacken, suddenly tightened again.

"I am not going to have my history period wrecked by a piece"—Mr O'Malley's voice gave a squeal of temper—"of bureaucratic frivolity. I intend to get through this quickly. And"—Mr O'Malley's voice now became musical, sadistic and languid—"any de—lays will in—ev—it—ably lead to three hours' detention on Sat—ur—day for the whole form."

A delighted smile came on Mr O'Malley's face, an open grin that raised his moustache. The otter seemed to be rising through the ripples.

"In alphabetical order I shall ask each boy in turn to tell me what he intends to do when he leaves this school and what religious denomination he belongs to. The replies," said Mr O'Malley with scorn, "as to all official enquiries, will, of course, be either dishonest or meaningless."

Mr O'Malley opened a large red book. He looked like a man, with knife and fork ready to enjoy an only too human meal.

"I'll take it alphabetically," he said, talking with his pen in his mouth. "Anderson—what will Anderson do when he leaves school?"

"Clerk, sir," said Anderson.

"Clerk, sir," mocked Mr O'Malley. "And what does Anderson think his religion is?"

"Church of England, sir," said Anderson.

"Church of England," said Mr O'Malley, taking his pen out of his mouth and making a note of it. "Agnew?"

"Clerk and Church of England, sir."

"Alton? Clerk and Church of England?"

"Yes, sir."

"Yes, sir. Liar, sir," said Mr O'Malley.

"Yes, sir."

"Andrews? Clerk and Church of England?"

"Yes, sir."

"Liar, sir," said Mr O'Malley savagely. "Next, sir? Come on, sir. Baker, sir?"

Henry Beluncle saw the question coming towards him. For the first time in his life, he saw coming to him a chance he had often dreamed of; a chance to play the Beluncle trick. On the subject of religion the Beluncles were experts. The word "God" was one of the commonest in use in their family. It was a painful word. Its meaning was entangled in family argument. The Deity was like some elderly member of the family, shut in the next room, constantly discussed, never to be disturbed, except by Mr Beluncle himself who alone seemed jolly enough to go in and speak to Him. God was a kind of manager and an interminable conversationalist; a huge draft of capricious garrulity always emerged.

3

For God, in the Beluncle family, was always changing His mind. Once God had been a Congregationalist; once a Methodist. He had been a Plymouth Brother, the several kinds of Baptist, a Unitarian, an Internationalist; later, as Mr Beluncle's business became more affluent, he had been a Steiner, a Theosophist, a New Theologian, a Christian Scientist, a Tubbite, and then had changed sex after Mrs Eddy to become a follower of Mrs Crowther, Mrs Beale, Mrs Klaxon and Mrs Parkinson—ladies who had deviated in turn from one another and the Truth. He had never been a Roman Catholic or a Jew.

Only once—it was just before the Deity's change of sex, Henry seemed to recall—had there been no God in the Beluncle family. It had been a period of warmth and happiness. They had all had a seaside holiday that year, the only holiday in the history of the family. Mr Beluncle himself had gone winkling. On Saturday afternoons Mr Beluncle went for walks with his arm round Mrs Beluncle's waist. There was fried fish in the evenings, a glass of stout now and then, and hot rides in charabancs to commons where strong-scented gorse grew and people came home singing. The air smelled of cigars. Mrs Beluncle was amorous and played the piano. Mr Beluncle read booklets on salmon fishing—there being a canal at the back of the house—and Mrs Beluncle used scent and was always warm-eyed, hot in the face and had frilly blouses on Sundays. Up a tree in the garden, Henry and his brother George smoked pipes made out of elderberry wood and left notes for little girls under stones in neighbouring gardens.

And then, as on a long summer afternoon, when the castle of delicate and crinkled white cloud that lies remote without moving over the thousand red roofs of a bosky suburb, swells and rises and turns into the immense and threatening marble mass of impending thunder, and there is the first grunt of a London storm, God came back. A book called Productive Prayer, in a red cover, three and sixpence post free, came into Mr Beluncle's soft hands. It was followed by one bearing the photograph of a fearless young man in horn-rimmed spectacles, called *Christ: Salesman*, and then by a pearl grey volume called *The Key to Infinity*. God came back but He had been cleaned of impurities: He was called Mind.

The simple change from God to Mind was like the change from gas to electric light to the Beluncles. Mrs Beluncle dropped out of the discussion at the first contact. She did not understand what "this here Mind" was; for the first time in her life she was prevented from confusing theological argument by diversions into autobiography. There was an assuaging notion that whereas even Mr Beluncle could not presume to be on equal terms with God, who according to the Bible was violent, jealous, revengeful and incalculable, he could (as the leading mind of the family) know Mind in the natural course of business and affairs.

Henry Beluncle sat in an exposed place in the front of Mr O'Malley's class. As Mr O'Malley's question came towards him, Henry vividly saw the incident in which his family's life had crystallised in a new form. The changes in Mr Beluncle's religion had corresponded very closely to the changes in his occupation and they had not always, by economic standards, been for the better. Wesleyans, Baptists, Internationalists had let one down. The Unitarian phase had been sharp, supercilious and fatal. But from Mind onwards, the Beluncles had been a little better off. And then Mind had taken Mr Beluncle—as far as the family could judge—out of the house rather more. If he was home late, delayed on Saturdays, unexpectedly away on Sundays, it was known that Mind was the cause. Mind appeared to move in higher circles socially than those of the Beluncle family, who indeed moved in no circles at all. (They held, as Mr Beluncle used to say, the fort.) Occasional news of the Hon. This, Lord That, Sir Somebody This or Lady Something else fell like a lucky bird-dropping upon the house. And if Mind led Mr Beluncle to slip an American word or two into his speech and despise his family a little, his family admired this in him.

In the old days before Mind, whenever Mr Beluncle lost his faith or, rather, found a new one "more in harmony with modern business" one thing always happened. The furniture van would be at the door at once. The taxi arrived. Mrs

Beluncle would be sobbing; Mr Beluncle would be catching two trains—one to put his family into and one for some business errand of his own. In the taxi, if Mrs Beluncle was still weeping, Mr Beluncle would sing:

"Tell me the old, old story"

and go on with warmth, putting his arm round Mrs Beluncle, to the second verse:

"Tell me the story simply,
For I forget so soon".

("Yes, you forget, you forget. I remember," Mrs Beluncle called out.)

Or, if the removal was especially disastrous, Mr Beluncle would sing a song to remind her of their courtship, like

"Oh dry those tears, oh calm those fears——
Life will be better tomorrow".

And Mr Beluncle himself would shed a tear in this song and turn his face shyly to the cab window, in case his family should see it.

It was in the period of one of these disastrous removals— an episode known in the family as "what happened at the High Street"—that Mind had appeared. The Beluncles had found themselves suddenly moved from a new villa in South London, to a basement flat in a reeking street within sound of the howling Thames, a street that appeared to have been cut through an immovable stench of railway smoke and vinegar. Henry and George were ill in bed. Leslie, their youngest brother, was ailing. Mrs Beluncle, who met disaster by outdoing it in the untidiness of her clothes—hiding her nice things so as to be ready to sell them—went about in an old coarse apron, her blouse undone, her hair down her back, her shoes broken. She had refused always the expense of doctors and dentists for herself and now had a long and bad attack of toothache. She sat in front of the kitchen range holding a piece of brown paper with pepper and vinegar on it to the fire, and then pressing it to her cheek, and as she did so, she rocked. Rocking led to soliloquy, soliloquy to cat-like moans, and her children sat at the corners of the dark kitchen, excited by the sudden squalor of their surroundings, watching her distantly. They did not dare to go near her, or she would grip an arm of one of them, with her strong working fingers, and with a terrifying expression of agony and drama cry out, as if she did not know them:

"Oh! If gran could see me now!"

It was into this room Mr Beluncle came, after a month away, with the smile, the bounce, the aplomb of a very highly tipped head waiter; and on his innocent lips was the word Mind. Gently and firmly, he took the brown paper from his wife; gently calmed the children; gently and firmly he told Mrs Beluncle about a man at the Northern Hotel, Doncaster, who had told him about Mind.

"Did Mind make toothache?" Mr Beluncle asked. "Of course he didn't. And yet you've just admitted Mind made everything that was made."

"You'll have to get your meal yourself. There's what's left in the saucepan," groaned Mrs Beluncle.

"So you just *think* you've got toothache," said Mr Beluncle kindly.

"You think you've had your dinner, go on," said Mrs Beluncle.

"It's an illusion of the physical senses," said Mr Beluncle, exalted. "Henry, you're supposed to be clever. Can a piece of bone feel anything?"

"Its nerves could perhaps," said Henry doubtfully.

"And did Mind make nerves?" asked Mr Beluncle scornfully.

"No," murmured Henry.

"Of course not. The boy understands, old dear. It's simple logic. Now put that paper away, the smell's awful. Let's have some supper. I've been travelling since seven o'clock this morning."

The children smiled, waiting for the light to dawn on the crouching figure of Mrs Beluncle. Suddenly she jumped up and screamed at their father.

7

"You wicked man, you dirty devil you, don't touch me. Talk about your sister, what about you? . . ."

The children were sent to bed in the next room. They listened but grew tired of the haggle of voices and dropped asleep. Henry woke up again, thinking it was morning, but the gaslight still shone through the fanlight over the door. He heard roars and shouts of fury coming from the kitchen. Mrs Beluncle was screaming out about someone called "that woman".

What had Mr Beluncle brought home? Some sublime and noble thing which Mrs Beluncle tore to pieces every evening like an enraged dog.

Night after night, month after month, Henry Beluncle listened. Was it the Open Seal? Was it the Key to Infinity —for the word Infinite came in with Mind? Was it Mrs Crowther's conference, Mrs Klaxon's call, the Science of the Last Purification, the Art of Salesmanship, Universal Brotherhood, or Mrs Parkinson's Group?

Henry Beluncle sat at his desk. His heart was racing. Even now he was not sure which kind of Mind had conquered his family.

"Belcher," said Mr O'Malley.

It was the name before Henry's on the list.

"Grocery," said Belcher. "And Church of England."

Henry swallowed. Vanity decided him. He plunged.

"Father's business, sir," said Henry Beluncle. "And Mrs Parkinson, sir."

"What?" exclaimed Mr O'Malley, putting down his pen.

"Mrs Parkinson, sir," said Henry.

It was not often that a smile of lyrical pleasure appeared on the small and injured face of Mr O'Malley, but now his bitterness went. The little bosses of his cheeks became rosy, his muddy eyes closed to long slits of delight, his short teeth showed along the length of his mouth and a long, almost soundless, laugh was going on in his head. He looked round the class from boy to boy, grinning with affection at each one, and then he turned to Henry Beluncle.

"Good God Almighty," said Mr O'Malley.

"Yes, sir," said Henry Beluncle, standing up at his desk.

"Your parents are followers of Mrs Parkinson?" said Mr O'Malley.

"My father, sir."

"Do you know what the teachings of Mrs Parkinson are, Beluncle?"

"Yes, sir. The Truth, sir."

"The Truth, sir. Balderdash, sir. Tommy rot, sir. Cheap, muddle-headed trash, sir."

Now he was on his feet, Henry felt no terror at all. He felt very strong. He had little idea of what the teachings of Mrs Parkinson were, but, hearing Mr O'Malley's attack, Henry was at once convinced of the Divine inspiration and absolute rightness of Mrs Parkinson.

"It is not, sir," said Henry, astonished at his own voice.

"How dare you contradict me, Beluncle!" said Mr O'Malley. "Do you stand there in your idiocy and tell me that if you fell out of that window, three floors into the street, and broke your neck, you would say it was a false belief and hadn't happened?"

A murmur of laughter came from the other boys.

"Yes, sir."

"Yes, sir; no, sir; yes, sir," mocked Mr O'Malley. "Would you, yes or no?"

"I would, sir."

"Oh no you wouldn't, sir," said Mr O'Malley. "Oh no you wouldn't. You couldn't, sir. You'd be dead, sir. Don't add impudence to stupidity. And tell your father from me that if he is stuffing you up with that nonsense he is a lunatic."

Mr O'Malley leaned back and presently a soft, long dove-like call came from him:

"Ooo. Ooo. Ooo," he said softly and leaned confidingly to the class. "Now I understand. Now we can begin to follow the mind of Beluncle. Beluncle is a superior person. Beluncle is a snob. Beluncle is a fake, isn't that so, Beluncle? A snob, Beluncle? A fake, Beluncle? Answer me, Beluncle?"

"No, sir."

"No, sir. Yes, sir. A fool, sir; a conceited ass, sir; a lunatic, sir."

"My father," Henry Beluncle shouted, "is not a lunatic."

The boys began to murmur. The captain of the form got up and said politely:

"Excuse me, sir. Beluncle has as much right to his religion as you have to yours."

"Sit down. He hasn't," said Mr O'Malley, very surprised.

But Henkel, the hot-tempered Jew, got up with a loud bang of his desk lid and shouted:

"His religion is as good as being an Irish Roman Catholic."

Mr O'Malley jumped to his feet, knocked his books off his desk and rushed up to within three paces of Henkel.

"How dare you speak to me like that," said Mr O'Malley. "I'm not Irish."

Three or four boys called out, "You've got an Irish name."

O'Malley waved his fist and rushed to where he thought the voices had come from.

"How dare you say I'm Irish," shouted Mr O'Malley. "How dare you associate me with that murderous lot of treacherous blackguards," he screamed at them.

The uproar in the class stopped at once. They were astounded by Mr O'Malley's outburst. They were not frightened by his rage. They sat back and waited to see, as connoisseurs, what form it would take next. What would Mr O'Malley do now? Which of his well-known antics would he now perform? The classical tirade against liars which all the boys could recite; the famous hair-pulling performance; the question torture of Anderson: Do your parents live in a house, Anderson? Is there running water there, Anderson? What is water, Anderson? Tell me some of the purposes of water, Anderson? Have you ever applied water to your person, Anderson? Answer me, Anderson. Answer me, Anderson. A small dance of exquisite pleasure follows and then a cooing voice. Are you going to answer me, Anderson? Don't you think you'd better answer me? And so on, the cooing voice rising and rising until at last Mr O'Malley leaps a yard forward with his hands out like claws with a sudden scream of, Answer! Anderson begins to blubber, is made to sit down, stand up, sit down, stand up and is left standing while Mr O'Malley walks to the other end of the form room, opens his mouth into a huge grin and picks his teeth with a match stick.

Which of these acts was it to be? Everyone could imitate them, Anderson best of all.

Mr O'Malley returned to his desk and sat down. His colour had become greenish but slowly it returned. He stared at the thirty boys, going over the desks one by one. Each boy noted the movement of the eyes as they checked him. Mr O'Malley seemed to be about to spring, for his hands held the edge of the desk, but he was steadying himself, while his heart quietened and his breath came back. For several minutes he remained like this and there was no sound. A master passing down the corridor looked admiringly through the window of the door at the sight of thirty Boystone boys motionless. Mr O'Malley's methods were famous. At last Mr O'Malley picked up his wooden pen and dipped it into the glass inkwell.

"Cowley," he said. "Future occupation? Religion? Come on."

There was a short flight of iron stairs at one end of the school building. A small court of admirers, sympathisers and critics surrounded Henry after school. These boys were all experts too. A hot argument about things Henry Beluncle had hardly heard of—so brief had been his family dips into the innumerable Christian sects—sprang up. The state of grace, the Real Presence, the Divine Mercy, Original Sin, the Thirty-nine Articles, were bandied about. Henry Beluncle said:

"Mrs Parkinson has cut all that out."

II

At twelve o'clock Mr Beluncle's brown eyes looked up, moving together like a pair of love birds—and who were they in love with but himself? He put his nail scissors away in their little chamois case and the case went into the waistcoat pocket on the happy navy blue hill of his stomach where fifty years of life lay entwined with one another. The machines had stopped working too. Presently the eighteen men could be heard leaving the factory. A week had ended and Mr Beluncle slackened and softened as the silence came to stand in his office. He looked out of the well-cleaned window at the wall of the factory opposite to his own and felt Saturday afternoon like a change of blood, the time when his office could have become a home to him. He went back to his desk and read again the country-house advertisements in *The Times* and was wandering among shooting-boxes and residences, sporting acres and paddocks, golf courses and mansions, travelling from one to the other in his car, seeing himself hit golf balls, ride horses, keep chickens, fish salmon, walk round his estate and stand before mantelpieces of all sizes. He was a short, deep, wide man, with grey hair kinked as if there were negro in him. His skin was kippered by a life of London smoke but it quickly flushed to an innocent country ruddiness at the taste of food: his face was bland, heavy in jowl, formless and kind, resting on a second chin like a bottom on an air cushion. It was the face of a man who was enjoying a wonderfully boyish meal, which got better with every mouthful; but in the lips and in the lines from the fleshy nose there was a refined, almost spiritual, arresting look of insult and contempt. Mr Beluncle was a snob about present pleasures; he was eager to drop old ones and to know the new. In his imaginary travels among the newspaper advertisements he got richer and richer, he moved from "well-appointed" residences to mansions and an occasional castle, he slowly raised his chin and insulted people right and left.

He did not notice that he was doing this and, in fact, as he read, he felt more and more amiable; he doubled the pay of his workers, bought a fur coat for his wife, sent messages of love and peace to the unhappy masses in India and China, set the Russians free, until, at the spendthrift summit, he remembered his son.

A son: a shy, desirous, passionate, protective, disgusted and incredulous play of feeling made its various marks on his face.

At once Mr Beluncle marched out of his office, down the short corridor, to the general offices where his son worked with Chilly, who was learning the business, and the clerks. Mr Beluncle was going to tell his son not to wait any more and to go home. "I am not an ordinary employer. I am your father," he was humming to himself. "Enjoy the sun, the fresh air, go home to your mother. You love her—or you ought to love her—think of her down there longing for you to get back." The generous impulse was the pleasanter for a sweet flavour of self-pity in it. "At that boy's age I worked till ten o'clock at night on Saturday," he said, and the sensation was that Progress had been created by him for others, out of his sufferings.

But in Mr Beluncle's dreams there was always a flaw. He opened the door of the general office, where half a dozen people worked. The first person he saw was this son of his, Henry, sitting at a long, high, old-fashioned mahogany desk that had been left when the office had been refurnished in the slump three or four years before. The boy had turned round from his desk on his high stool and was cleaning his nails with the edge of his season ticket. He was gazing in a sulky, childish, dejected dream at the sunlight on the factory wall, which could be seen from this window also. The boy was such a stubborn, unorganised weak replica of Mr Beluncle, with cheeks so young that one could cry out for care at the thought of a razor going over them. The father stopped short in horror and tenderness. A powerful feeling of anxiety possessed him. He forgot his intention in a shocked attempt to save the boy's character and life.

"One o'clock is your time," said Mr Beluncle. "I don't

like people idling away, watching the clock. The idle steal other peoples' time."

Mr Beluncle added the moral out of modesty, to escape the fault of random accusation.

The boy blushed and his jaw hardened with quick, young temper. The clerks held their cynical pens for a moment.

"I have nothing to do," Henry Beluncle said, rudely sticking up for himself.

"If you are working for me," Mr Beluncle said, his voice smoothing with a temper that was inexplicable to himself, it seemed to come from the small of his fat back, "it is your business to find something to do." He was shouting but only as someone shouts for help.

And Mr Beluncle went out fast banging the door, getting away quickly with the self-effacement of one who has saved a life and does not wish to get a medal for it. Too ashamed to meet the looks of the experienced clerks, the boy opened his stock books again. His neck, his ears, his cheeks had reddened and he sat in a storm of humiliation. With the ingratitude of the rescued he wished he had been left to drown.

Mr Beluncle marched back to his own room in a startled frame of mind. He had come down to earth; he was a man tortured, enslaved, tied down and unjustly treated by his own family.

He was followed into his office by his partner, a woman of forty-five, who was taller than himself, whose dark hair was dry but not yet grey and whose powerful uncoloured lips were crinkled and moved like irritable and exposed muscles.

"That is not the way to talk to your son," she said, and she was holding a pair of spectacles open in her hand. She had only lately taken to wearing glasses and was forming the habit of taking them off when she talked of private matters. Mr Beluncle, who had once admired her eyes, now took these sudden removals of the glasses as an uncalled-for reminder of his admiration.

He swung round to this surprise attack.

"Where were you?" he said.

"I was in the office. You didn't notice me," said Mrs

Truslove, speaking as if being conveniently invisible were a role, an achievement which had been painfully and satisfactorily built out of years of complaint. And in her white blouse and her grey coat and skirt, she had the neutrality, the protective colouring of irony and conscience.

"He is my employee," said Mr Beluncle.

"He is your son," said Mrs Truslove.

"Don't you start sticking up for him as if you were his mother," said Mr Beluncle, turning his head sharply over his shoulder as he shot this remark at her. And Mr Beluncle unmistakably conveyed, and meant to convey, that had he wished it, Mrs Truslove could have been the mother of his son; but that he had not so wished.

Mrs Truslove gave a shrug to one of her shoulders. She had picked up this foreign gesture from an Italian she had once worked for—it was the single feminine affectation in a woman who liked to be thought mannish, and had for Beluncle the irritation of a well-known habit—and she said that it was lucky for Mr Beluncle that she was *not* the boy's mother. She intended the ambiguity of this sentence.

And here Mr Beluncle found himself colouring in the large soft ears that stood out rather far from his puddingy head. He had been made, once more, to feel a foolish guilt by this woman who, unlike his wife, always looked him in the eyes.

"By Jove, that's good, Mrs. T. Ha. Ha!" Mr Beluncle guffawed with a coarsening cloud of laughter intended to cover retreat. He had built up his career, his business, his trade connections on humorousness. "My word, do you know what you jolly nearly suggested. I say . . . I say."

Mrs Truslove did not laugh. Once more Mr Beluncle was familiar with Mrs Truslove's inability to see a joke. He found reluctantly that he had to respect this curious trait in people.

"I am going to tell the boy to go," she said. "I won't have you speak to him like that in front of the staff. It is wounding to his pride," she said, "and it is bad for the firm."

Mr Beluncle's mouth stuck open with true astonishment. What he wished to say was "But that is what I *intended* to do.

That is what a father must do; break and harden the boy before the world does. What is wrong with that boy is he's afraid of me."

"*I'll* go and tell him," Mr Beluncle said. So Mr Beluncle, with the insulting look which he had gathered in his daydreams gone from his face, went back to the office smiling. That is to say he believed he was smiling. He was, in fact, scowling. Mr Beluncle opened the door.

"You here still? Why haven't you gone?" said Mr Beluncle.

"You told me not to go," the boy said.

"Don't flinch when I speak to you," said Mr Beluncle. "There is no need to do that. I mean, flinching conveys a bad impression. In fact," said Mr Beluncle, the idea just occurring to him, as ideas continually did—and feeling it would be rather unfriendly not to mention it—"it might convey to those who don't know you, that you were hiding something."

The boy, who was no taller than his father, stared directly at him as if he were hypnotised.

"That's all," said Mr Beluncle. "Go now and you won't miss the train."

Mr Beluncle returned to his own room strengthened.

"The damn fool was just sitting there!" he laughed to Mrs Truslove, and he went round to his side of their large desk and began one of his favourite defences against her stare. This defence was to lift a few papers from one side of his desk to the other. If she spoke he would stop; if she was silent he would begin a return game from the other pile.

"Leave your boy alone," she said. "He has done nothing wrong. It is only your bad conscience."

Mr Beluncle lowered a passing handful of letters to his blotter.

"Conscience!" he said. "I haven't got nothing on my conscience."

"Anything, father," said Mrs Truslove, correcting his English with quiet, unexpected pleasantness, and Mr Beluncle was too grateful for her change of mood to take up that word "father". He could have said, it was on the tip of his tongue to say "Why do you always say, 'father' in a certain way, what is the idea?"

"I am not a father," he wanted to say. She was his partner's widow, but this did not give her the right to call him "father" in her low, unmusical, ridiculing voice. It was not her business to remind him that Nature, in the form of woman, had taken the initiative from him, and had made him no better than thousands of other damn fools: the supremely ridiculous thing: the father of a family. The annoying thing about Mrs Truslove, during all the years she had been with him in the business since her husband's death, was this habit of telling him what a fortunate man he was, what a valuable and devoted wife, what pleasant children he had.

"Which way, father?" when she took his arm in the evening as they left the office—he could hear her saying it. When she knew what she did know about his life! When she could see with her own eyes how bad things were, why, for what purpose, did she correct and remind? But she did. She always ended by every day convincing him he had the happiest marriage on earth. He would go home in a dream of happiness—that is to say with the insulting expression on his face—and the first thing that happened when he got to the house was that he flew into a rage at the sight of them all, wished he had never met his wife or begotten his children, and would moan slowly round his lawn like a bee, taking the honey of self-pity from flower after flower, longing to get back to his business again.

III

On Saturdays Mr Beluncle and Mrs Truslove had lunch at a restaurant that was too expensive for her economical habit, and talked about the business. Occasionally, if she was pettish, he took her to the cinema. He had his car and he would drop her afterwards at her house and take a cup of tea with her. He would say to his wife, "I took Mrs. Truslove"

—(she was always spoken of formally)—"to the cinema and dropped her home. She's been difficult. I can't afford to quarrel with her."

The Saturday programme had once been a pleasure; it had become a duty and now he feared her. "It's a long story," he occasionally said.

For a few years during the Saturday lunches he had been inclined to indulge himself with a day-dream about her. He imagined he was married to her instead of to his lamentable wife. The dream would last through the car ride to her house. There, with a perplexing discretion, it vanished, perhaps because she used to change into shoes with lower heels which made her look shorter and so took away an advantage. An inch off her height made her desirable, for she was a handsome woman too, but the desirable was a quality which repelled him in women. "I am not a fool," he would think, and there was a positive pleasure in disappointing people, in showing them he was "fly". He could see through the whole bag of tricks. To be just, there were two other reasons: her sister was there and she was a cripple, and he was put out by the great love the sisters had for each other. It made a third party ridiculous and they were rudely inattentive. The other reason was inexplicable. They kept a canary.

"Why do you keep a canary," he often asked. "Why don't you keep a dog? A nice dog. An Aberdeen. That's what you ought to keep—not a canary. A canary can't wait on the mat for you when you come in."

Two women alone—they *would* have some silly trilling useless, sexless bird. Something in a cage. The natural cruelty of women. A canary was also, surely, a little common, the kind of thing his wife's horrible relations had; he hoped he had risen above that.

At one o'clock the last clerk went. His son had now gone. The best minutes of the week fell upon Mr Beluncle and Mrs Truslove like a spell. There was the simple childish excitement of being alone in the building. It was, in a sense, the marriage moment; not always happy, but always intimate. They took long looks at each other and sat there willing to be deluded by each other. "Avarice," Mr Beluncle would realise, "is at the bottom of her." And she, "He is not to be trusted with a penny." And after that, guiltily, she might come and put her arm round his shoulder or rub her cheek on his hair while he seemed to get pinker, fatter, shorter, as if he were allowing himself playfully to be squashed under her touch. She was a thin woman, but her bones were heavy. Or he might put his arm round her waist: by this peculiar method testing her mood. She could be wooden, she could be evasive, she could be yielding; another man might have been disturbed by her in that mood, but Mr Beluncle was not, or was not aware that he was disturbed. Today she went to the mantelpiece and rubbed her finger along the top of the clock that had belonged to her father.

"Dust," she said to him. She knew from long experience of Mr Beluncle that news of uncleanliness always brought him to his feet.

He went to the clock and said, "I shall have to talk to that woman." He put his hand on her waist but she moved away.

"Damn," said Mr Beluncle to himself. "She's been like this for a month."

Mrs Truslove's sulks were very long lasting, so long that he often forgot that they were there all the time. He had the impression that she had been sulking for ten years.

"After lunch," he said, "I thought I'd go to *Marbella*."

"Where is that?"

"It isn't a place. It's a house," he said.

"Oh, that house," she said.

"Would you like to come? You've never seen it."

"No, thank you," she said. "I cannot waste my time. You had better take your wife. I don't suppose the poor woman has ever seen it."

"She has seen it several times," said Beluncle. "And don't call her a poor woman."

"Several?" said Mrs Truslove. She was very surprised. "You are not seriously thinking of buying that house? You treat your family very badly."

Beluncle took this as a compliment. He liked it to be said

that he treated his family badly; that gave him a spacious chance of self-pity. But he was concerned by his partner's lack of perception. Was Mrs Truslove becoming stupid? That was to say, had she stopped listening to him and taking his concerns as her own?

Surely she knew that he thought of nothing but houses and furnishing them, day and night? Surely she knew he could not breathe where he was living at present, that it was a matter of life and death for him to "get out". Surely she must have noticed that out of his post in the morning he picked out the letters from the estate agents first, and often did not open his business letters at all; and then at least an hour and a half passed reading *The Times* advertisements. Surely she did not imagine he was wasting his time reading the news? Surely she was not accusing him of neglecting his business?

"That is where you and me—you and I? . . ." he hesitated shyly.

"You and I," she said.

"Thank you," he said. "Where you and I differ. What is a business? It is a place for making and selling things. What sells them? Personality. What is personality? Atmosphere. How can a man have the right personality if he doesn't live in the right atmosphere? It's like artists. An artist has to have a view. If he hasn't got a view, how can he be an artist? I consider it my job in this business to see that atmosphere doesn't dry up. Unless I have atmosphere," Beluncle said in despair, "I'm finished."

"Yes," Mrs Truslove's cold eye seemed to say, "you're finished."

Mr Beluncle thought she was just like his wife: she was ungrateful. In the past ten or fifteen years, he had taken her to dozens of houses within a sixty miles radius of London. He had been to some of these houses half a dozen times. He had invited her to the most intimate consideration of his life, in his talks about them. How he could not sleep on the ground floor, how he must have a bedroom to himself, how squalid it is for a married couple to undress in the same room, how vital is a lavatory downstairs. He thought of these journeys with her as an unguarded invitation to his inner life, a sharing of his imagination with her. The very house he lived in at the moment she had visited before his wife had seen it, and he was proud to think this was so. Mrs Truslove and himself in an empty house together: it was like a cleansing process, before the Beluncles, in all the squalor of living, rolled in and turned it, as he said, into a pigsty.

"Why shouldn't I be serious?" said Mr Beluncle. And, since being serious was part of the dream, his insulting expression was there.

"You can't afford it," said Mrs Truslove.

"Afford it?" he said. "I can afford what is right. If it is right for me to have that house or any other, nothing on earth"—and here Mr Beluncle made a very large gesture—"can prevent me from having it. And—I'll give you a thought there," said Mr Beluncle, now smiling so warmly that his brown eyes seemed to buzz like bees in his sunny creasing face, "—in case you are thinking of the price. There is only *one* price." Mr Beluncle said this solemnly, pointing a finger at her like an accusing salesman in an advertisement. "You think too much of figures, Mrs T., it's your training, I don't blame you, you're right to think of price; but if I believed every figure I have seen written down on paper in my lifetime"—and the word "life" led Mr Beluncle once more to make a large wide gesture upwards with both arms and to click the fingers of one hand very brilliantly as he did so, "—if I'd taken any notice of figures, where would I be now?"

"You'd be a rich man and not on the point of bankruptcy," said Mrs Truslove quietly.

"What?" said Mr Beluncle, dropping his arms and going as green as a gorgonzola.

"I said you are on the point of bankruptcy," said Mrs Truslove.

"I don't want to hear you use that word," said Mr Beluncle. "It's a funny word to use."

He looked furtively as if he had heard something sexually

indecent. Mrs Truslove herself lost some of her boldness after she had spoken, and she looked furtive, too.

They were both shocked by themselves. They had worked together in intimacy for years and had once or twice quarrelled, but they had never uttered or considered the indecent. And now, for a second or two, they had caught each other unappetisingly half-naked, he despondent, she cringing, their clothes on the floor. It was, for them, as near to a physical revelation as they would ever come.

Mr Beluncle was the first to recover respectability. His buzzing eyes became small, still and shrewd. His shoulders appeared to thicken and Mrs Truslove, who could usually meet his eyes, looked away with fear. His were shining. The glass of anger was on them when she looked at him again.

The interruption was sudden. The silence was long. Mr Beluncle walked himself up and down. When he stopped his colour had come back.

He got behind the defence of his desk again.

"I have made a great many mistakes in my life," he said in an elevated and injured manner and he took his glasses off and stretched his eyes.

"So have I," said Mrs Truslove. And she turned to the defence of her account books.

She collected them and put them in the safe. She was a tidy woman. Her side of the common desk was soon bare, except for its blotter, but that, too, she put away in a drawer. Mr Beluncle watched this sight blankly. When he went home his wife would be clearing up under his nose, in her sulking mood, too. He saw himself driving a car between two fits of female clearing-up and sulking.

At last Mr Beluncle went away to see that the building was locked up, saying the word "bankruptcy" on every floor and imagining himself in a foreign country. When he came back he was surprised to see Mrs Truslove had put on her hat and had her bag in her hand. They said as little as possible to each other, but she waited, as if she were tied to him, while he washed his hands and brushed his clothes. He spent two or three minutes at the mirror and he could see her round-shouldered figure, her face as deadened in its way as his own was now. She was, at any rate, waiting for him. He looked at his watch.

It would have been a thousand times better (Mr Beluncle's thoughts went by in jerky marching tune to the time of his annoyed steps, down the passage, through the warehouse and the factory, and out into the sour chemical smokiness of the grey and gritty London air which had pushed its way like a dry Cockney face into the yard), it would have been a thousand times better if Mrs Truslove had stopped whining about the death of her husband; if she had stopped carrying him about like an unhandy and reproachful statue which she seemed to set down in the corner of the office with her umbrella every day. It would have been a thousand times better if she had married a second time. Marriage would have knocked it out of her, he thought; though what was to be knocked out, he was not sure.

He led the way into the yard where his car was kept to protect it from the Bermondsey children. It was a dark blue saloon car and he walked all round it to see that it was clean and without a scratch. Mrs Truslove walked round it after him in a determined way. It was his car, but the firm had paid for it after six months of quarrelling about the expense, and Mrs Truslove walked round it like one preserving a right of way. Without her sanction he could not have bought it. She got in beside him.

Mr Beluncle drove out of the gateway, nearly hitting a barrow which had been left out of sight round the corner. This was a lucky incident, a fortunate distraction for both of them. Until Mr Beluncle nearly hit the barrow he had decided to pay Mrs Truslove out by breaking their Saturday habit of lunching together. He had decided to drive her coldly to her house, leave her there, and go straight home to his family. That would teach everyone a lesson, for his wife and family, who were always complaining that he never came home on Saturday afternoons, would be alarmed and put out, if he did what they wanted. He was sure of a bad reception and would give as good as he got.

Now the barrow received the rage that was intended impartially for his wife and his partner.

Mr Beluncle was subject to rage. A kind of artillery raised its barrels and spoke up in his soft and heavy body. No person was in sight in this narrow, cobbled back street between factory walls, to receive his attack. He shouted at the walls. He got out and shouted at the barrow. He came back into the car, after locking the factory gates, and turned on Mrs Truslove, telling her that she might have warned him. Mrs Truslove awoke from her sulk and was sarcastic. Cut by this, Mr Beluncle drove off to the top of the street and swung into the main road at a speed which would have been fatal on any day but a Saturday. A dog, a child, a late railway van escaped him in their turns. Mrs Truslove had her hand on his arm begging him to be careful. Physical terror on her part, physical excitement on his, cleared the air between them. Mrs Truslove hurriedly changed her mind and he hurriedly changed his; or rather he noted that like a sensible woman (and as he had known all along she would), she had "dropped all this nonsense" and was coming with him.

By four o'clock in the afternoon the offended widow of Mr Truslove had been driven for an hour and a half through the weekend traffic of inner and outer London to the suburban town of Sissing. Property was more expensive here than in the suburb of Boystone where Mr Beluncle lived, this being indeed its attraction for him.

"Smell the air!" he exclaimed to Mrs Truslove, and to him Sissing had the balmy perfume of the Ritz. "You can breathe here. It's bracing."

"Nice people," he said deferentially, nodding to the shopping crowds.

"Select," he said. "Exclusive."

He blew his horn suddenly and one or two of the exclusive scattered as his car took him up the avenue of the most exclusive part of this exclusive town.

Marbella was one of those large suburban houses which no family can now afford to occupy. It suggested a personage rather than a house, a minor royalty in flannels. There was so much collar and shirt-front of white balcony. There were top windows like eyes pouched by late rich dining, lower windows like a pair of bellies, the red face whiskered with creepers, the portico enlarged like a drinker's nose.

Mr Beluncle got out and smiled formally at the place. He would have liked to shake hands with it.

"I don't wonder your wife will not go in the car with you," Mrs Truslove said.

He pulled out the agent's keys and he made his way to his attack upon the house. More circulars were lying on the mat inside the door and one or two bills had been pushed in since Mr Beluncle had been there last time. He opened these bills and stood there lost in speculation about them and the previous owner. He forgot about his companion, who was standing in the dry, stationary, yellow air of the wide hall, watching him. These empty houses had all the same fatal effect upon her. She had resisted this one, hoping to keep to her resolution, hoping to keep the clarity of mind which had at last come to her after years of knowing him.

"They must have had the plumber," said Mr Beluncle, with the satisfaction of one who is spying his way into an unknown life. He read the bills with a sly, pettifogging patience, the rustic passion for detail, minuteness and thoroughness and poking his nose into things, which went oddly with the extravagance and violence of his temperament. His warm voice sounded like a bark in the stale and echoing house. He still had not moved from the door. This dazed hold-up at the door was so characteristic of him that she forgot everything except one thing. In this dead place he looked alive and young. She was in love with him. She had been in love with him for twenty years, she had been in love with him (she was now convinced) before she had married.

"Do you want to kill your wife," she said, "putting her into a huge house like this?"

Mr Beluncle walked into each room of the empty house with his usual look of satisfied insult.

"They'll have to alter that, of course. This must be taken down. They can treat that damp," he said, and got his knife out to test for dry rot. He was having a row with imaginary builders already.

The sound of their shoes going upstairs was alarmingly loud and in the passages and bedrooms the echo of his voice was harsher and richer. She followed him and was often a room behind him in the inspection, so that when she went into one he had just left, the stirred-up air seemed to be vibrating with him, and from the one next door where he was, his voice sounded like a choir of men singing. He banged doors that roused in her a kind of prudishness before noise.

Her lips became bluish with prudery and irony. Large, open-mouthed and expensive houses like this, well beyond his means and hers, started the miser in Mrs Truslove and, slipping the bag which held her cheque book on to her wrist, she took off her gloves, the better to rub her hands together. But she was captivated by one thing in the prospect of the Beluncle family. Self-improvement in every aspect—moral, social, financial, linguistic and æsthetic—was an hourly desire in her character. Like a schoolmistress she liked to rule and see others improved against their wills. To herself the amount of improvement, the amount of virtue, required by *Marbella*, would have been possible. But the Beluncles? Ethel Beluncle above all! They could never achieve it in the normal human span.

That was the outrage: that these struggling, bouncing, loquacious common little people should ever consider *Marbella*. And that was the added outrage: their bumptiousness entangled *her*. They lived (she reflected in kindly moments) in their imaginations. How she winced at the bounce, the boasting, the acting of Mr Beluncle. "I—I—I——" he went on. She had often groaned aloud. He heard her and he gave a sharp grin of pleasure in annoying her flat critical nature, for he never missed anything. He had infected her—for she

now regarded it as an infection—before her marriage, with
the unwilling belief that he could be anything he said he
was. He had simply to speak, to let his deep and changeable
voice strike not only her ear but her whole body. Her hands
themselves seemed to hear him. Her legs would move when
he spoke.

She and her husband used to talk about this electrifying
power of Mr Beluncle. Her husband had been just as captivated, just as offended as she was. They talked about him
in the secrecy of their engagement. They talked about him
all through their honeymoon. Beluncle seemed to lie in bed
between them. Mr Truslove had turned out to be a lover of
very limited performance, and Mrs Truslove had, after
marriage, gone through a period when, listening to her
husband's sleeping breath, she found her thoughts going out
of the bedroom window, up to London and back to Mr
Beluncle's office. And there, sharpened by dissatisfaction,
they perceived that Mr Beluncle had really bounced her
husband into the partnership; that she had really married
Mr Truslove because she was jealous of the attachment of
the two men for each other, or—and how often at this point
she had turned to her husband in their bed and had put her
arms round him—that she had married him in order to
protect him and to see that Mr Beluncle never bounced him
again.

In some way, Mr Beluncle had induced imaginary love in
her. He was never out of her mind, and by the fatal aid of her
prosaic nature she had accepted without protest the fact that
he was too full of himself to recognise this love.

Mrs Truslove was a very honest woman. She knew she was
not loved, but she had one tremendous satisfaction. Melancholy had had salt and flavour; she had stirred the jealousy
of Mrs Beluncle. There was no reason for this jealousy
and this increased Mrs Truslove's self-esteem; she thought
that she was entitled to that, or at any rate, that since it had
been put her way, she would be foolish not to take it up.

"Ethel will like the cupboards," she said as she and
Beluncle returned to the larger bedroom at the front of the

house. She knew that Ethel would not like the cupboards; that Ethel Beluncle in her slapdash fashion angered her husband by pushing anything into cupboards, out of sight.

Beluncle was too absorbed to answer.

"That is new," he said, pointing to a stain on a wall and affronted as if an intruder had been on his property.

He was on special and intimate terms with the plumbing. He had turned on the water at the main immediately they had gone into the house and presently there was the sound of a lavatory flushing, starting all the pipes and cisterns singing like birds. Mr Beluncle was an addicted flusher of lavatories in empty houses, being earnest for action and irked by the silence of these places. He came away, calling to Mrs Truslove with the jubilation of one who has just come from a friend.

He found her sitting on the sunny window-ledge of the room with her handbag and her gloves beside her.

"They work," he said cheerfully, as the pipes sang.

"When are you moving in?" she said.

"Trying to be funny?" he said.

"But what have we come for?" she said. "I thought you had decided."

"Who said I had decided?" said Mr Beluncle.

"No," said Mr Beluncle spaciously—a spacious "No" being a "Yes" to him. "It's the kind of house I would like. It's the kind of house I need. I need it now. I should like to go round and make an offer for it this minute. I mean, if it's shown to me that it's the right house."

"Shown?" said Mrs Truslove.

"If this is the right house for me then I can have it," declaimed Mr Beluncle. "If it's the wrong house then I don't want it. I wouldn't take it as a gift. I shall be guided to the right decision."

"Guided?" said Mrs Truslove.

This was an old game between them: the more Mr Beluncle was "shown" and "guided" the more Mrs Truslove asked how and why. It was like a game of cards: Mr Beluncle doubled.

"I shall *know*. By *knowing*," said Mr Beluncle, inflating. "There *may*, of course, be other houses," said Mr Beluncle, a little alarmed by the prospect of knowing and attractively shy about it. "I have one or two on my lists. I have seen them. But I *feel* this is the one. God wants us all to have the right house."

Mrs Truslove sighed. In her calculations, she was so prone to forget Mr Beluncle's special relationship with God, who was a joker in his pack.

"I hope God has given you the money," she said.

"God . . ." Mr Beluncle began to get in touch with the Almighty. But Mrs Truslove interrupted.

"You owe the bank nine hundred pounds," she said. "You owe your mother I don't know how much. You owe me three thousand pounds. Last year the business lost money, this year it is going to do the same except"—she said this sarcastically—"Mr Chilly is going to improve things. Have you any belief in Mr Chilly? I haven't. Do you know what you are living on? Your income comes out of your mother's pocket, your sister's pocket."

"Not my sister's," said Mr Beluncle curtly.

"I'm glad," said Mrs Truslove. "Then there's mine. You can't get any more money out of me, but there's Mr Chilly, of course, or does his money come from Lady Roads?"

Mr Beluncle was going to explain this tangled transaction but his partner went on:

"You will have to pay me back before you buy this house."

"The change of life, that's what it is, that has made her like this. Ethel is quite right," Mr Beluncle was thinking to himself. Aloud he said, keeping his temper, which was rising:

"So you have been saying for the best part of twelve months. And don't you worry, don't you fret yourself, don't you get worked up, you'll get it back, if I have to go and sing in the streets."

Mrs Truslove was sorry she had made Mr Beluncle overdo it, like this.

"Mr Chilly can pay me," she said.

"Mr. Chilly, the traveller," he said scornfully.

"No, he will become a director, you see. It will come from him," said Mrs Truslove with all her malice.

"Say it," said Mr Beluncle, who had a rose in his buttonhole and smelled it.

"Say what?"

"What you are thinking. Say I'm a fraud. Go on," said Mr Beluncle, taking the initiative. He was tired. He unbuttoned his blue jacket and sat down at the other end of the window-ledge. He took his brown trilby hat off and wiped the band. Everything (he recalled) was personal with women.

"You've been jealous of Chilly ever since he came into the firm. It was a mistake getting him in," he said.

"A mistake?" she said suspiciously. "Has *that* money gone too?"

"You know the money better than I," he said sharply.

"There is a far greater mistake than that," she said. And Mrs Truslove stood up to cry.

"Oh, God," said Mr Beluncle. He picked up his hat. There was dust on the crown and he flicked it with a coloured silk handkerchief he kept in his breast pocket.

Her tears, unlike his wife's, were brief. She was economical in weeping. She had not intended this quarrel.

She had come to her decision in a business-like way. She had seen solicitors, she had talked with accountants. She had taken advice—Mr Beluncle would not like this and a delicacy made her conceal the fact—from that Mr Cummings who had once worked for Beluncle years ago and who, after a quarrel, had shot up high in the business world and had lately bought one of those "gentlemen's residences" Mr Beluncle coveted. Truslove & Beluncle Ltd. had done well; but the riotous butterfly called Bulux Ltd., that had come out of that prosaic larva after her husband's death, had lived—the truth had to be faced—by going from flower to flower in search of capital. Small businesses survive by economy, meanness, slavery, not by adventure and dreams of greatness. She had been deluded by love; the humiliation was not that love had been denied to her, but the discovery that Mr Beluncle, who had bounced her husband and then herself, was not a great adventurer, not an intoxicating rogue, who went from one sharp deal to the next, building on a flourishing pile of liquidations and calamitous public issues, but a stern and meddling little dreamer. Mr Beluncle—it was the deepest wound—was a failure; he barked before he could bite. But in preparing to break with him, after the shock, she had been so practical, and so business-like, that she had not until then noticed what had happened to her life.

She had discovered this in the last half-hour as she had stood, frightened by its echoes, in the empty house. She could feel herself lying dead under the boards of it. Her life was like these empty rooms. Just as some family had moved out of this house so the years had moved out of her too.

Of course, she was jealous of Mr Chilly. That was the last shock and she knew it quite well. In her moralising way she had even argued that this pain was a just punishment for arousing what Mrs Beluncle had felt about *her*, for Mrs Truslove had a relish for the belief in punishment.

But the new jealousy had indicated the new desolation. She saw a side of Mr Beluncle she had never seen before; she saw that he had exploited her, that his imagination had drained her. He had destroyed her by inducing her to live virtuously on a delusion.

"I have just been useful to him and his wife," she said.

The filling cisterns sounded their rising, higher and more plaintive note. The sun of this hot summer, which everyone remarked on, and which made everyone smile, put a square of light before the red-tiled and broken fireplace of the room where they were sitting. Mr Beluncle, quick to forget his troubles, was thinking that here there would be a saving: the wallpaper could stay and he was itching to measure the length of the opposite wall. He could contain himself no longer and went to pace out the wall. Half-way, as he counted, and by way of apology, he said:

"You misjudge me, you know."

"Do I?" she said.

"We all misjudge each other," he went on. "It's fifteen feet. Yes, that's what we all do, we judge. Judge not, it says.

Fifteen by twelve. I'm not perfect, you're not perfect, no one is perfect. If I had my life over again, I'd do different. . . ."

She gave a small, quick glance of curiosity, in spite of herself. It faded quickly.

"You know," he said, "I married too young."

"My dear Philip, you have been saying that to me for the last fifteen years," she said. "I can't think why you say it."

But it was the final destroying sentence. For in what shame she now appeared to herself. He had said this before. And she had spent years calculating the rise and fall of its prospect for her.

She looked at the old, wide, fraying boards of this room with the remains of green linoleum surround which Mr Beluncle spoke of saving, at the wallpaper—a little faded —which was to be left. This (she understood) was to be Ethel Beluncle's room.

How many times she had wished Ethel Beluncle would drop down dead or fall in love with another man. The divorces she had dreamed. Scores of times she had day-dreamed that on a Saturday afternoon when everyone had gone, he would make love to her; or in her house, when her sister was out at her church; or in hotels when she had been away with him on business. So precise had been these dreams —she had even moved a sofa into his office from the ware-house—that, of course, when the moment could have arrived, the desire vanished; it had been exhausted by the imagination. Only when she was alone did the day-dreams once more put their intolerable paint upon her mind.

"Yes," said Mr Beluncle. "If I'd waited, if I hadn't rushed, I might have saved. I would have had capital. A young fellow's a fool to marry till he's turned thirty. You know," he said, walking into the square of sunlight to warm himself by an imaginary fire. "You know what I would like. I would like to go round the world. On a cruise. I once met a man who said he would like to go up in a balloon. I would. I've done with money. I don't want it. I never want to see another penny. . . ."

"If there is nothing more," she said, "I would like to go."

She did not hate him yet; but tomorrow (she thought) *that* will begin.

She dropped one of her gloves as they went out of the room and neither of them noticed it.

IV

Henry Beluncle was sitting in the front room of the station-master's house at Boystone. The railways of England are the oldest bureaucracy in the country and Mr Phibbs had the detachment of those belonging to an old culture which has reached the phase of contemplation.

Mr Phibbs's daughter was upstairs, changing the dress she wore in the chemist's library where she worked. The station-master, with the expression of one saying the word "mere" on his face, was talking to Henry. Mr Phibbs had "mere" sandy curls, creeper-like, in his hair, mere violet eyes, a merely ruddy complexion, and a blue serge suit that merely wanted brushing. His large friendly mouth seemed to be full of saliva when he talked lazily.

Mr Phibbs wore rimless glasses. His manner was idle, obstinate, not wishing to be disturbed. His large mouth pronounced the word "Yes" contemptuously (for he was essentially a "No" man), as "Cherss".

"Do you think it will keep fine this afternoon?" Henry asked.

Mr Phibbs's glance took a long time to cross the room and consider the sky.

"Cherss," he said. "June is always fine."

And by this he meant, to judge by his manner, "No" would be just as good an answer. If you were a reasonable young man, instead of being, quite naturally, a lunatic in love with my daughter, you would understand that it does not matter whether it is wet or fine. But, as a matter of plain sense, the world could become a reasonable place. War is unreasonable, cruelty is unreasonable, capitalism is unreasonable and so on.

He often dropped opinions like these before Henry Beluncle, like someone throwing crumbs to ducks on a pond. He had become used to the fact that, so often, the bread floated there sodden and untouched. Mr Phibbs asked Henry a few questions which he morally parsed, as he went along, into the reasonable and the unreasonable.

"What time did you leave?"—reasonable, all men want to leave their work—"your father's office": unreasonable, no man ought to be a capitalist or enjoy the capitalist succession.

"I caught the one-ten," Henry said.

"The twelve-thirty is better. It is a fast," said Mr Phibbs.

Mr Phibbs would not eat meat. He disputed with his Trades Union. He had a romantic love of strikes in the abstract, refused to strike when called upon to do so, joined societies in order to annoy them, was the plague of Mrs Parkinson's Group. He disturbed the members. Choosing a table top or a wall, he would give it a hard knock and say, scornfully, "There are people who actually believe that is real." When a train came into his station Mr Phibbs stood as if he were saying the same thing. Heresy and contradiction were Mr Phibbs's vanity. It was his wish to be the only heretic and the wish sprang from a beatific idleness and friendliness of mind.

Mr Phibbs had heard from his daughter Mary that it would not do for Mr Beluncle to know that his son had become friends with her. Mr Phibbs could see that love between the daughter of an official of the railway company and the son of a passenger had ideological dangers. Mr Beluncle was a small capitalist, the railway company would (he was sure) soon be nationalised. Mr Phibbs regarded the ideological difference as a kind of impassable Sahara, but he was willing to cross if he was sure Mr Beluncle would not.

"Cherss," Mr Phibbs was saying to Henry, "I like to see boys and girls going out together."

Mr Phibbs's glasses moved with a flash of instinctive opposition.

"Cherss," said Mr Phibbs, in the "no" sense, "but look at it another way. Take the railways. You are free to go to Inverness, or to Hetley"—the next station to Boystone on the London side; it was where Mrs Truslove lived and Henry was a little chilled whenever this place was mentioned— "but, don't forget, trains run on rails. . . ."

Mr Phibbs shifted happily in his chair and glittered with dialectical insinuation.

"There are time-tables," he went on. "The passenger is limited in his freedom. . . ."

The door opened and a large-boned girl of twenty-five, with reddish curls like her father's and a large mouth that was controlling a laugh or a scream, looked in.

"She won't be long," she said, looking at Henry from head to foot, as if she owned some part of him but had agreed to let her sister have the first choice.

Henry blushed.

She was followed by a sharp, dark girl who stood in the doorway and said:

"Whereabouts are you going?"

"Oh, I don't know," said Henry.

"All right," the girl said, "it's your business."

The girl giggled and also went. This girl was called Sis. Henry was sad that Mary Phibbs had sisters. He was horrified to think they talked about him when he was not there. He felt the dreaded beginning of those snobbish feelings which the Phibbs family awoke in him.

Mr Phibbs was continuing.

There were not only the time-tables, there were the signals, he was pointing out. A train is controlled by its signals. It would be unreasonable to find all the signals down.

"Yes," said Henry.

Mr Phibbs suspected this agreement.

"They can be up or down," he reasoned, but seeing no further opportunities of difference here, he went on to a favourite analogy.

"And then there are the points," he said. "People forget the points. They think of a train as something that goes straight on to its destination. It doesn't. A train can be switched."

"In love," said Mr Phibbs suddenly, as his youngest daughter came into the small sitting-room, "people are generally switched."

Mary Phibbs's young face blushed. She turned self-consciously to the window, showing the tip of one white tooth in the middle of her lips. The tip of this tooth was like a crystal of snow on her lips; or to Henry it seemed like the white key which had sounded the high small untrue note of her voice, for the Phibbs family inherited from their father a voice that came from a mouth with too large a tongue in it. She was a tall, fair girl with a small waist and hard, long, growing hips and she swayed to captivate him.

Mr Phibbs stood up with the mild resentment of the lazy, put his hands in his pockets, and went off like some tired engine out of the room.

Mary Phibbs said carefully and clearly: "Dadda is always tackful," and looked with more love at the closing door than at Henry, who was jealous. She stood on the far side of the dining-room table. Henry walked round the table and put his arm round Mary's waist. For a long time Mary had not allowed this, but he had worked his way through a phase of long handshakes, moving to the hand squeeze, the hand on her knee, the light hold on the forearm, and now he was at last allowed to put his arm round her waist, he felt it a duty to do this as often as possible. In doing this he had become aware that under her dress she wore other clothes; he had felt tucks, elastic, silk floating on a heavier material beneath. His growing knowledge of her clothes was a distress.

When he put his arm round her, Mary quickly turned, affecting to be surprised and tried to form her light eyebrows into a pleased frown. She pushed his shoulders gently and then with an "Oh you!" allowed herself to be given a short and awkward kiss on the lips. When he kissed her, Mary's small violet eyes had the distant studious look of her father's, for she was training herself to show Henry that she could read what was in his mind. "You can always tell by a boy's eyes," her sister had told her. Henry was watching the door in fear of the two sisters.

After this Mary smiled with nervous pride and the beautiful white tip of the tooth showed. They separated and Mary gave Henry a book.

"I have finished this one," she said. It was Browning's *The Ring and the Book*.

"The one I gave you on Tuesday," he exclaimed. "You've read it all?"

"Yes," she said.

"Did you like it?" he said.

"It was a beautiful book. It was deeper than Tennyson. Was it Tennyson you gave me last week?—no, it was Milton," she said.

"I can't read as fast as that," he said.

"I'm quick," said Miss Phibbs. "That is what Mr Turner says." (Mr Turner was the manager of the Lending Library where Miss Phibbs worked every day.) " 'Miss Phibbs,' he says—he calls the other girls by their Christian names but I don't like that—'Miss Phibbs, you're quick.' And," Mary added, "I am."

Henry frowned at the name of Mr Turner.

"I have brought you this," he said. "More's *Utopia*."

"Thank you," said Mary. " 'The books you read, Miss Phibbs,' Mr Turner says. He sounds quite surprised."

"Which part of *The Ring and the Book* did you like best?" asked Henry.

"What is that book?" said Mary.

"The one you've just given me," said Henry sternly.

"Oh, all of it, it was lovely," said Mary.

The door opened and the red-haired sister looked in again.

"You do lend Mary some books," said the sister. "She can't read them."

"Oh you!" said Mary, flushing and stamping her foot. "I read every page."

"In your sleep," said the sister. "It's bad for her eyes. Anyway, when are you two going out, spooning in here."

"Let us go," said Henry.

They fetched their bicycles from the back of the house and began their ride past the thousands of houses lying in the flat part of the town. This was the worst part of the journey for Henry.

Mary Phibbs always chattered during the first mile, trying to keep up with him, for he was going as fast as he could to get out of the neighbourhood. She was also struggling to keep her skirt from blowing. She had two subjects; the first was the goodness of her father. Mr Phibbs's three daughters were always expounding him. Her other subject was Mr Turner. Mr Phibbs's virtues were matched by Mr Turner's vices. Girls had been kissed by Mr Turner in the packing-room. They had been invited to the cinema. They had been asked to his flat in the evening. One girl had thrown *Pear's Encyclopædia* at him.

Mr Turner had invited her to his flat. Some noisy traffic passed at this point in Mary's story and Henry had to fall behind and then catch up in agony, to hear whether she had accepted.

"I'll go and tell him where he gets off!" said Henry. Mary said it was unnecessary. She had told Dadda about it.

Henry was now as jealous of Dadda as he was of Mr Turner. But Dadda had not acted. He had said, as far as Henry could see, that under private monopoly capitalism, the managers of chain stores suffered from a moral corruption that was bourgeois. It would vanish when they were nationalised.

The last allotments had been passed, the first hedges came up and the fields rolled to them, and almost human elms and oaks, with their imploring branches and stark trunks, shaded the road. Beyond Boystone Common the tarred road hung between heavy hills of deep bracken. A fine fair moustache of sweat had come to Mary's lip, her face was pink with energy. A steep hill forced them to get off their bicycles. They stood in the silence of the blue afternoon. They smiled and were delighted with each other. There were people walking across the common; otherwise they might have stopped there.

At the top of the hill they got on their bicycles again and the greenness of the country seemed to fill them so that they felt they were all the things they saw and every mile was like a long drink of new life. They came into country where there were village houses and farms, where countrified people were in their gardens or sitting at small windows and where the trees and the fields belonged to a world that made them laugh with pleasure, for it seemed to be dreaming itself. Other cyclists from London passed them, heads down, bare burned legs twinkling, drunk with the strong air, in the same holiday trance.

Shyness prevented Mary and Henry from stopping for many miles, but at last their hints became open. They stopped at a gate and went along the side of a field to a warm and nibbled bank.

"Here's a good place," said Henry.

Mary put on an air of unconcern, copying his, avoiding his eyes. They sat down a little apart; Henry pulled out a book of poetry. He had brought it many times before and it was still unread. They both smiled at its green cover with respectful hypocrisy. The book made Henry think highly of Mary and to Mary it was a guarantee of good behaviour.

When Henry came nearer to her and put his arm round her, and trembled at the heat of her skin, Mary studied the golden ants that crawled on the clay near their feet.

"Now he's looking for the other one. He can't find his hole. See what he'll do if I put a stick in his way. There you are, he's going round it," said Mary.

Henry's arm became tighter. She turned her head to look softly at him for a long time. Then she twisted away and taking him in both her arms pulled his head to her lap and kissed him. This afternoon she allowed him to undo the buttons of her blouse and she laughed at his disappointed face. Her large warm hand took his and took it to her breast and then she looked with pride on his hand.

"You are a funny boy," she said.

The pain of desire could not be borne. He got up and

walked across the field to see what was in the next one and when he came back she had done up her blouse.

He could still feel in his hand her small cool breast and the nipple that was like a soft pink crumb in his fingers, and he saw her mouth alter with the helplessness of physical love and her tongue show when this time he kissed her.

"I have been thinking about you," she said.

"When?"

"As you walked across the field."

"What?"

"I don't know," she said. "You looked sad. And you look proud."

They had to go before Henry's father came home and the green afternoon flew through them as they went back fast.

At Boystone when they said "Goodbye," his cheeks were burned by the sun. They leaned on their bicycles.

"Well," she said, pouting, "from what you say I don't see what call your father has to make a row with you. What about him and this Mrs Truslove?"

V

Hetley was three miles of streets and trees from Boystone. Some evenings George Beluncle got on his bicycle and waited at Boystone East for his father, or his brother; some evenings he went to Hetley. His father sometimes drove through Hetley when he took Mrs Truslove home and stopped at the garage which is on the Boystone Road after the roundabout.

One of his brothers was working; the other was still at school. George did not know how to occupy himself. He helped his mother with housework, he dug in the garden, he watched people go by in the street. In the middle of the morning he went out to the Public Library.

In the long hot reading-room men with nothing to do

were sitting at the tables or standing in groups by the newspaper stands. A smell of the municipality, the generic varnish of official oak, mixed with something rubbery, of town halls and the elementary schools to which George and his brother had been when they were young boys, closed the air of the Library.

"Don't wait for your father," his mother said. "Get a pen and answer an advertisement."

George lined up with the men at the newspaper stands, waiting his turn, but when it came he was bewildered by the print, and after staring for a short time, was soon pushed out of the way and ended with the hopeless ones, sitting at the yellow tables dozing over the magazines. To the smell of government they brought a sleepy human rankness, and George was soon overcome by it. It was not long before he was dozing.

In the afternoon Leslie, his younger brother, came home from school.

"Have you done that gardening I gave you to do?" Leslie said, mimicking his father's voice. "Here I am sweating my life out for you boys, and you lounge about all day doing nothing, you're getting round-shouldered."

George moved away from these sarcasms.

"I am going out," he called.

"Why," asked the baiting schoolboy, "doesn't he go on the dole? That is what I would do. Too snobbish, I suppose."

George went to Boystone station. The slowness of the afternoon lay like a hot unclimbable Alp between one hour and the next. He dawdled through the town, shop window by shop window, reading all the prices and notices, going over the contents so well known to him—the containers of sultanas and currants at the grocer's, the hairdresser's pictures, the ironmonger's tools and cans, and so on—sometimes following a man or some motherly woman. He stood on the kerb of the station yard, listening to the taxi drivers. An hour must pass before his father came. Every ten minutes or so a train came to the station and George watched the early city people come back. If they were laughing as they came out, he half laughed; if they grimaced, he grimaced; if they swung an umbrella, he walked a few steps swinging his arm. An argument started between two taxi drivers and George's face copied the changing expressions of their faces. He watched them over the neck of an eating horse.

After a time he went into the booking hall, buzzing in the web of his day-dreams, smiling at the people. He was wearing no hat. His fair hair was heavily greased, his trousers and his jacket were too short for him. He was not aware of the time going by, nor of boredom, for sometimes he was the first officer on a ship, sometimes a gentleman farmer, a pilot, a lorry driver, a financier, a police inspector, an engineer, a cabinet maker, a commercial traveller with a fast car. On the whole, he preferred a rank of some kind: to be a captain or major; or to have one of those prefixes that occur in newspaper headlines like ex-officer, ex-clubman, ex-manager, ex-chairman, vice-consul. He saw himself as a laddie, a chappie, a bloke, a type, one of those who fit perfectly into contemporary life by putting a touch of recalcitrance, a swagger without meaning into their characters.

A sportingly dressed young man in a canary-coloured pull-over and loud jacket came in with a couple of dogs. The young man was soon loudly drawling to a fair, fluffy girl as straight as a straw who hung on his arm and did dance steps as they looked at the magazines on the bookstall. George reached an exquisite torture of happiness.

"Ex-Army," thought George. "Abominable bloke. Hellish accent. Abominable!"

"Hellish" and "abominable" were words of praise for George.

The trains came, but no Mr Beluncle. George went back to his home sadly. He had been so certain he would meet his father and the failure had made him crave for him. He took Leslie's bicycle and went to Hetley and after cycling past Mrs Truslove's house there and seeing no car outside he went to Fred's garage.

George stood at the door of this wooden building. He could

see Fred's head above the bonnet of a car. George's eyes were glistening with sadness.

Fred got up from the other side of the car and straightened his thick body. He was a bald man of thirty-five with a war scar over one eye and this gave a look of sinister, complex interest to a simple, literal-minded man.

"Hullo," said Fred.

"I've been to meet my father," said George.

"Go on," said Fred. "Did you see him?"

"No."

"Not down at Truslove's?"

"No."

"Too bad," said Fred. He stared at George with slow sympathy.

George went over to the car and Fred bent down to work again.

"I see him down at Truslove's the day before yesterday," said Fred.

"He's often there," said George.

"He's got something there," said Fred, winking.

"He's always had her," said George.

"Dirty old man," said Fred. "I see them go by. Handsome."

George smiled with pleasure. He had boasted that his father had a mistress in Hetley, as a loud addition to his knowledge of sin and his blatant belief in it. His father was "abominable", "hellish": terms of admiration.

"Have you spoken to him about your job?" said Fred.

"Yes. Nothing's happened."

"It's bad for you being idle. You ought to tell him straight," said Fred.

"I have," said George.

"It isn't right," said Fred.

He put down his spanner and gazed at George across the wing of the car for a long time.

"I socked my old boy in the jaw when I was seventeen," said Fred. "Some row, I don't know what it was; I took his girl off him, I expect. My old man was all right, I respected him, but he liked one on the side now and again. So I socked him. We had no trouble after that. Don't worry, George. It'll come out in the wash."

Fred bent to the engine of the car and George came round to stand close to watch him.

"Bloody trouble at Pop's last night," said Fred. "Skippy got fresh with that tart. She was asking after you."

"Oh," said George.

"I'm going up there to fetch a van," Fred stood up. "You might hear of a job up at Pop's. It's no place for a girl."

"There was an ex-Army officer with a girl at Boystone station," said George. "Abominable lad with two dogs."

"Go on," said Fred. "What kind of dogs?"

"Sealyhams, I think," said George.

"Go on," said Fred, straightening up again to gaze at George. Fred was sincerely interested in everything George said. They were figures of romance to each other. Fred was married to a kind woman who was often in hospital. During the war, he had, he said, "mucked and split-arsed" his way round the British Empire. George, in Fred's eyes, was the son of a rich and tempestuous financier who had sporting estates all over England and kept a mistress in Hetley. A lassitude, if not a lack of imagination, in George and Fred, had created these imaginary figures and gave a restful flicker of interest to their relationship.

"He had a girl with him," said George, completing his picture of the officer.

"Go on," said Fred. "What colour hair?"

"Fair," said George.

"Cold," said Fred. "No good. Blondes aren't." And he went on with his work.

"Your brother gone to see his girl?" said Fred.

"I expect so," said George.

"He ought to see Molly up at Pop's, she'd put him right in a jiffy," Fred said. "Does your brother's girl go to your father's church?"

"Yes," said George.

"Molly would cure that too," he said. "We'll see Molly

when we go up. I hope her aunt isn't there, now there's a tart. Molly was asking after you, did I tell you that?"

"Yes," said George.

"What did she say? Something," he said, "I forget what. When we go up we can ask her what she said. If she's there," said Fred. "Perhaps it was about a job. She hears things."

"Does she?" said George.

"Come to think of it though," said Fred, "your old man wouldn't like it if you went up there with me. I better go up on my own."

George's face became miserable.

"I could stay in the car," said George.

"All right," said Fred. "That's an idea. That'd help me. I don't want anyone mucking round the car. Second thoughts, Molly's no good to you. Still, she was asking after you. Well, there," said Fred, pulling down the bonnet of the car. "There's that b—— done."

A smile of deep happiness came on George's face. He deeply loved bad language.

A black van was driven to the far door of the garage and two men got out.

"Leave her there," shouted Fred.

"Repent ye," Fred whispered to George.

On the body of the van were printed the words "The Wages of Sin is Death" in large yellow letters.

The two men walked round the car with quick steps and breathlessly. They tried the door-handles, they went to look at the tyres. They were whispering to each other in secret voices; very often their shoulders were touching. One of them was tired and fat and elderly and the sweat was running off his forehead. He was a jobbing gardener in Hetley. His name was Granger.

"Shall we fill her up now or in the morning? In the morning is better. And give her water then, eh? And the oil, don't let us forget the oil. Ah," whispered the old man with an anxiety that was sweet to him.

And he stepped back, wiping his face with a handkerchief and gazing at the car.

"It's a glory," he said. And then he leaned closer to the younger man. "You know what she is, I thought," and he touched the young man, "she's a worker for the Lord. She is." And he gave a covert giggle.

The younger man had grey hair and he was thin, straight and severe. He said, with a bitter grin:

"It bears its witness."

"Ah, that's it, that's it, what I told them," said the older man eagerly, cringing. "You mustn't look at the expense, I said, you must look at the witness she bears. Eh? Well, you must. Oh!" he broke off childishly. "Do you see what I nearly done? Do you see?"

"What?"

"Left 'em inside."

And he opened the door of the van and took out a heavy bundle of two or three hundred copies of a magazine and a rolled-up banner. His big, cracked, wooden-looking hands trembled as he picked up these things and gave the heavy bundle to his friend. Then, they locked the door again and once more stood back from the car and considered it. They stepped backwards a few yards from the car, as though it were a sacred object on which they must not turn their backs; and then the stout one again touched the arm of the other delicately and whispered: "Vogg, better mention it, perhaps?" Mr Vogg nodded. And together the two braced themselves to speak to Fred. It was Granger, the old man, who spoke. His whispering voice was fond, breathless and anxious; but now he spoke aloud in a whining, nasal and obsequious voice.

"Mister," he whined, "we have put the van there."

"Over there," said Vogg. His voice was deep, dead and blank.

"Will it be all right over there?" whined the stout man, insinuating and cadging.

"It won't harm no one there," said Vogg in a threatening voice.

"No, that's O.K.," said Fred, giving George Beluncle a nudge.

"O.K.," said the fat man, becoming aggressive, and he shambled rapidly up to Fred, feeling in his pocket for a tip; but half-way there he changed his mind. His hand went to his jacket pocket and, with a sudden brisk flick of experience, pulled out a tract and put it on the bonnet of the car which Fred was standing by.

"O.K.," said Vogg boldly, to Fred, looking him in the eye, man to man.

"O.K.," said Fred.

"That's Vogg, the paper man, opposite Truslove's, your old man's little job," said Fred. "Well, I'm going to pack it up. Are you coming?"

"I'd better get back," said George. And, refreshed by Fred, he said boastfully, "I'm going to tell him where he gets off."

"That's it," said Fred. "Give it him straight between the eyes."

VI

The two evangelists hurried out of the garage, close together, shoulders touching and whispering. In his earth-coloured skin, Granger looked like a frayed cigar stump: Vogg was bonier. His skin was tallow-coloured. Tortured by a sick stomach, Vogg had thin lips and his face was drawn by the habit of pain to a fanatical and cynical expression.

"It's a burden," whispered the fretful fatter man, as they jostled each other rapidly past the hoardings near Fred's garage. "Gladly, I think, I would lay myself down in the Saviour's bosom, on Jesu's breast, and enter our eternal rest. Yes, yes, I would, on Jesu's breast, beside *her* in the grave. I long for my eternal home."

"She's in the peace that passes understanding," said Vogg curtly.

They were speaking of Granger's dead wife.

"She is, she is," said the other eagerly, happily, breath-

47

lessly. "His yoke is easy but His burden light. And," he touched the arm of the other man with his free hand, "she wanted the glory so," he whimpered. "In hospital that's what she said, 'Give me the glory.' " And he looked enquiringly at Vogg.

Vogg ignored him.

"Look," said Vogg. He had stopped at a poster on the hoarding. They read: *Mrs Parkinson's Group. A Lecture: Is Death Real?*

The fat man smiled stupidly and then he spat.

Vogg glanced up and down the street. There was no one near. He put his fingers to the corner of the poster and tore half of it off the board, screwed up the paper and put it in his pocket.

"That's number eight," he said, as they walked quickly off.

This part of Hetley, removed from the arterial road, was Victorian in all its phases, from the grandiose, pillared houses of the early part of the century, to the sharp red jerry-built villas, already decayed, that were put up in the '80's. Nearly opposite to the latest and neatest villas was a row of shabby and defeated shops. They had been started eighty years ago for the use of the servants and mews families who worked for the prosperous people who had lived in the larger houses of the road. But now these houses were divided into flats and let off in rooms, the servants had gone, and the shops remained, half-empty places, their trade dying, owned by surviving invalids who scraped feebly out of the dark back rooms to their counters and whimpered about the changes in the neighbourhood.

Vogg's, the newsagents, had not been painted for years and its window was blurred by the dried runnels of dirty rain. The window contained some sheets of faded brown paper and one or two empty cigarette cartons. Vogg's few newspapers were on a rack in the doorway.

Vogg left his friend at the door. The inside of the shop was nearly as empty and dingy as the window. Its shelves were bare; the glass-covered show-case for cigars on the counter was empty. There were empty tobacco jars. The only saleable objects were a few comic papers and the district *Advertiser*. Old Vogg—this man's father—had been dead for ten years; the young one had let the trade go and merely kept on a newspaper round. When he went out on this round or when he went out selling badly bound and illustrated books on the Holy Land, he closed the shop. But if, when he was at home, the sharp new door bell went, Vogg would come out of the darkness at the back of the shop and look with blazing, upright, sarcastic amazement at the customer. No, he didn't sell ink, he had not got any tobacco or envelopes. If the customer wanted a paper he would curtly say they were all sold.

Vogg put his heavy bundle of papers on the counter and locked and bolted the door. Then he went inside to a staircase, past his bicycle, and went noisily upstairs. It was a dirty house, malodorous with the sour smells of cooking, lavatories, gas and the insidious acid smell of London dust and floor boards. He went into a wide high room above the shop. By one of its windows a very large woman was sitting in a raised chair that was bunched out with cushions and draped with a quilt. She was a woman of sixty with stained, violet cheeks and the alert eyes of a little girl. She had a small and pretty voice.

"Did you lock up?" Mrs Vogg asked.

And when he said he had done so, she asked if he had done the bolt too. To this he said he had also put the chain on and pulled down the blind. Then she asked:

"What was you doing, you was a time?"

"I put the papers on the counter," he said.

"You seemed so long," she sighed.

She asked all these questions out of an amiable smallness of mind and he answered them patiently and exactly while he leaned over to kiss her.

Their kiss made them both smile. David Vogg walked round the big room, passing the fireplace where the large mirror was. He looked into this with a look of exhilarated conceit. He now bared his teeth and squared his sharp shoulders and became overweening.

"Have you had your medicine?" he said.

"No, dear."

"You're a bad one," he said.

"Oh, I know I'm bad," she said with pleasure.

When he brought her medicine she told him about her day.

The two tall windows of the room were darkened by heavy green curtains and impressively the large mirror reflected, through its dust, a room which had only one picture on its dirty walls—an advertisement for tobacco. The floor was covered by linoleum and had only one rug, by the fireplace. There was a high, iron double bed, unmade, along one wall. The Voggs lived among smells rather than among things. Here there was a rich odour of sweet fruit, there of cheese and cooking; from chairs, the extraordinary breath of upholstery.

Mrs Vogg sat at the window most of the day, after her son had got her out of bed in the morning and had helped her to dress. She stood up, feebly modest, feebly ashamed, in her underclothes, the flesh coming like innocent chins over the cotton straps. She was pleased to have him as a slave. While she finished dressing he cleaned the room, got their breakfast and it was he who did most of the domestic work of the day; sometimes, on her swollen legs, she scraped with difficulty round the large table in the middle of the room, moving a plate from one end of it to the other. At the window she sat watching the street and the houses opposite, drowsing in innumerable childish secrets.

Mrs Vogg was wrapped in secrets. Every hour she made a few more. One or two central secrets gave her an innocent complacency. For no clear reason, unless it was some mysterious vanity or fear, she pretended that she came from North London. She was, in fact, the child of a Gloucestershire labourer. Then the older Vogg had not been the father of her son. She did not know who the father had been. She had made up a story for the late Vogg. Another secret was that she had not been married to Vogg. She had worked for him as a housekeeper before she became his mistress. She had never expected to be married. Vogg had often hated her son, but she had become necessary to the old man in his illnesses and he had left her his money. By surviving, Mrs Vogg had been at last rewarded; she saw herself as a wonderful collection of undisclosed facts, a passive and contented monument to all the crimes that were committed against ignorant girls and easily deceived women.

Mrs Vogg had peaceful blue eyes and small disappointed youthful lips. Out of the stale heap of clothes and flesh a precocious child was looking. When her eyes glanced at her arm or her knees, or when the arms or some part of her body moved, the impression was of a pair of animals in the same untidy basket looking strangely and mutely at each other.

The keeping of her own secrets had given Mrs Vogg a consolation in her illness; it had trained her to watch the secrets of other people. She supposed that everything she saw from her window was a concealed happening. A tradesman's van stopping at a house, a woman going out at ten and coming back at twelve, men knocking at doors, children crossing the street to another house, all the minute comings and goings of the day, were disclosures.

David Vogg shared his mother's taste. For her watching provided her with soothing, harmless comparisons with her own life: she was looking for events in the lives of others which would match and explain events in her own life. And it was her vanity that she saw nothing to equal them. David Vogg listened to her minute accounts. He sat close to her with his hands gripped between his knees, his eyes intent and searching, a line of sarcasm on one side of his face; and at every point he made a peculiar, wet-sounding noise like "Tiss-tiss" as he listened.

David Vogg listened for a motive that was different from his mother's. It had formed slowly in his childhood and had become a passion as he grew up. He was convinced that the streets he walked down, the people he saw or spoke to, were, in their varying ways, lies. His mother, in her watchful gossip, exposed some of these possible lies to him and calmed the anger he felt when he was alone and which had been strongest in him when his adoptive father had been alive and had cruelly separated him from her. Strengthened by her talk, he would get up at the end of it to cook a meal for her and say to himself as he stood over the gas stove in the small cupboard-like kitchen on the landing:

"The world is filled with sin, crawling with evil underneath the good appearance it puts on things; but you can see through it, you are superior. And you know one thing the world scoffs at: it is rushing to destruction and hell-fire."

Mrs Vogg worked her way down the gossip of the street as they sat together at the window. Presently a car drove up to one of the newer red villas which had long, cold, tiled paths to the gates. They were nearly opposite. The Voggs had to move in their chairs and lean back to see the car from this angle. Mrs Truslove got out of the car and was followed by Mr Beluncle into the house.

"It's his night," said Mrs. Vogg. "The sister is out. She must have gone to her church."

They nodded and they watched.

"She must have gone to her church. That's what I miss, Dave, not going out," said Mrs Vogg. "They come across the road. Mrs Johnson was pushing her."

David Vogg said: "Fornication: is that Christianity?"

As soon as she could Mrs Vogg changed the subject.

VII

Sunday. The one day of the week when Mr Beluncle was at home, the day his family gave to him.

The sun went up throwing off early heat like rings round the heart and body. The smells of the garden flowers came in at the open windows drawn in after flies and travelling bees. "The bee, the busy bee," Beluncle often said, of this moral creature. "Look how he gets his honey. He's a traveller. I was on the road ten years. To be a traveller was my highest ambition when I was a young man, the be-all and end-all."

A look of apology and surprise followed this confession.

Outside, the garden of the semi-detached house, with its six large trees and its well-trodden grass, was lying in the suave, summery silence. Beyond the villa, built in Boystone's yellow period, the suburban road and the red and yellow town round it were held in the same silence too. Later, the main roads would be noisy with traffic and as hot as an iron. The crowds would come out of the churches, the stations, the hospitals.

The Beluncles woke up; the youngest first. Leslie Beluncle was working on a system of electric bells and his bed was covered with screws, nuts and wires; now and then the boy lifted his head and looked at the poplar tree standing in the garden of the house opposite. He was dreaming. Then his head gave a pretty shake and his eyes opened nervously wide for a second or two and showed a crescent of white above the pupils. The doe eyes of all the Beluncles, except the small fish-grey salty eyes of Mrs Beluncle, displayed this circumflex of hardness and fright. In a moment the eyes became dreaming and tender again.

There were two beds in the next room. George was lying there dreaming sorrowfully, under the long lashes of his beautiful eyes, of the man at the garage whose wife had been taken suddenly to hospital. George was dissolved in sympathy; a masochist, he wished to be in hospital too. He was running through all the diseases he knew the names of. Henry Beluncle, the eldest of the boys, who was nineteen, was striving to recover the kisses of yesterday, but the memory was transfixed by the lies he had told when he got home and now he waited for eleven o'clock when he would see Mary Phibbs again. Grandmamma Beluncle had been awake since six o'clock and was thinking about her clothes. And, now and then, thought of telling her husband that, except for herself, she knew no woman whose clothes suited her, forgetting he was dead. The garden smells made her think of him.

Beluncle himself, her son, whose snores had ranged like cowboys through the house all the night in a loud undulating clatter, woke suddenly on a note like a shot. Clear-headed at once, he again set out occupying residences, sold all his

furniture, moved new furniture into shooting-boxes, maison-
ettes and mansions all over England, stopping between each
removal at certain hotels he had known when he was a commercial traveller, having old meals over again, recalling the
amounts of old orders. After these cavortings of the mind, his
soft, large face, which loosened and flattened into outer and
inner rings when his head lay on the pillow, hardened: his
hand went out to Mrs Parkinson's morocco-bound work,
Mind and Matter, on the table beside him. A scented marker,
which he smelled before he began to read, showed the place.
Mrs Parkinson was quoting Jesus:

In my father's house [he read] are many mansions. If it were
not so, I would have told you. I go to prepare a place for you.

In the front bedroom which she and her husband had once
shared, Mrs Beluncle slept on in her muddled bedclothes, her
long hair half over her face, which even in sleep seemed to
be shouting out an insult, from the wreckage of a night's
tormented, sheet-twisting and weeping dreams.

At the line: "I go to prepare a place for you," Beluncle
could not wait.

"Hullo," he called out from his room in a jolly voice.
"Hullo, hullo, hullo," he called.

In their rooms, all except Ethel Beluncle looked up and
frowned.

"You boys," he called. "Are you awake?"

There was no answer. Beluncle put down his book. There
was no doubting the Scriptures: a place had been prepared
for him. There were many mansions. Among the many
mansions of God's, there was one for him. Where was it?

"You boys. Get up," he called.

It was probably *Marbella*. If that was the one God had
chosen for him—and God would choose the best—then
nothing could prevent him having it. What could possibly
interfere with the purpose of omniscient, omnipresent God,
Good, Mind, Soul, Principle? The voice of Error, the Evil
One, might suggest ("Get up, you heard me," called Beluncle
genially. "Ethel, are you asleep?") that he was on the point

of bankruptcy; but who could doubt that if God provided
the mansion he would also provide the money to pay for it?

"I must work for Supply. God is Supply," muttered Mr
Beluncle.

"You boys! Ethel! I don't want to get angry," he called.
"I don't want to lose my temper. Greet the day. It's Sunday.
The sun is shining. The birds are singing . . ."

"That's a lie," said Henry in his room, to George. "There
are no birds singing."

George laughed too loudly.

"Get up," said Henry. "There will only be a row."

"Get up," shouted George to the youngest boy.

Then Ethel appeared in their rooms, with her hair dividing over her cheeks, and looking out from it like a savage
peeping in terror from an old tent.

"Get up," she said sharply. "You know what your father
is. I don't want the day ruined."

And she went downstairs in her nightgown with an old
coat thrown over it. They could hear her filling the kettle,
and presently George was called down.

"Take him his tea."

George carried the rattling tea cup to his father's room.
In his pyjamas Beluncle leaned on one elbow like a large
striped Turk.

"Take a little more care, you are spilling it. How old are
you?"

"Sixteen," said George.

"Don't be a fool. I know that," said Beluncle. "Look what
you have spilled. Open the window. Empty this saucer. It
is disgusting. Sixteen, and you cannot carry a cup of tea
upstairs. When I was sixteen, George, I was earning my
living."

George's dark eyes gazed appealingly at his father.

"Dad," he began, in a choking voice. "What about my
job?"

"Your job?" said Beluncle with astonishment. "*Your* job?"

"Yes, you said when I left school you would see about a
job," said George. "I left at Christmas."

Beluncle sipped his tea and frowned.

"*Your* job?" said Beluncle. "Why do you ask me about that today. You ask *me* to get you *your* job?"

"Yes," said George. "You said you would. You told me not to."

"There is only one job, one kind of work, George," said Beluncle kindly. "You ought to know that. You do know it, don't you?"

George's childish face grew long and sad and obstinate.

"God has the right work waiting for you when you are ready for it," said Beluncle. "Hasn't He?"

"I don't know," said George. "You said you'd ask Mr Miller."

"Now, George," said Beluncle sharply, "don't irritate me. At your age I found my own job. I didn't go to my father; in any case my father couldn't help me, he was a poor man. You are lucky having a father who is better off, but don't you go getting the idea that just because your father's got a business, you can just have anything you want, because that's the wrong idea. Now go and turn my bath on."

"You said yesterday, ask today," said George.

George turned away. His eyes shone with tears that did not fall and he walked slowly away, bewildered, carrying his love for his father away with him, like someone sent away with an unwanted load.

"You're a fool. I heard," whispered his eldest brother, outside the room. "He won't do anything."

"Shut up," said George, going to the bathroom and wiping his eyes sadly on his sleeve.

At half past ten Beluncle came downstairs. For an hour and a half they heard him bathing, caught a glimpse of him shaving, trying on new shirts, changing from one suit to another, oiling this side of his stiff grey curling hair and then the other, doing his chin exercises. His trousers looked like a pair of striped tigers as he sat taking his breakfast alone. It seemed likely that he was going to church, but it might not be so. He might sit so long over breakfast that he would be too late for church, and then, to their despair, he might

spend the morning walking up and down the lawn. Or he
might get out the car and drive to another church in London.
Or go to see his partner. The boys and Beluncle's wife hung
about the door outside the dining-room where he sat eating,
waiting for hints and clues.

Ethel Beluncle had more courage, but not much more,
than her sons. The more Beluncle dressed, the less she
dressed: their marriage had always been a duel. She had put
on an old skirt, her blouse was unbuttoned and her hair still
hung over her face and down her shoulders. The more he
sat, the more she stood. The more he was the lord, the more
she, vindictively, was the slave. The Beluncle boys hovered,
waiting to know if they would be free this day, waiting to
know what this Sunday would be like, whether Ethel Beluncle, by some small act, would tip the scale the other way
from the common Sunday quarrel.

Presently Beluncle stood up and came out into the small
hall into the heat of the morning. Stout and bland, he walked
lightly and gravely.

"Hat, stick, gloves," he said. He was astonished at the
sight of his family hanging about there idle.

"Get them," said Ethel, giving one of the boys a push.
And she herself went out into the garden and picked him a
red rose for his buttonhole. She brought it to him and he held
it to his nose.

"I would like," he said, "to be surrounded by roses.
Everywhere. I want colour, flowers, fragrance, richness."

And then his reddened, beard-blue face went suddenly
greenish as if he were going to faint and his thick lips went
small. His face began to shrivel with disgust.

"Oh," he said, holding the rose away from his clothes.
"Greenfly."

"Give it to me. I'll brush them off," said Ethel. "You're
not afraid of a fly."

"I don't want greenfly on my hands. They'll get on my
suit. I've only just paid for it; in fact, I haven't paid for it.
Are there any on it? I shall have to wash."

Three greenfly were brushed off the stem of the rose and

Ethel wiped them on her skirt and then she got the brush and, as he turned, she brushed him carefully.

"Henry," she said, when her husband's back was turned and she was on her knees brushing the back of his trouser legs. "Henry," she said, "wants to go out this afternoon."

"Out?" said Beluncle. "Henry does? Why?"

"I don't know. He said he wanted to go out," said Ethel, picking a piece of cotton off her husband's trousers.

"Where is Henry?" said Beluncle.

"You said you wanted to go out this afternoon, Henry," said Ethel. "Ask your father. You're nineteen years old, you're old enough to speak up for yourself. Don't leave me your dirty work."

"Dirty," George said, putting his hand to his mouth.

"I don't understand," said Beluncle. "Maybe my mind is clouded, or I am stupid—but *out*? Out on a Sunday? Isn't this the day, I don't know, I am just asking what you think, isn't this the day a boy would wish to be with his father whom he has not seen all the week. A father and son—they ought to be friends. I can tell you," and here Beluncle put his broad, bluish, clean-shaven chin out like a penitent martyr, "I regret every minute I did not spend in my father's company. . . ."

"Let him go out," said Ethel, in her tired voice. "He is young. You have only one life."

"You speak," said Beluncle, "as if I was old. I want us to be young together. And I'd like to correct your thought there: life is not finite. It is infinite. If Henry wants to go out, let him go out, but if he feels it would be more loving to be with his father, let him stay. You have got that clear, Henry, I hope. I don't stop you, but you will be sorry later on in life for every moment you do not spend with me. Give me my hat, Ethel."

Beluncle took the grey hat and placed it carefully on his head before the mirror.

Henry, who had stood resolved in the darkness of the passage leading to the kitchen, was now weak, afraid and secretive before his father. Before that warm, full, decided voice, his desires had gone. He had now only one desire, the desire not to burst into tears. Unknown to himself, his eyes glared at his father, but his sulking and vain young lips were uneasy. Tears would come hysterically to his eyes, his voice would waver, and passion, between love and hatred, disordered him. Every year he had been saying, "Perhaps next year I shall not cry when I speak to this male; perhaps next year I shall not feel this ungovernable shame and guilt which burn me up before I know where I am."

"Mother is wrong, I don't want to go out," he said. "I was," he invented quickly, "thinking we could go out in the car."

His victory won, Beluncle turned sharply on his son.

"The car belongs to the business. You seem to think it is yours. On twenty-five shillings a week you cannot afford to go joy-riding round the country."

"Seventeen and six," said Ethel, who was quick at figures.

It seemed to Beluncle that he was surrounded by a family who took everything from him and were trying to break him; but what especially he did not like was the physical appearance of his sons. They were growing to be men and he felt this was a sickness that was overtaking them, for their voices were thin, light and nasal, they were pompous and rash in their opinions, their feelings were evidently in a continuous lightheaded flutter, and their shyness embarrassed him. Every time he saw them he thought them half-grown and he could hardly resist striking them in their weak faces in which he could see the garbled lineaments of himself. "I'd like," he said apologetically, "to knock their blocks off." He ordered them, he thwarted them abruptly, he shouted at them, his violence growing troubled as they got older, but not from any conscious policy. They had been in him and now like three callow lunatics they were trying to get out.

"I will go and say goodbye to mother," he said, changing to a reverent voice, "while Henry and George clean their boots. They can't go to church with boots like that. I suppose you are going to church?" he said.

The two boys hesitated and Henry looked at the hot sky shaking on the green tongues of the trees.

"Make up your minds," said Beluncle, with detachment. "One either wants God or one don't . . . doesn't."

"No one," thought Henry, "understands my difficulties."

Beluncle went upstairs to his mother's bedroom. It was moving to see a man who loved his mother so much. The house was a small one and a good deal of old Mrs Beluncle's furniture was on the landing and in the rooms. There were two fenders in some rooms, two coal-scuttles, two clocks, two desks, two wardrobes; one carpet would be laid upon another. The furniture was duplicated because the old lady was unwilling to part with it and her son enjoyed having too much. Beluncle used to think that if he sold all his own furniture, there would still be his mother's, and every day he altered what he would sell if his mother died and daydreamed about the prices as he walked about the house.

Beluncle was a soft and dignified walker, and was able to surprise anyone in the house. The softness of his tread was a pleasure, a kind of virtue. He was a soft walker in his factory and constantly surprised men who ought to have been working. "Who is the master?" his grave face seemed to say when he made one of his quiet apprearances.

He went into his mother's bedroom. The small old lady was an early riser and was standing between the foot of her brass bedstead and the open door of her wardrobe, lost, as she often was, trying to remember which year of her life this was and which place. In her strong glasses she looked like an ant, rambling over the hummocks of her past life, and looking for the entrance to it, so that she could find where she began and could end. Her white hair was tightly done and pulled up from the back of her childish neck. The loose skin under her chin was like the skin of a little plucked chicken.

Downstairs Ethel Beluncle was saying,

"Hurry up. He has only gone to show himself to grandmamma."

Every day Mr Beluncle showed himself—and by that he meant the clothes he was wearing—to his mother.

He stepped into his mother's room and glanced into the open wardrobe as he passed it. The shelves and the drawers of this large piece of furniture were filled with house linen of all kinds. Beluncle knew the wardrobe was worth something, but he was never sure about the linen; his mother had stored up an enormous quantity and the embroidery of it represented a lifetime's work with crochet hook and needle. What was it worth? A hundred pounds? Two hundred pounds? Mr Beluncle forced up the price at an imaginary auction, bidding against himself.

The old lady had grown very deaf and did not hear him come into the room.

"Eh, Philip," she said, in a flat and reproachful voice when she saw him. She was reproaching him still for getting married.

"Well, well," she said, nodding her head.

"Well, mother," said Beluncle.

These words were exchanged with random emotion, like the idle shots that break up the silence of the slow dog-days of a battle. The old lady had put on a small black silk apron and now she slowly brought her hands together on it and, squeezing them together, seemed to be squeezing a small, hard, electric smile into her face.

"How do I look, mother?" said Beluncle.

"Eh," said the old lady cautiously, "is that a new suit?"

"I've had it five years, mother."

"Well, well, five years. You keep it well. I trained you to keep your clothes. You favour me and not your father. You keep your clothes, like I trained you."

"I lay," said the old lady, "—I lay *she* doesn't care for your clothes as I cared for them."

"There is no one like you," said Beluncle.

The old lady stepped close to her son and felt the cloth of his suit.

"Good quality," she said, "the very best. It will last you. Turn round, Philip."

Beluncle turned round.

"Eh, it's good. Your Ethel will not appreciate it," she said.

"It vexes me you should take it to that wicked church; you broke your father's heart following that woman."

She was speaking of Mrs Parkinson.

Beluncle turned round.

"I follow my conscience, mother, as my father followed his," said Beluncle, smiling. He was obliged to speak to the deaf woman in a very loud voice, but he liked speaking loudly.

"I would not follow my conscience to hell-fire," said his mother, smiling also. The two smiles were the same, they appeared in fixed, hostile circles on the faces of the son and the mother, but his smile was wide and bland and showed his very white false teeth. These had been put in in his twenties because they looked smarter than ordinary teeth, because he knew that the idea that he could spend a lot of money would impress his customers. Her smile was still switched on, fixed and burning neither more brightly nor more dimly.

"There is only one God," said Beluncle. "Father and I worshipped him in different ways."

The old lady did not hear this and looked vacantly.

"I say," said Beluncle, "there is only one God."

"One," he said.

The old lady now understood.

"Your father did not run after women and worship idols or graven images," said the old lady.

Beluncle smiled happily and his mother smiled happily too.

"Look," said Beluncle, taking his rose out of his button-hole. "I have brought you a rose from the garden. It is a red rose like father loved."

The old lady took the rose quickly and held it to her nose.

"Eh, your father loved roses," she said. "He liked big roses, the best that smell. It brings him back to me, it took away the smell of tobacco."

She put the rose on the dressing-table with delight and said in an excited voice:

"I lay Ethel didn't give your coat a brush. Wait, I will brush you. I can't have you going out with dust. You could never abide dust and dirt when you were a little boy. You cried if you were dirty. Dirty, you said, dirty, mummy. It is the way I brought you up, not like some mothers. I can hear you in the closet, I can, crying out, 'Mummy, mummy, dirty. Dirtee,' until I came to you." She was looking on her dressing-table for the brush.

"The brush is not here," she said blankly.

"It is in your drawer," Beluncle said. "Drawer—D—R—A—W—E—R. Oh dear. Over there."

"Have you been looking in my drawer?" said the old lady suspiciously, opening the drawer. "No, it isn't here, where is it?"

"You have forgotten," said Beluncle. "Put the rose in water."

"It is my silver brush. It has a bit of silver on the back," said the old lady fretfully. "My mother gave it to me when I was married, two brushes with real silver, not for the wide world would I lose it. She bought them in Leeds at Masons and it cost her a five-pound note. . . ."

The old lady stopped and turned to her son, standing stiffly with her small fists clenched. Suddenly, without warning, she screamed out:

"Philip!" she cried. "I have been robbed. I have had the burglars. This house is full of thieves. They have taken my brush to get a few shillings. . . ."

"Now, mother, calm yourself. No one robs you. I will not have you say there are thieves in my house. You have forgotten where you put your brush."

"No, I have been robbed. Robbers have been here. They have been to my wardrobe. I have been counting my sheets. Where are my two double sheets and the six little embroidered towels? They have stolen them."

"Who has stolen them? No one. Don't be stupid, mother. No one touches your things," said Beluncle. "Now be a good girl and be quiet."

"Time is getting on," said Ethel Beluncle in a kind and playful voice, coming into the room. She had been waiting outside the door.

"Robbers have taken my brush," said the old lady.

"You wicked child," said Ethel Beluncle, her quick temper putting two red marks on her cheeks. "No one robs you in this house."

"Ssh! Ssh! Ethel!" said Beluncle. "She was looking for her brush."

"Oh, this shouting! I could hear you all over the house. What does she want a brush for? I've got a brush," said Ethel.

"Just to brush my suit."

"I've done that for you," said Ethel. "Can't you leave yourself alone. Mother and son, I never saw anything like it. I don't know what you married for."

"Now, now, don't you start," said Beluncle.

"No, I am your wife. I will have my say," said Ethel. "There are no thieves in this house, grandmamma. I was brought up straight, straighter than some. There's your brush on the washstand—I can see it from here."

They watched the silenced old lady go slyly like a cat to the washstand.

"Eh," said the old lady. "I was testing you. I knew it was there."

"Say something, Philip. She's your mother. She's always making her insinuations. Look here, my lady, has anyone been taking your sheets? . . ."

"Ethel!" said Beluncle sternly.

"Or towels? Some missing, I bet."

"Mother," said Beluncle, "you mustn't say that people rob you. Everyone is kind to you in this house. You mustn't say things like that."

"Or 'my best embroidered pillow-cases'," mocked Ethel Beluncle.

"Eh," said the old lady, "the old are not wanted. Their own children turn on them. I am an old woman and no one wants me except for my money. They want me in my grave."

"Oh, her money—what did I tell you?" laughed Ethel Beluncle bitterly.

"I wish," said Ethel to her husband, "oh, how I wish and I wish, I begged and begged and prayed, but you wouldn't listen. I wish you had never touched her money. Her money, who wants it?"

Beluncle sighed and looked at his watch and then at his finger-nails. Unlike the dirty, broken, bitten finger-nails of his wife, his were well kept and the moons showed perfectly on each finger. He began tapping his fingers rapidly on the bed knob. When money was mentioned he always straightened his fingers and tapped them very fast on a table or chair or any object that was close to him.

"You used a funny word there, a peculiar expression," said Beluncle with pain. "When you say I *touched* her money, I don't know what idea is in your mind. 'Touch' is a peculiar word. I never, to use your expression, *touched* her money. I never *touched* anyone's money. If I hadn't looked after mother's money she would not have had a penny left by now."

"Oh, well, I hope there *is* a penny left," said Ethel. "She's counting it all up, like her sheets and towels, every night, mark my words. Mother and son, what a pair of squirrels. Your teeth are too sharp. A wife counts for nothing and never has. She got my rose off you, I see, that I picked specially."

"You must behave better to Ethel," said Beluncle, who spoke quietly to his wife and who had to shout loud slow words to his mother. "She is my wife, don't forget that. She does everything for you."

The old lady was frightened, but she kept her head steady on its weak neck.

"No one can bring your father back to me, nay he was good," she said. "I have no one to stand up for me against my own children."

And when Beluncle went, the old lady walked in quick small steps circling about her room, repeating the name of her husband and wailing for him in a frail voice; but soon her thoughts were changed by the sight of her store cupboard.

Downstairs, Beluncle called the two sons who were going

to church with him. They were a little taller than he was, taller, but round-shouldered, and he marched, upright like a drummer, between them to the high gate of the villa. The house stood at the corner of the road, and the solid green gate was wide enough for a car and six feet high.

"Open it for me," said Beluncle.

It was opened for him. They marched out as from the gate of a hill fort in troubled country. The group re-formed when the gate was closed and set out, once more, in step. There had been a war in the Beluncles' lifetime, but peace seemed to them the real war. The boys waited for Beluncle to speak. When they turned on to the dazzling Sunday pavement of the empty main road, he began using occasional phrases familiar to followers of Mrs Parkinson.

"To mortal seeming," Beluncle said gently, "there are many things that are not harmonious in our home. Your grandmother says things she does not mean, that puts your mother's back up because I do not need to tell you what your mother is like, and she says things she does not mean, too. That is her weakness. That is her, you might say, problem. It is our part not to accept false evidence of the material senses, to dismiss its unreality and to voice the Truth. All the time we should be voicing the Truth."

He paused. In the silence the Beluncles were marching like a regiment whose band has stopped, and there was only the sound of their shoes on the pavement. The Truth, they felt, was somewhere, somehow, being voiced, but not by them. A deep breath and the Beluncle band began again on a more musical note.

"I am afraid," said Beluncle, "I'm very much afraid your grandmother will not last the year. She is an old woman. Of course, you know and I know, there is no such thing as age. We are all made in the image and likeness of God and so we cannot be either young or old, can we, are you listening? Now, there's a man who has grown some good dahlias. What was I saying?"

"About grandmamma," said George.

"Oh yes," said Beluncle. "That's right. It would be better

if we lived in a larger house where we could all breathe and
that, of course, requires money," said Beluncle.

"To mortal sense," he added apologetically.

"In a manner of speaking," he said.

"Yes," said Henry.

"Yes," George said, "but grandmamma will leave you
some." The two brothers glanced quickly at each other when
this was said. "If grandmamma doesn't last, we could move
this year."

"That's a terrible thing to say; a funny thing, people
would say if they heard it said," said Beluncle.

"You said," said George in his innocent voice, "you didn't
think she'd last."

"Oh, God, God, God," Henry was saying to himself, but
acting the words to an imaginary audience. "I wish my father
would talk of something else. A literary subject, for example."

A few people were now walking in the streets and the
church bells were speaking out. The marrying bells of the
Church of England poured out. One or two people passed
in the opposite direction on the long walk towards the
Roman Catholic bell at the end of the town; other little pro-
cessions were making towards the Congregational chapel and
the chapels of the Baptists, the Wesleyans, the room of the
Plymouth Brothers, the disinfected hall of Vogg's Witnesses
in Andrews's backyard. Presbyterians there were, and
Methodists, Internationalists and the Spiritualists in the
room above the Laguna Café. All, the Beluncles reflected,
mysteriously going to their errors. Mr Beluncle once said:
"I want a religion I can breathe in."

"I want possibilities," he said.

"If I pray," he said, "I want an answer like when I ring
a bell."

Now they were in the middle of the town and groups of
twenty or thirty cyclists were making for the heap of green
country that seemed to be frying in the sun outside the town:
they passed with the soft throb of flying birds and Henry's
eyes followed them into yesterday. But the Beluncles were
making for a long row of cars that stood outside the closed

cinema, the cars belonging to the members of Mr Beluncle's church. Down a passage at the side of the cinema, in a little brick hall with a notice saying Dances, was the meeting-place of the society.

VIII

The church of the Parkinsonians was a place of flowers and smiles. The Parkinsonians smiled in the hall as they greeted each other. Out in the town they were proud of the ridicule they suffered and their faces reported to each other the week's tale of quiet triumphs. Mr Beluncle frowned in answer to the smiles for he did not care to be anonymous: the two boys followed their father's expressions. He did not like theirs to be different from his own and if he had had his way they would have had one face controlled from a central point; indeed God, as he said, was a radio station. They went to sit beside him in the rush-seated chairs in the middle of the hall.

The Parkinsonians—their correct name was The Church of the Last Purification, Toronto—were a healthy-looking collection of clean, smiling people, broad and bummy, whether male or female, and with the exception of one or two poor people among them, they dressed expensively. Among the summer dresses, the fine hats—some of them from Bond Street—and the scents, there sat living examples of prayer promptly answered; and the satisfaction of it seemed, in each case, to have added to the weight of the person. People who were converted to the Purification put on weight at once, as if it had been sent down to them by the Central Committee of the party.

About twelve men and sixty women, most of them middle-aged, sat in the little hall, smelling the flowers that were set in a wide copper bowl in the middle of the speaker's platform, quietly assured that soon they would move into a proper church building of their own when the funds increased—which they shortly would: ever-increasing funds were a sign of the Purification—and irked only by the playing of a small, ratty organ which was on evil terms with its player. This was Colonel Johnson, who was thought to play badly because he deviated in the doctrine. The organ thumped and gulped back at him after every two or three chords of Wostenholme and became malevolent when he improvised. A great number of the Purificationists had given up something as their religion took a larger place in their lives, and Colonel Johnson, grown mild after a career of war, wore the expression of one who had given up music.

Mr Beluncle sat glancing at his wrist-watch for he was always out to catch the leader of the meeting beginning late, and if this lady did so, he would find an opportunity of telling her afterwards in the brotherly manner enjoined by the teachings of the Purification, pointing out, perhaps, that order was the first law of God or that Divine Mind was never late. George Beluncle, in his slow-minded way, was gazing at the pictures round the walls of the hall and remembering which was which. These had been turned round and showed only their backs for they had distracting subjects: tavern scenes repugnant to those who had given up wines and spirits, dancing scenes disturbing to the senses. George Beluncle had resolved to take part in such scenes later on in life. George Beluncle was waiting, too, for the leader to appear from the door at the back of the platform. The door always opened as if by no human touch and presently, indeed, this happened. Lady Roads glided in. She was a large and bold woman, in a royal blue dress, who put on a tragic and exalted face when she came on to the platform. She had reddish-grey hair and large, sad malicious eyes. In a melancholy and shouting voice she announced the hymn, Colonel Johnson punched the organ, the organ hit back at Colonel Johnson, and the congregation rose to sing in voices of deafening refinement.

"Let us unite in silent prah," barked Lady Roads. The congregation closed their eyes.

Henry Beluncle glanced at the closed eyes of his father. He

was overcome by the sight of his father praying. To pray in company with his father embarrassed him. He felt that it was hypocritical and unfair to pray. For Henry Beluncle's prayers were radiant, passionate and severe; and if they were answered (as the prayers of those who followed the teachings of the Purification so often were), there would be such a transformation of his father's character that the father would no longer exist in his present physical or even spiritual form. Henry Beluncle's prayers might be compared to exalted and disinterested murder. To this, Henry Beluncle knew, his father would offer a victorious resistance; even so, it seemed deceitful and underhand to try such a thing. And there was not only this side to it: Henry Beluncle himself had no desire suddenly to become a child of Divine Love, for he saw that such a change would make him an anomaly in the family. Especially it would call upon him the scorn of his mother whom he deeply loved and who did not subscribe to this religion.

"No one understands my difficulties": it was Henry Beluncle's continual thought. If he and his father were reformed, where would Henry Beluncle's freedom go? He would be happy and, though his eyes moistened at the thought of this, he knew he despised happiness.

After one or two attempts at a prayer that would evade this central issue in his life, Henry Beluncle gave up and through his eyelashes took a cautious forest hunter's view of the congregation. He saw clearly the closed lids, so pale in her tawny face, of Lady Roads, and the freckles of her bosom like grains of cinnamon and milk. Her masterful lips now shrank into thin, short lines of dejection; her mildness and merryness had gone; she was betraying as she never did in her waking life, her unhappy marriage, her mania of sexual disgust. Below her, through a gap in the women's hats, Henry Beluncle could see Colonel Johnson, his chin raised and his eyes closed, no doubt thinking out his tactics with the next hymn. One or two pairs of eyes, when Henry looked round, were restless; Mr Phibbs's were wide open, happily musing. When someone said "Let us pray" the spirit of opposition in Mr Phibbs had replied "I am not a sheep." And there was modest Miss More, who felt too humble and worried to pray, and the trembling and acid Miss Wix, the white-faced enemy of Lady Roads. In the silence broken only by the sound of traffic on the High Street or the bang of a saucepan in a nearby house, Henry searched the congregation for the red dress and fair hair of Mary Phibbs. He knew she was here because of him, and he because of her. That, for him, was the one certain thing.

Lady Roads's eyes opened and her melancholy went. She read out the first verse of another hymn, and like many of the hymns of the Purification, it was a conundrum. She read:

> *If All is Mind and Mind is All,*
> *Man cannot sin and did not fall.*
> *Hold to this thought and we shall be*
> *At one with Mind in harmony.*

One of its high and jocose whistling notes came out of the organ—symbol of the Colonel's imperfect understanding of the teachings of the Purification—prolonging itself while he sought the cause, and did not stop until he crushed it with a chord. The congregation rose and now Henry Beluncle saw the Misses Phibbs, three of them, apart from their father, sitting on the far side of the hall. The eldest one turned boldly round, looking for Henry, and then whispered to the dark one, who looked round, too; and this one whispered to Mary, who did not turn, but one of her shoulders moved nervously and was higher than the other for the rest of the service.

The warm hour crawled by. The services of the Purification were eventless. The Scriptures were read; the works of the divinely inspired Mrs Parkinson were read. Her prose ground on, knocked into restful nullity by abstract nouns and remarkable alliterations; the word "infinite" tolled like a bell. George Beluncle, guessing the makes of the cars that whined past, woke up to find the service over and people everywhere talking and laughing.

Two of the Phibbs girls walked down the side of the hall to stare at Henry who had fallen in love with their sister, silently to flirt with him and to look defiantly at Mr Beluncle, who had not hidden his opinion that earthly love was a general error and that earthly love between a Beluncle and a Phibbs was a crime. Mr Phibbs was a friend of the heretical Miss Wix, whose weekly battles with Lady Roads were dividing the Purifiers; Mr Beluncle was a Roadsite. Mary Phibbs, blushing to the neck and even to her hands, was standing as near to Henry as she dared and talking to Miss Dykes, the crippled sister of Mrs Truslove, who was wheeled to the meeting every Sunday.

Henry and Mary Phibbs smiled secretly to each other across the body of the cripple and he knew that the cripple was watching them.

The fair hair of Mary Phibbs was crisp and in her long, young, unformed face her small eyes moved coquettishly after being still for so long in church. The colour of yesterday's sun was on her skin. She looked possessively at Henry and moved her lips to remind him of their kisses and then looked away. Henry glanced to see if his father was looking, but listened to the soft, flat voice of the girl, so slow, domestic, so maddening to him and yet so melting to his heart!

He said to her when they were out of earshot of the cripple. "Not this afternoon."

And he wanted to add: "You do not understand my difficulties."

"Oh, Henry, why?" said the girl.

Henry nodded to his father.

"Why are you afraid of him?" said the girl, putting on an obstinate look.

Henry looked nervously again, but his father was talking to Lady Roads. They would be talking about business, for Mr Beluncle thought that any conversation unconcerned with money was unspiritual.

"I am not afraid," said Henry. "It is my home, you do not know what it is like and how they quarrel."

"I am sorry for you, Henry," the girl said tenderly. "Dadda is sorry, too. It is very wrong."

Pride danced into Henry Beluncle's eyes: he was proud of

the family quarrels of the Beluncles, the continual mind-sharpening, heart-deadening warfare. He would have liked to begin, for example, by breaking Mary Phibbs of the love of the happiness of her family, a happiness he could only despise.

Henry Beluncle made an excuse to walk away from Mary Phibbs. In the very moment that his back was turned upon her, one of his imaginary pictures of her clicked into position in his heart, which throbbed quickly as he turned her into a beauty. He looked back but she had already hurried out of the building with her sisters and the young children she always gathered about her. The rest of the day he would try not to think of her as sitting in the small, camphor-smelling parlour of her house, where the walnut piano twanged and the torn music lay on the chairs, while one sister played and the other one sang ballads like *Parted*, *Friend O' Mine* and *Sea Fever*; but would work on some other scene for their love. In mid air seemed the happiest. There like two spirits they met and ran through the literature of love. The sensations of loving would pass over him, wave after lacy wave, as if he were lying in the shallow salt water of the sea's edge, and he wished he could pass the rest of the day alone in the helplessness of their continual touch.

The cripple sat on her wheeled chair at the back of the hall. She was a woman of thirty-nine. Her eyes were brilliant like a young girl's at a dance and she was eager for attention. A Sunday morning service and the mid-week meetings of the Purification were the two social moments of her life and she behaved with all the variableness of mood of a fanatical and adept hostess who interrupts conversations, attracts people to herself, and is always, after the first sentences, looking beyond the person she is talking to in case anything better is being missed. Miss Dykes was one of the best-dressed women in the congregation. She liked to wear small, high-heeled shoes on her useless feet, and she had a dozen pairs of shoes at home. Mrs Truslove, her sister, criticised this expense, but the cripple said with petulance that one day the Purification would heal her and she would walk. She must be ready then to live the years that she had wasted since she was thirteen years old. It was natural to receive these words with kindness and sadness and to think of her as a child. Miss Dykes had smooth grey hair brushed up from a high forehead, and a long sallow face. Her long, grey eyes cut into it and she seemed to belong to the grave and hard race of fairies, whose brilliance does not decline, who carry youth about like a copy that is truer than the original. She seemed stronger and longer lasting than human beings are.

"It was a beautiful service," said the humble Miss More, who had had her hair cropped after the 1914 War, so that the oppression of being a woman should not come between herself and God. "It was a great joy, such peace."

"Yes," said the fashionable cripple, studying and then dismissing the thick tweed coat and skirt which Miss More wore as a kind of marching uniform. "But I wanted to cry out"—and into the word "wanted" Miss Dykes put a yearning that darkened her eyes—"'Awake thou that sleepest. Arise from the dead.'"

Miss More blinked stolidly and her shoulders rounded with shame. Yes, it was true: she must arise from the dead. She must do more for others.

"Can I wheel you out?" she asked timidly, for she was a strong, broad woman and she thought that, without too much pride, she would offer her strength.

"Out!" said the cripple. "I'm not going yet. There are *hundreds* of people I haven't seen. Why is Miss Wix talking to Mr Phibbs? The atmosphere in this church is wrong; that is why I do not get my healing. They hold me back."

"It *is* wrong," said Miss More, and she felt "I must be wrong." She prayed slowly to correct this and the cripple saw that Miss More's broad face looked dazed.

"Awake, dear," said the cripple severely, "awake."

"This afternoon," thought Miss More, "I must make a special effort. She is right. I have become a burden to the Truth."

Miss More did not know how to leave; she knew only how to be replaced and Mr Beluncle now replaced her. He had wandered without noticing towards the cripple, whom he did not want to see.

"Your boy," snapped the cripple, "has picked the plainest of the Phibbses."

Mr Beluncle smiled cheerfully at the smell of war.

"I am not aware," he said, "that my boy is in a situation to *pick* any girl—to use your expression. He has all his work cut out reflecting the Divine Mind. We all of us have. And," Mr Beluncle smiled, "without wishing to suggest anything personal I came to this meeting to hear the Truth voiced and not to hear the false evidence of the material senses. Pardon my correction."

The cripple's eyes hardened and became like precious stones, brilliant with hatred.

"You are shelling my position," she said.

It was common for Miss Dykes to see herself as a military problem. On days when she was melancholy she would speak of Error putting down a barrage and advancing upon her. Or she would accuse Miss Wix of undermining her lines. She would speak of beating off the enemy attack all day. Then, like a storm dying away, the battle would vanish and her nature changed.

"Your mistake—just a loving word in season," said Beluncle, "in a brotherly way."

"You are not my brother, nor my brother-in-law," said the cripple, without rancour, for the cripple liked to make insinuations about Beluncle's relations with her sister, in order to enjoy the effect of them upon him. She said such things archly, with the licence of the *ingénue*.

Beluncle boiled up red and then opened his mouth, showed a row of teeth, and smiled knowingly.

"What's bitten you today?" he said. "Your tongue is your problem."

"Mr Beluncle and I are old friends," the cripple insinuated to Lady Roads, who approached again. "He comes to see me every day."

Now she had exhausted the company. It was Miss Dykes's faith that if she fulfilled the letter and the spirit of Mrs

Parkinson's teachings, she would one day rise up and walk. She believed this might happen in the middle of the prayers of the meeting and had often imagined the scene, how she would cry out her gratitude aloud, how at once she would be surrounded by the awe of people, some kneeling, some standing in doubt, and how God would speak through her lips. She wept when she thought of this. For her, there was no doubt that this would happen, and many, seeing her faith, were rebuked by the sight of it. Some truly longed for the miracle to occur; others were afraid of it; but many of the Purifiers had begun to resent the presence at their meetings of one with whom their religion had failed, for it made a bad impression on newcomers to the church. Others, the followers of Miss Wix, had no belief in the healing of Miss Dykes because she was, notoriously, treated by Lady Roads and they commonly said that if the miracle did occur it would not be the work of God, but an exercise of witchcraft, the result of hypnotism, Antichrist and wicked magic, which Lady Roads was known by them to practise.

"I have never met your wife," said Lady Roads, who enormously enjoyed the disputes she created in the church, to Mr Beluncle. "You always promise to bring her, but she does not come. She is not here this morning, is she?"

"No, she is not," said Beluncle.

"I shall call on her. I shall drop in unexpectedly," said Lady Roads in a masterful way.

"My wife," said Beluncle, resisting witchcraft, "is a peculiar woman. She is a recluse. She likes to be alone with her family."

"I don't believe it," said Lady Roads. "You are hiding her. I shall break in. I shall probably break in this afternoon."

"This afternoon would be inconvenient," said Beluncle, who saw himself putting the aristocracy in their place.

"Ha! Ha! Ha!" barked Lady Roads in her loud, man's voice. "I shall come round to catch you off your guard."

Now she was among her congregation, Lady Roads walked about smiling widely and laughing, as if she were going to eat them one by one, enjoying the way she frightened them. At the back of her mind was the thought, "These are all suburban middle-class people; they are all afraid of me."

When she went, Beluncle called quietly to his sons:

"George, Henry, come here."

They stood beside him and he looked at them with rage.

"What d'you mean by keeping me waiting like this?" he muttered to them. "You are unkind. You ought to be home helping your mother. You know we have no servants and yet you allow your mother to slave for you all day long; because of you she cannot leave the house. You think because you are here among people who keep servants that you are better than your mother, but let me tell you, you are not."

They marched out of the church, passing Mr Phibbs at the door. As a stationmaster he took up this post by nature, looking sardonically at each member of the congregation, conveying clearly to them that they were passengers. "To-day," he conveyed, "you are children of God. Tomorrow you will be season-ticket holders." Mr Beluncle would have passed him with a nod, but Mr Phibbs stood lazily in front of him in a familiar way. Mr Phibbs had a reddish moustache, a large soft thing, lying over his large, blabbing mouth, a moustache which might have been grown (and perhaps by some unfair means) to win a prize.

"How many understood what they heard this morning, Beluncle?" said Mr Phibbs, in his "mere" voice. "How many?"

"Understanding is a privilege," said Mr Beluncle. Mr Phibbs slowly studied the backs of the Beluncles from their necks to their heels as they walked away.

"There's a man whose coat needs a brush. What d'you know about the Phibbses?" said Beluncle sharply to his sons.

"The Phibbses?" said Henry innocently.

"Do I have to spell it?" said Beluncle.

George turned his head to smile secretly.

"You seem to be thick with them," said Beluncle. "They are not the class of people I would expect you to be thick with."

"I have seen them once or twice," said Henry.

"Not those girls, I hope," said Beluncle, marching faster. "Don't misunderstand me, when I use the word 'common', we are all children of God, but some just don't seem to have solved their problems."

"What problems?" said Henry coldly.

"Now it's no use you thinking yourself superior," said Beluncle. "You know what I mean. If you think you're superior you'd better get out, that's all there is to that."

Mr Beluncle's pace was fast. He suddenly said: "I can tell you one thing: I married too young. You might say from a mortal point of view, I was seemingly caught. If I had my life over again I wouldn't do the same. I think, by the way, I shall change my church. There's a better Purification meet-ing at Merford, nicer people, larger, freer. I can't breathe in that place."

To Mr Beluncle and Henry the promises of the day had already failed, and as they approached their house both father and son saw it with dismay. Only George Beluncle was happy. He had gone faithfully with his father; he did not like or understand the service; the Scriptures were a meaning-less tyranny and Mrs Parkinson's words passed over his head; all he asked was that presently his father would forget the strange trigonometry of his religion and notice his devotion and that it would please him. A consoling certainty that he could protect his father from the extravagances of his religion made George content.

"Open the gate, George," said Beluncle.

George ran ahead and opened the high, heavy wooden gate which distinguished his house from all the others in the road. It opened on what George called The Drive, but which was only a short path ten yards long going to the front door of the house.

"Shut the gate, George. Shut it right up. Now put up the bar," said Beluncle.

This was an extraordinary order and George hesitated.

"Do as I tell you," said Beluncle. "Help him, Henry. And bolt it." The heavy iron bar was lifted, the bolts were sent home.

"I don't want Lady Roads bursting in here while we're at home. I don't want," said Beluncle, "people sticking their noses in to see how we live. If you hear anyone at the gate you are not to go to it."

Then, when the gate was barred, the Beluncles advanced to the smell of their lunch.

IX

Meals were sacred to the Beluncles and Mr Beluncle regarded them as spiritual occasions. The more one ate, the more one was filled with Goodness. Eating was a blameless passion which annihilated the unprofitable ones. Once or twice Ethel Beluncle had blasphemously ruined the sacred Sunday meal by starting a quarrel, crying out as she planked the joint on the table, "Get your other woman to cook. I won't touch it," and leaving the room in hysterics. When Ethel Beluncle wished to be outrageous she ruined a meal. But this did not often happen. Most of their Sunday meals began awkwardly. Everyone knew that unpleasant topics might "come up", everyone did his best to talk about the food before them all, in order to prevent this happening. Indeed, that was the only safe thing to talk about and Beluncle himself responded to it. To carve a large joint was Mr Beluncle's joy. He changed his glasses first, in order to see it better. He stood up and sharpened his knife austerely, looking at the joint with the pity of the artist for his subject. Then he shook his head sadly,

"I don't know, I'm sure," he said.

"It seems a shame," he said, smiling across to his wife.

"Well," he said, "I suppose we must."

The family smiled upon him.

"I can't think what you're all waiting for," he said. And then, in went the fork and he began to carve, his face going hot with pleasure.

"Pass this to your grandmother," he said.

For it was generally appreciated that she was the one most likely to "bring up" unwanted topics and that to feed her quickly was the best way of keeping them down.

"That," said Leslie, the youngest, who was allowed to express the real feelings of the family, "that," he said, "should keep her quiet."

Beluncle carved away with the energy of a conductor working his orchestra through a piece of music. Murmurs of "Is it tender?" from Ethel, "Is it cooked enough?" were taken up by Beluncle in musical fashion with exclamations of mock despair, "I'm spoiling the look of this," and at last "Now it's poor father's turn." Eagerly vegetables were passed to Mr Beluncle, in the hope that he, too, like his mother, would forget his store of unhappy subjects. If he could be kept eating, if they all could be kept eating, virtue would be preserved. "For God's sake," Henry, the adolescent, prayed, "let us overeat." Only Ethel would not eat much, indeed as her husband grew larger and blander so she became leaner—or so it seemed—but, perhaps, she could be made to smile and even to laugh. If Leslie could be provoked to impertinence then the feast would pass off without harm. The eyes, even Mr Beluncle's, often turned to him.

For a while the normal conversation of the Beluncles was practised. "It's nicely done," said Beluncle.

"Is it nicely done?" asked Ethel. "I always have trouble with that oven. I had the dampers in and still it did not seem to heat up, not to say 'eat," said Ethel.

"Heat," said Leslie.

"You want the top damper out," said Beluncle.

"I don't understand it," said Ethel.

"I remember," said Beluncle, "a wonderful piece of beef I had at the Waverley. Was it the Waverley? When I was travelling for Milders and Spoons, just before we started in business; but if you want mutton the Welsh are the best places. I used to know the chef at the Hotspur and he used to say to me, 'We heard you were coming, Mr Beluncle. I've got the nicest piece I've seen in twenty years. Tonight you can be kind to yourself.' "

"What?" said the grandmother.

Leslie sat beside her and acted as her telephone.

"He said you starved him when he was a boy," said Leslie. "He never got a decent meal until he went to an hotel."

"Eh," said the grandmother, enjoying this irony. "I fed him on the best. The best Mr Battle ever had. 'Eh, I want the best, Mr Battle,' I used to say, and he used to say, 'Mrs Beluncle, you know I keep it for you and I know it won't be spoiled in your hands, there are some in this town I wouldn't sell it to.' "

"They wouldn't sell *you* the best," Leslie called to his mother. "Look how she's putting it away."

"Leslie!" said Beluncle.

"If you've got a good range," said Ethel, with a tact uncommon in her, "that's the whole thing in a nutshell."

"How much did you burn on that old Cromwell we had at home?" said Beluncle to his mother.

That was another safe subject. They could now go on to soft coal, hard coal, boiler nuts, gas coke and anthracite, with diversions to steam coal, large coal, slow coal and the price of it, which was cheaper in which year. And from there, the question of grates was taken up. Open grates, closed grates, boilers, old kitcheners and new ovens, wicked great things that ate it up like ships, furious small things that roared like engines. And the grandmother recalled older grates and open grates and spits, and "some" she knew (dangerously leaving the subject) had fires in their bedrooms. Mr Beluncle supplied prices, tonnages, measurements, figures of consumption and speculated upon them, worked out what a ten-roomed house used, or a house like Lady Roads's which had thirteen bedrooms and four reception rooms, and contrasted this with the consumption of several large hotels, going all over England for examples.

"Grandmamma has got something on her mind," said Leslie.

Mr Beluncle stopped and the old lady said:

"Your father always sorted the coal into sizes and stacked it in the cellar with his own hands. It looked beautiful, as

81

neat as a brick wall, it was a shame to touch it. And we had to be careful," she said, with a malicious look at Ethel, "not like some in London that throw it on with a bucket."

"Wearing a man's life out for a bucket of coal," said Ethel.

"Mother doesn't look so well," said Beluncle.

"Did you see what she ate?" said Leslie.

"You said she didn't look well before. *I* don't feel well," said Ethel.

"I doubt if she'll last till Christmas. The money's safe," said Leslie.

"Now then, Leslie," said Beluncle.

"What did he say?" said the grandmother.

"I said Christmas is coming," said Leslie.

"Eh, I always do well at Christmas," said the grandmother.

"You bet you do. You'd raise hell if you didn't," said Leslie.

"Leslie, I won't have language," said Beluncle. "And you mustn't say things. It's not kind. . . ."

" 'It's not necessary, it's not Christian,' " the boy quoted. " 'It's not God-protected, God-directed'—but someone has got to find the cash."

Everyone smiled, even Beluncle smiled, at Leslie. The youngest of them, he seemed much the older, much older than his nervous brothers. Leslie was the privileged one and all listened to him with relief when he brought out the scandals of the family. How Mr Beluncle had already got possession of some of his mother's money and was now preparing to get his sister's share, how Mr Beluncle helped himself to money from everyone he met, and so on. Mr Beluncle was defeated by his son: he laughed uncomfortably. Ethel watched her husband as every dart went home. George grinned vacantly, delighted to see his God destroyed before his eyes. Only Henry sat cold and reserved and unsmiling, angry that shameful things should be publicly said.

"I am an intellectual," he said to himself. "I must get out of this. To think that no one in this house has read Anatole France."

"What's the matter with Henry?" Beluncle said.

"Nothing," said Henry.

"I thought," said Beluncle, "there was. You looked as though you were thinking. As though you had thoughts. Great thoughts, I have no doubt. Tell us the thought for today. From Shakespeare or something. Don't keep it to yourself. Be sociable."

George was delighted to see his elder brother attacked.

"I never have a great thought," said Henry coldly.

"A pity. I thought you could enlighten us," said Beluncle.

The sunlight made tall triangles on the porridge-coloured wallpaper close to the windows and caught the corners of the oak mantelpiece, picking out the brown ornaments with the Scottish proverbs upon them. The dining-room of the Beluncles was used by Mr Beluncle alone during the week, but on Sundays the family moved there. Some of the furniture in this room was too large and each piece represented a crisis in the early financial life of the family. There was a piano which had been the subject of a writ. Pressing calls, angry letters, a solicitor's threat, had pressed around the sideboard. For a year or two the carpet lay like a lawsuit: Beluncle had said it was "on trial" or "on approval". The dining-table of black oak had been unsaleable in one of Mr Beluncle's misfortunes, and had remained like a black sheep in the family, almost sacred because it had turned out not to be an asset. Other pieces of furniture came from Mr Beluncle's furniture factory, and it was understood that, technically, the chairs—he made chairs—were not part of the home, but were on loan from the directors of the business, who, he conveyed, were always enquiring about them. To Mr Beluncle the furniture of the house was, in a poetical sense, stock and his most common remark was "Be careful with it. It may have to go back." This gave the Beluncles the sensation that their home was a warehouse and the furniture insubstantial—it might vanish or land them in the courts—and, on the other hand, that Mr Beluncle was their real furniture, his conversation their carpet, his anger their utensils, his person their armchairs. They were sitting, treading, reclining on him and this was an emotional experience. He himself regarded his home indifferently. The happiest years of his life had been spent in large commercial hotels, and when he bought furniture, he bought it unconsciously for one of them. His highest praise for any object was that it was "too large".

Henry ate little and kept his eyes on the things in the room. Half-way through every Sunday meal, doubt appeared in his mind. If God did not make Evil, where did Evil come from? Ever since he had openly declared his belief in the Purification he had begun to doubt it. Lady Roads had opened her large eyes upon him, Colonel Johnson had asked him to tea, Mr Phibbs had told him Evil was all in the class system, Mary Phibbs had said her father knew. In vain: Henry was still dogged by the sense of evil, by the reality of pain, the conviction of sin.

"Henry," said Ethel, now that her husband had stopped questioning him. "Henry. Eat up. What is the matter?"

"Nothing," said Henry.

"If Henry thinks he's being superior by not eating, that is where he is wrong," said Beluncle. "Digs at thirty shillings a week will make him thin. He'll soon come running back."

"Have you been at him?" said Ethel, who was out for justice for her sons.

"No," Henry answered quickly, seeing that his father, refreshed by food, was ready for dispute.

"Prig," said George, under his breath.

"I may have been giving Henry advice, but he doesn't want his father's advice. Oh, no. His father's an old fool. When I was nineteen I thought my father a fool."

"Well, he was. You often told me," said Ethel. "He gave in to her," said Ethel, nodding to the grandmother. "Yes, dear, no dear, as you please, dear. I can hear him. The little queen of Mixham in the Mud."

"Well," said Beluncle, "we needn't be vulgar."

"Henry wants to go out," said George, not wishing a quarrel to be lost in his mother's reminiscences.

"I thought you settled that," said Ethel. "You Beluncles

are worse than dogs at a bone. Thank God *we* were not brought up like that. Let him go out. You were young once."

"Yes, and I should like to be young again," said Beluncle earnestly. "I would appreciate my father as I didn't do; no, I didn't appreciate my father enough. And now he's dead I regret it. A thousand times I regret it." And Mr. Beluncle with emotion raised the corner of his table napkin to his eye. "Henry knows as well as I do that if his love of his father means nothing to him, there's nothing to stop him going out. And, by the by, youth and age: I'll give you a thought there. It's in your own consciousness, as a man thinketh in his heart so he will be, if he thinks he's old then he will be old. A man believes he is young and he is young. Your grand-mother—take your grandmother . . ."

The old lady, having eaten, was now asleep. They had sat long at the table and she looked, under her glasses, like a pale, little stuffed frog.

"She thinks she is seventy-seven. The world thinks she is seventy-seven. That belief is pinned on to her. But what is seventy-seven? Just an expression. Two figures. Seven and seven. It might just as well be six and six. That's all there is to it. I met a man yesterday who was eighty-four," said Beluncle genially.

"Well, come to the point," said Ethel. "Remember I'm stupid. I never had any education."

"Henry," said Beluncle, pushing his chair back, stretch-ing out his legs and tenting his fingers, "Henry is young. Henry is sentimental. Henry, I have no doubt, thinks he's in love. He may think he can deceive me, but he can't deceive me. I am not a fool. I keep my ears and eyes open. Does he tell his father? Does he make his father his friend? Does he try to be close to his father? Does he ask his father to share his thoughts, his secrets? No! Henry doesn't want to be close. Isn't that so?" He paused.

"Henry deceives. It is not his father's business."

"I'll never forget the row when you told your father you was in love," said Ethel, "with that silly girl in the chemist's shop. And what about me?"

Beluncle wagged his head patiently, waiting for her to end.

"My father did not have the understanding."

The blood made a dark cloud on Henry's face and anger dried his mouth.

"I'm not in love, I'm not in love," shouted Henry. "I tell you I am not.

"I wish I were," he cried out.

"I wish I could be in love," he said. "You do not love mother, you told us this morning. . . ." But tears filled Henry's eyes, he was choking with sobs he could not govern. To his astonishment no quarrel started. The rest of the family were silent, watching him with fear, with curiosity and with a peculiar pride. His mother looked sternly at him with the ironical amusement of a young girl, and even tidied her hair at the back as she did so.

"Grandmamma doesn't give a . . ." said Leslie.

"Leslie!" said Ethel, stopping him.

Beluncle gazed at Leslie and forgave him.

"That is not," he said (but he was not referring to anything in particular), "what we are taught by the Science of Purification."

And being launched on this, enlarged upon it, his pleasant deep voice rumbling on like a bluebottle in the room, going round and round. Love was Divine, he said. Love was getting up when you are called, not making a mess in the bathroom, coming when you are sent for, being prompt, punctual, tidy; not shutting yourself up unsociably with books, keeping the garden tidy, doing your job properly, getting to know nice people, seeking first the kingdom of Heaven, respecting the home, not kicking the furniture. . . .

The tears dried and burned on Henry's face. "Burned dry the wandering Beduin," he was thinking, "with gazing eyes": only words came to his mind. "Wandering", "gazing" —were those the best words? He gave in before the warm waves of Beluncle's voice and was carried listlessly to the centre of his father's affairs.

"It is no use saying we cannot love, for love is God and we are all like Him. When I go to my factory and make furniture, to mortal sense I seem to be making wardrobes, armchairs, and so on, but really I am spreading love." Mr Beluncle raised his short heavy arms and was himself struck by the luxuriousness of his soft pink hands which seemed to smooth the very air. "And the more I spread love, the more orders I get, and it's right for me to have orders because orders are giving love. It is not money we want, it is love."

"What I can't understand," Ethel said, "is why you had such a bad year last year."

"That is where you show your lack of understanding, if you will allow me to say so," said Beluncle. "If you had more understanding you would not speak of last year as a bad year. We live in an eternal now."

"Ah, now, now, now," the word drummed on Henry's brain. "Now the wandering Beduin . . ."

"Oh, talk English. You mean I'm ignorant," said Ethel. "I am. An ordinary school, St. Mary's, Church of England, till I was thirteen and then I was apprenticed. I can't talk, but I know the difference between sixpence and a shilling."

"It's sixpence," said Leslie, and Ethel looked frightened when he said this.

"Your mother is talking," Beluncle said. "Let her finish what she has to say."

"Oh, it's of no importance what I have to say," said Ethel, looking sideways, and speaking to the top of the curtain pole. "I thought you had a bad year last year, but perhaps my hearing is going wrong. Gran suffered from her ears too. You had to have that money from grandmamma here because it was bad. It's all right as long as it's straight."

"It's all right. Carry on," Leslie said. "Grandmamma's well away."

"It looks to me that Divine Love means someone puts up the money," Ethel said.

Beluncle's rosy face became pale in patches and he looked stern.

"You've finished, I hope," said Beluncle. "You have told us what is on your mind."

"No, I haven't," said Ethel. "I've never finished. I never shall."

"Well, women have to have the last word," said Beluncle amiably. "My father used to say, I can see him saying it, in our kitchen, he must have been my age—that's funny when you think of it—he used to say a man's betrayers are in his own home, those you think love you are the ones who wound you, strangle you, it seems that where you'd think there would be gratitude, the carnal mind tries hardest to put most hate. He used to say to mother there 'May God forgive you, you wicked woman.' I have heard him, after they'd been having words."

No one answered this, but all gazed at grandmamma. They could see the small stone house where she used to live, with a monkey puzzle in front of it like a moustache. The smell of the house came back to them. To Ethel the smell of soap from a scrubbed table, to the boys the smell of country bacon and the deep, hanging odours of fruit and of damp in the parlour; there was a smell that seemed to come from the tropical leafage and flowers of the country carpet. However far back they went, from father to grandfather, from grandfather to great-grandfather, there was God in their family, sitting obdurate in one room of the house and saying to their guilty minds: Thou shalt have no other Gods before me.

Henry gazed across to the window and to the short lime trees. The wind was playing on the leaves, turning them from shade to sun, from pale to dark; brushed like a bird's breast. In places he could see small changing tears of sky. Gone three o'clock, how long they sat! He imagined himself on some country common and fitfully his imagination tried to bring Mary with him, but she was always dropping back on the road and vanishing while he, consuming his freedom, went on. There was only himself. After his shout and his tears, his body seemed to be bruised and his throat ached.

George was thinking: now he has done, he has finished everything, he has reduced them all. There is only himself and myself left, we can go away and forget them all. I don't

mind what he says to me, what he does to me. He looked
appealingly at his father and Beluncle frowned and parted
his lips in rebuke. George smiled a little, looking forward
softly to the attack.

But it did not come. Leslie straightened lazily in his
chair.

"Listen," he said.

"What?" said Ethel.

"Someone at the gate," said Leslie.

"Silence," said Beluncle. "Listen."

They heard the heavy green wooden gate being shaken.

"Someone trying to get in," said Ethel.

"Lady Roads," said George.

"Did you bolt that gate as I asked you?" Beluncle asked.
"A quarter past three, what an hour to call."

"We sit and sit," said Ethel.

"They're still shaking it," said Leslie.

Beluncle got up and gave quick orders.

"Is the front door shut? What about the kitchen door?
No one is to go to the windows. Sit still."

All were now standing except the grandmother. They
were stopped by Beluncle's contradictory orders.

"Talk quietly," said Beluncle. "Now, quickly, quietly,
clear these things away."

Each one took plates or glasses from the table and hurried
from the room with them.

"What about her?" said Leslie, pointing to the grandmother.

"Let mother sleep," said Beluncle. "Confound you. Can't
you move quietly?"

A madness had seized the Beluncle family. Each, as he
dashed with a plate to the kitchen, was astonished by the
frenzy of the other. Why is he rushing about like a lunatic?
So their eyes taunted one another. A half laugh of hysteria
was on their lips. Any moment we may be caught, we may
be exposed, the whole pack of cards will come down. In the
room, giving orders, estimating the sleep of his mother, peeping through the curtains to see if the gates were still shaking,

Mr Beluncle said, as each member of the family came back into the hot room:

"I don't want people to see how we live."

"How we live!" mocked Henry, as they passed one another.

"How we live," laughed George, under his breath.

"Do her good this Lady What's It," said Ethel. "Do her good. Let her see. Let the world see. Let them see what I have been through."

But she was possessed of a spirit as fanatical as her husband's.

The table was clear and, having given his orders, Mr Beluncle went to the small dark room at the back of the house where he sometimes sat alone; the others crowded into the small kitchen and listened at the closed door. In his room, Mr Beluncle brushed his coat and then nervously pulled a dozen or so unread magazines, issued by the Purification, out of their wrappers—for it would create a bad impression, if the caller really were Lady Roads, when she saw the literature of their religion unread—and sat with a scornful expression on his face, waiting.

"Tidy yourself, Ethel," he said, when she recklessly came into the room. "I can't imagine she will break in, but take that apron off, do."

"She can see me as I am and as you have made me," said Ethel angrily, but she obeyed him. She took off the apron and closed the door of the room. They were talking in quick, lowered voices, with the tenseness of their campaign. One of the boys, after creeping up the passage, reported that the gate was still. He had come into the room. Suddenly there was a new sound. There was a clatter at the front door.

"What's that?" said Beluncle.

The noise rose and a woman's shouting was heard.

"She's in. She's got in," said Beluncle, and went out in three strides, his neck swelling and his fists clenched. The front door was wide open.

In the dining-room the grandmother had slept, forgotten, through the noise, with her small head sunk like a kitten's as the family bumped past her. She could have wished to dream about her husband, but he rarely came into her sleep; though often he was on the edge of the dream, a presence felt in the next room. She had two kinds of dreams: ones that were grotesquely comical, not fitting—so full of antics they were—to an old lady and she woke up ashamed; others that were about her childhood and the people she had known in her village at that time. As the Beluncles bumped past her she was dreaming she was at a railway junction and that luggage, containing her linen, her silver and clothes, was being lost.

Now she opened her eyes.

She found herself alone. There was no one in the room. There was no tablecloth. There were no knives, forks or plates, no food before her; and the room was silent. The table itself shone like the varnished wood of a coffin. The grandmother was frightened. She did not remember where she was. She called out her husband's name.

"Ernest," she called, "they have taken everything away."

No voice answered her and she got down from her chair with a small thump and half fell, half walked to the door.

The hall too was empty.

"Ernest, Ethel!" she cried. "Help me. They have robbed me. Help me."

To the deaf, all places are silent, but the Beluncles were clattering behind the closed door of their kitchen. She was sure she had been abandoned. She opened the front door and ran out into the garden shouting towards the gate. It was still: if anybody had called they had gone away.

"Robbers. Thieves. Help me. God help me. God help me," cried out the grandmother.

"They have stolen my money," she cried.

Beluncle, striding out into the garden, saw her tugging at the bolt of the heavy wooden gate.

"Mother," commanded Beluncle, taking her small arm and looking down at her.

"Eh," she said, breaking into tears and hiding her small white head against his coat. "Thieves have robbed me. God, take me to your father. Pray God, take me to him."

"Now, quiet, mother, quiet," said Beluncle. "I am here. No one has robbed you. What would the neighbours think if they heard you say that? They would say it is very unkind of you, you naughty girl. And that we weren't looking after you. They might even get the idea I was robbing you and that would be a terrible thing, your own son robbing you, your own daughter."

The old lady sobbed under his arm.

"Look at all those roses. Aren't they sweet? I gave you one this morning, didn't I? Smell one? Just come over here and smell this one—that's it," said Beluncle, looking over his shoulder apprehensively at the gate while his mother smelled a rose. "That's it," said Beluncle, drawing her away. "That's enough. You will take all the smell out of the flower, ha! ha! Now here is a handkerchief, let me dry your eyes."

She lifted her head, took off her glasses, and allowed him to dab her eyes, and when he had done this she gave herself a small shake and smiled bleakly at first and then a little slyly at him before she put her glasses over her frail lids which were like plum petals, shrunken and a little stained.

"It is Ethel who is robbing me, my son," said his mother. "Ethel is taking the things from my room. Three sheets have gone. She says she has given them to the laundry man. I lay," said the old lady mournfully and slyly, "she lies in them with him. I will speak out. I am your mother and you are my son until she took you from me. Now the Lord has taken your father."

"Now, mother," said Beluncle severely, "I shall have to get angry with you if you speak like that and then I shall break a commandment. I honour my father and mother. You will break a commandment, too, you will be bearing false witness. You remember that? Thou shalt not bear false witness against thy neighbour. We must not break the commandments and that is one thing I never do. I keep the commandments and so must you because father can see and God can see too. He sees in our hearts, doesn't He? He sees His image in our hearts. Now you be good."

They were at the door and Ethel was there to help the old lady up the step.

"She's all right, Ethel," he said. "She woke up in the room and was frightened."

Ethel took the old lady's arm and led her into the house and sat her in a chair.

"You poor thing," Ethel said, and knelt by her chair and held her small hand.

"Go and put the kettle on," said Ethel to her husband fiercely.

"Oh, dear Lord, take me to him. Take me. Take me," said the old lady.

"He is with you and watching you all the time, looking after you," said Ethel. "Up in the sky he is watching you and caring for you. I believe that, dear. I don't follow these new-fangled ideas. I believe God is in Heaven. My mother is there and my daddy. Look, I will tell you something. When I was a little girl I had an Uncle Ted. You've often heard me talk about my Uncle Ted. The big man who was deaf and he sold fish. . . ."

The old lady brightened.

"Eh," she said, "there is money in fish. We were in trade when I was a girl. I like trade. . . ."

"Uncle Ted was my favourite. He used to come over on a horse and he always brought me a present."

"Aye," said the old lady. "The presents I had when I was a girl. I've kept them all."

"You have, old dear," said Ethel, under her breath, and then in her story-telling voice she went on, "and d'you know what he brought me once? Do you know? This brooch."

And Ethel unpinned a small brooch with a dove on it from her brown frock and gave it to the old lady, who held it covetously.

"It's gold, real gold. It belonged to his mother," said Ethel.

"Eh, I've always liked a bit of gold," said the old lady.

"I will give it to you," said Ethel. "Wait. Let me pin it to your blouse."

"Eh," said the old lady. "Eh, well, I don't know, Ethel. I don't say but what it isn't nice, though it's not as good as the one I had from my mother."

"Of course not, you old devil," said Ethel, under her breath. "Isn't it, dear?"

"Nay, it's poor stuff really. Shoddy," said the grandmother, as pleased as a queen. "But I will keep it."

And then she started to weep and said:

"I have done wrong to say things about you, Ethel. I didn't think you were a good girl when he brought you to me, but you are good. You're the only one who loves me. You take no notice of the things I say. It's my son and my daughter who have broken my heart, from the very first when he brought you with the baby at the breast and not a penny in his pocket, asking for money. We emptied the saving box for him. He will take everything I have. Thank the good Lord God I have got you. While I've got you I am not alone."

X

The slow Sunday passed. The grandmother sat upstairs in her room and dozed over a love story. In the dining-room where they had had their lunch, Mr Beluncle slept amid his harassed property, and Ethel listened to his loud and crusading snore, a snore that seemed to go burning out on quest after quest. What was he dreaming? Nothing. He never dreamed when he was asleep, only when he was awake. Ethel sat knitting and going over incidents of her life, seeing it all so dramatically, so vividly, so crowded with people and misfortune, so densely inhabited by the dead, that her nervous face grew lined and haggard as she relived it all and she felt ill. She had indigestion.

"I have ruined him," she said to herself with a certain satisfaction mixed in with her remorse. Then she straightened herself. He was immovable. Ruin did not affect him. In terror she imagined herself going to his funeral. In the carriage was his partner, "the brains of the business", as she was called, whom Ethel Beluncle hated with all her heart.

"*You* have been his ruin," she said to Mrs Truslove. The untruth of this pleased her. It was one more of the myths she lived by.

"I am," she concluded, scared because Beluncle's snoring had broken off and he slept now in a gently whistling interval. A melancholy, watery sound, pitiable and feeble, came from him and commonly this led to waking up. "I am," she murmured hurriedly, to make things right with herself because one of his eyes opened with accusation, "a wicked girl." But the eye closed and since he did not wake, and his snoring began again, her thoughts went back to her honeymoon when she had first heard the snore, the first indication to her that there was more in love than she thought.

XI

In his bedroom at the top of the house, sitting on a tin trunk because there was no chair there, Henry was reading a French book, losing himself in the foreign tongue and the foreign country.

George was in the garden standing close to the neighbour's fence and Leslie was sitting up in one of the fruit trees looking out happily into the street and the world beyond. But George was stooping by the fence and looking through a hole in the paling. He was studying the couple next door and putting his life at their disposal: how often he wished to give himself to his father, would clean his boots, brush his clothes, bring his paper, and his sadness grew as his father ignored him. Then George behaved badly—swore, went unwashed, lay late in bed, talked loudly of the things that annoyed his father: anything to attract his father's notice and even to be attacked by him. To be the scoundrel and waster of the family was becoming George's ambition: to be drunk, the gambler, the "hellish lad" with a powerful motor-bicycle. George could see the garden seat next door and first of all only the feet and legs of the couple. By the movements of the feet, suddenly turning, the couple must be making love: particularly George admired the heavy brogues of the man, and the calves of the woman. George altered his position; now he could see the couple were holding hands, and the man, who had a short red beard, kissed his wife. George watched the wrestling dance of the two pairs of hands.

"Darling, shall I make the tea?" the man said.

George sighed at the man's voice.

"No, dearest, let me."

George, in imagination, rushed into their house, put the kettle on, laid the tray and then smiling brought it to them. He put the tray down, then he joined their hands and made them kiss each other. He was their slave, their son, lost in them, walking with them in their love.

George loved the clothes of the man. He loved his brown sports jacket, his flannel trousers, his socks, and after that, the man inside them. George tried to walk as the man walked and to talk in his voice. Carefully, as he watched them through the hole in the fence, George copied all the expressions of their faces: their adoration, their sulks, their talking faces and their kissing faces.

"George! What are you doing?"

Mr Beluncle, clogged by his sleep and puzzled by his boredom, had come out for some air. George turned with a happy smile to his father. Mr Beluncle saw before him a fair-haired youth whose clothes were too small for him. This suit of clothes was worn only on Sundays and had not yet been allowed for everyday wear; now, clearly, it would be useless, he would have to buy the boy a new suit. Why should he? Why was the boy not earning his living?

"Take that silly grin off your face," said Beluncle plaintively. "Why are you wearing out your best suit? Why haven't you changed it? Look at the knees of the trousers, you know it has got to last another year. Have you filled up the car? Why not? That is unkind of you. You know I'm going out."

The boy was astonished: he threw over his slavery to the couple next door, and childishly admiring the unexpectedness of his father, he started off to the house.

"Where are you going?" said the father.

"To get a can of water for the car—you said," said the boy.

"Who said?" said Beluncle. "I said you had not filled it."

The boy stopped like a puzzled dog. Mr Beluncle turned his back and then leaned down to smell a sweet william. He was peeping through George's hole in the fence.

"Are we going out?" said the boy eagerly.

"Who said 'we'?" said Beluncle. "I may be going out. I don't know."

Mr Beluncle turned and, looking with contempt at the boy, jingled his keys.

"You'd better fill it," said Beluncle.

"Here," said Beluncle. "Come back. Why don't you come at once when I say? Where is your brother Henry?"

Leslie's voice came mockingly out of the tree.

"Upstairs in his room, reading."

"Tell him to come down and be sociable," said Beluncle, and walked to the tree.

Leslie looked down at him, and just as Beluncle was about to give a roar, Leslie parodied his father's voice:

"Haven't I told you time and time again not to sleep after lunch. Mrs Truslove doesn't sleep in the afternoon."

Beluncle found himself blushing and he turned away to walk round the garden, working the smile from his face.

"Come down, there's a good boy," he said. "We're going out. I want you to stay with grandmamma."

"But grandmamma *talks*," said the boy, and Beluncle turned to reply to this insinuation, but changed his mind and walked on.

George went up to Henry's room at the top of the house.

Below, Mrs Beluncle was playing her repertoire of Sunday hymns and, tiring of them, had moved on to *Sea Fever*. This playing always brought Henry down because he liked to sing and had a good opinion of his voice.

"You've got to come down," said George. "We are going out in the car."

"What mood is he in?" said Henry.

"Filthy," said George, with sincere pleasure.

"Are they having a row?"

"No," said George. "She hasn't started anything."

"He starts them, not her," said Henry.

"You always take her side," said George.

"You always take his," said Henry.

"There's the car," said George.

They looked out of the window and saw Mr Beluncle admiring his car and dusting it. As he did this he looked to the house for help. He hated doing things alone.

When they were all downstairs Henry said to his father: "George said we are going out."

"Who said anything about going out?" said Beluncle.

"Oh, you've brought it round to have a look at," said Ethel.

"That car has got to be taken care of. I don't want it ruined," said Beluncle. "It cost a lot of money."

"Are you selling it?" Ethel said.

"Let us have some tea," said Beluncle.

"You're just like your mother with your things," said Ethel.

Beluncle himself did not know whether he was going out. He liked to look at his car. He like to touch it, especially to run his fingers, when it was dusted, over the warm coachwork. He now went off and washed his hands. He liked to glow with the feeling that he owned a motor-car; ideally, he would have liked it in the house. It horrified him that his family should get inside it, mark it, scratch it. He wanted to be alone in it, feeling that it was an addition of wheels, engine and coachwork to himself: he thought of himself as a kind of car. He felt this about his clothes, his shoes, his

98

house, his factory, about all *things*. Most of his life was passed in thinking of new things he could have.

It annoyed him to see his family thinking, assuming that they would go out in his car, and he punished them for this; he would not tell them whether he was going out or not. Often on Sundays he had had the car brought round, watched the rising and falling emotions of his family and had driven it back thirty yards into the garage. He had, in his imagination, sold it, bought another; sold that one and then, gradually, buying, selling, exchanging, he had come back to his original car. These day-dreams exhausted him and he looked sponge-faced and pale at his family. "Why can't I have the life I want?" he said.

Mr Beluncle put his cup into its saucer and handed the cup across the table to his wife.

"More," he said.

If they were going to torture him by making him take them out they could wait till he had a third cup of tea.

"I don't know what you are all hanging about for, but if you are going out with me you must hurry. The afternoon's gone."

"We're waiting for *you*."

"For me!" Beluncle stood up and gazed at them superciliously.

"You astonish me," he said.

They got out at last into the car and Leslie stood at the gate, winking at them.

Mocking his mother's voice, he said:

"I am going to the other woman." He was nodding to the grandmother's window. "Have you decided where you are going?"

The boy had the ever-smiling, ridiculing face of an elderly man. He listened to the argument going on in the car.

"Come on," the boy said. "Make your minds up. Which one is it? *Uplands? Lyndhurst? Marbella?*"

Very suddenly the car shot forward and swung out of the short road without caution into the middle of the main road.

XII

The Beluncles drove ten miles to *Marbella*.

"Well," said Mr Beluncle, getting out of the car with his family, and since they were eager to go into the house, he held them back. They watched him. It appeared to be a meeting between two personages and it was hard to know who was more important: Mr Beluncle or the house.

Mr Beluncle spoke to it privately.

"Here we are again. Be a little discreet, will you? This is my wife and there are two of my sons, at the awkward age, as you see. If you don't mind we will not mention I was here yesterday with my partner. My wife is a peculiar woman with peculiar ideas, a recluse really, she has imagination. To mortal sense she is jealous. And let me explain that expression to you. She may not wish to admit it but what does it matter what she wishes to admit? She can't avoid facts. As a matter of fact, we are all made in the image and likeness of God and she therefore *can't* be jealous. It is merely the five mortal senses that make her seem so. All the same, if you don't mind, we will say nothing about it. And, by the way, don't mention the price either. Now, if you don't mind, we will go in. If you don't mind my mentioning it," said Mr Beluncle in a jolly voice, figuratively pinching the fat arm of the house and, on principle, putting it in the wrong, "you *have* let the creeper get into your gutters, haven't you?"

And now Mr Beluncle turned to his subdued family and marched them in.

"There's only one thing wrong with this place," Mr Beluncle said. "It wants living in."

And the navy blue flannel jacket he had changed into during the afternoon came open when he said this for he had raised both arms on the word "wants" as if the house were some large, low-necked widow who was inviting him to shower her with presents. And indeed, as he walked his family round, van-loads of furniture seemed to pour out of his talking mouth. Pictures went up on the walls, gongs sounded, carpets raced up the stairs, curtains hung from the windows, fires were lit and the kitchen hummed.

Henry and George went to the top floor and looked at the view of the town from the window. Between the tops of the rich trees that stood as thick as crinkled kale in this hilly district, they saw the immense steep roofs of adjacent properties, saw pieces of half-timbered façade, white gates and then, decently below, the monotonous rows of sharp, cheaper roofs, where the houses were like dull trains lying idle in a railway siding.

"Like Beduins, the Beluncles . . ." Henry sourly began to ruin the line of his poem that never progressed beyond this line.

"D'you remember Thatcher Street?" said George, with an ashamed grin, in a low voice.

"Five b," replied Henry secretively.

Every year or two, the Beluncles moved house. They had lived in seedy streets, in slums, in mediocre avenues, in a large number of pinch-faced villas. They were ashamed, in a house like *Marbella*, of these vicissitudes and were making plans, as they gazed at the town, to assume a manner which would conceal them. Yet, more deeply, they were proud of the insecurity which had entered every crevice of their lives. The boys' eyes exchanged a secret agreement.

"Let us be snobs," they suggested.

They went down to the room which was to be Mrs Beluncle's bedroom; their parents were still downstairs. The first thing George saw was a woman's black glove lying on the floor, curled up like a dead mole. George looked a long time at the glove, then slowly smiled at it; he called Henry and nodded to the glove. George smiled at it.

"Mrs Truslove's glove," he said.

They both smiled now. They listened for sounds of their father's steps. He was still downstairs.

"How d'you know?" Henry asked.

"I know it," said George. It was one of his small pieces of information, one of the sacred secrets. Henry, the elder, knew everything; George knew nothing, except the little he knew, and that was his vanity. That little, that ignorance, was precious to him and he let out only a little at a time.

George picked up the glove.

"Show it to me," said Henry, who took everything.

"No," said George, squeezing the glove out of sight in his hand. He put the glove into his pocket.

"*She's* been here," smiled Henry.

They both laughed privately. Then George let out another small piece of information.

"Yesterday, they were here."

"How d'you know?"

George would not say for a long time. Then he said:

"I saw them. Fred brought me this way in his Riley. We saw the car outside."

"Good Lord," said Henry. "Let me see the glove." He felt a desire to touch it.

"No," said George.

"You'd better give it to me. I'll take it to her at the office."

"No," said George. His importance was growing.

"What were you going to do with it?"

"Keep it," he said simply.

It was precious because it was a concern of his father's.

"And then," said Henry with anger, "he has the hypocrisy to go for me because I was with Mary—while he ruins mother's life and our lives."

They broke off, for Mr and Mrs Beluncle were now coming up the stairs. The sun was going down, large and clear in its last bold circle behind blackening firs, and the shadows were moving out fast on the lawns and roads of Sissing and then vanishing into the neutral sunless light of a town evening.

A bird was singing in the garden of *Marbella* and Beluncle came into the room eagerly to open the window and to call his wife to listen to it.

"Listen," he said. "It is happy. This is its home. It lives here. There's a lesson for you—that bird doesn't worry."

Mrs Beluncle hunched her shoulders and looked in a cowed, mistrustful way at the fat bird high on the tree.

XIII

"Good afternoon, Mrs Beluncle," said the newly married woman from next door, looking over the fence. "I have been watching you. How hard you work! I have made a cup of tea. I will bring it in, if I may. I cannot bear to see you working so hard, when I do nothing."

Mrs Beluncle answered in a refined voice.

The two women went into Mrs Beluncle's kitchen, and while this athletic woman with bare legs and strong intellectual-looking toes looking gravely through the straps of her sandals sat talking in the voice of un-numbered Summer Schools, Mrs Beluncle shrank and huddled and blinked her little mousey lashes. To be so bare, so sun-burned, so political! To be so good at badminton, singing, economics and sex! Shyness coloured Mrs Beluncle; how was she going to listen when the woman told her what a wonderful lover her husband was; how was Mrs Beluncle going to avoid telling the woman how many orgasms she had in a week and what, in any case, was an orgasm? Such a shudder of jealousy went through her when she saw the large green eyes of the woman looking over the fence and swallowing up her sons.

"We often talk about you, Mrs Beluncle," the young woman said. "You never go out. Your husband comes home late. He looks so important. We think you have a rotten time. We don't think it is right. We think a woman ought to have a better life. I wouldn't stand it. I would rebel."

"Fight for yourself, Mrs Beluncle," said the woman.

Mrs Beluncle was delighted by this attack on her husband. She wished he were there to hear it.

"We're socialists," said the woman, in a grave voice. "I expect you are not."

Mrs Beluncle did not know how to answer this.

"The boys used to bring something like that back from school," said Mrs Beluncle. "Socialism, fascism, religion— we get a lot of that in the house. I don't listen. I don't understand it. I leave it to father. I was brought up in the poor old Church of England, say what you like about it."

"Yesterday we saw you all go out in the car. We're always watching you. 'There go the Beluncles,' we say," said the woman.

"People who are in love," thought Mrs Beluncle, "are like that. Everything interests them."

"We were going to see a house," she said.

"Oh—you aren't going to move?" said the woman. "Don't do that. We love looking at you."

"You could all have a much better life, we think," said the young woman disinterestedly.

"Do you know," said Mrs Beluncle, "I've moved house twelve times. The van comes," said Mrs Beluncle, rolling her eyes. "Out it all comes. In it all goes. And out it all comes again. There we are. We've moved."

Mrs Beluncle sent out a sudden peal of laughter, covered her face with her fingers and looked through them at the surprised woman, who had the air of one carefully filling all the information on a form.

"You say we interest you. Listen to this," cried Mrs Beluncle with excitement. "Sometimes we go up. Sometimes we go down. But we move. It's like a scenic railway. Sometimes a cab fetches us, sometimes we walk. Sometimes we *have* to move. Oh dear!

"It's because we can't *breathe*," said Mrs Beluncle. "One day you'll look out of the window and you'll say, 'Where are the Beluncles?' Gone. Yes, we may be moving to Balmoral Castle. I expect the King would move out. Or we may just be floating about in the air. Or we may just stay. But even if we stay, we'll be moving in our heads, as you might say. Don't laugh, it will kill me."

The woman smiled reprovingly. Tears of laughter ran down Mrs Beluncle's cheeks.

"That will teach him," said Mrs Beluncle to herself, wiping the tears from her face when the neighbour had gone. "It is about time people here knew who we are and what we are. We are a problem and no mistake. What a terrible thing, I could see right up her legs. Well, some women are large and some small. There it is."

Now she had said all this to the neighbour, Mrs Beluncle was remorseful. She had exposed her husband and he was not strong enough to be exposed. And she was afraid too: perhaps the grandmother had heard her.

During the day the old lady had looked several times into the scullery. The two women had quarrelled violently often about the washing and Mrs Beluncle had forced her to remain in her room. This victory had to be paid for. On Mondays, the memory of a lifetime's laundry powerfully rose in the old lady's mind and sometimes—perhaps in vengeance for being prevented from advising and scolding— she opened her window and threw out clothes and parcels on to the lawn.

"You are sleeping, you old dear," said Mrs Beluncle, peeping into the old lady's room, and went to lie on her own bed.

"I oughtn't to have spoken like that to that woman. I could bite my tongue off. He's right. My tongue is my worst enemy. I say things and I don't mean them. . . ."

She was lying on her bed, pulling the pins out of her long hair, and her fingers opened with surprise.

"That's how I got him," she said, astonished by this thought.

Poor dad dead, kicked by a horse, and he'd known the horse for years, every day out with it. Herself, a young girl, a young limb, working in the shop. She would see half a dozen shop windows shaken by the trams. Inside, gaslight, the heavy breath of stale gas, a smell like blankets being ironed, and herself behind the counter in the haberdashery. Beedle & Rootes were drapers and outfitters.

The assistants stood at the counters in the morning and then, from the door of Bespoke Tailoring at the turn of the main stairs, came a warning cough and a clear whisper.

"Half a dog in a tram," the voice said. It was the voice of her sister's young man. He was dead now and the sister too. All London rumbling round them.

Her sister's young man had the gift of saying peoples' names backwards and Half a Dog in a Tram was the shop version of Yerfdog Nitram: Godfrey Martin, the name of the manager.

Godfrey Martin was a mere moth, plagued by anxiety, one hand generally under the back of his tail coat to convey, perhaps, an illusion of backbone or an attempt at authority. When the disgusting Mr Boucher caught Mr Godfrey Martin looking up at the ceiling in agony or ecstasy, Mr Boucher said loudly: "He's found it."

Some girls laughed outright. Ethel laughed. (She laughed even now remembering it! "I could write a book about the way he laughed.") Others turned their backs and giggled into the shelves and boxes; some ducked below the counter. Others, like Miss Parkes with the goitre, affected not to hear; and Miss Mulhouse "looked volumes". Mr Boucher was as bald as a toad with his eyes too high in his head, splay-footed and sunk into the belly-basin of middle age. His nostrils spread like a foot over his face. Every morning he made this joke.

Mr Martin walked up the shop.

"Miss Ethel," he said, "are you tidied and dusted underneath?"

"Miss Parkes," he said, "I want to look at your sundries."

Remarks that might have passed through one ear and out at the other, but for Mr Boucher. He clasped his thighs, sniggered, danced, ducked and then stood still and winked like a lighthouse. Beedle & Rootes survived—that is to say, its staff survived—because Mr Boucher had discovered that, even on their low level, life had a higher and a lower meaning.

And then Ethel Carter saw the man who was to be her husband. He flashed in as terse and smart as a swallow and all laughter stopped, all blushes were blotted up, all eyes stared. That was the impression she had: it was the first arresting, painful stroke of love. Life had been light-hearted and endurable at Beedle & Rootes before he came there.

Beluncle! What a name! A young shop-walker—without a day's experience. He had walked into the shoes of an old man who had walked off somewhere on to the streets, to gutter away without a pension in one of the back rooms of London. Short, country-faced, black-crested, with his small moustache like a butterfly and his eyes killing and indignant, Beluncle whizzed after customers, enfiladed them, waltzed them from counter to counter. If Martin spoke to him Beluncle flicked an imaginary piece of cotton off his sleeve afterwards: Beluncle drove the laughter out of the shop. They saw their damnation. His very coat made Martin's look green and despicable. The staff could not bear this. They hated the poverty of their life to be exposed.

"How they hated poor dad," Ethel thought. "Boucher couldn't bear him."

"Miss Parkah, forwahd," Boucher mocked.

"Miss Tums—evah been had?"

This Beluncle was clean. His shirts were clean, his collars were clean, his boots were clean. He was superior. He said so himself. Washed in the blood of the Lamb. Beedle & Rootes couldn't bear cleanliness. His food agreed with him, and their afternoons were tortured by indigestion. He walked quickly; they were a flat-footed, shuffling lot. He did not drink on Saturday nights and was never sick on the stairs. He didn't come out in horrible pleasure spots, like Harrison, or smell of girl's scent and thieved cigars, like Boucher.

"I could be Prime Minister tomorrow if I wanted," said Beluncle.

"This is a free countreh. If a mehn has push he can get anywheah."

Push, Mrs Beluncle thought. Push he's got, look where he's pushed us now. What were we? Nothing.

On Sundays he went to chapel and took a Bible class in the afternoon.

" 'And the Lord said unto Moses.' I was as bad as the rest," she thought. "It made you bad, just seeing him."

One morning his spats were down the lavatory, his hair oil was spilled on the floor. Glue was put on his chair in the basement kitchen off the stockrooms where the staff had their meals. But the glue was a failure; Beluncle was particular—

"Just like his mother. Is she still asleep? I must go and see in a minute and take the old bitch—I mustn't use that word—her tea"—he always dusted a chair before he sat on it. The Lord God Almighty ("Elk Nuleb" was his shop name) takes his seat. Rolls of cloth toppled on him, piles of boxes fell down from shelves as he passed, extra polish was put on the floor at the bottom of the main stairs where he stood viewing his hands from different angles. He was sent on false journeys.

"You sent for meh, sir."

"Naow, I didn't," Godfrey Martin sneered.

"No reason to dash," said Godfrey Martin.

"Running after next week's salary," Boucher said.

"Some of you people haven't earned last yeah's," said Beluncle.

Poor dad, they hated him, Ethel remembered. I was as bad as the rest. I was wicked. I was in love. And there came back to her memory, with a shudder of fear still, the afternoon which had decided it all, the awful afternoon when she was in the window "dressing" for Mr Godfrey Martin.

"Miss Ethel," said Mr Godfrey Martin, a slave to his disastrous habit, "take off your nightgown."

She took the nightgown off the model. It was the slack time after lunch when the day slowed down, when the hands of the watched clock moved slowly like a pair of flies over the face. Beluncle himself was standing in his public way, as if he were footman to himself, and Ethel looked ruinously back at him many times from the window. She asked him afterwards whether he had had an eyeful, staring, staring, nothing but stare, all the afternoon. Was he in love with her already, even at that time? When did he first fall in love with her? Was it before that? No, he said— he liked disappointing people: that was his favourite kind of truthfulness—"as a mattah of fact" he had not "observed hah" in the window. He was looking through her, through the window, to the window of Gamble's Stores on the other side of the street and he was thinking of the future. Beedle & Roote's lace buyer was back from Nottingham and Beluncle admired this man. Even more he admired this man's job. He was estimating how much Lucas earned and whether he made anything out of his expenses. Beluncle was wondering whether he wouldn't march over the road to Gamble's and ask for the manager and apply for that kind of job with Gamble's. That was why he walked thoughtfully towards the window where Mr Martin and Ethel were working.

"Take off your nightgown, Miss Ethel," Mr Martin said. The nightgown dropped to the floor and Mr Martin bent to pick it up; he backed towards the window entrance as he bent. The striped seat of Mr Martin's trousers gleamed like a divided mind beyond the partition. Ethel pouted her lips and put her head on one side, nodding to the groping figure of Mr Martin. And then Beluncle saw this pretty girl, the youngest, the shyest, the most timid in the shop, make a gesture so bold, so immodest with her hand that he saw he was being challenged. Mr Beluncle was too exuberantly shy himself to resist a challenge. He swung his own hand down hard out of his day-dream and caught Mr Martin a full slap on the backside which sent the manager down head first in the window. Two women passing by outside opened their mouths and pointed.

"Caught you bending, Lucas," Beluncle said, thinking he had caught the buyer and not the manager.

Even now, the terror of that scene started Ethel Beluncle's heart. The nerve of it, the wickedness of it! She did not laugh. She was driven back to a primitive terror, a fear which, though it changed its form as the years went by, was always there: the fear, the shame, the horror of losing a job, of getting the sack. And her fear, too, was the measure of her fear of Beluncle and her love of him too: she had lost him *his* job. Yes, she had begun by ruining him. A woman like Mrs Truslove would never have done a thing like that.

"Come to my office," said Mr Martin to Beluncle.

Half an hour later, Beluncle came down the stairs. He was wearing a hat; he was carrying a bag. He was going. He was sacked. Furtively, frozen, pitying, the assistants watched him pass with consternation.

"Are you leaving, Mr Beluncle?" cried Miss Parkes, in a small hysterical voice, speaking for them all. Beluncle turned. Freed from his official, shop-walking smirk, Beluncle shook his shoulders, flushed ingenuously, stuck his chin out.

"My name's Walker," he said. "Going opposite."

Ethel ran from her counter and stood with him at the door.

"Oh, I'm ever so sorry, Mr Beluncle," she said.

"Come to chapel with me on Sunday," he said, looking down at her small shoulders.

It was religion from the start, she thought. Wesleyans, or Presbyterians; no, that wasn't it; it must have been Methodists, count your blessings and see Brother Tintack is counting his, pray on Sundays, prey all the week. Hallelujah, thought Ethel, and keep your hands off. One Bank Holiday, at Hampstead Fair, when they were on the roundabouts, he rising up in the air on his horse and she going down beside him on hers, she remembered him saying, "That's the difference. You don't have to pay to worship at the chapel. No pew rents."

"No what?" she shouted, because of the thump and skirl of the steam organ.

"No pew rents," he yelled. "Nothing to pay. Worship God freely."

"Poor old dad," said Ethel voluptuously, putting a leg off the bed. "He wanted everything free."

She walked to the dressing-table and sat down there on the cane-seated chair.

Mrs Beluncle's bedroom indicated their past. "If that wardrobe could talk," Mrs Beluncle said.

They had bought this suite when they had got married two years after the spanking of Godfrey Martin. Beluncle had changed his job three or four times. He was a man relations mistrusted. Within three months he had started a Dyeing and Cleaning business in a bad street. Within six months they were out on the bad street—and—it was the first shock—the suite had "gone back". Ethel Beluncle discovered that furniture was not furniture to her brisk young husband: it was stock, capital. So was her engagement ring. She had the sensation that Beluncle would have pawned her if he could. He certainly sent her to his mother's while he made another attack upon the world.

"Where are we moving to?" This became one of the commonest questions. "From me to you. To me. Lower. To you." The years were marked by the voices of van-men moving the wardrobe.

"Well, I've kept it nice," she said of her bedroom. "It was a good thing I did, they wouldn't have taken it back".

Some men would have drunk it, some would have put it on horses. Some would have thrown it away on women. Some, also, would have died.

"I will say that for dad, he's good-living. I know I carry on about Mrs Truslove's, but she's never got him. No, he's true. I just make that up about Mrs Truslove to punish him for the rest," said Mrs Beluncle. "To annoy him, to annoy her."

And now Mrs Beluncle did her hair and as each strand was put into place and her small head looked larger, a pink, flashing, sulky expression settled in her cheeks, and she could not help despising Mrs Truslove and her husband, alone together in that office all day, for being so prim and well behaved. The hypocrites, if they want to, why don't they? If they don't want to, what are they sitting there for? Mrs Beluncle put up the last coil of hair and took the pin out of her mouth. As if she cared! But if they ever did, she would tear them to pieces.

"Oh, I'm a wicked girl," Mrs Beluncle obstinately exclaimed to the mirror, for she had just torn Mrs Truslove to pieces all over the floor. "I'm a woman. If gran were alive, she'd knock the life out of me. I've stood in his way."

Mrs Beluncle's mind was a kind of cinema in which she sat, watching the extraordinary black-and-white dramas of her life and perfecting them. It was a shock when the reel came to an end and the lights went up; and now she had done her hair and was putting her skirt on, she was surprised and a little disappointed to see there was no one in the room threatening to knock the life out of her. The day without her husband was long.

"I wonder if the old b. is awake," she said, going down the passage to the grandmother's room.

"Eh, I was thinking you had forgotten me," the old lady said. She had been up for half an hour, washing and dressing, waiting to be fetched.

"You don't think what I have to do. You just stand there to be waited on," said Mrs Beluncle, aloud, because she knew the old lady was too deaf to hear.

"I've come to bring you down to tea," she shouted in the old lady's ear. "Have you got your shawl?"

"Eh, I feel hungry," the old lady said. "I think of those who are in want. The beggars that come to the door."

"We get no beggars here," shouted Ethel kindly. "I say we get no beggars here, you're thinking of the country."

"Give once and they think you're soft," said the old lady. "Once I did to a man that came from Castleton, two slices of bread and butter and a slice of my seed cake, and he came again. 'Eh,' I said. 'I can't spare my cake for them as don't work.' People came for my cake from far and wide, but we never gave to the miners."

"No, you wouldn't. I can hear you," said Ethel, taking her to the dining-room. "You're a hard lot."

When Ethel brought the tea the old lady ate greedily and slipped two buns in her sewing-bag to take back to her room with her. After that she tried to slip a third one in. Ethel Beluncle pretended not to see, but it reminded her of something.

"Grandma," said Ethel, "you've been at the window again."

"Nay," said grandmamma, "I've been sleeping."

"Don't tell lies," said Ethel. "You have. What's this?"

And Ethel put a brown-paper parcel on the table. The parcel was dusty with soil at one end and had torn leaves caught in the string. It was addressed in faint, scratchy writing to Constance Beluncle, The Manor, Snagworth.

"It was in the flower bed," said Ethel. "Now, listen, you threw it out of the window, didn't you? You're a naughty girl—if you do that you know what I'll do to you—I'll put you to bed."

"Nay, I never," said the old lady.

"I'll put you to bed without any supper," Ethel shouted. "It's silly throwing parcels out of the window, they don't get posted that way," she shouted; "if you want to send things to Connie, ask me or Philip. We'll do it properly. Connie hasn't been at Snagworth for twenty-five years."

The little violet veins showed as the old lady's face went pale.

"What is in it?" said Ethel.

"Eh, poor Connie, I doubt but what she's hungry," said the old lady.

"Thirsty more like, if I know her," said Ethel. And she opened the parcel. Inside was a crumbling muddle of old buns and cakes.

"You poor old soul. You poor mean old soul," said Ethel quietly.

"She's a bad girl. A bad daughter," shouted the old lady. "A harlot. She won't have no money of mine. She broke my heart and my husband's heart. She sent him to the grave. The shame killed him. I doubt but what she's paying for her sins."

"A harlot, that's what you called me when dad brought me to see you, a clean-living London girl, more clean-living than your lot with your Connie carrying on with that man at the Manor, and going off with Thompson at the Mill, churchwarden, too," said Ethel firmly. "I haven't forgiven you. I'll never forgive you. And now I've got you on my hands—what for? What did your precious son bring you here for. It makes me laugh. I'd have gone on the streets if I had been brought up by you. It must have been a prison, praying all day, making your two children stand up for their meals, thrashing poor dad because he was out after seven at night; I wonder they didn't end in gaol."

Then she shouted: "Don't you worry about Connie. She's

all right. Why don't you see her? Ask her to come here and forgive her."

"Nay, it's her place to ask," said the old lady.

"Your husband says it's her place to ask," the old lady said slyly.

"What d'you mean my husband says," asked Ethel.

"I doubt but what he wants all the money for himself," said the old lady. "Brother and sister," wailed the old lady, suddenly crying. "Oh, love of God, take me to Thine arms. My children have broken my heart. Oh, love of God, take me to my husband."

Ethel put down her cup and said fiercely:

"Philip has written her. He has begged her to come. He has been to see her. He doesn't want your money," she said.

The old lady went on lamenting.

"Philip," declaimed Ethel to herself, "if you don't pay that money back at once, I'll leave you. I'll go anywhere. If you're trying to touch Connie's money, I'll . . ."

"Here," said Ethel, getting up and going to the drawer of a table by the window. She was getting a piece of note-paper and an envelope. There was a fern on the table; behind the fern was the lace curtain of the window and through the curtain Ethel could see the windows of the houses opposite. Like a long row of narrow rebuking faces they looked; faces that, by dint of staring for so many years at her own house, had come closer and closer, peering into her life.

"Here," she said. "Pen and paper. Write to Connie. Tell her to come on Saturday. Tell her she's to have your share of the money."

"Nay," said the old lady, "you hypocrite."

Mrs Beluncle dropped the paper on the table, which was covered with a grey and blue cloth.

"What did you call me?" she said.

"Nay, Ethel, you hypocrite," said the old lady. "Eh, I knew it when he brought you to me."

"How dare you. What d'you mean?" cried Ethel.

"Eh, what use is it bringing Connie here? He's had the money."

"Who has?"

"Your husband. Eh, I've no doubt you schemed him to it."

"Don't tell lies," cried Ethel. "My husband hasn't touched Connie's money. How dare you say so. You've got the shares and he had only his own share of it."

"He's got all of it now," said the old lady. Her tears had stopped. "He's got Connie's money too."

"Philip, Philip, Philip, what have you done now? What have you been up to behind my back?" Ethel cried to herself. "You swore you wouldn't."

The room seemed to rock. With sickly slowness the curtains seemed to come down from the windows, the carpets seemed to roll up on the floor, the voices of men moving the furniture could be heard. She saw herself alone in a gradually emptying house, her mother dead, her sisters dead, no one to go to, no one to be with, but this old accusing lady. "Boys," cried Ethel's heart. "Come home, come near me. Here. George, Henry, Leslie. Look what he has done."

"When——" Ethel began by shouting, but she brought a chair—being too giddy to stand—close to the old lady and spoke in a normal voice in her ear. "When did you give him Connie's money? Did you sign something? Did you sign papers?"

The old lady's mind did not grasp these questions. Since her husband's death she had signed so many things. She was lost among the jogging, confusing pictures of her life and these pictures were captioned by words from the Bible. Above all, the word Harlot, kept returning to her. All women outside her own chapel at Snagworth and some within it were Harlots and many even from other villages; it was her name for women whose clothes she coveted. It had been her mild husband's favourite word when he took the day off from his carpenter's bench and went preaching. It brought the sound of his voice back to her and that she longed for. But one thing the old lady could understand was that her daughter-in-law was distressed and that the younger woman's heart was at her mercy.

"Eh," the grandmother said lucidly. "If the money is with Mrs Truslove, it is safe. She is a good woman and a good daughter to her father and mother. She could not wrong me. Eh, she has been the making of Philip."

"She has," said Ethel boldly. "Don't think I don't see your little game."

"A better woman never walked," said the old lady. "Young and good-looking. I had looks when I was young."

"You don't catch me like this," said Ethel. "She has done dad the world of good," she said for the old lady to hear.

"Aye," nodded the old lady, with malice. "If things had been different. But a man's always carried away and what his mother says counts for nothing."

"Yes," said Ethel amiably. "I wish I had taken gran's advice before I got married. I say I wish I had taken gran's advice."

The old lady took Ethel's meaning and her satisfaction went. She had failed to rouse Ethel's temper.

"Oh ah, oh ah," the old lady moaned like a child, pitying herself.

"Now then, my girl," said Ethel sharply, banging the cups on the tray and clearing the table. "None of that. You behave yourself. You could make me cry once, but you can't do it now. I know you. I'm going to get Connie down here and then we'll see who's who and what's what, flat on the table."

At six Ethel heard the whistle of a train; an hour later Henry came home. Ethel did not ask, but she knew that in that hour the boy had been seeing his girl. Ethel blushed with this knowledge as he stood beside her in the kitchen making jokes about the people in the factory. Everyone was mentioned except Mrs Truslove; the boy was obeying his father—"There is no need to repeat anything Mrs Truslove says. It does not matter, but it will be more harmonious if you don't." Ethel laughed at the boy's jokes but she could not hold out for long.

"Did Mrs Truslove say anything?" she said.

"No," said the boy.

"I thought perhaps she might have," she wheedled.

"Oh, do stop about Mrs Truslove, mother," the boy said angrily. "You're only jealous."

"Jealous!" Her eyes sparkled with mockery. "What d'you know about it?"

"Everything," said the boy coldly. "You needn't carry on as you do."

"Oh," she laughed. "Fancy you thinking that is jealousy. You'll be thinking you're in love next."

She could see she had wounded him. He walked away to the sitting-room, which was kept for his father's use alone.

"He looks ill. He has gone thin and haggard. It's his age," she thought with repentance, and when she had settled her cooking she went to see him. He was sitting at the table reading, looking up words in a dictionary, and writing them down.

"What are you reading?" she said, looking over his shoulder.

"It's French. You won't understand it," he said sulkily.

"What good will that do you, tiring yourself out, after your work."

"When I go to France," he said.

"And leave the business. I thought you liked being there. With Mrs Truslove"—she could never resist it—"so refined."

"It's a trap," he said. "I can't stand him any longer. I can't stand working with him. I hate furniture."

"You mustn't talk about your father like that. He is your father."

"You say worse about him."

"He's my husband. I love him."

"Love him! And all these rows? I'll bet you'll have one tonight. When we were children—nothing but rows and rows."

"Pooh," she said. "You don't understand what love is. You may think you do, just because you kiss some silly girl."

"And if you do know," said Ethel, flushing with suspicion, "if you've been touching a girl, doing what you've no business to do, I don't want anything to do with you."

But he wouldn't, I know he wouldn't, he's like his father, she thought. I oughtn't to say that to him and upset his pride. It's what I do to his father, Ethel thought with embarrassment.

The boy scowled and then smirked. She wished she had not seen this expression on his face and she was in half a mind to put on her hat, rush out and warn this girl of his against him.

"Ask no questions, hear no lies," she laughed, when she got back to her kitchen. "It's a trap. What does he know about traps, with hardly a hair on his chin or his body."

"What a lot I have got into," she thought.

XIV

"I must try to pay the paper bill again," said Mrs Truslove, looking into her bag as she got ready to go. "I've been twice to Vogg's this week."

"He's open, I think," said Miss Dykes from her couch at the window. "He doesn't bother about his bills. Why should you?"

"I don't like it. It's slack," said Mrs Truslove. "People who are easygoing about money are always dishonest in the end."

"Beluncle," said Miss Dykes, venturing this information, and then hurriedly covered it with, "I don't know what the Voggs live on."

"Dust," said Mrs Truslove. "I never put my bag down on the counter. I can't have lost my glove there."

Mrs Truslove went off in the fluster of her anxieties and crossed the road.

"Everyone sees it. What a fool I have been," Mrs Truslove took her words down the ringing tiled path, through the limited odours of the fiercely flowering suburban gardens and across the road. "He has been unfaithful not to my body, but to my life. And what is my life? It is my money, left me by my husband, the security I married that man for. He has been unfaithful to my safety."

Half-way across the road, cautiously looking at a distant car, blobbed with sunlight like a fly's wings, Mrs Truslove changed sides:

"No one knows it. No one realises it. Except him. I've told him. I've told him everything. *She* is jealous. How dare she say Mr Beluncle has ruined me."

The blue tarred road became a river and she seemed to sink drowning into his arms, and they went down together in a brilliant suffocating dream of ruin. With all her heart she wished to be ruined by him.

"All my savings gone!"

It was like a conquest, a rape.

"I have never heard such wicked nonsense," she said, this time aloud, as she stepped into the shade of the opposite pavement.

The Truslove's iron gate closed, Mrs Vogg turned at her open window and watched her walk across. Later on in the day Mrs Vogg would have the pleasure of hearing from her son what the mistress of Mr Beluncle wanted.

The loud bell struck as she went into the empty shop; the morning sun was coming in over the window-screen and making a long band across the wall close to the ceiling. Vogg came in from the side door, and walked silently round the two counters and put the tips of his fingers on the counter where Mrs Truslove was waiting. He stood stiff as a sentry and looked, without speaking, not quite in her face, but a little over her shoulder.

"I have come to pay you my bill," she said to Vogg. "I came yesterday and the day before, but you were closed."

"I've got no one to look after the shop when I go out," he said.

He took the bill and her money and wrote out the receipt slowly in pencil.

On the counter was a booklet. She read the headline as he wrote: Millions Now Living Will Never Die, she read. She could see her mother's large skull-like grin when Vogg had handed her this paper years ago. How different from the womanish, chattering old man, the elder "Hospital" Vogg (as people in the street used to call him), the son was. Her father had known him, as he had known all these shop-keepers, and Mrs Truslove used to go to the shop when she was a child. She remembered the boy had become a merchant seaman for a time and had left the sea when his father's illnesses had become worse.

"How is your mother?" Mrs Truslove asked.

"The same," he said, in his deep voice.

"I often see her at the window," said Mrs Truslove.

Vogg made a small smile. He had known her by sight for many years too. He remembered her as a stolid and large young girl who ignored him when he passed her in the street. In his teens he had often walked behind her, copying her step. Then he remembered her courtship, her marriage to Mr Truslove. They watched that from the window. The sight of Mr Truslove with his arm round her bottle waist and both of them tamely, amorously walking had made him jeer. Mr Truslove had died while Vogg was at sea, and he did not recognise the busy woman he found when he returned. Money leads to money. The death of her husband had made her thin, frivolous and rich.

The Bible had first made Vogg distinguish between the rich and the poor. Mrs Truslove was the human being who had seemed to him a sample of the rich. When he saw her go down the road now, her skirt, as it moved to her walk, seemed to him to scoff at the people in every garden she passed. When Beluncle went in and out of her house—and he was there two or three days a week—Vogg saw her become gay and beautiful; then, as time went on, tired-looking and strained but even better dressed. In the winter she wore a fur coat. Lady Roads (the Voggs quickly picked up the names of everyone's visitors in the street) used to call on the crippled sister and she wore a fur coat, too. Vogg saw a postman's daughter rising in the world and jealousy turned to hatred. He listened to the flat, literal and harmless reports of his mother, who, without knowing it, was feeding the jealousy of her son, and now—the dull grind of jealousy turning to the more gratifying sense of persecution—he was convinced that Mrs Truslove and her sister were as he said "spitting in their faces". All the gates in the street had their different sounds and the Voggs could distinguish each of them. When the road was quiet the peculiar sound of the iron gate of the Trusloves, though it was not opposite their shop, would always bring Vogg to the window.

Vogg wrote the receipt and gave it to Mrs Truslove, who said kindly, "Your mother ought to go out in this lovely weather," as she was leaving the shop.

"She can't move," said Vogg, and he hoped he conveyed the injustice of that, when every day Miss Dykes was wheeled out in her chair.

Vogg went to the door when Mrs Truslove had gone and watched her from the doorstep. The tea-brown stains under her eyes had seemed to him disturbingly sinful, her metallic, finished and scrupulous voice was brisk with the vice of the world. He went to the door for air.

Vogg returned to the small room at the back of the shop, opened his Bible and read:

> And he cried mightily with a strong voice, saying Babylon the great is fallen, is fallen, and is become the habitation of devils, and the hold of every foul spirit and a cage of every unclean and hateful bird.
>
> For all the nations have drunk of the wine of the wrath of her fornication, and the Kings of the earth have committed fornication with her, and the Merchants of the earth are waxed rich through the abundance of her delicacies.
>
> And I heard another voice from heaven, saying, Come out of her, my people, that ye be not partakers of her sins, and that ye receive not of her plagues.

The woman drunk with the blood of the saints, the one upon whose head was a name written Mystery, Babylon the Great, the Mother of Harlots and Abomination of the Earth, filled the imagination of Vogg. She was Mrs Truslove; she was Lady Roads; she was Mrs Parkinson; but underneath the emotion that the words created in him, was another and frightening notion that came, as he knew, closest to his own secret thoughts: the woman was his mother. He shut the book with fear. When he could master himself, he went up the stairs to the sitting-room to speak to his mother, looking at her simple face and chatting with her until the sickening passion went away.

XV

In the morning Mr Beluncle and his son caught the 8.10 train from Boystone to London. East Boystone station was a quarter of an hour's walk away, through the speckled greenery of pleasant suburban streets and up the side of a chestnut-shaded park. To enjoy the morning shade in the summer and to listen to birds singing in the gardens as he walked was Mr Beluncle's delight and he often spoke of it; but he had rarely experienced it. He found himself, as a rule, running to the station in seven minutes and said he could do it in six. His habit of early rising was the cause of the rush for it gave him his favourite delusion of timelessness.

And then, just before he left, Mrs Beluncle was apt to remind him that he had not given her the housekeeping money and George Beluncle, spaciously rejected at all other times, would make his final demand:

"When are you going to see about my job?"

Mr Beluncle's departure was then likely to be delayed by a moral explosion which left George gazing with sadness after him and saying, "If only he would let me drive him in the car. I would do *anything*." And Mrs Beluncle rushed to an upstairs window to watch anxiously that her husband did not get run over in his rage.

Mr Beluncle and his son Henry would do a short scamper to the corner of the road, a length of only thirty yards, in which Mr Beluncle was in a running battle of words with his son. In the main road he would march for twenty yards or so and then, with a sergeant shout of "Now!" he would trot again and only pull up when Mr Stein, the Swiss, came out of his garden gate ahead. Mr Stein was in the handbag trade and once or twice made humorous remarks in such good English that Mr Beluncle did what he could to avoid him. Mr Beluncle thought that one managing director ought not to see another run.

"Mr Stein," said Henry, as they trotted. It was his duty to warn his father.

They pulled up and walked at once.

"I want to talk to you, my boy, very seriously," said Mr Beluncle, dropping into a walk. "I don't want to go on at you. I don't want you to think I'm lecturing you. . . ."

"Mr Stein is running," said Henry.

"What's the damn' fool running for," said Mr Beluncle. But glancing at his watch, he saw that Mr Stein was right. "Another thing," said Mr Beluncle, beginning to trot again. "This wouldn't happen if only you'd get up in the morning. If your mother wouldn't come out with damn' silly questions at the last minute."

Mr Stein had turned the corner where the park began and the Beluncles, left without an omen, trotted erratically out of step and in honest bewilderment.

"I don't want," said Mr Beluncle breathlessly, "don't want—run on your toes like you were taught at school—I'm not lecturing you, I'm—warning—you. I don't need to say anything—I'm sure you know, you're bound to know . . ."

Mr Beluncle slowed down to a walk and got his breath.

"You read a lot of books," he said, "novels, poetry—French books, I believe. You don't want me to tell you anything, you know it," Mr Beluncle burst out. "I don't want to waste my time telling you what you know which," said Mr Beluncle, dropping suddenly from breathless irritation into deep-lunged reasonableness of the man-to-man kind, "which, of course, you do."

They turned the corner.

"He's running," said Henry.

"There's nothing I like to see less than a man running for

a train. It shows his character. You know what I'm talking about?"

"Yes," said Henry.

"About women," said Mr Beluncle, with hatred. "Girls. You're at the age—we had better run—when you see girls, meet girls—when girls speak to you. Perhaps you may speak to a girl yourself. That's when you've got to be chary—we can walk a bit—I mean you might speak to a girl, I don't say you do, I don't say you have, at least I hope you don't—that's all right, but the next thing is that a girl might start calling you 'her boy'; you hear them. 'My boy,' they say. What is the expression, you know it better than me? Boy friend?"

"Yes," said Henry.

"Stein's running, why didn't you tell me?" said Beluncle, starting to run once more. "They see no harm in it," said Mr Beluncle pleasantly. " 'He's my boy'—you hear them.

"It's their nature," said Mr Beluncle indignantly.

"You might call it their business," Mr Beluncle said bitterly. "To get hold of a boy.

"It's what," he said, with a tragic growl, "they're on earth for, to mortal sense. We know enough to rise above that. What I'm getting at is this. A customer of mine, I won't mention no names—sent his son up to his Glasgow office, decent young man, your age and, of course, there's a girl in the office like Miss Vanner in ours. I suppose this girl looks at him and says here's a nice young man, doing well, got a good position, nephew of the manager—I don't say she did but this is how their minds work, it's their nature—and they get talking and . . ."

They came to the end of the park where the road rises to the station at East Boystone and from which the up-line signals could be seen.

"It's down, dad," said Henry.

"Damn," said Mr Beluncle, pulling out his watch again, looking for Mr Stein, who was finally out of sight, in the blessedness of passing the ticket collector. "It can't be."

The race began once more, Mr Beluncle's rage rising

against the rise in the road; he had not enough breath to spare.

"The long and short of it," said Mr Beluncle, "was that that girl had a baby and it cost his father four hundred pounds to get out of it. I just want to tell you I haven't got four hundred pounds."

The last ten yards were done in silence. Father and son ran down the long tunnel to the platform steps just as the 8.10 train was rumbling above them and the ticket collector was shutting the gates. Seeing Mr Beluncle he maliciously turned his back, but seeing his son behind him, he relented. The two rushed through.

"Get a seat," shouted Mr Beluncle, going to his first-class carriage. His son went to the third-class.

The Bulux (Beauty and Luxury) factory, originally Beluncle & Truslove, was the size of a drill-hall or a chapel, with a hearth-stoned doorstep and a brass plate. It was no cleaner than any of the other buildings in the yellow street that ran close to the bowling railway arches of that low-lying part of London, an area of hops, hide warehouses, breweries and solid Victorian public-houses that sent out a sour smell of beer and matrons at the street corners—it was no cleaner than any other building, but to Henry Beluncle it seemed so. Or to any other member of the Beluncle family when they went there. To him the brick seemed to have been scrubbed down that morning lest a speck of soot should flake down upon his father's white fingers. Mr Beluncle had set up a kind of home from home in this building. His gramophone was in one of the office cupboards, his Worcester china, his substantial cases of silver, his riding boots; they were part of a cache which Mr Beluncle did not speak of at his home; just as at his West End showroom there was another cache: two radiograms, two or three fine French clocks in enamel or marble, more silver and china, a huge silver loving cup— for loving, as a general spiritual idea, appealed to Mr

Beluncle—in fact, a few hundred pounds' worth of private treasure whose existence was unknown, or so he supposed, to Mrs Truslove. There was more down at a bank in Bournemouth, and two more burial mounds in Godalming and Colchester, the knowledge of which Mr Beluncle hid from everyone. If the worst came to the worst he could go and squat ruminatively on his hoards.

When Henry had taken the glove from his brother, the business of giving it to his father or to Mrs Truslove seemed very simple to him. Now he was in the office, walking with the morning's letters to put on their desk, he understood the thing was impossible. The whole peculiar value of the glove lay in the secret it held; to hand it to either of them would be like the blasphemy of dishonouring them.

"Take your hand out of your pocket, my boy," said Beluncle kindly, when he came in. He was holding the glove, wringing it in his anxious hand, and he nearly pulled it out in his confusion.

"What have you got in your pocket?" said his father. "You'll knock it out of shape and you can't afford a new suit. . . ."

But before Mr Beluncle had finished there was a lucky interruption; an umbrella fell down in the passage, the door was opened, and a high undue voice exclaimed:

"My lords, ladies and gentlemen, pray silence." Mr Chilly came in. Or rather it seemed that a pair of astonishing pointed shoes had done so, bearing with them the summary figure of Mr Chilly, who only lightly inhabited them. Mr Chilly was a very tall man met by the cold and enquiring glances of seated people, older and earlier at work, than himself. "I'm sorry," he said in a whisper, taking his greeting back with modesty, "I disturb.

"I'm late," said Mr Chilly, asking for sympathy and getting none: "I know I'm late."

"It is general knowledge," said Mr Beluncle, scoring a point with his smile.

Mr Chilly was a good-looking man with long legs and a slight frame bending very easily as if on a hinge, under a double-breasted waistcoat. He was a man who had been ruined by his innumerable advantages. The fact of being a gentleman had been one liability, though he could be said to be vain of all his liabilities. He watched his restless hands, surprised they had remembered to come with him. He had the air of a man trying to remember to make gestures suggesting strength and efficiency, and looked to see that his clothes hung right first.

"I was late because I brought you a present," said Mr Chilly.

"A present. I hoped it would be an order," said Mr Beluncle.

"An order!" exclaimed Mr Chilly, seeing already how wrong he had been.

"I didn't think of that. . . . Oh dear, sir.

"It's a hydrangea, sir," said Mr Chilly.

The attraction of Mr Chilly for Mr Beluncle was that of one extravagant man for another.

Mr Chilly went outside and came back with the plant. With a bow which annoyed the two partners, who could not bear his manners, he put the plant between them on their desk. As he did so he smiled at Mrs Truslove.

"For you," he said to her. "For both of you," he said to both of them. "No, that is not right," said Mr Chilly, standing back to consider them in relation to the plant. "You cannot see each other."

They could not and Mr Chilly leaned across and lifted the pot away.

"Not on the desk," said Mrs Truslove.

"On the window-sill?" said Mr Chilly.

"It will interfere with the telephone," said Mr Beluncle.

"Not on the filing cabinet," said Mrs Truslove.

"Oh dear," said Mr Chilly.

"Try the mantelpiece," said Mrs Truslove.

"There's no room there," said Mr Beluncle, getting up.

"Problem!" Mr Chilly halted. "On the floor. I love flowers spread on the ground."

Now he was on his feet, Mr Beluncle became interested.

"It will be kicked there," said Mrs Truslove.

"Oh, not my flowers kicked," said Mr Chilly, kneeling down to pick up the pot.

"There's a stand in the warehouse," said Mr Beluncle.

"It is sold," said Mrs Truslove. "Mr Beluncle, have you rung Abbotts?"

And she put a glare behind the question.

"Time is getting on," she said. "Put it on your desk, Mr Chilly."

"Oh, but it's for you, not *me*," said Mr Chilly. "Don't let me cause a *situation*. Don't let there be a *thing*—it is for you. A little colour."

Mr Beluncle got up and put the pot on the window-sill.

"No," he said, stepping back. "That is not right."

"On the shelf?" suggested Mr Chilly.

Mr Beluncle and he considered the shelf.

"Too high," said Beluncle.

"We must keep it dusted," Mr Beluncle said. "How do you water them?"

The telephone bell rang and Mr Beluncle turned to scowl at it until Mrs Truslove answered it.

"We are colourful people," said Beluncle, moving out of the room to get away from the telephone. "I said," Mr Beluncle was speaking for the firm, "we are colourful people."

Mr Chilly followed Mr Beluncle to the waiting-room.

"What a brilliant idea!" said Mr Chilly. And Mr Beluncle frowned again at the note of excess in Mr Chilly's diction. "For the customers, while they wait."

"We do not want an expensive plant to die of neglect," called Mrs Truslove from her office.

Out of politeness Mr Chilly would have replied, but Mr Beluncle prevented this. He allowed himself a general reflection.

"I should like a window in this room, a large window, Queen Anne, Georgian, Tudor, something really period— see the idea?—and a dozen, two or three dozen of these banked up with indirect lighting. Massed," said Mr Beluncle.

"Like Claridges," cried Mr Chilly.

"I like mass," said Mr Beluncle, opening his hands, and then Mr Chilly's phrase struck him. "You can't afford to go to Claridges," he said.

"It was one thing I could not stand about the retail trade when I was young—there was no mass. It was all pennies and ha'pennies," he said.

"Why don't we mass them?" said Mr Chilly, making a dart towards the table and waving his hands as if he were making passes over the flower in its pot, so that it grew into scores of plants.

But Mr Beluncle was already leaving the waiting-room and going back to his office. Unguardedly Mr Chilly followed him and said enthusiastically:

"Let us buy a dozen and bank them up to begin with, sir."

Mr Beluncle walked before his assistant into his office, walked as far as the window, measuring his steps, and then turned round and gazed at Chilly.

"What did you say?" he said, in a quiet voice.

"I beg your pardon, sir," said Chilly, noticing the change in Mr Beluncle's manner. "I fear I got thrilled. I am sorry, sir."

"Let *us* buy?" enquired Mr Beluncle.

"Us? You made use of a *plural*, Chilly," said Mr Beluncle.

"A plural, sir? I am sorry, sir," said Chilly. "Frightfully. Have I offended—sort of committed a solecism? I was just thrilled. Enthusiasm for a brilliant idea, just enthusiasm. Carried, as the accountants say,"—Mr Chilly's eyes seemed to be seeking the next word in the air—"forward."

Mr Chilly gave a quick glance at Mrs Truslove as he said this. Mrs Truslove glanced at him. Was he being ironical?

"Don't let there be any misunderstanding," said Beluncle. "In this House, we are never offended. Offended is a word we do not use. Surprised, perhaps. Interested always."

Mr Chilly waited obediently. One of the things that always impressed him about Mr Beluncle, one of the things that he admired, was Mr Beluncle's ability to make a statement and then appear to lean physically upon it.

"I am a blunt man," said Mr Beluncle.

"Blunt to the point of being plain-spoken," said Mr Beluncle.

"Frank," added Mr Beluncle, and at this word softened a little and put his hands in his pockets.

"Strictly speaking, Chilly," said Mr Beluncle, "you are not 'us'."

"Oh no, sir. I quite understand, sir," said Chilly.

"I do not know what is, or shall I say *was*—if it was—in your mind. I don't want you to misunderstand me when I say that 'us' is not a word that has occurred to me or to Mrs Truslove as regards 'you' . . ."

"Oh, please, sir, I assure . . ." said Mr Chilly.

Mr Beluncle held up his hand.

"I do not know what was in your mind," continued Mr Beluncle, "but I think you should understand this is, if I may say so, a very unusual firm. I doubt if there is any firm in England quite like it, perhaps not in the world. It is and always has been God's business—I won't go into that now. I feel, I should say we feel, Mrs Truslove and myself, that we are a family here and you are almost one of the family. A kind of adopted son. But not 'us'. I don't know if I have made my meaning clear."

"But perfectly, sir, perfectly," said Mr Chilly.

Mr Chilly stood on the office carpet like one nailed there by the tips of his pointed shoes and swaying in a useless attempt to get away. Now Mr Beluncle released him. Mr Beluncle slipped away sideways to his desk, where he stood shuffling his letters into new arrangements, putting the urgent ones underneath, the ones which did not need to be answered on top. Among these letters were slips of paper in Mr Beluncle's own handwriting, slips that were propped against his inkstand for a day or two before returning to one of the heaps of papers. On these slips were written sentences like "All things come to him who waits" or the opposite sentiment, "Do it now." Or "Don't let your work get on your mind; keep your mind on your work." Sometimes the message was metaphysical: "Eternity = Now." And Mr Beluncle might place it next to a letter beginning "May we draw your

attention to the enclosed account" with the satisfaction of
one playing patience with his correspondence.

"I do not say, of course," said Mr Beluncle, covering a bill
with a text, "that the question of your being 'us' could not
arise. I do not say it should not arise. I merely say that it
has not arisen. There might be a time when it could, I don't
say come up—but when it could be visualised."

And Mr Beluncle had the sporting air of a yachtsman,
looking through binoculars, at a very distant scene.

Mr Chilly's eyes shone and Mr Beluncle suddenly gave a
sweeping, flashing smile that washed the subject out of the
room.

"One hydrangea is enough, Chilly," he said. "They cost
you money."

"You are right, sir," said Chilly. "It was a silly idea of
mine. Even two would have been too many."

The surrender of Mr Chilly warmed Mr Beluncle; all sur-
renders made him generous.

"Ah," he said genially, and coming from his desk and
taking Chilly by the arm, he led him towards the door—
"I'll give you a thought: there is no such thing as too much
or too little. All we can do is to give—to give and give. There
is only what is right." They reached the door. Chilly opened
it and Mr Beluncle patted him on the shoulder. "If it's right
for you to come into partnership"—Mr Chilly was now going
through the doorway—"nothing can stop you. Nothing.
Nothing can stop what is right—provided, of course," added
Mr Beluncle briskly, "a proper agreement is drawn up and
the terms are satisfactory. The world turns on terms."

"I feel such a child in business," said Chilly, from the
darkness of the passage outside.

"It's all experience," said Mr Beluncle. "There's nothing
in business but experience. You're lucky: *I* had to buy
mine."

Then Mr Beluncle returned.

"Close the door. There's a draught," said Mrs Truslove.

"I'm so sorry," said Mr Chilly, coming back to close the
door.

When Mr Chilly had gone, Mr Beluncle sat again at his desk.

"I have a lot to do this morning," said Mrs Truslove. "Chilly wastes our time."

Mr Beluncle took up some letters in self-protection. Mrs Truslove had the ability to work on her books, to add up figures and balance accounts, and at the same time, to complain about having to do this and keep up a running critical mutter. This faculty had been a sign of gaiety in their early days together. The lively fashion in which she could do three or four things at once had been his admiration and there had been an excitement in piling more and more work upon a widow so clever.

"So please don't interrupt me," said Mrs Truslove, her pen running up the column on the page. "I think you ought to have a word with Lady Roads about Chilly. He's an idiot. He's quite useless here."

"That is prejudice," said Beluncle, pretending to read a letter. "He comes of a very good family."

"This business has always been run by people of very bad family," said Mrs Truslove.

"Chilly has got a lot to learn," said Beluncle. "When I was his age I was . . ."

"He will never learn. He has run through two fortunes already," said Mrs Truslove.

"I would not call them fortunes," said Beluncle, putting down his paper, to float about on a favourite subject. "I happen to know the figures. His father left him a bit, but what he had from his mother is in trust. He can't touch that. It's very hard that a man can't touch his capital. It is unjust. It is a denial of the Divine Law of Justice."

"It's fortunate," said Mrs Truslove, "because he is a fool."

Mr Beluncle opened his eyes.

"I don't know what is in your mind. You seem to have got the hump or something. Anyone would think you thought his money was not safe with us."

"Well, is it?" said Mrs Truslove.

"Safe!" said Beluncle, his face becoming suddenly fierce with the smile of a cold, newly risen sun. "Is anything safe? What is safety? Has this business ever been run on safety?"

Mrs Truslove did not answer.

"I've never been safe," Mr Beluncle declaimed radiantly. "I scorn safety. The world is risk, adventure, creation—in other words," added Mr Beluncle, correcting his exuberance, "unfoldment."

They were dangerously near their argument of Saturday afternoon in the empty house but Mr Beluncle, after the first shock of it, had soon persuaded himself that it had not been important and, in any case, he liked talking. It was a way of turning realities into unrealities and that was rather urgent.

"You seem to suggest there is something not quite straight in our arrangement with Chilly. He is learning a trade. He is picking up all our business secrets. What is to prevent him from being another Cummings"—Mr Cummings had had a short stay in the firm some years before—"pumping us dry, and taking off all our customers?"

Mrs Truslove smiled as she worked.

"I think you were jealous of Cummings," she said.

"Jealous, good God," said Mr Beluncle. "Jealous of Cummings!"

"You said Ethel was jealous of me, you said I was jealous of you. But it was you—you were jealous of Cummings," said Mrs Truslove.

Mr Beluncle blinked. He hated the past; if there was any one thing that astonished him more than any other it was the fact that he was married (so to say) to two women, entirely different in character, but alike in their love of the past and their skill in darting back into it. Mr Beluncle had a poor memory of the past. He could hardly remember one year from another. He was about to say "But you hated Cummings" when it unhappily struck him that a quotation from the Bible would transpose the dispute to the moral plane where it would become more congenial and more manageable.

"Let the Dead bury their Dead," he said, and was so

delighted by the aptness of the quotation that he scribbled it out on a piece of paper and propped it against Mrs Truslove's side of their common inkstand. He was so busy doing this that he did not notice Mrs Truslove's pale stare. She dropped her pen.

"You heartless man," she said. "Seventeen years ago today. Today. This very day. And you say that to me. Jack died seventeen years ago today. Don't touch me."

For Mr Beluncle had got up.

"I'm sorry. I forgot. What date is it? The 17th? I didn't know . . ." stammered Mr Beluncle. And then, suspiciously, "Are you sure?"

"Am I sure?" she said coldly. "You forgot. What else have you forgotten?"

Mr Beluncle did not like this. The fact was that quite naturally he forgot everything. Sometimes in an insincere way he wished that he did not forget; it would be so useful, in small skirmishes of this kind, if he did remember; but in a larger way—he stuck to it—to let the dead bury their dead was the best thing. He had a suspicion, too, that Jack Truslove had not died on the 17th; the more alarming suspicion that Mrs Truslove was saying he had died on the 17th for some particular convenience of her feeling that he had not yet penetrated. She had said this because she had something else on her mind. Tactfully Mr Beluncle put out his hand, moving to take back the text he had given her and to throw it away, but Mrs Truslove was too quick for him. She took the paper and put it into her handbag.

"I shall keep that," she said. "I shall remember it."

And then she said something which made Beluncle open his mouth.

"I saw Mr Cummings at the station this morning. He asked me to dine with him," she said.

"To dine with Cummings!"

"Yes," she said, "to dine with Cummings!"

"I hope he is sober," said Mr Beluncle, for Mr Cummings was one of those efficient drinkers who seemed, to Mr Beluncle's astonishment, to run brilliantly on alcohol to the top of the ladder. He had long ago zigzagged upwards into financial worlds well out of Beluncle's reach.

"He has offered me a job," she said.

Mr Beluncle studied his partner and his friend. So often she had spoken of leaving Bulux that he supposed it was one of the womanish threats that would go on for years. They had been serious enough to drive him to a forestalling move: the introduction of Mr Chilly. Mr Beluncle was certain that she would change her mind when Mr Chilly appeared and her tenacity since then had confirmed him in his adroitness.

"There are times," Mr Beluncle said, "—there are times, Linda, when I do not understand you."

"I will say it again," said Mrs Truslove. "Mr Cummings has offered me a very good job."

"You are taking it?" said Mr Beluncle coldly.

"I am considering it," said Mrs Truslove.

Mr Beluncle studied Mrs Truslove's person, beginning with her black hair parted in the middle, moving down her face. Mr Beluncle's journeying eyes stopped at the edge of her blouse, as at the edge of a precipice.

Mrs Truslove's dangerous blouse took his memory back to a scene of years ago when he walked into the office and had found her lifting Mr Cummings's hand from her shoulder when she was bending near the safe.

"I suppose," said Mr Beluncle, who would have liked to have been offered a job, too, it was such a pleasure, "he is offering you a large salary."

"I suppose so," said Mrs Truslove. "There would be no point in a small one."

"Well," said Mr Beluncle, separating his hands as if he had just washed them and was now going to dry them. "If there is one thing I am proud to say of myself, it is that money has never governed *my* life. Money has never entered *my* calculations. I have seen the hell it creates, the lives it wrecks. I thank heaven that, in my small way, I have run my life not on money . . ."

"What have you run it on?" said Mrs Truslove.

"What?" said Mr Beluncle.

"I say, what have you run your life on?"

"On love. Love, that is it! On giving, not getting. On love," said Beluncle, with feeling.

"Philip," said Mrs Truslove, "that kind of talk doesn't work with me any more." She got up and pressed a bell by the fireplace. "I have rung for coffee. You have never loved anyone but yourself. You are a hypocrite."

Mr Beluncle did not smile, but his face, which had become very pale, began to gleam and even to glister like a round cheese with spectacles on it. He had been wrong. He had supposed that in the calm of Sunday their quarrel of Saturday was forgotten.

"Hypocrite," he said aloud. "I am a hypocrite. Thank you very much. So that is how it is."

He went to the office door, put on a bowler hat and took down a white dust-coat and put it on, and then walked, exalted, strangely satisfied in the desire for unjust punishment, out of the office. He went down the passage under a cliff of cheap piled-up chairs, the unsold surplus of a large foreign order, then through a pair of clean swing-doors and afterwards through a pair of thumbed and dirty doors into the factory, where the air was suddenly as hot as a drinker's face too near. The smell of varnish and timber was evident. On the first of the three steps going down to the factory he stopped.

Mr Beluncle's white dust-coats were longer than those garments usually are and his stout figure looked womanish and like a priest's in them. He had these coats slightly starched and they were blindingly clean.

"His nibs," one of the men whispered.

Mr Beluncle did not hear this but he was aware of it. The sight of him put a furtiveness in the movements of his workmen and Mr Beluncle found a pleasure in this. His eye discovered at once who was pretending to work, who was talking about horses, who had just come back from a stolen smoke. But, as he stood there now, Mr Beluncle was really standing in an imaginary pulpit and he was saying to them all:

"I have just been called a hypocrite. What do you think of that? Would you agree? I doubt if you would. You are not women, you are men. You are large and tolerant. You know the world. But let me tell you this: it doesn't matter what I think or what you think, or Mrs Truslove, or my wife, or my sons. The question we ought always to ask ourselves is, What does God think? God sees into the heart, and when He looks at me and you does He say 'There's a hypocrite' or 'There's a murderer' or 'There's a thief'? How could the Divine Mind think such a thing? Unimaginable, isn't it?"

The exultation of a moral victory rose in Mr Beluncle and, in the midst of it, it seemed to him that he heard a voice, as clear as the inner voice of conscience but much friendlier, speaking to him. Mr Beluncle's father had heard such a voice, after being stripped of his rank and thrown out of the army when he was young. "Come ye out from them and be ye separate," the Voice had said to his father. "Preach the kingdom."

Mr Beluncle senior had heard the call; and he had been in the furniture trade too. So it did not surprise Mr Beluncle junior that a Voice should speak to *him*; on the contrary he would have raised an enquiring eyebrow if It had not. What the Voice said to Mr Beluncle junior were words as enlarging as those his father had heard.

"Go to the West End," the voice said. "You are wasted here. You cannot breathe. Get outside, have a shave, go to the bank. Go to the West End."

XVI

Mr Beluncle walked to London Bridge. He did not dare to take a taxi until he had crossed the river for he felt Mrs Truslove might have some means of watching him anywhere within half a mile of his factory.

"A terrible thing," he said. "I am fifty-five. Really, I would not mind being dead. All you have to do is to hang yourself."

He enacted the scene, and just as he was being cut down, he saw not his own body, but Jack Truslove's body in the mortuary at Birmingham.

"Served him right," said Mr Beluncle. "Oh no, I didn't mean that. Good heavens, why did I say that? What I meant was, *in a sense*, it served him right. There's no doubt about it—he deceived me. No good ever comes of deceit."

Mr Beluncle stopped outside a tie shop. "Many a time I have bought a shirt or tie here," said Mr Beluncle, "in the early days."

The same shop, with the same narrow, pinch-faced window, and the same shirts and ties for the office people round about who could not afford better.

"Damn' fool I must have been," said Mr Beluncle, for he had his shirts made expensively in the West End now.

"I used to wear spotted bows," he said. He shuddered cynically: the shop brought to his mind again Truslove's great, sly deceit. Truslove was a one-tie man; a faded piece of green poplin used to hang parsimoniously from his neck like a suicide's halter; his straying, sandpapering voice had the weakness of one who had started to hang himself the night before and then had not had the will to go on. He was a tall, soldierly shabby man with a sunken chest, who seemed to look over the tops of everyone's head at some distant place, like the blind looking for something they have lost. At first Truslove was a customer of Beluncle's agency, one of those lonely, friendly ones who buy so as to make an excuse for interminable chats. He liked making quotations from poetry in a depressed voice. One of these Mr Beluncle always remembered. "It irks me not if men my garments wear," Mr Truslove was fond of saying. Afterwards Mr Beluncle used to laugh with Miss Dykes, his secretary, a plump and stolid, homely girl.

"His garments! He'd have a job to give them away." Mr Truslove was the most shabbily dressed man in the trade. Why? What was the matter with Mr Truslove? What did he want? What was wrong? He was doing quite well on a few patents. What was he after? Mr Beluncle used to ask his secretary, who was too solemn to enjoy rhetorical questions. He used to ask his wife.

"It's a funny world," he said. "Here am I without a penny, but I've got faith. That man Truslove has got capital and not even the faith to buy himself a decent tie. And confound me," said Mr Beluncle, "if I don't tell him so."

Mr Beluncle did tell him. Mr Beluncle told Mr Truslove this with tremendous emotion.

"I'll tell you something, Truslove. You don't know you're born. You know the trade. You've made a chair that would sell all over the world, but you just peddle it about in ones and twos. You haven't even given it a name. You can't sell a thing without a name. And you can't sell it without faith."

Mr Truslove's wintry eyes moistened.

"I can't make a chair like that, I haven't the capital, but if I had you'd see the Beluncle Chair all over England," cried Mr Beluncle.

"Uncle's Chair," murmured Mr Truslove, in his flat and weary voice.

"The Beluncle Chair," corrected Mr Beluncle.

"Uncle's Chair," repeated Mr Truslove suicidally.

"Uncle's?" said Mr Beluncle, offended at the play on his name.

"No offence," said Mr Truslove, in the voice of one pausing before he cut his throat. "I give you the idea."

"Don't *you* give *me* ideas," said Mr Beluncle warmly and in a scornful temper because he saw Truslove's idea was a good one. "I've got all I can manage. I'm so full of ideas, I'm afraid I'll burst a blood vessel. Give me the capital."

It was a sudden wooing, but that is what Truslove did.

Truslove & Beluncle: it was like a marriage and Uncle's Chair was the child of it. Even now, all these years afterwards and Truslove long dead, Mr Beluncle felt the nuptial buzz of those early months. Mr Beluncle saved Mr Truslove by his faith; Mr Truslove saved Mr Beluncle by his capital. And it was like a marriage by the offence it caused; there had been nothing but quarrels ever since. Miss Dykes, the solemn, heavy young secretary who had slaved for Mr Beluncle, who had a crippled sister and an invalid mother, and who often went without her pay for two or three weeks when Mr Beluncle's agency was in a bad way, who had once or twice paid Mr Beluncle's train fare to Scotland (where he had business) out of her own pocket, and had only got half of it back, was jealous of Mr Truslove at once. Mrs Beluncle, who had liked Mr Truslove because he looked ill, now turned against him too. Mrs Beluncle suspected the motives of everyone who helped her husband; why did people back a certain bankrupt? They were giving him money in order to ruin him.

"What's he after? That's what I can't make out. You're so blind. You're so full of yourself. You believe everything they tell you," she said. "You don't listen to your own wife."

She was quite right, Mr Beluncle often thought; but the poor woman had her mother's temper and spoiled her intuitions by wrapping them up in unending yards of rage.

Mr Beluncle walked on slowly from the tie shop with a short laugh of indignation. Ten weeks after Truslove had become his partner the betrayal had come.

Mr Beluncle went home and stood fizzing like a black old-fashioned bomb in the hall of his house.

"Eth," he said, "I've had a blow."

"Phil," Mrs Beluncle cried, "not the High Street?"

"The High Street?" he said. "Why are you digging that up. What's the High Street got to do with it. Forget the High Street."

"I thought someone had come about Connie or the High Street," she said.

"Take this from me," said Mr Beluncle, hardening his face, which he rarely did, squaring his jaw, and looking as though he would hit the next person who spoke to him. "No one is going to come about Connie or the High Street. I don't know what you mean."

"But, Phil—it was never paid. We went . . . I mean . . ."

"Ethel," said Mr Beluncle, softening sadly, "you don't understand business. When Medalls opened up in the High Street he took a risk. It was none of Connie's business. The landlord took a risk. The manufacturers took a risk. That's what business is—risk. You never did and yet you were a business girl. Forget the High Street. The High Street does not exist. It's finished."

Beluncle started to laugh in an uncomfortable way.

"It's Truslove—Jack. He's married Miss Dykes. Don't sit looking at me. I say, he's married Miss Dykes—that's all."

"But, Phil . . ."

Mr Beluncle said it had gone on under his nose for months and he had not noticed. That he was rather proud of; he hoped he had more important things to do in life than to notice sex. Yet they ought to have told him. They hadn't even asked. It might have been thoroughly inconvenient for him to have them married. And then, surely, if the girl had wanted to marry she ought, in a platonic way, to have married him, not Truslove. For Truslove was not free to marry; he was, so to say, married to him, Mr Beluncle. And what a disgusting thought it was; that long bony man with ginger hair on his arms—and probably on his legs too—in bed with that poor fat girl; Mr Beluncle wanted to rush into the bedroom and save her, or at any rate to lie between them, in case, in the middle of the night, she started telling Mr Truslove confidential business matters which she must have picked up while she was working with him.

"I don't mean anything Wrong," said Mr Beluncle to himself, exhausted by his torment, and speaking in that pathetic inner voice which he sometimes used for intro-spection, "but I thought she was in love with me."

His wife's reply to all this was typical of her. In a flash, woman-like, she changed from her long dislike of Miss Dykes and Mr Truslove, to infatuation with them.

"I said, you never listen, you never do, I—I—I, all the time, I said, he wanted something when he came to you," she said tenderly. "He was lonely."

"Lonely?" said Mr Beluncle. He had never heard of such a thing.

"Wanted something, someone—human," said Mrs Beluncle.

"Pooh," said Mr Beluncle.

And then: "Poor girl," she said.

"Poor girl," burst out Mr Beluncle, in open jealousy. "She trapped him. She feathered her nest. Feathered it!" said Mr Beluncle, flopping into a chair which seemed to him noticeably cold and unfeathered. "Poor girl!" he jeered.

"He's dying," said Mrs Beluncle, tears coming to her eyes. "Like my sister. I've seen it before. I can hear his chest now, like a lift going up and down."

"A lift?" said Mr Beluncle with terror—for sometimes his wife's images were too wild for his sensibility. "That's a peculiar thing to say. I mean to say, have some sense, a lift in a man's chest. How can a man's chest sound as if it had a lift? . . ."

' Going up and coming down. I can hear it. My poor sister," said Ethel.

Mr Beluncle was relieved. He knew when his wife mentioned her sister she was never describing anything likely to be repeated in human experience.

And there, Mr Beluncle turned out to be wrong again. There were more betrayals. Six months after the marriage of Miss Dykes and Mr Truslove the girl's mother died. Two years after that the partnership came to an end: Mr Truslove dropped dead in the corridor of a train going to Birmingham, where he was to introduce a new idea of his—the Long Uncle Chair for (as he said dismally, glancing at his own legs) long uncles.

XVII

Mr Beluncle went to Birmingham for the body of his partner. The death shocked him. He had loved Truslove. The flat voice, the small eyes, the lankiness, the uncouthness, the calmness of Truslove, had had a powerful effect on him; they had excited his heart and his senses. "David and Jonathan we were," he said.

And yet, Beluncle thought, when he saw his friend's body in the mortuary (and but for the strong arm of the young widow he would have fainted at the sight of it), Truslove had his faults. The parable of the talents, perhaps applied to him; perhaps the story of the centurion; one must give up everything. Truslove was mean, exact, prudent, curbing. Men with a little capital always were. And when he and the widow walked out in the industrial rain and he put his umbrella up and took her surprisingly thin, hard arm which was not soft like Ethel's, he felt wild with hunger, wanted to take a larger room at the hotel, have a bottle of champagne, eat ham and hire cars. He wanted to show this girl who had worked for him three years ago, and whom he didn't forgive for so secretly marrying his partner and who would come into his money, how these things were done.

She would not let him. Her face was set and dirty with grief, not red like his own; she did not weep. She stopped him at the undertaker's, where she insisted on coming, when he was about to spread himself on the funeral. She had complained about the expense of the hotel. She obliged him to go to a poor teashop where they had eaten scrambled eggs and there was a thumb mark on his plate.

One triumph Beluncle had, after the funeral—when he had been obscured by two or three relatives—Mrs Truslove and himself travelled first-class back to London and he reserved the compartment. This was an important victory, for Truslove had introduced the cautious notion of third-class travel in the firm. When the train came out of the foul station tunnel into the smoky sunlight and the smell of coal and sulphur staled the carriage, Mrs Truslove was weeping. They were her first tears. Mr Beluncle sat opposite to her for three hours, saying little to her and watching.

"There has been a death," he said, in a low, discreet voice, to the ticket inspector, handing him two third-class tickets and a half-crown tip. The inspector murmured and went. She was too dazed to notice or to stop him hiring a car when they got to London.

At Mrs Truslove's house when the car got there, no blinds

were drawn. The house had been visited by Beluncle once or, perhaps, twice before and had made an impression of hardness and damp on him. Beluncle did not object to the house. What disturbed him was that inside and out it had a dingy austerity which recalled to him the house of his parents and, also, that the Dykes had lived there for seventeen years. The extraordinary thing was that Truslove had not taken his wife away from it, but had moved in with her. Economy again. Truslove had been one of nature's lodgers. His bicycle was in the hall.

The front room of the house was a bed-sitting-room, occupied by the crippled sister of Mrs Truslove; a room at the back was the sitting-room, beyond that was a kitchen. When they got to the house, Mrs Truslove rushed straight upstairs and left Mr Beluncle in the sitting-room. The furniture of the older Dykes (the father had been a postman) was in this room, and every object, the old-fashioned vases on the overmantle, the horsehair sofa, the hard chairs, the fantastic sideboard with its little mirrors, indicated people who never spent money on new things if the old or the second-hand would do. Beluncle's estimating eye reckoned how much they would get for the lot in a sale.

But soon the door was opened and gently struck the cloth-covered table which stood against the wall; the canary, which Beluncle had not noticed, began to sing and in, very softly on the oiled wheels of her chair, came Mrs Truslove's sister.

The bearings made a soft tick as it moved, a kind of winding sound. Judy Dykes had the air of a peculiar human clock, some doll-like, wooden Swiss invention. She was a very pretty woman in those days. Her voice had a childish sing-song and this evening it was electric and eager and happy.

"I have to wait till my sister comes down," she said. "Tell me about it. Now do stop!" she called to the excited canary.

Beluncle said afterwards that this mechanical woman seemed to be preparing some trick on him, as the figure in a jack-in-the-box might. He sat down uncomfortably and told her about the funeral. He looked at the sideboard, hoping to be given a drink, but the room, indeed the house, was odourless as though no one ate or cooked or drank there.

"I can't believe it," Beluncle said. "I knew he had a bad chest, but the heart to go like that. I can't credit it. It's no good saying I can, I just can't.''

In his black clothes (bought for the funeral), his black tie and with the heavy black blob of his close-shaven beard like a loose dark bib on his cheeks, his jaw and his large personal chin, Beluncle looked like the king of all mourners in full black blossom. The cripple studied his clothes with a smile of appreciation as he talked, and so fixed her eyes on his white teeth that he was embarrassed and brought out a black-bordered handkerchief and blew his nose, which brought tears to his eyes.

"It hasn't happened," said the cripple pleasantly.

"That's how it seems," said Beluncle.

"It's like a dream," he said.

"It *is* a dream," said the cripple.

Mr Beluncle was giving a second touch to his nose with the handkerchief when she said this and stopped to look over the black border at her face. It was gay, smiling; the childish voice had vehemence and zest and that oddity and authority which is fixed, like a device, in voices that are speaking in private quotation.

"He is not dead," the cripple quoted. "He has discovered that he has not died. He has opened his eyes and has discovered that it has not happened. He is here, wishing we could realise it. He has exposed the biggest lie of all.''

Miss Dykes smiled like a hard-headed, story-telling child. Mr Beluncle put his handkerchief away.

"He has moved," said the cripple, "on to another plane.''

"Well," said Beluncle afterwards to his wife, "I felt a damn' fool. You could have knocked me over with a feather.''

But what he meant was that he had felt like knocking Miss Dykes over.

He looked at her shrewdly. She was an echo. These were not her views; she was, he recalled, a follower of Mrs Parkinson's. An appetite was awakened.

But the cripple like a reciting child had finished her piece and did not say any more.

"We shall have to sell the house," the cripple said. "With the money we can go away to the sea. That is what I have always wanted to do. I was always on to Mr Truslove about it, but Mr Truslove was obstinate. Now she is free."

It was plain to anybody, Beluncle said, when he told his wife about this conversation, that there had been no love lost between Mr Truslove and the cripple. "Not Jack," he said, "but *Mr* Truslove, *Mr* Truslove. Very strange."

"Why did *she* take him to live with a sister? A sister is a woman," said Mrs Beluncle.

Mr Beluncle took off his black clothes that night and Ethel took each garment from him.

"A coathanger, old girl. Is that a mark on the trousers? Let me fold them," he said.

"These must have cost you a penny," she said.

"You never know when you won't be going to a funeral," Beluncle said. "Where are those trousers I wore at our wedding?"

There were ten other suits in the wardrobe which they shared, her two or three frocks being shouldered into a corner by these masculine clothes. When he was in his shirt and pants, he realised the drama was over and the reality was that money might be withdrawn from the firm.

Mrs Truslove made a visit to the Beluncles on a Sunday afternoon in February. She was wearing a navy-blue coat of good lasting material, well cut, new gloves and a hat which Mrs Beluncle said would have suited the right person. Mr and Mrs Beluncle were astonished by the woman who sat on the edge of the seat of their small sofa. Mrs Beluncle felt she had been deceived. She recognised her only by her height and her voice. The plump secretary had gone. The widow was thin.

"I did not think," Mrs Truslove said in a melancholy voice, "when I went to work with Mr. Beluncle, that I would be left with a business."

"How d'you mean?" said Mrs Beluncle.

"My husband's share was the greater," said Mrs Truslove.

"I never know about business," said Mrs Beluncle, who knew very well, but her husband had never told her he had a smaller share; he always spoke of it as if the firm was his and that out of affection for Jack Truslove he had given him a little corner in it.

The question was, Mrs Truslove said, what Mr Beluncle wanted to do.

"And what *I* want to do," said Mrs Truslove.

"I shall see her to the station," Beluncle whispered to his wife.

"Oh, Phil, *do*," said Ethel earnestly. She was pulled by opposite feelings that Mrs Truslove ought to be kept in the house for ever and that she ought to be sent as far away as possible.

"Phil, she's flirting with her money. It's woman-like," she said.

Another morning, with soap on one side of his face and holding his razor, he said:

"She wants to come back: that's the trouble. They can't live on what he's left."

"Back!" said Mrs Beluncle. "Don't you. You can't take on a woman twice."

Mr Beluncle reached London Bridge and crossed the river.

"Ethel was right," he said and, in the fancy that by crossing water, even the commercial Thames, he had cast off the scent and Mrs Truslove could see him and wail after him no more, he took a taxi and wondered how he could disguise this expense in his accounts.

XVIII

The general office of Bulux was next to the windowless waiting-room. In the general office sat Miss Vanner, a heavy and scheming girl, sleepy and self-protectively quarrelsome. Even her heavy breasts seemed to be quarrelling inside her jersey, as resentfully she typed. She had large and beautiful dark blue eyes and dark blushes quickly flowered on her cheeks in some continual, unpeaceful, private struggle.

"Haven't you anything better to do than stare?" she said to Henry many times during the day.

"Henry," said Mr Andrews, the carrot-haired invoice clerk, a man who sat itching on a high stool. He steered a tormented course through his accounts with one hand gripped in his trouser pocket like a cyclist holding to one handlebar.

"Henry," said Mr Andrews, "*they* are for one pair of eyes alone: the Lancelot of Ladbroke Grove. . . ."

"There is no necessity to be disgusting," said Miss Vanner, with sullen pleasure.

" 'Eyes', did I say?" said Mr Andrews, never defeated in the rearguard actions of embittered lechery. "Hands."

"Oh, you married men!" said Miss Vanner, waking up into indignation. "The only gentleman in this office is Mr Chilly. He has manners and a clean mind. A girl doesn't often see manners."

Miss Vanner felt safer and stronger when she called herself a "girl".

"There are fairies at the bottom of my garden," said Mr Andrews.

But here Mr Cook, the delivery clerk, intervened. A married man with five daughters, with little spots from his wife's cooking on his waistcoat, Mr Cook simmered away on his stool like some puffing kettle, content to wait. Mr Cook worshipped the married state and Miss Vanner (who was engaged to be married) was a semi-sacred object to him. He was sorry for the lewd, unhappy and hen-pecked Andrews who always tried to bring disgrace on the married condition; and, quickly to redress a balance, Mr Cook would talk to Miss Vanner about the pleasure of family holidays by the sea, the sad bulletin of a daughter's health, the amusement to be got out of a bossy wife and would invite Miss Vanner to his house at Ilford, where she could see his modest work of art: five daughters and their mother, all sitting round a table and making fun of him. The ends of Mr Cook's grey moustache nearly met under his lips. He was the ringed bull, domesticated, and with grey hairs on his chest. Mr Chilly might have manners, but for virtue, Mr Cook conveyed, give him the good old-fashioned steam roller of steady paternity. It was Mr Cook's sadness that Mr Beluncle did not appear to appreciate him.

"Damn' fool," Mr Beluncle used to shout when he came back from a visit to the general office to enquire why Mr Cook had let the van go without the Nottingham order or had lost a sale catalogue. For Mr Cook lived in a mild pomp of incompetence.

Mr Chilly came into the room and sat at the long desk close to the door. Miss Vanner lowered her beautiful eyes and, taking a contralto's long breath, gave a loud exhibition of perfect typing, very fast. To Mr Chilly she was sending a blameless message in code; if she had to speak she did so in an artificial voice. To a question like "What did Mr Beluncle say?" she replied, "I am not the recipient of his confidence." But it was Miss Vanner's unhappiness that she was able to speak in this well-staged manner to Henry, to Mr Andrews or to Mr Cook; but not to Mr Chilly, the only man who would appreciate it.

When Mr Chilly said:

"Miss Vanner, would you add to your very many services by typing this with your fair hand?" Miss Vanner was unable to say more than "Oh" or "What?" and could never look him in the eye.

"He is the only man who has had the courtesy to escort me to the bus," she snapped. "A girl notices," she added.

When "a girl" was alone in an office "full of men" (she conveyed) she expected her unique dangers and discomforts to be appreciated. They were, after all, her attractions. Miss Vanner left every evening with a beautiful flash of reproach at the workmen and the office staff. She was sighing for the sexy anonymity of a large office. And she arrived every morning with the sullenness of one beginning a great defensive battle in an exposed position against Henry Beluncle's entranced adolescent stare, against Mr Andrews's reminiscence of the stark facts of married life, even against the modest example of Mr Cook's powerful domesticity; against, above all, her stupefied, headlong, helpless attraction to the manners of Mr Chilly. Before all, except him, she fell back on the solid ground of her engagement to be married. Never was a girl so engaged, Mr Andrews said. Before Mr Chilly her engagement receded, until it was a dulled mark on the horizon of her memory.

But Mr Chilly had eyes for one person alone: Mr Beluncle. Sitting near the door, on his stool, with one long foot on the floor, tapping it, ready to spring to the summons, Mr Chilly lived in the exclamatory state of one who has no clear idea of what he is supposed to be doing. To get customers, of course, was his duty; not to approach customers the firm already had; on the other hand, not to neglect them. On these points Mr Beluncle was touchy. To find out about the business, to learn, was Mr Chilly's task; on the other hand, not to pry, not to find out too much. To assume and yet not to assume; to lay the golden egg but to keep out of the way until he laid another. The only certain duty of Mr Chilly was gratitude. He must show a meaningless alacrity in what Mr Beluncle called "his unique opportunity": a unique opportunity to lay one more golden egg. For six months he had found this mystery took up all his time. Another duty was to strengthen his character. The surest way of doing that was to think continually of Mr Beluncle. Mr Chilly was one of society's natural voids and the danger was that he would be filled—it had happened in his past life—with what was undesirable. He hoped that past would not return. Mr Beluncle, the firm of Bulux, filled him; but there was the prick of a fear—which sometimes made him jump down from his stool and fly out to the factory or to Mr Beluncle's room in a panic—that resolution might, at any moment, start to leak again, that his character would collapse and that the void would once more appear.

Panic struck Mr Chilly especially on those days when Mr Beluncle left the factory for the West End: left alone, Mr Chilly felt a large rise of self-confidence, a desire to go out and give orders, to make huge changes in the firm, as a kind of gift of gratitude to Mr Beluncle. This emotion was followed by terror, the leaking feeling. Someone must fill him quickly lest he collapse and vanish, leaving a ghostly warmth on the seat of his stool.

Lunch-time came. When Mr Beluncle was there Mr Chilly took lunch with him and Mrs Truslove in their office. But when he was not, the struggle broke out in Mr Chilly.

"I think I shall toddle," he said, his keen eye misting a little.

The question was—when the toddling moment came—how much longer had Mr Chilly to prove himself? How much longer was needed before he was certain that he would not slip back?

Today, before lunch-time came, Mr Chilly hurried through the factory, head in air, his yellow hair lifting in two slices at the back, as he flew through into the yard where the vans waited. Gazing over the empty yard with the look of an injured angel whose master spirit has dodged him, Mr Chilly re-entered the factory and, very fast, flew back. The men at their benches rolled their eyes. After a quarter of an hour, Mr Chilly sailed through again, his eyes blinking very fast as if a fury of thought were propelling him. No Mr Beluncle. Mr Chilly was caught in a whirl of poetic importance: it had, after all, been suggested to him that one day he might become a director of the business.

"I shall be on the Board. I shall be on the Board," Mr Chilly's heart was singing. He was anxious merely to show himself to everyone, to expose himself to some imaginary Press camera; but especially to Mr Beluncle, to remind him, not by words, but by the simple, unaffected sight of himself, of their conversation.

He was met by Mrs Truslove, to whom he bowed.

"Mr Beluncle has gone to the West End," she said in a voice that suggested Golders Green cemetery. The rapid blinking of Mr Chilly's eyes stopped and the ecstasy went out of his face.

"Oh!" he exclaimed pettishly.

The life of Mr Chilly suddenly became a desert. Mrs Truslove went back to her room and Mr Chilly was about to follow her, for he must have some human being to lean on, but peremptorily her telephone rang and he turned emptily away. He went to the general office and looked there for help. But Henry had gone, Mr Andrews had gone and Miss Vanner was closing her typewriter.

"I think I shall toddle," said Mr Chilly to no one in particular. And then, before he knew what he was saying, he said to Miss Vanner:

"Fair lady, would you care to have luncheon with me?"

The blushes of Miss Vanner were heavy and plum-coloured.

"You don't want to," she said sulkily.

"But I asked you," said Mr Chilly. "I would be charmed if you are free."

"I don't mind," said Miss Vanner. "I'm always," said Miss Vanner, searching vainly for a word, "elastic," she said.

Mr Chilly's heart sank as he waited for Miss Vanner in the doorway of the building and sank lower as he took her to a bus. She sat beside him, pushing her shoulders and breasts and legs this way and that as if two parts of herself, the engaged and the disengaged, were shoving sullenly against each other.

"This is a mistake," said Mr Chilly to himself as they went through the carpeted bar of a restaurant a mile from the office, where many managers, directors and salesmen of the neighbourhood gathered. Mr Chilly felt he had a notice on his back saying "Unfaithful to Mr Beluncle". In the restaurant the first person he saw was a large man shouting with some drinking friends: the Devil, the Satan of their trade, the ruthless overbearing swindler and competitor.

"Cummings," said Miss Vanner, with importance.

"Good God!" said Chilly, with fear. "Has he seen me?"

"Cummings is nothing," said Miss Vanner largely, taking power from the nervousness of Mr Chilly.

"He doesn't own the restaurant," she said.

Mr Chilly was surprised by this information. He looked over the top of the menu, gazing at Cummings, fascinated by him, endeavouring even to attract his attention against his own will.

"Crab salad, lobster," murmured Mr Chilly mechanically, disregarding Miss Vanner, still staring at Cummings.

"I can't. It repeats," said Miss Vanner.

"Disagrees, I mean," Miss Vanner corrected herself, very angry with herself for the vulgarity. "I am aware that I have had it.

"I'll have whatever you have," she said.

Mr Chilly looked at her warily.

"This is a terrible mistake," Mr Chilly said to himself; he considered Miss Vanner carefully through the meal, and the less flattering his conclusions were, the more polite and charming he became. A full stomach and Mr Chilly's politeness put Miss Vanner more at her ease. She began to talk freely and then recklessly about the firm. After every sentence she scowled: she knew this was a most tactless way in which to talk to Mr Chilly.

"Mrs Truslove's the cuckoo in the nest, you can see that plain as a pikestaff," said Miss Vanner. "His wife can't stand her. The boy's terrified of him.

"I'm sorry for that boy. I'm sorry for Mr Beluncle," said Miss Vanner. (Miss Vanner's sorrow was a way of punishing them.)

You could see what was happening: Mr Beluncle spent so much time keeping the peace with his wife and keeping Mrs Truslove quiet about the money, his mind was taken off the business. It was going to pieces. The last time they had the accountants in, they warned him. And the bank manager. They ought never to have quarrelled with Cummings years ago.

"That," said the young Miss Vanner in a slow, hammering moral tone, raising and lowering her chin with each word, "that is where things went wrong."

Mr Chilly listened. The information of Miss Vanner did

not make its impression on him in a direct fashion; it made him silently apologise to her for his conclusions of half an hour earlier and revise them in her favour. She was a very beautiful and attractive girl; and her scandalous talk gave her a restful and seductive squalor. In his pre-Beluncle days, Mr Chilly had had a tendency to sink into squalor; the sensations were returning. Their familiarity pleased him.

"It was a personal quarrel," said Miss Vanner, "of course."

"But you were not there then," said Mr Chilly, not doubting Miss Vanner, but allowing her miraculous powers of travelling up and down time wherever she wanted to be. His remark was admiration.

"No," said Miss Vanner. And then she was at last able to speak the kind of sentence she wished she could always speak. "No," she said, "I was informed by a reliable source."

And she sat up like a queen.

"Cummings was trying to get *friendly*," said Miss Vanner. "I don't say they ever did actually get *friendly*, but he used to go out with her. Mr Beluncle would not agree to it—what business was it of his if they were going out? You've only got one life.

"Haven't you?" said Miss Vanner to stir Mr Chilly, who had picked up the menu again and was looking over the top of it towards Mr Cummings. He was still trumpeting at a distant table.

"You say interesting things," said Mr Chilly, coming down from his agitation.

"Handsome," said Mr Chilly, hearing his own voice with astonishment. He had been thinking, really, what a handsome woman Mrs Truslove was.

"I always thought you were in love with Henry," said Mr Chilly, with a high laugh.

"Pooh," said Miss Vanner, "that kid. I mean child. I'm going to be married. What put Henry into your head?"

"It's a great pity," said Mr Chilly, "that you should be married."

("This is frightful," Mr Chilly said, "I must stop saying things like this.")

"Why is it a pity? My boy and I have been friendly for years. We've been going out since we were sixteen," said Miss Vanner. "He wants the bird sometimes," she sighed.

"I will give it him one of these days," said Mr Chilly, and knocked his glass over with a great gesture, but catching it before it fell. "Taking a beautiful girl like you."

"He's so jealous," said Miss Vanner. "When you're engaged that doesn't give you the right to be jealous. A girl is often attracted. Some are friendly with several, not that I agree with that. I thought you were attracted to Mrs Truslove. Everyone says so in the office."

"I should say Mrs Truslove is attractive to many men," said Mr Chilly coldly.

"It's funny about her hair—have you ever noticed it? The way she does it? It's been like that ever since I was there," said Miss Vanner. "It doesn't suit her, not at her age. She must be getting on. I was surprised when you asked me out this morning. Had you been thinking about it or did you just think you would? I didn't think I interested you. Or was it just curiosity?"

"You've got lovely hands," said Mr Chilly, kicking himself the moment he said this because he had not, in fact, looked at Miss Vanner's hands. He had often admired Mrs Truslove's.

"It's funny you should mention them because I like them and so does my fiancé," said Miss Vanner. "I didn't know you asked me out because you were attracted. I'd never thought of you wanting to be *friendly*. When the cat's away the mice will play—Mr Beluncle's gone to the showroom, hasn't he?"

"I'm sorry to bring this lunch to a close," said Mr Chilly, suddenly brought to his senses by the name of Mr Beluncle, "but I must fly."

A toddle ended in a dash. He dashed for his bill, he dashed with Miss Vanner to the bus. So far ahead of her was his mind dashing that he hardly spoke to her; and when, accidentally, he looked at her his eye was cold, wondering who she was. He stepped into the warm building with the sense of one returning to the womb and did not even nod to Miss Vanner as they parted.

XIX

In the middle of the afternoon an unnerving thing happened to Mr Chilly. He sold two tables.

"Oh, how I wish Mr Beluncle were here!" said Mr Chilly to Henry. "Where is the order book? Look, I've forgotten the carbon paper, lend me your pen. I can't remember—is this the address of the shop? Or is this the office."

Mr Chilly flew to the foreman two or three times to be certain of the stock numbers.

"Put 'Terms—Cash'," said Henry.

"Oh—is that right?" said Mr Chilly. "I've never done this before. Shall I ring up Mr Beluncle? Oh, I do hope it's all right."

"If we've got the tables," said Henry.

"How d'you mean? I saw them," said Mr Chilly.

"He means," said the foreman, "unless they're sold."

"Good God," said Mr Chilly. "I never thought of that."

"Mr Beluncle may have sold them," said the foreman. The art of increasing the natural doubts of Mr Chilly was well advanced in the firm. "Are they going by rail?"

"He didn't say," said Mr Chilly.

"Oh," said the foreman.

"Why d'you say 'Oh' like that?" said Mr Chilly.

"If they're not going by rail who's collecting them? I mean who's paying delivery?"

"Pay delivery?" exclaimed Mr Chilly. "He never mentioned it."

The foreman did not answer but returned to his small desk against the wall at the end of the factory.

"Henry," said Mr Chilly, holding Henry's arm and walking towards the office, "I am in despair."

"What was the price?" said Henry.

"Henry!" said Mr Chilly. "Bring me the book quickly. Suppose I was looking at the wrong list."

"It's quite clear, Mr Chilly," said Henry.

"*Mr* Chilly, *Mr* Chilly," said Mr Chilly. "Don't be so impersonal, so hard. Everard—please. Say 'Everard', Henry. No, go on. Say it."

"Everard," said Henry.

"Oh dear, that's better," said Mr Chilly. "You sometimes freeze me. One would think one wasn't liked. One would have the impression one was thought a fool. You do think I'm a fool, don't you, Henry? Don't deny it. Don't deny you have often thought Everard is a fool."

"I never . . ." began Henry Beluncle.

"Oh, you and your father are so strong, so sensible. Everything is easy to you. You are a born businessman, a shrewd, quick, practical—look at your hands, show them to me. No, I mean it, show them to me. . . ."

They were standing by an empty table where the men's tea cans stood near the entrance to the factory. Henry Beluncle blushed and glanced nervously towards the men. Henry showed his hands and Mr Chilly raised them.

"The hands," said Mr Chilly, "of a practical, ambitious, successful man. Have you seen the ghastly hands of Miss Vanner? Meat, Henry, chilblained meat. Mine . . ."

Mr Chilly dropped Henry's hands and held his own up in a despair that gradually changed to interest and then to discreet admiration.

"Mine are different," said Mr Chilly coolly. "Artistic—some would say. I have no doubt," said Mr Chilly with satisfaction, "the proletariat is looking at us with vulgar interest. I will go. I leave you, Henry, who *know* the men," said Mr Chilly, "to soothe their troubled breasts."

XX

"I'm sorry I'm late," Lady Roads was roughly calling up the stairs to the landing outside her office. It was a room looking on to the traffic, over one of the banks in Boystone. Mr Beluncle was standing on the landing with his hat off and his head bowed, forcefully mourning the minutes that were dying around him. Time, he felt, fluttered away from him like pound notes as he waited. He could feel himself ticking like a taxi while this woman, always late, kept him waiting.

Lady Roads was thrown up on the landing on a wave of shouts, breasts first, hitching her skirt at the waist.

"I've been raising the dead," Lady Roads laughed. She enjoyed Mr Beluncle's startled look.

"He wanted to die," said Lady Roads, "but I wouldn't let him. They're so sweet," said Lady Roads with the wistfulness of the masterly, "when they try to die and they can't."

Mr Beluncle liked geniality, but only in himself. At one of the doors on the landing the displeased figure of Miss Wix appeared. She was trembling at the chin, trembling with all she knew, all she feared. Lady Roads had the loud shabbiness of wealth, Miss Wix the shiny shabbiness of poverty. At home with the parents who disliked her, Miss Wix cooked on a paraffin stove, a small meal which she ate alone. With it she drank a cup of some liquid which tasted like tea and coffee mixed and which was free of caffein and tannin, those deleterious drugs that play on our senses. She was married to a bicycle on which she rode gracefully through Boystone, thinking of practical household repairs, her religion and often of the nephew she had brought up and whom she had held so often to her uninflected chest.

"Kitty," Lady Roads said loudly, waving an envelope at her. "For you. From Toronto. I found it in my box."

Miss Wix's trembling head gave a shaking evasive look at Lady Roads's bosom. She was frightened of those bold breasts which had suckled children. She dreaded and even hated the bosom of Lady Roads and often spoke of it curtly to her followers in the church. Lady Roads, she said, was probably a secret Roman Catholic and worked "through sex".

Suspiciously Miss Wix took the letter from Lady Roads's fat and pretty hand and Lady Roads opened upon her one of her long, sly, sensual smiles.

"Come on, Mr Beluncle," said Lady Roads, "when I can find my bloody keys."

Miss Wix had gone back into her own room, and as Lady Roads led the way into hers with the dipping walk of a large woman, she said:

"That was a letter from headquarters. Poor Kitty has been writing to them complaining that I get all the patients. She says I get them by personality and not by prayer. Sit down."

"It is hard to realise," Mr Beluncle said, "that woman is a Divine Idea."

Lady Roads's room had linoleum on the floor and was furnished by a trestle table in deal with the green-bound works of Mrs Parkinson in twelve volumes on it and a large cocoa-coloured photogravure of one of the Parkinsonian temples which resembled a famous block of offices. The Purification was, in essence, an office religion, a way of finding the Almighty in the proper files. There were two deck chairs in Lady Roads's room. Mr Beluncle looked with annoyance at them. Why no Bulux chair here? The Parkinsonians ought to support one another. If not Uncle's Chair why not Model Three?

Lady Roads sat down and dropped things about her as if she were on a beach. She crossed her strong legs and exposed an unclean garter. She laughed again.

"I know what Kitty has been up to," said Lady Roads. "She wants to get me thrown off the register. She doesn't get the cases."

"Terrible," said Mr Beluncle, who was very shocked, but he felt better after hearing a scandal.

"Oh!"—Lady Roads was melancholy—"our movement stirs up all the hate in human nature. And I'll tell you something between ourselves." Lady Roads gave him an even slyer look. "I opened that letter by mistake. It was in my box. I stuck it up again. If"—she winked—"it *was* a mistake." She started to heave herself out of her chair. "I must go and tell her. No," she said, relapsing, "talk to me first. How's your boy? Here"—and she pulled a bag of toffees out of her pocket. "Have a sweet?"

"No, thank you," said Mr. Beluncle, but Lady Roads put a large toffee in her cheek.

"I'm listening," she said.

"You are speaking about Henry," said Mr Beluncle apologetically. "Well, I suppose the answer is that he has the belief in youth."

"I'm always on the side of youth. The young people always come to me," said Lady Roads. "The future of our movement is with youth. Bring the youth. Call the youth. They long for a leader."

"I was not aware," said Mr Beluncle politely, "that the Divine Mind had any age."

"I'm fifty-two," said Lady Roads.

"I'm surprised to hear you give voice to that," said Mr Beluncle, with a little indulgence.

"No," he said genially. "Henry is at the age when he knows everything. A father . . ."

"Has he got any girls?" said Lady Roads. "He ought to see a lot of girls."

"He has no time for girls. A man who works for me has his mind fully occupied," said Mr Beluncle firmly.

"It's sweet to see them in love," said Lady Roads tenderly and looking voluptuously at Mr Beluncle.

"He may have spoken to a girl. I don't know," said Mr Beluncle, on guard.

"Oh, who?" said Lady Roads.

"Oh, no one," said Mr Beluncle. "I imagine he always thinks he's in love."

"That's the wonderful thing about our movement," said Lady Roads. "It takes sex out of love."

Mr Beluncle blushed on behalf of Lady Roads.

"We have got to make youth take sex out of love," she said with bitterness.

Mr Beluncle allowed her to go on. There was confusion in the teaching of Mrs Parkinson about love between the sexes. Miss Wix was of the party that believed it to be forbidden. She was surrounded by a group of celibate girls and women who had left their husbands. Lady Roads believed that marriage was permissible if sexual intercourse could be eliminated. Mr Beluncle had not joined the movement in order to argue; he did not care for the subject to be talked about: it suggested enquiry into other peoples' lives and Mr Beluncle was against that. It took attention from his life. He noticed that sex was discussed everywhere but he preferred to manœuvre out of the way; the sexual instinct interfered with the acquisitive.

"I don't want sex," he thought of saying to Lady Roads. "I want more of God, more and more. Manna is what I want—every day." He had occasional doubts about Lady Roads: like himself she had a strong mind in a strong body. She was very spiritual, of course; her spirituality was strengthened by the fact that her husband had been a railway director worth—well, Mr Beluncle had made a note of the figure somewhere. Mr Beluncle regarded this sum with reverence and with innocence.

But the time had come to interrupt Lady Roads.

"Talking of getting the sex out of love or the love out of sex, what you were saying," said Mr Beluncle, who got no pleasure out of frankness. "I should like to get the accountants out of my office. They've been in a week."

"Always a trying time," said Lady Roads tactfully.

"Well, your office is not your own. They're in and out, wanting to know this and that, things you can't remember. Twopence here, threepence there. It's marvellous really. An accountant," Mr Beluncle said, with deprecation, "is a man who deals with figures. That's his business, what he has been trained to; he knows five is more than four and two is less than three. He writes down a lot of figures on paper and he looks at them and he *believes* what he sees. That's the point: he actually believes it. They hypnotise him. I suppose the biggest lies that have ever been told are on balance sheets. You can add it up this way, you can add it up that, and every time you can get a different answer. That's the point. As Shakespeare says, it's all in your own mind."

Mr Beluncle paused.

"No," said Mr Beluncle, "if I'd listened to accountants or believed figures, I'd be out on the street. But there it is, it's their profession, they've got to believe it, or *they'd* be on the streets. I tell Mrs Truslove this every day, but well—— Still, I didn't come to talk about that. I'm going to be frank with you—and why shouldn't I be frank with you?" said Mr Beluncle, in his intimate voice. "The fact is we can't afford to carry your nephew as things are. I say, as things are. If we are going to go on carrying Everard—we call him Everard—to be plain about it, we feel, Mrs Truslove feels, I feel, that in common justice Everard ought to support us by carrying us more than he does. I feel, we both feel, Mrs Truslove and I feel, that we have done something for Everard. He came to us and—to be quite honest with you, he's a very nice boy . . ."

"He's thirty-five," said Lady Roads.

"But we had to teach him everything. I don't say he doesn't know the privilege he has had, I hadn't thought of it as a privilege myself but Mrs Truslove said to me only yesterday, 'He has to realise he is privileged in working for us,' and Mrs Truslove is just, very just. I will say that about her if I go down to my grave, Mrs Truslove is a just woman though she has not yet seemed to want—why do I say 'not want'? We all want them, in fact we have them whether we want them or not, they're here and now—the teachings of Mrs Parkinson."

"You mean," said Lady Roads, "it's a question of money?"

"Well," said Mr Beluncle, smiling abundantly, "you always come to the point. I wouldn't have put it quite that way. We think we want money, I may think I want money to buy a house with, I've seen a house which looks to be the right idea, in fact I'm sure it is, if God wants it for me, but what we want is substance, ideas. Seek ye first. I would have said if there was a need of money in my business it was not for me to outline to God how it would be met, I don't say that Everard has to bring in more money but if God wants him to be the channel, well," said Mr Beluncle, with rebuking charm, "it is not for me to obstruct him. He would get seven per cent free of tax."

He stopped and frowned. Lady Roads was rustling her bag of sweets.

"Go on," she said, "I'm listening. Do have one though. They are the kind Mrs Parkinson used to eat."

"Really," said Mr Beluncle, very impressed. "In that case, may I see? What are they called?"

And while he was taking a sweet, a door banged on the landing.

"There goes poor Kitty," Lady Roads chuckled. "Do go on. You want Everard to put up more capital. . . ."

"Don't mistake me," said Mr Beluncle, holding up the palms of both hands. "To mortal belief, capital is necessary to business—there it is, why conceal it? I would have put it in different words. I would have said that giving is the lesson of life. It may be, I don't say it is, that Everard's problem is like the world's problem—we can always give more than we do."

Mr Beluncle saw himself suddenly and shyly in a dramatic light.

"I just want to give the whole time," said Mr Beluncle, "—to pour out."

XXI

At his home in the morning, Mr Beluncle said, "I shall be early tonight."

"Oh, I *am* glad," said Mrs Beluncle. "You're not often early. I get the pip shut up with gran. I never go out. I sit here waiting for you, longing for you to come home; but, there it is, I say, it's for us. You're working for us. It's being alone stirs up my imagination. Do come early—just once. Leave it all to this man Chilly and to Mrs Truslove."

Mr Beluncle and his wife both saw they were drifting as usual to the dangerous subject. They hesitated on the edge of it and then drew back. There was a pleasure in the old quarrel. It was easy going over the old ground again, visiting old jealousies, repeating familiar accusations, remembering slammed doors and fits of hysteria and their hot repertoire of criminal charges which broke up the boredom of their lives. The certainty that they would be doing this for the rest of their lives made them pause. What a long time to go; they must invent some new arguments. Their genius had reached one of its infertile periods.

"I would like to have supper early. I am going to the lecture," said Mr Beluncle. "Will you come?"

"Oh," said Mrs Beluncle, "I thought you were coming home to see me. No, I won't come. How can I go when I haven't got any clothes to wear with all those women? I would have thought you had enough of God."

"That's a surprising thing to say, old girl," said Mr Beluncle amiably. "Perhaps you don't realise what you've said. Had enough of the infinite! How can you?"

"Oh well," mumbled Mrs Beluncle, without ill nature. "I'm a heathen. I've seen the posters. Van Hook, who is Van Hook? This lecturer."

"It's Van der Hoek," Henry said.

"We had a dog called Van when I was a child. He died. Van, Van, Van, I called out all night when I was little. It broke my heart. Oh, how I loved him. I would have died for him." Mrs Beluncle was surprised by herself. "Where is everything now?" she asked with fear.

Henry and George Beluncle moved closer to their mother and looked curiously at her and she saw the lost, tender gaze in their eyes that were usually so fiercely, warmly young.

"That's my religion," said Mrs Beluncle. "Love a thing while it's here. We shall all die."

Mr Beluncle was bored.

"I want you boys to come to the lecture. Mr Van der Hoek is one of the Big Three in the movement. That man gave up a thousand pounds a year in dentistry for Mrs Parkinson. Sacrificed everything. I don't know what he makes now. Three thousand perhaps," said Mr Beluncle.

Afterwards Henry told George he was not going to the lecture.

"Other things to do?" said Mrs Beluncle ironically.

"No," said Henry.

To George he said, "This house is a prison. I am trapped in it. Wherever I go I am stopped. My letters are opened. They are watched and counted. . . ."

"You never have any letters," said George.

"I have," said Henry. "I used to have. Mary used to write letters to me but I had to stop. You know there was a row."

"Well, what d'you want to write letters for?" said George. "I never write letters."

"I can't talk to anyone," said Henry. "Why should one feel gratitude?"

Then Mrs Beluncle wheedled George.

"What has Henry been saying to you?"

"Carrying on. He is the eldest," said George.

"He was talking about this girl he goes out with," suggested Mrs Beluncle.

"He wasn't," said George.

"You can't deceive me," said Mrs Beluncle. "I am a woman. None of you can deceive me. I read you all like a twopenny book. You and your father. Going to a lecture my backside. Do you think I don't know?"

"You're just out to make trouble," said George. "We shall be having 'the other woman' next."

"Clever, aren't you?" said Mrs Beluncle. "Do you think I'd let another woman ruin my life, not likely. Mrs Truslove is my greatest friend. You boys think you know everything, but you don't."

"We've seen a lot," said George stubbornly.

"Now then, stop that, I won't have it, what you've seen. You've no business to see," said Mrs Beluncle sharply.

"Well," said George, "why don't you make him get me a job?"

"What has happened to you lately," said Mrs Beluncle suspiciously, "speaking up for yourself. Eh? What have you been doing down at Fred's?"

Leslie, who had been packing his school books, came in and answered for George gaily:

"Aunt Connie, all over again. Look at the way he stands, round-shouldered. It must be some woman."

Mrs Beluncle moved round the breakfast table picking up the plates as she went and then at the top was arrested by a new thought:

"We're all mad," she said, looking to them, panic-stricken, for confirmation.

In the evening Henry came home early from Bulux. He had seen Mary in her shop in the town for two or three minutes. He had decided to go to the lecture in order to be where she was, held by the same building, to think about her.

"We shall not be able to speak," he thought, "but we shall be with each other."

He would sit behind her so that he could see her neck which he loved more than any other part of her; and perhaps her tooth when she smiled and her small puzzled pretending blue eyes. Under the words of Mr Van der Hoek, he would (as it were) creep and their souls would depart from the meeting. Their souls would shed their clothes and somewhere, rising in the summer air until they were almost out of sight, they would be clasped virginally together, talking about abstract subjects of a literary turn.

Leslie saw Henry in the garden and came out to smile with a schoolboy's tempting smile.

"You've changed your mind about the lecture?" Leslie said. "Have you lost your faith? O'Malley takes us for English and he often asks after you. 'Does your brother still believe in that nonsense?' he asked me one day last term."

"What d'you say?"

"I get him into an argument," said Leslie. "You never got him on to the infallibility of the Pope, did you? You funked it I expect. And Lourdes. When we've got him going, I get up and say, 'You know, sir, you are not supposed to introduce religious propaganda.'"

Leslie studied Henry's morbid face. Leslie was the one who watched for them all to provide drama for him, like some curious, dispassionate elderly man. The last-comer to the family, he found in them material for moralising and argument. He had appointed himself the elder. But he demanded events: for him something new must continually be happening.

"Are *you* going?" said Henry.

"I can't," said Leslie. "Mesmerism with its cree—ping fingers makes its seen—is—ter passes over the so-called hu—man mind." Mr Van der Hoek had been criticised for rolling his eyes, making slow, mesmeric movements with his hands during his last lecture. Lady Roads had admired this. "You realise," she barked excitedly around the meeting hall afterwards to her friends and supporters, "who he was referring to? The Roman Catholic Church." Miss Wix's face sickened. Anything, she pointed out, that suggested the laying on of hands, for good or for evil, had been forbidden precisely on page 274 of Mrs Parkinson's book. Mr Phibbs said that the lecturer looked as though he was going to lay his hands on something sooner or later if he could.

"Why can't you come?" said Henry.

"Grandma," said Leslie. "You never know. Suppose she kicked the bucket."

"You're always talking about that," Henry rebuked.

"I only say what you all think," said Leslie. "As a matter of fact, I'm the only one who really cares for her. She's interesting. She had four petticoats on yesterday."

"You sound as though you don't want to miss anything."

"Not exactly," said Leslie. "It would be bad if mother was alone when it happens. It's funny you should mention it though. I want to see what happens. If you'd take my advice," said the patronising boy, "you'd try and get interested in the family. It's terrible, we all know that, but it's the only family you'll have. Of course you want to be free. I've never been interested in freedom. I'm the youngest and I'm spoiled. You used to be jolly nice to me."

"Let's walk up and down while we talk," said Henry.

"Like the old man. Do you ever notice that. He says let's walk up and down. You say the same, rather lordly—like him. No, go on, don't stop because I said that. You know I often think about the family. It's rotten. Sinking ship. The rats are getting ready to leave. You'll leave it, George will leave it, Mrs Truslove will leave it."

"She's not in the family. She's in the business."

"The business is the family. I shan't leave. You *can't* leave this family."

"You're wrong, man," said Henry. "You can leave it tomorrow. I mean, I can."

"I'll tell you about myself," said Leslie. "I've got my maths but I'll soon knock that off. Before I go in—have you got any friends to talk to? No, I bet. It's the same with me. I don't talk to anyone at school much. You've got to realise we're a peculiar case. I've been checking up at school; other chaps are happy but they're boring. This is more interesting. Look," he said eagerly, "go to the lecture, you'll see your girl, there'll be a row . . . go on. . . ."

"That's my business," said Henry.

"All right. I'll go back to grandma," said Leslie. "You talk to George about it but you ought to talk to me. I'm more reliable. I could give you advice. If you take my advice. . . ."

Henry cuffed at his brother's head, but Leslie dodged.

"All right," said Leslie. "I'm not offended. You'll learn by experience, that's one thing life has taught me." He had begun his mimicry again. He went away grinning. "I'm going to grandma, she's failing, she's failing. . . ."

"Shut up," called Henry.

Leslie came back and said seriously:

"I am the one who loves her. That's what none of you realise."

But another question was troubling Henry and he followed Leslie this time to the kitchen door, saying:

"Just a minute, Leslie. You said just now Mrs Truslove was part of the family. What d'you mean? Do you know anything?"

Leslie went inside and sat down at the kitchen table and took his school books from their case.

"What do you know?" said Henry, following.

"I keep my ears and eyes open," Leslie said.

He opened a geometry book and showed Henry the red ticks made by the master, turning the pages to show that not once had he been wrong. The word written on one page: Excellent.

"See," said Leslie. "Excellent. Every page. The same with everything." He pulled out his exercise books and showed his brother the other pages. "Everything's right.

"You know what my tragedy is," said Leslie, in the manner of Mr Beluncle. "And I don't want you to think I am one of those men who blame their failures on women, saying that women have ruined their lives. . . ."

Mrs Beluncle and George came into the room and she listened in her worried way while Henry and George stood smiling.

"My tragedy is that I've got no ambition," said Leslie.

"Thank goodness," said Mrs Beluncle. "We've seen a lot."

"There you are," said Leslie to them all. "You've had it all and look what it's done to you. Not one of you with a pound in the Post Office. I've got forty-seven pounds fifteen shillings, and I'm not putting it into Bulux either."

They laughed, but they looked nervously at the book. How often he had said he had watched them all and had learned his lesson. If she had any sense—and, more important, if she had any left, Leslie said—his grandmother would leave all her money to him.

"And," he added, with a disquieting look at them, "she probably will."

XXII

"She's done her front," Mrs Vogg said. And she sighed as she saw the blue-and-white tiles of the path shine before the door of one of the opposite houses. A woman there with a handkerchief round her head went inside and shut the door.

David Vogg grunted and went on reading the newspaper. He had not shaved and he wore no collar. Now and again his body pressed back into the chair as if he were more closely entrenching himself against the news he found in the world. He read every word, in every column, slowly, going from the news items into the advertisements. Occasionally he read aloud the testimonial written on behalf of a patent medicine. His mother liked these testimonials. They had been an interest of the older Vogg. Mrs Vogg and he had always been drawn close together by the magic of patent medicine.

"It didn't do dad any good," David Vogg said, after one of these readings.

"No," sighed Mrs Vogg.

The mother and the son reposed with a little conceit and satisfaction upon the impregnable nature of the father's illnesses. David Vogg reflected, with pride, that sin had been the cause of these maladies: the sins of his father's father. Generations of sin, Vogg mused with arrogance, had been inflicted like a whipping upon himself.

Mrs Vogg glanced at her son. He had not been out of the house for three days. He was sinking into one of his moods. She feared he was thinking of going back to sea. She turned again to look out of the window. Pigeons she liked. As their bold slate bodies flew over the roofs like slowly flung stones she had another pleasurable memory of the elder Vogg. He would sit in the yard at the back waiting for his pigeons to return in the afternoons and it was during one afternoon, when a late bird had come back from Northampton, that he went into the kitchen and first put his arms round her while she was standing at the sink. After that, every place in the house had its secret for her, for Mr Vogg never made love in a bed. This was his distinction. And the pigeons, so destructive of time, by their inconstant arrivals, always seemed to make a suggestion to him. By some accident of genius, Vogg had satisfied her strongest passion: the love of secrets.

A gate whined.

"Miss Dykes is going out. Mrs Johnson does walk fast for a big woman. They're going up to Hoppners, to the shop. They're talking to Sydney Childs, he's sweeping. 'Good morning, good morning,'" Mrs Vogg's lips politely formed the words that she imagined Miss Dykes to be saying.

David Vogg got up and looked out of the window. He was not drawn by the sight of Miss Dykes or Mrs Johnson, but by a mechanical interest in her chair. It was fairly new and its metal caught the sunlight—the Voggs believed that Mr Beluncle had bought it—and Vogg hissed with unguarded pleasure through his teeth at the sight of it. *He*, he reflected, had a car.

"Why don't you go out on a lovely day like this?" said Mrs Vogg, holding him by the cuff.

David Vogg shook his head and went back to his paper. Mrs Vogg watched him as the morning passed and he knew she was watching him. He became irritable; when she fell asleep in the afternoon he sulked and went out to seek importance.

Vogg's suitcase which contained his books was heavy and pulled his wrist out of his sleeve, showing the inky tattoo mark on his arm. He walked into the poorer side of Hetley near the gasworks, his mouth twisted by the pain of his load, and then he began his calls. Knock at the door, or ring, case on the ground beside him, the orange-coloured book on Palestine with the pictures ready in his hand.

"Good afternoon. Can I interest you in a book?"

The doors slamming in his face, the rude refusals did not dismay him, nor did the prevaricating smiles deceive. He stood back. People in these streets were frightened of one thing and another, the rent collector, the school inspector, or simply of men who put their foot in the door. They always looked first at his feet. Vogg stood back scornfully. Going away to the next door, he thought these mean, pink, untidy streets would cry out, like the avenues of the rich, when Babylon burned. He smiled not entirely in self-righteousness; when Babylon burned, perhaps before that, when he saw the disaster coming, he would be back at sea, and such grey sheets of water slapped in his ears sometimes, that he was dazed as he walked.

Occasionally he would find householders who were willing to stand at their door and listen to him. He spoke to them in a low, deep, insinuating voice and one or two women, who did not listen to the words, put their hands to their hair or took a deep breath quietly, raising their breasts and half smiling, and would lean over to look at the coloured pictures. Then his voice changed and a deep half-chanted note would take its place, a small sweat would glister on his forehead. He said suddenly:

"Cast off your sins and kneel to the Lord. Fall on your knees before the Judgment Seat."

As he passed from house to house, people laughed behind his back and some were indignant, some argued, but Vogg was indifferent to this.

As the hard sun went lower in the London fume, Vogg's walk came to an end. He despised those who worked; they were slaves on the treadmill of Mammon, as old Vogg, his adoptive father, had been. Vogg always broke his journeys at the recreation gardens between Boystone and Hetley. If anyone sat near him he gave them one of his pamphlets. When his feet were rested he went on to Boystone to see his friend.

There are two church spires in Boystone High Street.
Vogg hated these spires. It astonished him that these monu-
ments to pride and hypocrisy could still stand. When he
spoke of the wickedness of the flesh, it was not really of flesh
but of stone he thought: of those grey smoky granite buildings. He often pictured these churches on fire.

He had taken a bus from Hetley recreation ground. He
showed his books to the conductor. At Boystone market the
women were in cotton dresses and the Jews were at their
stalls. Vogg hated the Jews. They often came up if he was
showing someone a book in the market and were itching to
see him sell one and to watch his methods. Once or twice they
had whistled up friends, anxious to see that ecstatic thing to
them—a sale. And six months before this time the thing had
succeeded. A Jewish greengrocer had sold a book for him
and always grinned at him now when he passed.

"Sailor man," the Jew called him. Vogg heard the whine
of the sea in his ears when this happened, and now Boystone
market was the confusing, undermining sea to him and he
avoided the Jew for unsettling him.

Vogg got out of the market and walked down to Boystone
East. The two churches burned. The Public Library, filled
with the dreadful fruits of the Tree of Knowledge, caved in.
He came to the largest cinema: the Royal. It was an old-
fashioned house approached by a long, wide, ascending
passage with posters on the walls, a kind of tunnel, like a
gullet or a mouth, that breathed out warm air. It was an
entrance to hell, filled with tobacco smoke and women.

What made the Royal seem wicked to Vogg? It was a
place of pleasure; but the crowning wickedness was a notice
saying, Seats 2s., 1s. 6d., 9d. It was the pay for pleasure that
convinced Vogg of its wickedness. All over the world, in
ports, he could think of pleasures that stripped seamen of
their money. He knew that the Royal filled up with the
ordinary people of Boystone; yet when he thought of them
there, his imagination became licentious. The moment they
were in there, in the darkness, their clothes came off them.
The Royal was packed with the naked.

As he passed, a new word struck him at the entrance. It was printed on a poster. It was the word "Free".

Vogg went on past the Royal to the station. The clock outside the wine company's shop, beckoning to drunkenness, said twenty minutes past five with its black sad hands.

Granger was standing on the kerb at the station entrance. With an experienced flick of his wet thumb, Granger was handing out tracts to people as they came off the London trains. A litter of these discarded tracts blew about the station yard.

Vogg went to him quietly.

"Whatcha," said the old man meekly. In his earthy face the eyes glittered modestly like toiling ants.

"Good evening," said Vogg, with contempt, which the old man caught.

"I've been casting the bread," the old man whispered timidly.

Vogg did not answer.

"Oh, the manifold mercies," he whined to ingratiate himself.

Vogg nodded and stood beside him.

"Pack it up," said Vogg.

The old man was shocked.

"Not stop?" he said incredulously.

"You're only making a mess," said Vogg, nodding to the tracts blowing about the yard.

"It's the word," pleaded the old man.

"Come up to the Royal," said Vogg. "I want to show you something."

"All that way," pleaded the old man. "My poor feet are caning me. We were going to the cricket, you said, in the van."

"There's a call at the Royal. I heard a call," said Vogg. The old man turned in awe. He smiled with wonder and connivance at Vogg.

"All right," he said. "Was it"—he lowered his speech and came close to Vogg—"the Voice?"

"You don't have to *hear* a Voice," said Vogg.

A tragic expression came upon the old man's solid face, as if he had heard a farewell.

"It's written up," said Vogg sternly. "You've got to use your eyes."

The old man sighed but held back; but Vogg walked away and he was forced to hurry after him.

After falling into their curious walk, as if together they had become a shambling, four-legged animal, they went up to the Royal Cinema, stared at a poster. The poster said: *A Free Lecture on the Science of Purification. Speaker: Elias Van der Hoek. Is Death Real?*

"Many false prophets shall arise," chanted the older man.

"Free," said Vogg. "Tonight. Eight o'clock," said Vogg, shutting him up.

"What's that?" said the old man stupidly.

"We've got to bear witness," said Vogg. "It's free.

"In there," he nodded to the cinema.

"Did the Voice say?" asked the old man, drawing back.

"I said," said Vogg. "What's up with you?

"Lies," Vogg shouted suddenly, very loudly, to the street.

An errand boy turned round and stopped. The proprietor of the cinema was strolling up the long passage to take the last of the sun.

"Not go to the cricket?" pleaded the older man.

"Lies," shouted Vogg, ignoring him.

The proprietor heard the word, but by the time he had got to the entrance, Vogg and the old man had moved slowly away.

"If I was vouchsafed a new pair," the older man said, pointing to his boots, "I could get along quicker. These are murder."

"I've got a pair of my father's back home," said Vogg impatiently. "We'll pick them up."

And then Vogg explained to the older man: there was a call to go to the lecture of Mr Van der Hoek and shout. They were to sit at the back near the exit and first Vogg was to get up and shout; after that the older man; and then both together.

"Shout what?" said the older man anxiously.

"You shout 'Blasphemy against our Lord and Saviour Jesus Christ'," said Vogg. "I'll shout 'Lies'. Then you shout out 'Lies', and I'll do 'Blasphemy'."

"No, you do 'Blasphemy' and what was it? I forget so easy. I'll do 'Lies'. I've got more voice for a short word."

"And they all of one accord began to make excuses," said Vogg.

"Ah!" sighed the older man. "The dear Bosom. That's where by rights I ought to lay my head."

XXIII

The hands had gone and all the clerks.

"And so," said Mr Chilly, "it is going to its lecture."

He stood beside Henry and put his arm round his shoulder. Quietly he squeezed. Henry moved sulkily away from Mr Chilly.

"Innocent eyes," he said, letting Henry go.

Henry looked with provoking scorn at Mr Chilly. Mr Chilly was in one of his frightening moods. Henry hated Mr Chilly to address him in the third person, though he clung to Mr Chilly's explanation that he had picked up the habit in Italy. Mr Chilly's life in Italy bewitched Henry. Once or twice Mr Chilly said, "I will take you there." And then the invitation died in his eyes.

"Let me look at its eyes. No, no. It is innocent."

Twice already Mr Chilly had kissed him on the top of the head, once had held the top of his head lightly for a moment, murmuring:

"Celtic. Celtic. A pity. The Celts destroy civilisation."

Henry felt large, rough and uncouth when Mr Chilly behaved like this; but if he saw Mary Phibbs soon afterwards she complained of his vanity and started garrulous praises of her father or spoke of more wickednesses of the shop manager.

"It is going to hear that evil does not exist," said Mr Chilly. "And yet it admires Balzac, Shakespeare, and is just going to read Dostoevsky. If evil does not exist, what is going to happen to literature?"

This was the Everard Chilly Henry could not resist.

Mr Chilly listened gravely to Henry's arguments.

"It is not astonished," said Mr Chilly, "that a good lady called Mrs Parkinson, whose husband had a shoe-repairing business in Toronto, has solved the problem that has, I mean, wrecked the minds of theologians, I mean, for two thousand years—the origin of evil."

"Many," Henry argued, "have come near to the Truth."

Henry thought, "How we have all misjudged Mr Chilly." He looked at Mr Chilly's handsome nose; a little coloured at the tip, was it? The cheekbones marked by redness? Did Mr Chilly drink? The irony of Mr Chilly's foolish voice was infuriating and disturbing. Mr Chilly looked at his watch.

"My dear," he exclaimed, "you must fly."

He was dismissed.

"I could never tell all this to Mary," Henry thought. "Everyone thinks I ought to have another girl. No one seems to understand my situation. Is the Purification true? Do I love Mary? Why am I not thirty-five? If I could be like Mr Chilly and yet not be a fool! The great mistake in my life is not belonging to the upper classes."

Henry wished to say good night to Mr Chilly, but he had left the room.

Mr Chilly himself had gone to Mrs Truslove's office.

"Thank God," he thought, "now I am going to wipe out that horrible business with Miss Vanner. Oh, I am so ashamed. Mrs Truslove is coming to dine with me. We will toddle along."

Mr Beluncle's departure had left the usual void. Mr Chilly could feel the wonderful emptiness opening in him, alarming, sinister, yet irresistible. He opened the door marked Private and stopped dead, so suddenly that his foot kicked the door, the handle slipped from his hand and the door went wide to the wall. Mr Beluncle had *not* gone. He was there.

"I'm so sorry," said Mr Chilly.

Mr Beluncle's face was pinker than he remembered it and was fixed in a handsome smile that seemed like the frank smile of a brilliant portrait in oils. The lips beautifully smiled; the eyes, enlarged by happiness, reflected the smile of the face.

"Oh, sir!" said Mr Chilly, with a shout of laughter. Mr Beluncle had gone mad. Mr Beluncle was having a lark. Mr Beluncle was having a romp with Mrs Truslove and had put her hat on his head. There was Mr Beluncle dressed up in a woman's hat.

The smile went when Mr Chilly laughed and the big face became set, large and masterful, in one of Mr Beluncle's well-known facial manœuvres.

"How d'you do?" said a woman's voice. "I am waiting for Mr Beluncle. I am his sister."

"Oh, what a fool! How stupid! For the moment I thought you were Mr Beluncle. I beg your pardon," said Mr Chilly. "I'll get him at once."

He turned round and then back again, making a circle.

"But of course, he's gone," he said. "He went an hour ago. They should have told you."

Now he saw his folly. Those handsome eyes were longer than her brother's. The large face was painted, the jaw soft and strong, the hair showing under the hat was brown. She was wearing a tight black dress. A little cigarette ash dropped on one of the creases of the bust, and one fine leg showed, bent at the bold knee that looked like another face beyond the desk. It was hard to guess in what odd attitude Miss Beluncle was sitting. She was a woman who changed the air of the room in which she sat; she used a strong scent that, after the first breath, had a bitterness in it which puzzled Mr Chilly's sensitive nose. Large, electric, deeply-breathing, Miss Beluncle sat before her brother's papers and Mr Chilly felt that he had been wired and instantly given a violent change of current. Miss Beluncle's voice was slow, low and questioning.

"Who?" she said.

"When you came in," said Mr Chilly, "did they tell you?"

"Who told me?" repeated Miss Beluncle. "No one told me. I came in and sat down"—and she put both her hands on the desk. "Here," she said, and touched the arm of the chair. An emphatic woman. A small chin appeared under the jaw.

"I came in at the main door—do you call it the main door? Yes or no? All right," she said. "And there was no one in the passage. Isn't that so? I asked no one."

Miss Beluncle seemed to accuse him of wilfully saying something else, but she was still smiling generously.

She laughed a small isolated laugh which was like a speech to someone else in the room—indeed Mr Chilly turned round to see who it might be.

"I came in," she resumed.

Mr Chilly saw she was like her brother. She was not a woman to be contradicted.

"When did my brother go? You say he has gone. If he has gone, when was that?"

"An hour ago."

"An hour. All right, an hour. You said at five o'clock. Still, let it go," accused Miss Beluncle.

Mr Chilly looked at his watch.

"Yes, five o'clock, about an hour," said Mr Chilly, very politely.

"So what?" said Miss Beluncle.

"I beg your pardon?" said Mr Chilly.

"Where is he? I don't want to know when he went, where is he? You keep saying he went an hour ago or five o'clock, I don't know what you mean, it doesn't matter. Oh," she said, surprising herself, "I see. You are with him in this."

Miss Beluncle lifted a bold white arm and made a kind of semaphore signal, indicating the office, the factory.

"Yes, I mean, I work here," said Mr Chilly. "We're just closing. I think Mrs Truslove is about. Shall I go and fetch her? She will soon be back."

"What's she doing here?" said Miss Beluncle. And then

she laughed quietly to herself. "Of course. Mrs Truslove. I didn't ask for her. I want my brother. It is no good your saying he's gone an hour ago or five o'clock or six or seven, what did you say?"

"Five," said Mr Chilly, hypnotised by Miss Beluncle.

"I called at his house on Sunday to see my mother in his house," said Miss Beluncle fiercely. And then she smiled. "On Sunday. The gate was locked. I pushed at the handle." Miss Beluncle raised both arms and began to push an imaginary door about the desk. "I pushed it, using my strength—you don't understand. I would say you didn't understand anything. Don't pretend."

Miss Beluncle suddenly stood up and her face redoubled its redness and became crimson and then purple.

"It's no good lying to me," she said powerfully. "You've got him here. You're defending him. She's my mother as well as his. And locking her up in an old box. I rattled it, I tell you"—she stepped out from behind the desk and advanced on Mr Chilly. "—like this, back and forth, back and forth, on Sunday and it wasn't five o'clock or an hour ago, three, two, I don't know what it was. . . ."

Miss Beluncle's face became gloomy and the skin over the fine jaw folded and thickened.

"Oh, all right," she said, becoming calm. And she smiled voluptuously at Mr Chilly.

"He has stolen my money," she said.

"Who?" said Mr Chilly.

"Don't stand there pretending and lying," said Miss Beluncle, raising her arm and suddenly striking at Mr Chilly. "My brother. And tell him this. He can f—— off."

Mr Chilly stood away. He switched on a hurried anxious smile.

"I'll get Mrs Truslove," he said. "I'm just an assistant here." And he went to the door. There was a crash as he left and Mr Chilly saw Miss Beluncle knock a chair over and then strike a pile of papers off Mr Beluncle's desk.

"What was that?" Miss Beluncle accused him.

Mr Chilly ran. He heard the door slam behind him.

"Mrs Truslove," he called. "Could you come?"

Mrs Truslove came up the steps with her towel and her handbag in her hands.

"Miss Beluncle is here," he said. "I'm afraid she's . . . I don't know what she is . . ."

"Oh, God," said Mrs Truslove. "Not Connie again?"

Miss Beluncle was lying on the floor when they came in.

"Open the window, Everard," said Mrs Truslove. "One can smell it right down the passage. I hate sour drink."

She was lying asleep with a smile amorous and content on her face. Her mouth opened, the smile died on her cheeks, which had now gone violet at the cheekbones, and she snored the profound, ranging and aggressive Beluncle snore.

"Poor woman," said Mrs Truslove. "This is the end of our dinner, I'm afraid, Everard."

"Oh no, no," said Mr Chilly absently, looking at the fine body, the beautiful legs, with admiration.

XXIV

All the way in the train to Boystone, Henry watched his faith go out of the window, sheet by sheet, like leaves out of a book. At some stations, a page or two blew back, but, once more, it flew out again to lie and stain and decay in the back gardens. "If I could be reborn," he thought, "and never see these houses again. If I could be everyone I see and not myself."

But as the crowd moved into the Royal Cinema, as someone said, "He's here. There's Mr Van der Hoek's car," his faith returned. How could so many well-dressed people be deceived? In the expectant hall, before the dead, slightly dirty, white screen of the cinema, he forgot everything in his search for Mary's head.

"There's Mr Phibbs," said his brother George, to their father.

"You'd think he'd wear a hard collar," said Mr Beluncle.

Henry did not look, but patiently searched for a glimpse of Mary's fair hair. He could not see her, but there in front, on the other side of the hall, she must be growing like a single flower.

Faith came washing boldly back at the sight of Mr Van der Hoek on the platform. A very tall and heavy man, in a frock-coat and with white-lined waistcoat, he sent smile after smile spinning over the heads of the audience, and everyone was whispering and fidgeting with pleasure. "Look, Mr Van der Hoek. He is smiling. So sane, so sensible, so kind, so good, so inspired. Who says there is anything peculiar about the Purification? We are normal."

Faith boomed as Mr Van der Hoek stood up, his body reposing against his fine shoulders, his good-natured legs carrying him gratefully. And then, like cream pleasantly poured upon some fruit pie whose pastry was crisp and dry to the teeth, the words of Mr Van der Hoek gradually covered the audience. Henry's mind woke up. Mr Beluncle grew stouter with pleasure. George's head drooped wistfully. Then Henry's mind began happily to wander and, at last, for a moment, he saw Mary's head. He could not see her face, but her chin was lifted and sometimes she slightly turned, at some good point of Mr Van der Hoek's, to glance at her sister. And, by a movement of her shoulder, Henry guessed she was holding her sister's hand in that incredible affection which played in her family like some simple little fountain.

Earnestly Henry tried to follow her good example and to listen closely to Mr Van der Hoek. And for a time he managed this; but, inexplicably, Henry's thoughts went to Mr Chilly and he began to compare Mr Chilly's trousers, well cut and sharply creased, with Mr Van der Hoek's. Were they as well creased? And then, a terrible thing happened. Henry's faith went. Henry's fancy unbuttoned Mr Van der Hoek's trousers from their braces. Slowly he lowered them, crumpling their creases. He pulled Mr Van der Hoek's trousers down to his ankles. He removed his underpants. Fighting with all his might against the impulse, he exposed the mild and thoughtful private organs of the lecturer. Hurriedly Henry pulled back the underpants. Hastily he struggled to haul up the trousers and he was in the midst of this when the air of the hall seemed to freeze, every human body in it stiffened, and a wide empty hollow opened in the air. There was a shuffle of chairs and a man's voice was shouting out at the back of the hall.

"Blasphemy on the name of our Lord Jesus Christ!" and

"Lies! Lies!" and again

"Blasphemy!"

Four hundred heads turned. Mr Beluncle said to his sons: "Don't look round. Don't look round."

There was a scuffling sound and Mr Phibbs, to Henry's pride, rushed quietly up the hall to the back. But Mr Van der Hoek's voice went on uninterrupted. Only the raising of his pale eyelids showed that he had noticed the interruption.

"The creeping, sin-i-ster forces of animal magnetism . . ." he was saying, slowly raising his hands before him in the well-known, the very controversial gesture.

But Henry's heart and mind were at the back of the hall, out in the street, where the man must be and he was pursuing him, begging him to say *why* it was all lies, why it was blasphemy. His heart rocked and went on rocking. Lies, lies, lies—he could still hear the voice, and he felt it was his own crying out as he drowned.

After the lecture Mr Beluncle took his sons into the circle of people who were congratulating the lecturer.

"This is my son," said Mr Beluncle expansively. "He thinks he knows everything."

"Well, you know," said Mr Van der Hoek, expanding even more than Mr Beluncle, "he does, too. He is the child of God."

Mr Beluncle and Mr Van der Hoek went on expanding before each other.

XXV

They sat for two hours beside the body of Miss Beluncle and in low voices they talked about her. Mr Chilly gazed. She was a woman of forty, he supposed, but Mrs Truslove said severely that she must be fifty-seven.

"She has been a great trouble to the family," said Mrs Truslove, speaking with some dignity, as if trouble were an immensely respectable thing, "since she was a girl. A great trouble to old Mrs Beluncle.

"Men," said Mrs Truslove.

Mr Chilly nodded his head respectfully. The snoring had now stopped and the moaning, too; Miss Beluncle moved voluptuously in her sleep and blew a small bubble.

"We shall have to take her home," said Mr Chilly sadly.

"I am so glad Mr Beluncle wasn't here," said Mrs Truslove.

"Yes, he would be upset," said Mr Chilly.

"It doesn't upset me, you know," said Mr Chilly. "I mean, I feel rather exhilarated."

"It is disgusting," said Mrs Truslove.

"I was absolutely plastered . . ." Mr Chilly began, and then he caught Mrs Truslove's eye.

How extraordinary, he thought. I was going to dine with Mrs Truslove. I admire her very much. I don't know what would have happened. I am in a peculiar state. Goodness knows what I said to Miss Vanner. And poor Henry. Here I am looking at this beautiful woman. I can't take my eyes off her. Why?

And a voice answered Mr Chilly. The voice said, "She is a wreck. That is what gets you." He felt he had found a complement. Mr Beluncle his saviour, Miss Beluncle his wrecker. If Mrs Truslove had not been there he would have touched the sleeping woman's brow.

Later on, they called a taxi and took Miss Beluncle to her flat in St. John's Wood, a small place filled with what could only be called the ill-assorted loot of love. A mantelpiece was

alive with signed photographs which made Mrs Truslove
wince. Miss Beluncle excused herself weakly and they stayed
while she went to bed. She begged them to have a teeny,
tiddley little one for the road, but Mrs Truslove refused and
Mr Chilly reluctantly did so.

"She wants to thank you," said Mrs Truslove, coming out
of the bedroom.

Mr Chilly went in and the lady patted the bed for him to
sit down.

"Get rid of her," said Miss Beluncle.

"I'm afraid, I mean, I'm awfully sorry," said Mr Chilly.
"I'm taking her to dinner . . . I . . . I would love . . ."

"Give me a ring. Here's the number," she said, stretch-
ing out her arm and taking his hand. "Soon," she said.
"Tomorrow."

"Yes," said Mr Chilly.

"Oh, I feel awful. I look awful," she said. "Don't say I
don't, I do."

She was about to start another quarrel.

This is life, thought Mr Chilly, as he dined with Mrs Truslove, hardly hearing what she said. She was moralising about
the character of the Beluncles, their power of exploitation,
their habit of destroying human beings, the inevitable softening in their lives.

This is life, he thought, and saw a white arm coming across
the table again and again to him, and large threatening lips.

It was about now, while they were drinking coffee and
Mrs Truslove was beginning a disagreeable dispute about
paying her share of the bill, Mr Chilly thought, that he
would have been saying, "You have lovely hands." Now
that could not happen. He admired Mrs Truslove. He
admired Mr Beluncle. He thought "poor Henry" rather
sweet; but here in Miss Constance Beluncle were the disastrous, the irresistible forces of nature.

XXVI

"Why are you so late? I have been waiting for you," the cripple said to her sister.

"I told you I was going out," said Mrs Truslove. She was used to being questioned but it was late, she was tired and she thought, "How awful to have to account for oneself the whole time."

"With Mr Cummings?" said the cripple, avid for news.

"No, no," said Mrs Truslove, with weary annoyance. "With Everard."

"Oh," said the cripple knowingly.

"It is not 'oh' at all," said Mrs Truslove. "I am going with Mr Cummings tomorrow, if you want to know all my business."

"Don't get cross," said the cripple.

"I'm tired," said Mrs Truslove.

"You are tired of me," said the cripple.

"No. But can't I come in without having to say everything?" said Mrs Truslove.

The cripple looked injured.

"No," her face clearly said. "You are mine, the whole of you, every minute of you."

"If Cummings offers you that job," said the cripple, "take it. Get out of Beluncles. I have seen that very clearly lately. It's an infatuation with you."

"It is my money," said Mrs Truslove, with bitterness, "that is infatuated."

After she had said this, the pain of her situation was renewed. She wished now her passion for Beluncle was over, that she could speak of it. She had been on the point of speaking to Everard Chilly about it; under his folly, she guessed he would at least understand ruin. But she had not spoken; she knew she would confess in a tone that would sound like a reprimand to his youthfulness. It was distasteful to be so unattractive.

But the cripple spoke, from habit. Her real subject was waiting on her lips.

"An awful thing happened," said the cripple.

"What?"

"Vogg was at the lecture. Vogg from opposite. Mr Van der Hoek had been speaking for about twenty minutes when someone got up at the back of the hall and started shouting."

"Shouting? Shouting what?"

"I didn't hear. Shouting terribly. Words. I don't know." The cripple covered her ears with her hands.

"Everyone was there," she said excitedly. "Mr Edwards was there, Mr Phibbs rushed up from the front—and Mr Langton . . ."

"But what for?"

"Vogg and a man. They were shouting out."

"Yes, but what?"

"I didn't hear," repeated the cripple, covering her ears. "But Mr Van der Hoek was wonderful. He went straight on, the power of Truth is in that man. Mr Phibbs just leaned over and tapped the man on the shoulder and it was Vogg. Vogg!

"I . . . no, no. I mustn't hate him. It was wonderful after that. The calm. The uplift. Not a cough the whole evening. Why do we have to get our papers from Vogg?" the cripple said.

"We don't have to," said Mrs Truslove. "You've had too much excitement. You ought to be in bed."

Miss Dykes chattered on. She had spoken to Mr Van der Hoek. He had moved down from the crowd that stood around him afterwards to speak to her. He was like a big brother. "Well," he said. The broad, lazy goodness of that "Well". She had told him how badly she felt about the man crying out in the middle of the meeting. It made her ashamed for the town.

"And that is true," she said. "I felt awful. As if I had cried out myself. I blushed at the time, and Mrs Angel who was in front, her neck went quite red. But Mr Van der Hoek said, 'Well,' he said, so plainly, so wise, so human, oh I don't know, so like a man, dear, 'Well, I guess I had to know pretty sharp that there's only one Voice.' "

"And that," enquired Mrs Truslove, "was his?"

"It was wonderful," said Miss Dykes, staring at the carpet. Suddenly Miss Dykes gave a cry: "My foot, my right foot. It moved. Did you see it? It moved. Look.

"It moved. I'm sure it moved."

"You saw the shadow of my arm. I just moved it from the back of your chair," Mrs Truslove said.

"No, it wasn't a shadow. I saw it move. Wait. Watch."

They sat silently, looking at Miss Dykes's feet in their black suède shoes with the high heels. They sat without speaking and Mrs Truslove could hear her sister's intense breathing. She seemed to be dragging her breath through her teeth.

Mrs Truslove held her tongue and pity relaxed and filled out her face. She looked ten years older as she leaned sadly to one side, concealing a yawn. This cry—that her sister had seen her foot move—had so often been heard. In excitement, after a meeting perhaps or simply on some boring evening when she was getting no attention, the cry would come.

"My foot has moved. I swear."

It had curiously the effect of a deliberate cruelty inflicted upon those around her, not upon herself.

Mrs Truslove hardened herself and let the minutes slip by. She had no pain, she thought, that she could put upon anybody.

"Why didn't you wear your brown pair this evening, the ones with the diamanté; those are my favourites?" Mrs Truslove tactfully said.

"With black!" said the cripple, waking up. "Linda! Really! No, my dark green I might have worn, or the black lizard, but no, I'm funny. I *felt* like these."

The spell was broken. The cripple could always be distracted by talk of clothes. The sisters returned to talk of the lecture.

On the following afternoon Lady Roads came to the cripple's house. She visited her every week. Mr Van der Hoek had been staying with Lady Roads, and after she had

had a lecturer to stay, Lady Roads's batteries were re-charged, by all the scandal of the movement which she adroitly got out of visiting speakers. Lady Roads felt she was missing something in her tedious work in Boystone. One got interested in people in Boystone, but the important people of the movement had no time for that. They were decisive.

Lady Roads was brusque and melancholy with the cripple.

"As far as I'm concerned," she said harshly, "you're healed. You're walking. I see it and I'm not going to say any more about it. The work's done."

Miss Dykes's heart hardened with fear and resentment when she heard this. Healed. Walking. She did not want to be healed. She cringed with terror.

"Love more!" barked Lady Roads, like a man.

Miss Dykes winced. She moved her hands in an impulse to cling to one of the cardigans of this hard-corseted motherly woman and to beg her not to desert her. She was distracted by Lady Roads's clothes. Today she was dressed in a low-necked, pink silk jumper and her large breasts rested on top of a corset which must have been pulled on anyhow. The colour of her skirt was ginger and she was wearing—Miss Dykes was quick to see—odd stockings.

"I want to be married," Miss Dykes had once said to Lady Roads. Lady Roads was a sentimental woman and a warm matchmaker, but of the kind who like to drive people to the altar and then violently pull them back from it at the last moment. She knew that those she had driven into marriage always turned upon her afterwards. She pretended not to understand why.

"No woman would want to marry if she knew what mar-riage means," Lady Roads said. "For men, marriage means sex and nothing else."

"I suppose it does," said the cripple demurely. Then boldly, "I want that so much."

Lady Roads regarded her patient with a pity which was really disgust and dislike.

"That is a great obstruction to your healing," she said.

After long struggles with herself Miss Dykes had conquered her day-dreams. She waited twice a week to see the large, sad, broken eyes of her healer, the clumsy assuring bosom in the wrong blouse, the woman victim abused once by a husband whom Miss Dykes now had come to hate with jealous desire—though she had never seen him—to hear the warm, harsh voice that made her mind wake up. She innocently adored Lady Roads's title, which seemed to come into the room like a shadow with her. If she could only walk, Miss Dykes thought, she would see her more, she would not be left behind but would go off with her in her motor-car, to her house, wherever she went, never leaving her side, willing to be bullied, in an ecstasy of gratitude, in a desire to replace the man who had wounded her body. The wound—Miss Dykes was to be its guardian.

Now she heard that Lady Roads was not going to pray for her any more. Miss Dykes listened and gazed, and by a large effort of her love made an attempt to agree.

"Stop thinking about yourself," said Lady Roads. "Love more. Heal other people. That is what you must do. When I leave this room, begin healing other people with Love and Truth."

Yes, yes, yes, Miss Dykes's thoughts went on like panicking fingers on the keys of a piano.

"I will help her," Miss Dykes thought. "Buy her clothes. Poor darling, she gives so much of her life to others, she never has time to think of them. The pink with that ginger is terrible. No, I am wrong. I must not seem to be criticising her, for if God wanted pink and ginger together like that, it would be right—but God probably wouldn't want *that* pink."

Lady Roads left. The room became insipid.

Agitatedly Miss Dykes filled her heart with love. Quickly moving to those near at hand, she started to love her sister and Mr Beluncle and her housekeeper. But these people were too close to her. She moved her chair to the window, and drawing back the dark blue curtain, she sat preparing to love the world. A brewer's van drawn by a horse had stopped at one of the shops across the street.

The horse is an idea of strength and fidelity (she saw), the van is a useful thing. What was beer? The Parkinsonians were teetotallers and non-smokers. What could be the spiritual significance of a notorious evil?

"It is refreshment," she thought doubtfully. "Where streams of living water flow . . . No."

And to her memory came the difficult figure of her sister's new friends, Mr Cummings and Mr Chilly.

Love Mr Cummings? In two hours she had become as jealous of Mr Cummings as she had been of Mr Beluncle. When Mr Beluncle came to the house she always went off to bed or to the next room. To listen, lying stiffly and still for one change in the monotone of the voices, for a run of new notes, for whispers, for a sound of love.

"I must love him, not hate him," she insisted.

She closed her eyes to pray. When she opened them again, at the sound of a car, she half believed that Mr Cummings and Mr Chilly had been whipped out of their office chairs and had come flying to her door, drawn by her irresistible prayer.

The street was empty now. A road like a glum and vacant face, flat under the maudlin London haze. Their father's ugly presentation clock twanged. Miss Dykes's heart closed and love went out of her head. For solid years at a time she had seen endless, narrow folds of dirty woollen cloud such as now slanted over the dark blue slates and the red chimneys, a dirty raftering as heavy as time itself. "This that I am having now and seeing now is my life. I have been thinking that life is something that is going to happen."

And that was how, she thought, the old people in the row of decaying shops must feel. That decay was their life. And so she came to look at Vogg's, the nearest one. The weak daylight made the upper windows impenetrable, but there, slowly it occurred to the cripple, Mrs Vogg might be. Her eye was moving from the edge of Vogg's shop to the empty hairdresser's next door, was indeed on the last bricks of the Vogg shop, on the frontier between the two sets of lives and about to forget them.

And then, with the inner roar of a vision in the mind, like shop shutters going up in the morning, the revelation came to her. Mrs Vogg was the woman she must love. Mrs Vogg was the woman like herself, a woman at a window unable to move. And she must love Vogg, the man who had cried out—one hand went to her ear—those words.

The heart of Miss Dykes opened again. Love Vogg. Love Vogg. Love Mrs Vogg.

XXVII

"I had dinner with Everard last night," said Mrs Truslove across the desk to Mr Beluncle, who was working out figures. He had calculated the imaginary cost of *Marbella*. This had led to an imaginary estimate of his debts and his income; that was horrifying. Mr Beluncle then went into an imaginary inquest on the prospects of next year's money.

The first principle clearly was, Ye must be born again. So he gave birth to the firm again in a different form. He put the letters P.B. for Philip Beluncle at the top of the page, constructed a genealogical tree of directors and shareholders beneath it, branched into several lines of production.

Suppose Mrs Parkinson's Group increased its churches at the rate of five, no, say ten, a year; say each held two hundred, no five, well, put seven hundred people. That is seven thousand chairs. Seven thousand at cost was . . . But now he was into the question of cost and profit: the fairy tale of figures began to enchant. That was Mrs Parkinson alone. The actual population of England was—what was it? (Mrs Truslove saw him get *Whitaker's* from the shelf)—forty-five millions. That meant, how many chairs? Well, how many chairs in a house? How many houses? Yes, Mr Beluncle thought, and we're only talking of chairs. What about three-piece suites? This is modern business, Mr Beluncle hummed to himself, statistics, planning, analysis. It was what Mr Van der Hoek had said in his lecture! God was the great planner.

Mr Beluncle woke up. "What did you say?" he said.

"I dined with Chilly," she said.

"What on earth did you do that for?" he said.

His memory whizzed back like a film to Mr Truslove. Another betrayal. Surely, at her age, she was not going to start again.

"I thought you were dining with Cummings," he said.

"That is tonight," she said.

Two blows. He felt—but no one seemed to know what he felt. Quite frankly he did not like people to dine with each other. Not his sons. Not his wife. No one. They were all like vultures pulling his flesh off him. They tore themselves out of him, leaving large raw wounds. Beluncle froze.

"Chilly," he said, "doesn't realise what a privilege he has in working for us."

"I am not usually taken with Everard," she said. "He behaves well in difficult situations. He was surprisingly sympathetic and tolerant. It was not easy for him."

"Nor for me," said Mrs Truslove.

"What are you talking about?" Mr Beluncle asked.

"Your sister was here last night, after you left," she said.

"Constance!" said Beluncle, putting his pencil in his ear.

"Drunk," said Mrs Truslove, "on the floor."

Beluncle listened to the story and his fingers tapped on his desk.

"Why wasn't the door locked? The outside door is supposed to be locked at half-past five," he said.

"It is no use losing your hair," she said.

"What did she say?" said Beluncle. "Was Chilly there? Did she talk to Chilly?"

"Of course," said Mrs Truslove. "She's in a bad way. The gas was turned off at her flat. We tried to make her some coffee."

"Her flat! You took her home!" gasped Mr Beluncle.

"What did she want?" said Mr Beluncle.

Mrs Truslove hesitated. She could not resist it.

"What all the Beluncles want—" she said, "cash."

"Don't be funny, Linda. That girl has been helping herself

to other people's money all her life," Mr Beluncle shouted out suddenly. "She's been rich. Do you think she'd give me a penny when I was down? Not a penny. Shut the door in my face, my own sister. Now she comes here."

"You told me," she said, repenting. But again, she could not resist saying:

"Poor Philip. They're all after him."

"Poor," said Beluncle, pulling himself together. "She was here a fortnight ago, after you had gone. I didn't mention it. I knew she was about. That was why I had the gate locked at home the other Sunday. . . ."

"You told me it was Lady Roads. Oh, Philip."

"Well, Lady Roads. Perhaps it was. I don't know," he said.

"But," his anger started again but now coldly, "let us have this clear. I won't have her here. I won't have her talk to Chilly. I'll go and see her. I don't want my business trotted round all over the place.

"*You* seem to think it's all right," he said.

"It's not a nice thing for me," he said. "I've led a decent life. She killed my father. She won't write to her own mother."

"But it's her mother she wants to see," said Mrs Truslove. "She says you have written to her telling her not to come. I don't know what is going on but she seems to think you are stopping her seeing her mother."

Mr Beluncle stood up. When his face took a greenish bruised colour, his grey close curls looked like a wig and he seemed to have been compressed for an explosion of frightening violence. The violence of Mr Beluncle frightened Mrs Truslove and went to her entrails, woke up not her old love but a total powerlessness in his hands. She could not disguise from herself her longing to be attacked by him and the irony she used in self-defence was simple provocation. She had, she believed, come to the end of her love for him; but she had not come to the end of that ambiguous compulsion which comes from the hatred in love.

"Constance can come down to see us tomorrow," he said

quietly. "What is to prevent her? There are trains. She can come. 'You come,' I said to her. 'But remember,' I said, 'mother is an old woman. Her mind wanders. A shock might kill. You don't want to kill your mother,' I said. 'If you can take that responsibility, well and good,' I said. 'It's up to you. I can't take it.' And why does Constance want to come? Is it love? Does she think of her mother's love for her? Does she care about her in her old age? Has she made a single sacrifice? You would have thought she would have been a daughter as I have been a son. No, she wants money, as you said just now, you're quite right, to pour down her throat. And then, how do we know that it would be convenient for her mother to give her money? It might be very inconvenient. How can I say? I don't know how it seems to you," he said more calmly, "how life seems to you, but to me it seems you work, you sow and others reap. But God sees into the heart. What would my father say if he were alive to see the money he saved for years thrown away on drink in a fortnight? Constance thinks she wants money, but we none of us want money. You don't, I don't, Connie doesn't. What we want is to purify our hearts—that's what Purification means. My father would say, I can hear him saying it," said Mr Beluncle, very moved and shyly wiping an eye with the back of a finger, "I have lived my life for nothing."

Mr Beluncle looked at her hard as he spoke and she looked as steadily at him, her eyes softening when he spoke of his father, for she thought of hers, and then hardening again. He got up in order to face her eyes and began again:

"When did she come?"

He wanted to hear every detail of the story again. And when he heard it, he wanted to go home at once to his wife and to tell her. She would storm, she would say terrible things, but she would understand him. And he would warn her to keep the gate locked.

XXVIII

Mary Phibbs saw him before he saw her. He was coming fast down the hill which hung like a stone waterfall between the trees and houses. He was nearly at the lamp standard on the Boystone side of the second railway bridge, which was one of their meeting-places. He took long steps, his chin was stuck out as if he were looking for a fight, his head was down staring at the pavement, though sometimes he looked up in a shy fierce manner as if the light were too strong. When he saw her, he slowed down and smiled all over his face as if he had been suddenly let out of a cage. A cage, a dream: these were what he lived in. She looked away to the wall to hide her confidence. She was taller than he was and, remembering how Sis said she was clumsy, she put out her hands to give herself a graceful floating appearance, and pretended not to see him. She was concealing a smile. In one hand she was carrying the book he had given her.

He was an impatient boy, wrapped up in himself, Sis said, morbid. "It's funny our Mary liking him, but she's young."

The letters he wrote to her! "You'll have to get a new drawer, Mary," Sis said. And the words he uses. He talked about love at once, before he felt it. Talk doesn't make feelings. Sis said, "You want to say No, Mary, you're too young, and say you will always treasure his friendship. Have you got a snap of him? Fancy, our Mary! Only yesterday I was pushing her in a pram and now she's blushing." In bed at night it was, "Don't squeeze me so tight, Mary, you're choking me and you're pushing me out. I'm not Henry." "Oh, Sis, how can you say?" "Well, when you are married to him, you'll be in bed, silly girl." "Don't talk like that, Sis, it isn't right." "I bet you talk about it, Mary, you two." "No, we don't." "Oh, so pure, so pi, go on, tell us, Mary, what does he say? Go on, Mary." "Nothing, Sis, truly." "Pooh, he sounds dry, too wrapped up, the family's a stuck-up lot. That's what Dadda says. Has he kissed you, Mary?" "Yes." "Where?" "Never you mind." "He hasn't ever kissed you,

you'd like him to, but he hasn't." "Yes, he has, Sis, in the birch woods." "Cuddle and squeeze, Mary, I *am* surprised! Well, Mary, as long as you keep your self-respect." "We trust each other, Sis." "Oh, so you *have* talked! I've caught you out, you little sinner."

Sis put her arm round her and her hands on Mary's small breasts and yawned with boredom. "Oh I'm so fagged, Mary," Sis said. "I've been at it all day. What's life for? it makes you wonder. There's a new boy, he asked me to a dance, but I don't know. Doesn't Henry dance? Bring him, Mary." "Oh, he couldn't, he doesn't dance, his father wouldn't let him." "His father! Oh, Mary!" and Sis laughed into the pillow. "I'm making this pillow wet. How can his father stop him?" "He's strict, Sis. He's afraid of his father, Sis. Mr Beluncle is not like dad." "Well, he's got to choose, Mary, be sensible, between you and his father, a boy can't play fast and loose, I'd tell him straight. That sort let you down." "Stop it, Sis. Henry's not like that. I won't speak to you if you go on like that." "Oh," said Sis, "did you wind that blessed alarm? Thank goodness." "Oh well, you keep so close, you don't tell us anything, Mary. Are you asleep, Mary? I'm sorry I said anything. Have I upset you?" "No." "Girl, you're not crying?" "No." "Mary." And Sis laughed quietly and stroked her sister's back. "I know how you feel, Mary. You wish it was Henry stroking you. You do, I know you do. Isn't it lovely when he strokes you like I am? Oh, when Tom did, there I'm telling you, I don't mind, I used to feel . . ." she shuddered. "My, your cheeks are burning. You're blushing. He doesn't, does he?" "Yes," whispered Mary. "What—I can't hear you, Mary. *Yes*, did you say? But, Mary, Mary girl, I shall have to shake you—listen. Don't let him do any more, will you? It's wrong." "I never did, Sis. We wouldn't think of it." "I'm glad to hear of it, Mary. You'll have a lot more boys, it's soft to get potty on one."

Henry and Mary exchanged books. They were walking to the countrified edge of the town where the birch woods were falling to the builders at the south end. The trees went on trembling as if they had faces between them, till they stopped at the edge of the small, clay cliffs of Boystone pond, where youths stopped their motor-bicycles and threw stones into the water.

"Sis," said Mary, "says I must be in love. She used to say it was calf love, but now she says it is love. Sis says you ought to speak out to your father. I mean, it is him or us, isn't it? I often think I'll give him a piece of my mind."

"You mustn't," said Henry, thinking of his father's sarcastic smile. Between Langford Avenue and Dean Road they spoke of Mr Beluncle, getting off the subject quickly for it led to Mr Chilly. What would Mr Chilly think of her?

"Let's sit down," Henry said.

"If we can find a place," said Mary, blushing. "In there I'll tear my dress. You should have heard Sis the last time I tore my green. You know my green?"

"We can go round by the gate."

"When mother was a girl," Mary said, climbing over, "it was considered wrong for a girl to show more than her ankles, not that I think much to shorts, except on bicycles."

And sitting by the tree, as he put his arm round her and kissed her and put his hand into her small cold breasts, she pulled her frock down modestly over her legs.

"You worry me," she said, feeling his skin burn against hers. "I often worry about you. Last night, I was thinking about you. Sis was asleep . . ."

"You sleep with Sis?" he said sharply, his hand going still on her breast.

"Of course," she said. "Silly boy. Where do you think I sleep? I was thinking—you carry on too much. You're so wrapped up. I don't mean morbid. You've got your thoughts. I was thinking about you. When you're walking you look proud—there, I've given myself away. I wasn't going to tell you, you'll think it is flattery."

"Last night, was that?" he said. "What time was it?"

"Late," she said. "A good thing Sis was asleep. You never think of me."

"I do. Last night I did."

"Pooh," she said. "Only last night?"

"Every night," he said. "All the time."

"You don't. You say you do. Do you really?"

"Yes."

"Sis says we're too young and dad laughs. And mum, she looks so wise."

"You talk about it to them?" said Henry, taking his arm away and looking at her.

"We've got no secrets in our family. It would be wrong to have secrets."

"I don't tell anyone. I don't want to," he said. "I've got to get home soon, before he gets back. It's deceiving, I know."

"People who stop you when they've got no right get themselves deceived," she said.

"It starts the whole thing—mother, Mrs Truslove, everything," said Henry boastfully.

It was time for Henry to tell one of his stories. Mary hated his stories with all her heart. She hated not the stories themselves but their importance to him and his pride in them. She believed them but they frightened her. "You exaggerate," she said.

"But it's true," he said.

"That is why I hate it," she said. "And you laugh!"

She tried to distract him by talking about her family, but there was little to be said of them.

"Dadda and mother have never had a cross word in their lives," said Mary complacently. "We laugh at them. He loves her and she loves him. That's how it ought to be. If she's ill he never leaves her side; if he is ill, she hardly speaks to us. She has eyes for him alone. Like two doves."

"Mine quarrel the whole time," said Henry proudly. "They never stop. Five nights of the week they're at it, hammer and tongs."

"That isn't love," said Mary. "It can't be."

"They oughtn't to have married," said Henry fiercely.

"He kisses her when he comes in. He sits and holds her hand on the sofa," said Mary. "Oh, you two, Sis says. Jealous? Dadda says. You have to smile."

Henry could hear his father's voice after he had come from a church meeting. "That man Phibbs is nothing but a damn' fool. Soft, socialistic, something wrong there. It's the Miss Wix lot."

Henry's spirits sank and he took his arm from Mary's soft, heavy arm for a moment, to strike for the shore away from the happiness where the Phibbses swayed in the listless contentment of the drowned. He also wanted to gesticulate.

"We used to listen at night to them," said Henry. "It was Mrs Parkinson, the Trusloves or the business. When we were at Romwich it was terrible."

He did not tell the true shames of Romwich: the carpetless house, half the furniture gone, the man knocking at the front door one morning and his mother answering. "Name of Beluncle?" the man said. And his mother's lie that had held them transfixed in whispering and watching for days. "No one of that name here," Mrs Beluncle said. "You not Mrs Beluncle?" "I'm the maid. Carter here"—her mother's name. Her voice was clear and firm and the man went. They watched him cross the road from behind the lace curtains of the front room.

"Mum, you said a lie."

"Shut your mouth."

"She said she was the maid because she was dirty in her apron," Henry explained. And that they had all believed.

"Oh," Mrs Beluncle suddenly moaned, and rocked tears out of herself in a chair. "It's the High Street, the summons, you wicked man."

Henry did not tell Mary that part of the story. He jumped to the end of the family's life at Romwich. There was a difference in mental kind between himself and Mary, the difference between the wounded and the unwounded. He did not wish for sympathy. He did not wish for love. He wished to show himself. It was a kind of honesty which was to make clear to her that there was a distance between them, and that to be loved she must be like him. From the beginning his conversations were a warning; what he said of others, he was saying of himself.

The week they had left Romwich was the end of happiness and the beginning of passion. People talked about the war he did not remember; but the real war had begun during that week. He was a soldier in it, encamped, bored, drastic, never secure.

There was a white fog one morning outside the Beluncles' window, a fog like cold bed-clothes over the town. No one wanted to get up. They knew something was wrong when instead of his mother coming in and saying, "Get up you boys, you'll be late for school," in came Mr Beluncle already dressed.

"Are you going now?" George asked, fearing that his father was going away.

"Get up, there's good children," said Mr Beluncle gently. And his voice seemed to forgive them.

They got up in hurried silence and went downstairs. There were two strapped suitcases in the dark hall and against the dining-room window was the wall of white fog. The morning milk cart could be heard somewhere, crawling and rattling in it. They sat at the table. Their mother came in with her yellow hair done, her hat and coat on. It was frightening to see her in her best clothes and not in her apron. She looked like a woman and not a mother. She was sniffing tears from her face. She banged a plate down hard in each place, and with each bang, came a large sob as if she had a bird inside her.

"Get and eat it," she said, and went out. The food might have been poisoned. Mr Beluncle followed her at a distance, stood still in the room, smiled. Too startled to eat, the children smiled boldly at him. "We are ready to be on your side," their eyes said.

"Come on in, Ethel," Mr Beluncle called in a tired voice from the door, and then went to find her. Once more she came in with a teapot and carrying her large handbag, too; and, at the same distance, Mr Beluncle was following her. This time he had the expression of one silently whistling.

Down went the teapot on the table and some tea gulped out of the spout and made a small pool on the cloth. That annoyed Mr Beluncle.

"The cloth," he said sharply, and opened his mouth to say the price of it, but did not do so. Moaning, sobbing, Mrs Beluncle wandered in a dazed way round the table, talking to herself. They watched her with interest. Was she mad?

"Sit down," said Beluncle quietly.

"Oh," Mrs Beluncle suddenly screamed, "don't you dare talk to me." The children lowered their eyes and very slowly raised their forks to their mouths.

"Is Grandma Carter dead?" said George, out of feeling for the squalor of tragedy.

"Stop that boy saying wicked things," cried out Mrs Beluncle.

"Get on with your breakfast, George," said Mr Beluncle.

"Where are you going, mum?" said Henry.

"Away," said Mrs Beluncle, looking at Henry with contempt, "—away from the lot of you."

Leslie was out of his chair and under the table at once. George dropped his knife and fork and cried into his plate. Henry's heart rang inside him like a hammer, in hard, regular, workshop blows.

"*She*'ll look after you, no doubt," cried Mrs Beluncle. "*She*'ll do it all, without a maid. You'll have *her*. . . ."

"Who?" said Henry.

"Bring that woman down here," cried Mrs Beluncle, pointing to their father. He smiled apologetically and kindly at them.

"Your mother is upset, not very well, has a headache," he said. He hummed, at a loss, and then began to sing. " 'Oh dry those tears, oh calm those fears,' " Mr Beluncle sang.

"Ah, ha, ha!" laughed Mrs Beluncle, in hysteria, pushing past her husband, and because she laughed, the children laughed too. Leslie came out from one side of the table to look.

They were ashamed by their laughter. They stopped laughing when they saw their mother stop and look at them with the quivering fear of a cornered rabbit. Her fear created fear in them. She gave them one incredulous look and then left the room for the hall. They heard her open the front door. Henry ran from the table to the hall. George followed him. Leslie took a piece of bacon from a plate and remained in the room, undecided, eating it; Mr Beluncle tickled his neck as he passed the little boy and went out to her. Leslie went round to the other plates.

She was standing in the hall, pulling at a brown fur with a fox's head on it. It had bead eyes and little soft paws; it was a fur that smelled of train tunnels, and with that round her, though she could be a pretty woman, she looked choked and wolfish.

"Ah," she said, "you think you have trapped me here, chaining me up like that dog outside, with three young children, look at their stockings all holes, you made a mistake.

"A large mistake," she said. "I'm going."

Mr Beluncle was not outwardly alarmed but stood back at the foot of the stairs to make room for them. The hall was tiny. The builder at Romwich (Mr Beluncle had said) had never tried swinging a cat in it. Mr Beluncle stood back like a producer.

"You'll understand this better when you're grown up," he said to Henry, who stood weighing up his father and his mother. And to his wife, he said:

"The door is open. There is nothing to stop you."

"I'm going. I'm going, I tell you," said Mrs Beluncle. They were all suddenly indignant with her.

"I'm staying with dad," said George, taking his father's hand. Henry's heart had gone; he swayed from one party to the other and while he swayed his mother gave him a sharp look.

"Henry," she said, "come here." And at the same time, she put out her hard hand, caught his wrist and pulled. Henry looked back at his father for forgiveness, but Mr Beluncle smiled.

"Get your coat on," she said to Henry.

"You're hurting my wrists."

"Here," she said, and she pulled his coat off the peg, dragging other coats down with it; and still holding him she made him put it on. He stepped away when his hand was free, but she caught him by the wrist violently.

"You're to come with me," she said.

And she opened the door wide, the fog came in like an inane and wet, white face, and Henry was pulled after her, looking back to signal, "I am sorry. You see how it is. I am forced."

Leslie, the small boy, laughed.

"You'll laugh," Mrs Beluncle said, pulling Henry into the front garden, "on the other side of your face when they drag the canal."

"You've forgotten the suitcase," called Mr Beluncle.

Confused by the sudden jeer, the sudden dead silence of a London street where the fog had stopped all traffic, hurt by his mother's grip on his wrist, Henry half trotted to keep up with her racing step.

"Don't run, mother.

"I can't keep up."

He was pulling her back, ashamed of her. Her small face in its fur was as keen as a rat's, intense, hunting, unhearing. He was glad of the emptiness of the street, dreaded this boy or that coming out of the gates of their houses. He was glad of high hedges to the gardens, and he ducked by the low ones.

"Where are we going?" he asked. "Let me go."

And yet, also, he felt enormously important at being alone with her. Their steps raised hard echoes in the fog along the walls of the houses which could be known only by their smells. They turned the corner at the bottom of the street. They crossed the next road blindly. They took a sudden turn to the right. He could not guess where they were going and she did not speak once.

And then the ground softened and he saw they were under the trees going to the park, and through its wide stone gates they went, stumbling over the soft riding way and across to the high banks of spilling laurels where the fog seemed to hang over them in grey waves and to come blowing down as cold as sea water.

They took an asphalt path, then left it for the grass, and now into empty acres of whiteness they went, as if the place were a steppe in some slow and noiseless blizzard. Then he heard within two or three yards of them the cluck of water-fowl, secluded and untroubled, on their empty lake.

Now he understood. His mother intended to throw herself into the lake. It was a relief knowing this. He knew he could stop her. And he also knew, in the same moment, she would attempt nothing of the kind. They would follow the rail—he would make her follow the rail—round and round they would go. He could see the small curved concrete edge of the artificial lake and the sly, flat face of the London water, with its long, dirty mackerel ripples like his father's city smile.

Now he had got her to the far side and had slowed her down, because this place always enchanted them. There was a little island and its two small bays. There the swans dipped their coarse and smutty necks and drew them out like hawsers. The path out of the park was by the island and it was simple to take her out and to the wretched, humiliated, walk home. He looked at her face. There was no change in it, except that it was reddened by the cold, damp walk; she did not show a sign of defeat. They walked to their door. Mr Beluncle, thoughtfully, had left it open.

XXIX

"Your poor mother," said Mary.

"She didn't mean to drown herself. Just acting," he said. Now he wished he had not told her.

"D'you know what they did? They fried fish. All the rows in our house end up in frying plaice. QUANtities of it."

The bluish savorous smoke of frying fish clouding in the house was really what he remembered; and the feeling of gentleness, softness and delicious languor after violence. Yet happiness, love, serenity, trust and truth were less after violence too. Another rock crumbled off the island on which one tried to live.

Mary looked at him, woodenly and with disapproval. He had laughed, or his eyes had laughed, through the last part of the story.

"We must go," he said.

"You know," he said, to punish her for not laughing with him, "I'm going to clear out of this country. When I'm twenty-one. I'm going. They can't stop me."

He was standing up.

"Abroad," he said.

"Oh," she said, in an offended voice, "you speak as if you didn't like Boystone."

"Good Lord," he said, "I hate it. Don't you?"

"I love it. I never want to leave it," she said. "Dadda does too.

"Perhaps," she said, "you don't love me, you say you love me, do you know what love is?"

"I do love you," he said.

And then, with one of his sharp, sudden violent changes of mood, he embraced her softly while she sulked. And he whispered to her.

She moved away and would not speak and he feared he had offended her. They walked slowly away from the place and he said, "I am sorry."

"You must not say things like that," she said, looking away from him. "It is wrong." And when he did not answer she said, "I am not beautiful."

"You do not trust me," he said.

"I trust you," she said. "Don't look angry or sad. I would like to."

This utterly silenced them until she laughed.

Mary repeated, "You look sad, you look angry or sad. I want to," she said. "Look, we've flattened the grass. You remember when we went to the Common we found the grass still flattened. You said, 'Perhaps we have had lodgers.' "

"No one could have found that place," he said eagerly.

They brushed the grass from their clothes and her small eyes were brilliant in her coloured face. "A button seems to have undone itself," she said. When she tidied her hair, raising both her arms to it, she knew she looked five years older, a grown woman and beautiful. They walked away and two people with a child passed them. Henry and Mary put on an air of unconcern. "They might have caught us," she said. And, looking round, hoping the other couple were watching them, she took Henry's arm. The other couple did turn and she felt proud.

"I like people to see us," she said.

Henry hated it. He hated her to say it and to show that he was in her possession, folded up and put away and taken out again, like his grandmother's linen.

"It's a lovely sky, I like the red in it," she said, putting her head on one side and putting some of the sky away too. "Sunsets make me feel sad and yet I'm happy. We used to come up here with mother on Sunday evenings but the rabbits have gone with all this building."

"We sometimes go out in the car," Henry said, "never walk."

"Oh, that car! It makes me cross, really it makes me cross," said Mary petulantly. "I wouldn't want one. It's materialistic. It's what's wrong with the church, Dadda says."

And Mary held her head high and primly. The field gates clicked, shutting the evening away behind them, and then click and click behind them again as the other slow couples took the well-known path, letting them into the fields.

"They're all going where we've been," said Mary, squeezing his hand with deep pleasure.

"Yes," said Henry, squeezing in return, but his spirits sank. That was, he thought, the hell of Boystone.

Upon the hard pavement of Deans Road, Henry said "Lights" and squares of yellow were chequered at different levels in the avenue. "I must hurry." The houses stood like trains.

Henry's heart thumped and then started to race. He was

trying to bring himself to say what had been in his mind all
the evening, what he had been thinking as he walked, head
down, to meet her at the railway bridge.

"I've stopped believing in the Purification," he said.

Mary took her hand from his arm and stopped dead to
look at him.

"Henry," she said.

"I have. It isn't true. I know it isn't. I can't go on with
it. It isn't honest. When that man called out last night 'Lies',
you know—I knew he was right."

"Oh, Henry, you haven't?"

She looked at his head, his body, his hands and feet; for the
first time, she seemed to be looking at the whole of him.

"I have," he said.

"You can't," she said.

The unhappiness, the desolation in her voice shocked him
and he went to take her hand, but she stepped away, fearing
to be touched by his unbelief.

"You have stopped loving me," she said. "Henry, you
have. That is what you are trying to say. You have stopped."

The appalled, deserted look on her face, the anguish in it,
the incredulous dread, made him aware for the first time that
she was not an extension of himself, but another human
being. It was she, now, who was distant from him, not he
alone distant from her.

"I haven't," he said. "I'm talking about the Purification.
I *can't* believe it. Please, I love you."

Anger, so uncommon in her, filled her cheeks. There were
tears in her eyes. She snapped at him:

"Telling me like this, at the last moment, after what you
said to me, when you asked, it's not you. It's like a coward,"
she said. And she started to walk fast away from him. He
hurried after her. He tried to explain.

"It's your father. That is what the teaching of Lady
Roads does. Miss Wix always said so. She drives everyone
out of the movement. I have heard her say it in our house,"
Mary said. And she stopped again.

"Henry, it isn't true?" she said.

"It is," he said, and he could not control a small hysterical smile of vanity.

"Oh," she said, taking both his hands, "you must be unhappy, poor boy."

"I'm not," he said. "I feel free."

"Free!" she said, horrified by him and looking at him with fear. "How can you be free? You don't know what you're saying."

They started to move on again.

"Please see Miss Wix," she said. "Please talk to her. I will. Talk to Dadda. Oh, Henry, this is a terrible thing. Say you will try to get back your faith. I will pray. I will do anything."

The sky had jumped darkly over the thousands of trivial chimneys of the pink town, and then hung like the sheet of a circus tent over the pool of lights by the bridge where they stopped. He tried once more to explain, but she looked away up and down the road nervously.

"You must go," she said, thinking of him.

"If you have stopped loving me it will break my heart," she said. "Oh, you have made me unhappy, saying it like this, at the last moment. When we cannot talk. It is a terrible thing you've done." She took her hand away and, not wishing to look at him, hurried away. She did not look back.

Henry watched her in the dusk, in consternation and with remorse.

XXX

Sis said, speaking to the flowered wallpaper, "Tom was terrible. He said I had the loveliest body of any woman, like Venus. When we were down at Worthing by the sea. Of course. Well, I mean! But one day," Sis said, "accidentally —it was quite an accident—I left the door of the room open and—oh, Mary, I could die when I think—he saw! But Tom was like that, all eyes. Your Henry wouldn't want to, he'd be too deep in a book, that's what's so soft about him. Though I expect all men are alike—if Henry is a man, Mary, I mean you say he's a man," she laughed, "but you can't prove it. You're up in the clouds, you're so pious, so pure, thinking of heaven all the time, higher things. And you're right, Mary. Henry's got a good job. Have you seen those houses going up in the Avenue? I was thinking 'One of those would do for Henry and Mary.' Why don't you take him round that way? Boys don't think, Mary, they're funny. Women have got to make them, they'd just drag on for years and you're too quiet and patient. Not like me; well, look at me and Tom. It wasn't that I didn't like him, but you could see what he was like, stick to nothing. I'm like that too."

"Sis," said Mary, "Henry wants to go abroad. To learn."

"Learn what?" said Sis. "Is he? What's he going abroad for?

"Here, Mary—oh, you're crying. Mary dear, don't. Here, Mary, you haven't been playing the little hypocrite with us all, have you? You haven't . . ."

"No," sobbed Mary. "It will break my heart. I shall die if he goes. I shall kill myself, Sis."

"Now then, Mary, don't be silly. You won't. Look, Mary, you're too good, you're too in the air, in the clouds. You know what I think. You've made him suffer, that's what it is. Men are funny, they suffer with it and girls are cruel without meaning. I don't say they haven't got to look after themselves. I see it now. I was like you. I made Tom suffer. That's why he went. Oh, Mary, I could kill myself now, I was a fool. There now, I've told you something I didn't mean to. I don't mean you ought to give in to a man, no girl ought to do that; but as long as you keep your self-respect, that's the important thing, Mary, and if it happens then it's no one's fault and a decent man will stand by you. Henry's a decent boy, he's got his religion. I know it tells us not to, I used to pray about it. 'If it's right,' I used to pray. Tom used to say, 'It's either me or the religion. I'm a man.' And he was. Still, I don't suppose Henry suffers like Tom did. I tortured Tom, Mary, I see it now, I tortured him."

"I would not do a thing like that, Sis," said Mary. "It would be wrong. It would be wicked. I wouldn't trap Henry."

"Trap Henry," Sis laughed. "You've got a chance, you silly fool. He'll be on the boat to Timbuctoo, before you wake up. Who's talking about trapping? All I'm saying," said Sis, "only you don't listen, get Dadda to ask his *intentions*. I suppose you've got a right to know that—or perhaps you like being trodden on by a lousy bookworm."

"Sis, I hate you. I hate you."

"Stop it, Mary, you're tearing my night-gown."

"Oh, Sis, I'm sorry. I think I'm out of my mind. It isn't true what I told you. He said he loved me. Tonight he said it. I know it was love."

They lay silently listening to the alarm clock and watching the flash of the electric trains.

"Sis," Mary said, "Henry's stopped the Purification. He says it's lies. He's saying terrible things about it. I'm so upset. That's what upset me."

"Girl, don't worry about that. That's nothing. Tom was like that. He just made fun of it all the time. Henry'll get over it. I often don't believe it myself."

"Oh, Sis!"

"Well, I go hot and cold. Once you're married he'll come back to it. A wife has power. He's young."

"He's stopped everything, Sis."

"You speak to Miss Wix about it, Mary. A woman can do anything, Mary, don't you forget that, she has her ways. Boys are fools. I could see that with Tom. I'd only got to look at him and his hands were everywhere. Next time you see Henry when you're out, in some shady nook, Mary, if you see, it'll all come back if you make it. I mean for his sake you can make it. I wouldn't let Tom, that's where I was a fool, but Tom hadn't got it to lose, not faith, I mean; but Henry—well, it wouldn't be wrong. If you love someone and it's just that would bring his faith back . . ."

"Stop it, Sis," Mary said.

"Well, they want it," said Sis bitterly. "I know how I lost Tom and Tom hadn't got faith."

Mary's head ached.

"Oh," she thought, "if I could get his faith back I would. I would do anything. I will pray."

And, as Sis heavily slept, Mary lay trying to pray.

XXXI

Mrs Beluncle was happy. She was going over a few funerals with her youngest son: her father's funeral, her sister's, her mother's; visiting their cemeteries. Then she went on to the dead pets of her childhood. There was, for example, a marmoset called Dick. What Leslie wanted to know was whether any of the relations left any money and what they did with it. Were there any misers among them?

"I admire misers," Leslie said in his frosty middle-aged way.

"Dick, our marmoset, didn't leave a penny," said Mrs Beluncle, a little afraid of the boy's shrewd look.

"Pity," he said. "There's money in marmosets, I bet, if you know how to go about it. I made a lot out of those rabbits George gave me, you remember, years ago; silly fool, I'd have bought them from him and still made a profit."

"Well, you're a cure," said Mrs Beluncle.

"I'm going to leave a lot of money," said Leslie, "if I live till I'm fifty. I might not see fifty. By the way, has Dad insured us? I suppose not. Short-sighted. He never realises anything about life. When I think of you all, I think you are wasting my time."

Mrs Beluncle did not know whether to laugh at her youngest son.

There was a knock at the door and Mrs Beluncle dropped the spoon out of her saucer.

"My nerves," said Leslie, turning into an actor at once. "You know I suffer from nerves something chronic."

He got up.

"Don't go," said Mrs Beluncle, in a panic. "Wait. I can't

bear a knock. That means you didn't lock the gate like your father said."

"Aunt Connie again?" said Leslie.

"You wicked boy. What d'you mean?" said Mrs Beluncle.

"The harlot," said Leslie, rolling his eyes.

They were sitting in the front room and Mrs Beluncle had edged to the window and was looking through the curtain.

"It's a man," said Mrs Beluncle.

"It's all right," said Leslie, "he's going. It's old Repent-Ye Vogg. Wages of Sin. A boy at school pinched his banner last term. I could have bought it, but where would you sell a thing like that?"

"Oh dear," said Mrs Beluncle, going back to her tea, "I hope your father is all right. I'm always so frightened that it's something for your father. People used to come. The High Street—but they wouldn't come now, would they? I mean it's a long time ago. Isn't it?"

"Was I born then?"

"You were a baby in arms," said Mrs Beluncle.

"All the best things happened before I was born," said Leslie. "Was that when we had the writ for the piano?"

"Stop it," said Mrs Beluncle. "There was trouble."

"I ought," said Leslie, "to have been born first. I could have saved you a lot. I can't understand why dad never had a fire. It would have given him a decent start."

"You're a deedy one," said Mrs Beluncle.

XXXII

David Vogg walked away from the Beluncles' and went next door and then worked his way up the short street. It was his first day out after the meeting.

He had quarrelled with the old man when they came out of the hall.

"You didn't stir yourself much," he had said. "I must be

deaf. I didn't hear you. Who was it bore the Witness, eh? Go on, who? Eh?"

The old man, when the moment came, had sat fast in his chair and had not called out. It was Vogg alone who had shouted.

"It was these boots. You was going to get me a pair of your dad's," the old man whined. "They're like irons, these 'ere. They weighed me down like Satan under the floor. Once I'm down I can't get up."

"You don't speak with your feet," Vogg said.

The old man cringed.

"I was too full of the glory," he said sheepishly. "The glory came down on me. I couldn't open my mouth." He said to himself: "It's youth. If *she* had been alive, I would have done it. With no one in the house I've got so as I can't talk."

Vogg was ill immediately after his shouting. He was always wonderful for a couple of hours and then knives started to cut him up inside. All the bloody ships he had sailed in ripping him up. He came home and washed himself at the sink and retched. He was at sea and the house rolled. The pain had started like a rat under the ribs.

His mother had wanted him to get a doctor. Why doctors? he said. Doctors practise medicine, medicine is knowledge, knowledge comes from the Tree. Like the churches, the schools, the temples of learning, the factories, the palaces of the rich, the parliaments, the banks, the hospitals too would come rolling down into the fire, the slates and the glass pouring down like marbles, the walls swelling out to burst like drowned women and crushing the rich, the educated, the popes, the bishops and the Parkinsonians in their cars, beneath them; and in the bloody darkness, with the heavens on fire, the poor and oppressed would arise and swarm like dungworms in their millions to the throne of grace.

Millions? He had lain on his bed with the pain scissoring in his stomach and that was the thought he came back to. Would it be millions? It might only be thousands. How many would be saved? Whom had God chosen? That was an argument he used to have with the old man sometimes. There were all the prophets to add up, and then there was the old man's wife and Vogg; under a hundred they made it. As he lay there the numbers lessened. Very few would be left. Only a handful out of the millions of dead since the earth began. The faces of specific sinners, faces jacked open by screams, ridged and furry with iniquity, appeared to him like faces on playing cards. Starting with the street: Mrs Haxted, the grocer: adultery in the top room on Tuesdays. Galton: drunkenness. Faber: hypocrisy—he was in the Salvation Army. Mrs Truslove: adultery three evenings a week between six and eight and on Saturday afternoons. Mr Beluncle, gluttony and adultery. Mrs Johnson, the housekeeper: lewdness. Miss Dykes . . .

Vogg was divided in mind about the cripple. Her religion was wicked, the false god worshipped. It was, after the Roman Catholic Church, the most wicked of religions. But she was a cripple. The sins of her fathers had crippled her. Was she downtrodden enough to be saved?

"What is the matter, dear. Is your old stomach paining you?" his mother said.

He told her about the lecture and how he had shouted out. Mrs Vogg listened proudly. She had only the slightest knowledge of his religion, but she was lazily proud to think her son had made trouble. All the housework, he does, she said, gets me up in the morning, dresses me, cooks the breakfast, cooks all the meals, a good son. What's making trouble matter? Let him make it. The world owes it to him.

And she had a fantasy that one day when he was making trouble somewhere, a man's voice would suddenly cry out:

"Stop that or I'll belt you."

Her son's father, whoever or wherever he was, suddenly appearing. "David'll kick up a row until his father comes," she affectionately thought.

Still, when she heard his story she wanted to soothe him.

"Don't let it get on your mind, dear," she said. "Don't

worry about it. Everyone will have forgotten about it to-morrow."

Forgotten! Mrs Vogg saw she had said the wrong thing. That was what drove him out of the house again when the pain weakened; the fear that the silly public would have forgotten all about him.

He stood at Boystone East station to sell his paper. He counted twenty known followers of Mrs Parkinson going to the trains. He was showing himself. He was aware of every pair of eyes and there was a slight smile on his face. He was determined to be watched. He felt that standing or waiting he cut a mark in the air. The pain inside him made him think this.

XXXIII

Vogg put his suitcase down at the end of the road where the Beluncles lived, for the weight pulled his ribs out of his stomach. He thought he was going to split and his stomach rolled over. He started on again looking at the sky in agony, and when he got to Boystone market he felt too weak to go on. He bought two buns, got into the Hetley bus and made for home. Buns always stopped the pain and at Hetley when he got off it was small and dull.

To be without pain, after three days and nights of it, enlarged the mind of Vogg. He looked about him as he walked and the excited energy he had known immediately after the meeting came back to him. And more, for there was the energy or the power which came from the con-templation of the pain he had suffered. He had passed through one crisis; he was ready for another.

The pigeons were tipping in circles over the street as he walked past the large houses towards his shop. He watched them and fell into a day-dream about old Vogg's pigeons. Pigeons took him back to his childhood. Watching in the yard with Vogg, he had had his earliest introduction to injus-

tice. Pigeon racing, the old man said, wasn't straight. There
were men who fixed their clocks. The big fellows won the
prizes. They could build big lofts and employ a couple of
loftmen to feed them. Some of the first to go to hell-fire
would be the men with big lofts; after that the bloody railway porters who, racing men themselves, would put the
crate of birds in the wrong train at the junction. There were
men like Dykes, the postman, who wouldn't tell you anything, close as oysters, dirty, wily, cunning men. "I'd spit
out half the teeth in my head to have a look inside Dykes's
brain for five minutes, he's deep," old Vogg used to say
when Vogg was a boy.

Vogg was eating his second bun as he walked, watching
the sky, and the dough stuck dryly in his throat. A pair of
birds came down on a chimney and he watched them bob-
bing there like a pair of clockwork toys up to their tricks. He
stopped. And then one flew off and Vogg, looking from the
chimney to the house, was taken aback. He was brought
abruptly and fast back from his childhood when he saw,
as if he had never seen it before, that the house was the
Dykeses'.

An extraordinary sense, like a revelation of his true state
during the last three days since the meeting, came to him.
He had been lonely. When he had stood up in the Royal
Cinema, he had seen not a single known face. Except Miss
Dykes's. She had been wheeled in at the back of the hall, and
she had even smiled at him. It was her smile, excited and
proud, which had given him the will to get up; *she* at any
rate would know who he was. He was shouting, in a sense,
at the lecturer, just to show *her*. He knew now that to show
himself to her would have a definite effect. She knew. She
had heard. The town saw him and probably had no recol-
lection or knowledge of his act. Vogg's vanity was roused,
his feeling of loneliness went. He crossed the road to the
Dykeses' house and, stirred by the familiar whine of its iron
gate, knocked at the door.

"It is that Vogg," said Mrs Johnson to the cripple. She
was not sitting in her chair but on the long couch which was

put by the window in her room, with her feet in the sunlight, reading and drowsing.

"Oh, Mrs Johnson!" said the cripple. Her heart raced with fear. "But are you sure he asked for me? He didn't ask for my sister? Is it about the papers?"

"Love Vogg. Love Vogg," Miss Dykes hurriedly prayed.

"No, dear," said Mrs Johnson. "It was you he asked for. I've got him on the step."

"Child of God. Child of God," Miss Dykes murmured in a panic.

"Oh, ask him in, ask him in, don't keep him on the step."

"It's all right, dear," said Mrs Johnson. "I put the chain on. You leave the door open, next thing they step in and they steal your umbrellas. It happened when I was a girl at my Uncle Tom's."

"Fetch him in," Miss Dykes said, proud in her sudden calm. "I will see him."

It might be, she thought, an answer to her prayer. For days she had loved. She could nearly see and feel the love pouring from her eyes and her mouth and her heart like a pure stream of light across the road to the shop. She was numb and serene with the steady stream of the sentences of her prayers, dulled by the monotonous brilliance of the light which was broken only by short crimson flashes (like those one sees when staring into the face of the sun). It was the swooning crisis when the nerves collapse and the self dissolves and ripples away into weakness, nothingness, the liquid of a kind of death. Those moments went and then the long struggle of desire began again, the will revived it, the bones of her forehead began to ache with her striving until the light of her vision began once more to pound upon her.

"Mrs Johnson dear," she said. "Put the rug over me. Is my hair straight? I have prayed for him to come."

"You pray for funny things, miss," said Mrs Johnson formally, to show detachment from a prayer which, being directed to one of her own class, was a folly to her. Mrs Johnson had a profound conviction that prayer should not extend beyond the people of one's own station. "Don't you give anything to Vogg, miss. His father was lame with the doors that slammed on his foot. They're hawkers."

Mrs Johnson arranged Miss Dykes's cushions while she was saying this and then this wide-bummed woman went to the door.

"She says to come in," said Mrs Johnson scornfully. She watched for him to wipe his feet on the mat; and when he did not, watched for his hand to go to his head and take off his hat; but instead his hand went to his pocket, he slipped a tract into her surprised hand. "I'm daft," she said. Vogg never wore a hat.

Annoyed with herself, she closed the door after him. When he went into the room she looked at the dusty prints of his shoes on her shining brown linoleum. Mr Vogg's profound voice seemed to tumble like coals into a cellar. It was, to Mrs Johnson's mind, an offence and she went back to her kitchen and shut it out.

"Good afternoon, Mr Vogg," Miss Dykes said, putting out a hand, in her playful and magical manner. "Sit down."

Vogg did not answer, but he sat down. Three days of pain had put pale blue circles under his eyes and drawn his mouth tight and his lips down. He was wearing his sharp-shouldered navy-blue suit. He sat very upright with his knees together and she was startled by the fingers of his hands. She had not remembered seeing such separate fingers; such a tiny and disparate crew. The green tops of his tracts were showing in his jacket pocket. Mr Vogg looked melancholy, energetic and ill. He ignored the room and, in a sense, was not in it; . but was like some incongruous figure cut out of shiny paper, and pasted awkwardly upon a drawing.

"I bring a message to you," said Mr Vogg.

Miss Dykes's heart sank with disappointment. She had expected—she did not know what she had expected. Perhaps that Mr Vogg would fall on his knees with contrition; per- haps that he would beg her pardon. She had imagined him listening, beaten, but longing for the Truth.

Now, he said, he had come simply with some message! Her sister had put an advertisement in his window for a lawn mower. Perhaps it was about that? Or the distributors had forgotten to send one of her pattern magazines. Her lips drooped. She had dropped from her burning flights towards the sun, into the familiar desert of unanswered prayers.

"What is it? Who from?" she said, putting as good a face on it as she could.

Mr Vogg took his hands from his knees and let his arms hang loosely and straight as if his joints had gone. The fingers nearly touched the floor. The effect was to thrust his chest forward. There was a kind of prolonged mechanical flash from his false teeth, a rapid, lifeless heliograph signal. He said:

"I bring you a message from our Lord and Saviour Jesus Christ."

Miss Dykes's heart was jerked with fear and while she searched for a word to say, the voice of Mr Vogg broke, as if some gear had been let in and a loud machine began to grind:

"The Day of Judgment is at hand. The Lord cometh in the hour no man knoweth," he said. "I charge you: Come out from them and be ye separate. Three nights ago in the Royal Cinema, the voice of God was heard crying, 'Lies, lies', to the wickedness that dwells in high places. I bore witness to the Truth. I exposed to all the world the wickedness of the prostitute you worship, this Mrs Parkinson, daughter of the whores of Babylon."

Miss Dykes was shaking with terror, but her will and anger broke it down. Weeks of loving went from her heart.

"How dare you speak like that of Mrs Parkinson and our movement," she said. "Mrs Parkinson is the purest soul on earth, the messenger of Love and God to this age, cleansing the lepers, healing the sick and redeeming man from his slavery to the senses."

Mr Vogg did not interrupt. A flow of recited words always pleased him and he listened, but as automatically as he spoke. Miss Dykes was emboldened:

"And if this is the message you have come to give, I can

tell you it is not from Christ Jesus, the highest expression of Love that ever trod this earth, but from animal magnetism and evil. And that it is powerless to hurt the child of God. And, what is more, Mr Vogg, you are the image and likeness of God and you cannot be brought into subjection by this wicked thing."

Mechanically Mr Vogg nodded, the heliograph flashed. The message came back, monotonously, without expression.

"I have read your literature. I know your arguments. They are from your father the Devil and the lusts of your father ye will do. The world is four thousand two hundred and fifty-two years old and the Word of God has gone out, gathering his people together before the judgment; the day is decided. Search the scriptures and you will find it. There will be wars and rumours of wars, millions will be slaughtered and the cities fall, like it says, and the house of the harlot will burn. This is the witness I bear."

Miss Dykes smiled.

"You have no power over me," said Miss Dykes, in a trembling voice. "No power at all. Truth is all power. God is power. Not evil. I am the image of God. The image that means reflection. There is no power, no power. . . ."

Miss Dykes was losing her way.

"You are the child of darkness, not the child of light," Mr Vogg effortlesssly continued. "You are a harlot in the house of harlots. You were born in wickedness and lust and fornication."

Mr Vogg's manner changed a little. An edge came upon his voice, some local inflection from that part of London.

"You and your sister, your father who was a liar and a robber and your mother a harlot before you. You are liars and daughters of liars and worshippers of Belial. . . ."

"How dare, how—how dare you, Mr Vogg, speak of my sister and——" The rug fell off Miss Dykes's body, agitated by her movements. She made a move to pick it up, but it was beyond the reach of her hands and she could not, though she strained to do so, stretch to get it. She wriggled her body. "My feet," she was crying to herself. "I must cover my feet," for Mr Vogg was looking obscenely at them. It was the first movement his head had made.

"You say it's the Truth," he said. "Why doesn't it heal you? Why can't you walk?" he said.

And now his impersonality had gone. He stood up and the face was cut into the lines of its illness and his deep voice was quieter with personal rancour.

"I know the reason. Everyone in this street knows the reason. God crippled you for the sins of your father. The cheating postman who stole the letters, the dirty racer, a gambler. And your mother drinking every night in The Butcher's Arms and paying for it out of what she earned on her back."

"Stop it! Get out! Mrs Johnson!" called Miss Dykes. "Pick up that rug, give it to me."

She wriggled vainly to ease herself down the couch.

Above all to cover her feet, to hide them from him.

"Your sister three times a week with a City man, in this house, in this very room," said Mr Vogg.

"You're mad. If I could get at you!" cried Miss Dykes. The sweat was heavily seeded in her scarlet face, the shoes had fallen off her feet and she was helpless to reach her skirt which had worked over her knees and on one side, the side he stood, her thigh and its suspender were uncovered. It was the last shame.

"Mrs Johnson!" she screamed out. "Let me get at you. I will kill you."

Mr Vogg did not move. He stood there, looking at her, without a smile on his face. He grimaced, as if he were cut out of wood. There was a thump. Miss Dykes, in her last effort, had lost her balance and rolled off the couch. It had been mounted on high wooden blocks so that she could watch the street when she lay there. She fell heavily on her back and rolled over, dragging the rug with one hand.

"How dare you talk about my sister," she called out from the floor, in spite of the shock of her fall from the bed. "My sister has never . . . You hateful . . ."

The sound of steps came from the kitchen and Mrs

Johnson came into the room. She could not see the figure of Miss Dykes but could hear her grovelling and her voice and she could see Mr Vogg looking down. And she saw Mr Vogg step back and say, "No! Get away. Get away," and hold his hands up.

Mrs Johnson took three steps across the room to him and then she cried out, "What have you done? She's having a fit. She's having a fit."

Miss Dykes, who had turned over on her stomach, suddenly raised her buttocks and fell, then raised them again; the right leg moved in a half-sprawling move, sideways. She fell on to one knee and they both saw her raise herself on it. "I'll kill you. I'll kill you," she was muttering.

"She's moving. She's crawling," Mr Vogg said, backing away to the fireplace. "Keep her away. Keep her away from me. Keep her away."

"Dear," cried Mrs Johnson, going down on her knees to hold the cripple, and as she did so, the cripple rose to her knees and her left leg now sprawled and she half raised herself to Mrs Johnson's arms. The sweat poured from her face and her chest and had soaked her blouse.

"Kill him. Let me get to him," Miss Dykes was shouting, and she struggled against Mrs Johnson's body, tearing at her apron and her blouse, striking Mrs Johnson with her fists.

"Quiet, quiet," gasped Mrs Johnson. "Help me."

But Vogg had got to the corner of the room; he was grimacing with fear.

"Keep her away. Keep her away."

In the enormous strength of her rage, Miss Dykes pushed Mrs Johnson. Her blouse was torn down to her waist. Miss Dykes pushed against the corner of the table and Mrs Johnson tottered and loosened a hand to save herself. She let go of the cripple and Miss Dykes fell again.

She fell, not under the table, but sideways and half across the corner of it. And there she half hung, gripping the table by the edge.

"She can walk. Look. She can walk," sneered Vogg, in his corner. And indeed the right leg bent and then straightened and for a few seconds Miss Dykes stood like a drunken woman, before she slithered down again to where she had been half lying before.

"It's a sham," he called. "She can walk all the time."

"Don't stand there like a man," called Mrs Johnson. "Help me with her."

"Kill him," groaned Miss Dykes, pulling herself up by the table leg once more. "Don't let him go."

XXXIV

"She has walked three steps," the doctor said. He was a thin, elderly man with tobacco-stained fingers, gentle manners and a nose that had once been broken.

"It's a miracle," said Mr Beluncle. "I don't understand you medical men. You attack us but we do the job all the same."

"It's interesting," said the doctor gently. "Did you see it?"

"They phoned me at the office and I brought Mrs Truslove down at once," said Mr Beluncle, beginning a long personal narrative.

"That was yesterday," said the doctor. "There has been shock."

"You call it shock," said Mr Beluncle. "I call it God. I call it a miracle."

"I call it Nature really," said the doctor modestly.

"Just like that, suddenly, she saw the Truth," said Lady Roads, who came into the room now. "I've been treating her for years."

"I know," said the doctor. "I believe whatever I see. It has often happened. I expect in your religion you get a lot of cases."

"Often," said Mr Beluncle scornfully. "Not in medical science. And may I make a correction there if you will pardon me. If she had died you would call it Nature too!

I would like to say this is a purely normal happening. We are normal people." Mr Beluncle put his head in the air and walked up and down.

"Nothing could be more normal than Mr Beluncle," Lady Roads said slyly to the doctor.

"Normal! I am normality," said Mr Beluncle, with aggressive good humour. "Or to use a word I prefer, the word of that American President—what was his name?—never mind—normalcy."

"I wonder what his blood pressure is," the doctor said to himself.

Tears had been running down Mrs Johnson's cheeks again, they saw when she brought the tea in.

"My baby," she said. "He tried to kill her."

"Now, Mrs Johnson," said Lady Roads. "We ought to be filled with joy."

Mrs Johnson looked oddly across to the couch. There was a long tear at the side of the cover.

"Who tried to kill her?" asked the doctor.

"That beast, that dirty beast," Mrs Johnson cried out. "If I could get hold of him. Hanging is too good for a man like that."

She went to the door and the doctor got up and followed her.

"We must protect ourselves against evil," said Lady Roads, closing her eyes. "I must speak to the doctor. He isn't hostile. But Mrs Johnson is upset. It's very important for the movement not to speak of this yet. I think it would be a good thing to get your sister away from here, dear," she said to Mrs Truslove. "I will have her to stay with me. You can both come. I have seen it before. If God does something wonderful people can't stand it. They hate it. They tear you to pieces rather than admit the Truth; the devil gets into them."

Mrs Truslove did not answer but her heart cried:

"This is the beginning. They are taking her away. She belongs to me no more. I must not be selfish but what have I got now?" And she looked at Mr Beluncle with one of those incredulous regards of farewell which had come to her eyes unwished for on now numberless days. "Nothing."

And she could not restrain the cynical and ferocious thought: "If this had happened years before, if I had been alone in my house, I would have had him. She gives me my freedom now I am virtuous and do not want it."

"This," said Mr Beluncle, "is going to make a lot of difference to our lives. No one knows what Mrs Truslove has had to bear all these years; she has felt the strain. I have seen it. It isn't always easy."

"What has happened to me," Mrs Truslove asked herself, startled by his remark, "that I cannot be grateful for that? He has always been careful to read only half my thoughts."

He stayed there the evening, after the doctor had gone, and outstayed Lady Roads. Miss Dykes was at last asleep. Mrs Truslove came out of the room quietly and blinked at their radiant faces.

There was, she said, going to be trouble with Mrs Johnson. Mr Beluncle listened to her account of her sister's behaviour. They had had to let her try to walk a step or two and then listen to her accuse them of trying to stop her.

Mr Beluncle took her into the small narrow back garden and heard the evening radios bawling away, one overpowering machine drowning the others. There were instances of applause and laughter, like the roaring of packed-in animals.

"This," said Mr Beluncle, "has given me certainty. I know what to do. Now cheer up. It's wiped the floor with the doctor, you could see that."

Mrs Truslove's hand was on his arm. She was not drawn closer to him, she had never felt so far away, but she needed his support.

"I am worried about that poor wretch Vogg," she said. "I wonder if I ought to go and see him. If it's true what Mrs Johnson keeps saying, that he broke into the house and tried to get at Judy—what was he trying to do? To rape her, do you think?—we ought to see the police."

"Now calm yourself," said Mr Beluncle, shocked by the

word "rape". "We've heard what happened from Judy. It is a very wonderful thing. She sent for him, called him over, it was very brave of her, to speak to him about the meeting. It's a lesson to us all; expose the lie, as Lady Roads said, and the healing comes. Personally I feel humble, very humble," said Mr Beluncle, stopping in the middle of the grass plot and addressing the neighbouring gardens.

"Women like Mrs Johnson—they're like my wife, their imagination runs away with them."

"Why does Mrs Johnson *say* he broke in? I think Judy is going to die," said Mrs Truslove.

"Die!" exclaimed Mr Beluncle. "This is the beginning of life. Personally, I feel I am beginning life all over again. She's not going to die."

Mr Beluncle spoke with anger: "When we have seen with our own eyes a wonderful manifestation of Divine Love," he said loudly.

"But we didn't see anything with our own eyes," said Mrs Truslove.

"We have seen her walk," said Mr Beluncle, "that is what I am grateful for. I can tell you the world is not the same place for me, after this. I feel I have been changed. A wonderful thing has happened. In a way it is frightening. I could easily be frightened now. But I am not."

Mrs Truslove did not answer.

"I feel," said Mr Beluncle, modestly looking away, "I can see the future all around me."

"For me—well, you can see, it might destroy my life," she said.

"Destroy?" he said. "It can't. Destroy? I don't understand."

She had not meant to be threatening, but she could see that he took her words in that way. It was not a complete shock that he thought of what had happened only as something that would affect himself.

XXXV

There was one simple change Mr Beluncle had not reckoned with. There was confusion, happiness, apprehension at Hetley and he was out of it. Mrs Truslove stayed with her sister. Mr Beluncle drove there on the third morning on his way to the office. What he expected to see was a woman radiant and walking. What he saw was Miss Dykes sitting in an armchair with a stick beside her. She got up for half a minute, swayed on her legs, reached for her sister's arm, took a very small step and then sat down. Her eyes terrified Beluncle. They were larger than they had been, more brilliant, ecstatic and sunken. She looked gaunt and ten years older. When no one was watching she got up again and walked two steps to the mantelpiece and held it. There was a small annoyance: she was a little deaf. And Beluncle heard that she had been deaf when she was a young child.

Mr Beluncle drove on to his office. "Make way, make way," his car horn spoke out in the clogging traffic on the London road. "A miracle has occurred. It may be my turn next. It will be."

In the following days, when Mrs Truslove rang him up at his office, she sounded tangled in happiness and fear, in a private entanglement so close that when he spoke of business affairs her voice seemed to go off the line. To get her to listen to one or two practical things was like chasing a fly down that impersonal wire.

"I shan't come in this week. I don't know about next," she said. "I may go to the Roadses'."

Mr Beluncle could not hide his shock of displeasure. If anyone ought to be going for a rest, if anyone ought to be going to Lady Roads's house, it was himself. Yes, that is what he felt like—a thorough rest.

He missed Mrs Truslove. Despondently, resentfully, with misgiving, he sat alone at his desk, looked at her empty chair—and what did he feel? It was very odd, but he felt hungry.

It was as if he had been nibbling off her for years, and his first independent act in her absence was to have coffee and biscuits brought in earlier.

"I see you have brought only three biscuits," he said to the girl.

"I thought you being alone, sir," she said.

"Now, Mildred," he said, with a forgiving smile, "pull yourself together. Did I change the order?"

"I'm sorry, sir," said Mildred. She brought in three more biscuits.

Mr Beluncle felt better after eating his partner's biscuits.

It was unnerving to pass a morning in which he answered all the telephone calls, read the letters and the newspapers and had no one to bicker with. He had always felt that if there was any truth in her accusation that he was lazy and incompetent, it was because she prevented him from following his plans. He had only to go out of the room intending to speak to one of the clerks, for her to say, "If you are going to the warehouse you had better speak to So-and-So," or if he had planned a morning in the West End showroom, she would be certain to say something that would prevent him from going, as if she knew how to read his mind and automatically thwart it. Now she was away—and he realised with a shock that she had not been away more than two days in fifteen years—he was lost. He spent hours trying to think of what he ought to do, how she would contradict it and how he must do what he supposed she would want if she were there. He was screwed up to an extraordinary pitch of loyalty and duplicity.

But he came back to the important new fact: the miracle. Mr Beluncle was a believing man. He believed everything. He believed both versions of the miracle. He believed that Miss Dykes had heroically sent for Mr Vogg and had calmly been transfigured and healed by her courageous affirmations. He also believed that Vogg had attacked her and she had floored him by miraculously rising to her feet. He also believed that it did not matter what had happened: the interpretation was everything. This led him to the

conclusion that if he was expecting miracles in his own life—
and he was expecting them, rather peremptorily too—a
good deal of boldness and severity was necessary.

Mr Beluncle began his week by rebuking the people in
his office and his factory. By the end of the week, Mr Cook
was flustered to the point of being almost unable to hold
his pen, Miss Vanner was talking of giving her notice, Mr
Andrews was tensely whistling to himself, one of the workmen was sacked, the others were watchful and resentful,
Mr Chilly had been spoken to about not pulling his weight
and Henry found himself working hard for the first time in
his life. Mr Beluncle had turned down a Canadian order
because it was not large enough and had had several rude
telephone calls.

Certain crucial letters were put on Mrs Truslove's side of
the desk. They were all financial; one or two were urgent.
They represented future disputes with his partner. Mr
Beluncle evaded them. A successful evasion made him feel
as efficient as an unavoidable facing of facts did. He had been
able to evade the awkward fact of his sister's visit and when
he thought he ought to see her, or feared that she would call
again, he said, to his imaginary interlocutor:

"There has been a miracle. You understand we must
postpone our talk."

He was on good terms with his wife this week. He had
been able to say that, without wishing to be unkind, it was
a relief to be on one's own again; and Mrs Beluncle was
pleased about that. "She has interfered with you. She has
held you back," she said. She was also able to sympathise
with him in the amount of work he had to do. And even
when she changed her mind and perversely took the opposite
view: that Mrs Truslove had "a steadying hand", that she
hoped she would "come back before something went wrong",
this was a good point too. To hear his wife saying a good
word for Mrs Truslove was a relief, a pleasure.

It was always a question what to tell his wife. In the end
he always told her everything; occasionally that succeeded;
at other times, he regretted it. He had begun by telling her

that the cripple had had some attack, some crisis, and he had been on the point of telling her about the miracle itself, but he remembered Lady Roads's warning; and his wife, strangely determined to be pleasant about everything this week, made the warning unnecessary. Mrs Beluncle loved a good illness. The illness of the cripple, the fact of having to look after a crippled sister, had been Mrs Beluncle's one never broken bond of liking for the hated woman. It gave her a kind of respectability, almost a certificate of chastity in widowhood, admitted her to that hushed court of calamity in which Mrs Beluncle was a genteel lady-in-waiting. What calmed Mrs Beluncle was the notion that the cripple was getting worse and she could see that this must be a test of her husband's faith. She had no doubt in her mind that the Purification would be unable to do anything for the cripple; but her love for her husband, the strongest feeling in her life, made her hope that his faith would survive the test for his sake. Perhaps, if things went well, "that woman" Mrs Truslove would join the Purification: it would be happier if she did. Mrs Beluncle did not quite admire Mrs Truslove for sharing her own (Mrs Beluncle's) total rejection of her husband's religion. She would have preferred Mrs Truslove to be different from herself.

As the week went by, Mr Beluncle's efficiency had created a kind of hollow. He had decided so fast, rebuked so sternly, evaded so promptly, that he found time on his hands. From Hetley he picked up the latest news: Miss Dykes had continued to walk. Mrs Truslove, telling him not to come down, telephoned this news to him; her voice was worried, and became high-pitched with anxiety. She was having difficulties with Mrs Johnson. She had gone to see Mr Vogg and Vogg was out. There was a rumour that he had gone away. An ambulance had come for Mrs Vogg.

Mrs Truslove was keeping him off. He put down the receiver, injured and puzzled. The thought struck him that perhaps she would never come back.

Mr Beluncle felt suddenly cold and sick, but he quickly mastered that feeling. He repeated his phrase: "There has been a miracle." It occurred to him that he kept on saying this, but that he was not acting on it. How to act in the knowledge of the miraculous?

Quite clearly, as if a voice had spoken to him, Mr Beluncle heard the words:

"See the agents about *Marbella*. Make an offer."

XXXVI

When he left his office, and stepped into the street, a shower of gold seemed to him to fall upon his shoulders, his sleeves, his trousers. He took a taxi, on the south side of London Bridge—he took it on the north side when Mrs Truslove was at the office—and sat in the long expensive drive to the West End. He disliked driving his own car in the London traffic and one of Mrs Truslove's meannesses was that she would never let him have a chauffeur. He paid off the taxi at the top of Bond Street.

There began then one of Mr Beluncle's bouts of imaginary shopping and general expenditure. First of all he started valuing property, worked out the return of corner sites. In each shop window he calculated turnover. He bought and sold dozens of passing cars. He equipped himself with all kinds of luxurious stationery, trunks, suitcases, picnic baskets, pictures, shirts, ties. In the middle of this, he quite unexpectedly bought a lobster. This was a real purchase. He had the idea of taking the lobster back to his office and eating it there and, forgetting *Marbella* for a moment, he looked for a taxi to take him back.

There was no taxi, but he found that he was outside a silversmith's. Mr Beluncle had a special feeling for silver. He loved it, but not entirely for itself. When he gazed at a window filled with silver, his desire rose, but it was not for the silver itself; he had heard of families, in certain straits, "selling their silver", and of large sums being "got" for it. Just when they were bankrupt, penniless, finished, they suddenly "sold some of the silver", took a little out of the hoard and adroitly lived on the proceeds. In the past crises of his life, it would have made all the difference if Mrs Beluncle had had silver to sell. One may or may not be short of money, but Bond Street cried to heaven of the indispensable affirmations of property. He had once sold his wife's rings in his young days. Suppose she had *not* had rings! "Buy silver"—it was an imperative.

Mr Beluncle went into the shop and after the first shock of hearing the prices, they began to bemuse him.

Ten pounds was his price; but in a short time fifty, seventy, a hundred and fifty, three hundred and twenty-five murmured the poetry of numbers into his glowing ears. In a pause he saw himself in one of the shop mirrors: it was like seeing someone bidding against him in an auction. He returned to his dabbling on the counter with new zest. He heard himself estimating, as he walked out of the shop, with a small silver tray, as he looked back at a much larger and presumptuously tarnished one in a case by the window, that he must have saved two hundred pounds.

And now, with his tray Mr Beluncle was floating. He had drunk the champagne of expense. To see him walking down the street now, was to see a nabob, exalted, sublimely contemptuous in the face. What some men find in a woman's winding arms he had in this glorious expense. He got into a taxi, went to Victoria, took a first-class ticket and in an hour had hired a car from the country station to the house. There was a small shock for him in the train. He had got his tray but where was the lobster? It was gone. He had lost it, left it somewhere.

There stood *Marbella*, the florid, the dissolute villa, the clubman, the company director. The sky was heavy and grey at Sissing and the house, overcrowded by its trees and creepers, was sunk in a postprandial nap which brought out the obduracy of its character; its plain view that it was uninterested in anyone who had not got the money.

"The last man who lived in you," Mr Beluncle argued back, "thought he was on top of the world. A year after he moved in his wife died. And she found he had embezzled twenty thousand pounds. She is out of her mind."

The house grunted.

"That's nothing to do with me. Have you got the cash?"

Mr. Beluncle said sharply:

"Surtees had it before. The biggest man in eggs. I knew Surtees when he was nothing. I sold him his first desk and I had a job getting the money. Two wives divorced him. Do you call that happiness? And his son killed in a motor accident. His favourite son."

The house said: "You're trying to beat me down."

"Look at your filthy condition. It is deplorable."

Mr Beluncle was at the back poking at some creeper in the kitchen gutter.

"Leave me alone," said the house.

A yard of rusted gutter suddenly fell off and struck Mr Beluncle on the arm. He jumped back with the pain.

"Confound," said Mr Beluncle. "A suit just back from the cleaners."

His arm went hard with the pain which he had small capacity to endure. He brushed his coat and pulling back his sleeve he saw a blue ridge on his skin where he had been struck.

Mr Beluncle looked round to see whom he could rage at. There was no one. His conversation could not go on after this insult. He walked to the estate agents' and burst out, "That place is falling to pieces. It is a positive danger. I nearly lost my life. Another inch and someone would have had an action for damages. It's your business, as the agents of the vendor . . ."

Yet, that perhaps was the crisis? The miracle was on its way.

At five o'clock he took a slow train back to Hetley to see Mrs Truslove. He did not say a word to her about the house or his journey. But it struck him, when he saw Mrs Truslove holding her sister on the edge of the lawn and in conversation with neighbours on the other side of the fence, that there was something very stupid about them all. If he were to take his clothes off, they would see printed in huge letters all over his body the words he had said to the estate agents an hour before.

"I will put the offer in writing tonight."

His mystery made him feel modest.

XXXVII

The day was ending. Desire gratified had brought with it a mood of austere and absent lassitude, a benign serenity of mind. Mr Beluncle had been in too many trains and he was tired. He got out of the train at Boystone, wondering what on earth had made him leave his car in London, thinking with self-pity of the uphill walk home under the evening birdsong of the avenues, past houses filled with armchairs where less-disturbed men than he was had long been sitting with their pleasant wives. His behaviour about his car had been as impulsive as his marriage.

"What a man goes home to, he never knows, my father used to say."

"D'evening, Beluncle."

Mr Beluncle felt something like a large, rank, dusty friendly dog pushing against him on the platform, changing step to walk with him. He looked up. The stationmaster, the really superfluous man of Mr Beluncle's life: Mr Phibbs. A gingery, low-class man, like an Airedale.

Mr Phibbs grinned ironically.

"Wonderful news," said Mr Phibbs in his "mere" voice, looking at the last coach of the train go out in a blue electric flash over Boystone bridge.

"I don't get you," said Mr Beluncle, plainly indicating that it was a matter of principle for him not to "get" Mr Phibbs.

"The world is a wonderful place," he added.

"Cherss," said Mr Phibbs. "And people don't realise it."

I

Mr Phibbs did not drop Mr Beluncle at the ticket barrier. He walked through the gate with him into the echoing subway up which tired people were climbing.

"I'm referring," said Mr Phibbs, in his indiscreet voice, "to Miss Dykes." And Mr Phibbs, it seemed to Mr Beluncle, was announcing this through a megaphone.

That, at any rate, was his effect. Bumping Mr Beluncle's shoulder in a brotherly way, as he stuck his long legs forward, Mr Phibbs pointed out that it was just what the Church needed, and that in his job he had remarkable opportunities of putting in a word for the Truth to some of the passengers. He'd told quite a few.

How the devil had Phibbs heard?

Mr Beluncle was deeply annoyed. Mr Phibbs began to explain the miracle, pointing out that it was natural when Mr Beluncle said it was wonderful; and when Mr Beluncle agreed it was natural, stopping him on the station slope and asking him:

"Cherss, but what do we mean by Nature?"

Mr Beluncle hurried on, but the long figure of Mr Phibbs moved closer to him. He would walk part of the way. He was going off duty.

"It's unwise to talk about it," said Mr Beluncle. "Lady Roads was very clear about that. We must not let our good be evil spoken of."

Mr Phibbs was delighted to hear this. Always, in his idleness, searching for new chances of heresy, Mr Phibbs said in the presence of one of his porters as they went outside:

"Cherss. Miss Wix was saying we must remember all healings are not of God. How do we know God healed Miss Dykes? Eh?" And he picked an ear.

Mr Beluncle stopped. He gave his umbrella a gentle tap as he looked from Mr Phibbs's stained navy-blue waistcoat to his face.

"I shouldn't," he smiled with condescension, "pay much attention to the thought of Miss Wix. It is not usually helpful."

"A reasonable man like you, Beluncle," said Mr Phibbs,

with a genial familiarity that enraged Mr Beluncle. "No reasonable man can help seeing through Lady Roads."

"I am not aware," said Mr Beluncle, "that anything *sees*, except the Divine Mind."

And he shook Mr Phibbs off with these words.

The fool! The second-rate imbecile! Mr Beluncle roared up the streets to his house. Why do they have such a man in the Church? What a man! What a family! Followers of Miss Wix. My God, Mr Beluncle reflected, wherever Truth is how subtle the perversion. We cannot be too severe, too strict, too careful if we wish to enter the Kingdom. A boy, like my son, Henry, carried away by people like the Phibbses! No wonder, thought Mr Beluncle in violent alarm, we don't get miracles in our home. My God, it was Henry who told that Phibbs girl. Henry must have heard me talking on the phone.

It was worse than that: he had been on the edge of the miracle; no, he had been floating in the vision of it all day; and Phibbs had put him in a temper and had taken it from him at the last moment. It had gone.

He was a little calmer when the garden of his house came distantly in sight. The miracle reappeared for a moment, like a mirage. Perhaps . . . But Mr Beluncle checked himself with horror at the peculiar thoughts that could come into the minds of right-thinking men and he hastily said:

"I hope nothing has happened to mother, today."

XXXVIII

The two boys, George and Henry, put their bicycles away in the shed and walked under the trees towards the back door of the house. George was saying that up at Pop's there was an abominable laddie called Penrose with a motor-bicycle who slept with the tart called Valery; Pop had been in prison and Fred had pointed out a car thief and the boys of the North Road gang. As he spoke George could smell the sour

smell of old tea leaves and melting margarine that hung
about Pop's café, and he glowed with importance and
pleasure in the low company. All these men seemed great
men to George; not as great as his father, but when his
father ignored his love he turned to them. "I am in the
middle of the family," he thought, "I am going to be the
bad son; perhaps that will attract their attention."

Valery had come and sat on his knee to annoy one of the
lorry drivers. George was delighted by this experience.

"You're lucky," said Leslie to his brothers in the kitchen.
"He is not home yet. You just scraped in in time."

Leslie laughed at their relief.

A small compressed dark storm cloud travelled fast up the
main road towards the house. An hour later than his usual
time Mr Beluncle was coming home.

"Here he comes," said George, standing behind a laurel
bush at the corner of the garden. Mr Beluncle's face was
serious, pale and his eyes were lowered most of the time as
he came along. The boy ran back to warn his mother, who
looked slyly at her family and put on a sullen expression.

"There is going to be a row," said Henry.

Mrs Beluncle went to meet her husband.

"Oh, I've been so worried. I thought there had been an
accident," she said.

"Your father is calling to you," said Mrs Beluncle, going
to her sons. They read in her face that they were wrong. She
was not going to quarrel this evening.

The three boys waited and then George was pushed forward because he had most of the love.

"My shoes, old boy," said Mr Beluncle in a kind, tired
absent voice from his chair in the front room. Mr Beluncle
raised one leg and George knelt smiling with pleasure to
undo his father's shoes.

The grandmother stood beside her son's chair, thickly
smiling.

"Half past eight," she said. "What a time to get back. I
never 'eard of such an hour. It's only ten minutes ago they've
come in with those bicycles, both of them. Running round

with all the street urchins and the bad company in the public-houses."

The grandmother smiled with delight.

"When you was a young man," she said to Mr Beluncle, "you came in at seven and your poor father had to get the whip to you. Eh, poor man, it hurt me to see him so put out. No supper you had. Sent you to bed with a good whipping from his belt," said the grandmother sentimentally, looking with love at her son. "It's what made a man of you. Your poor father's arm ached."

"Yes," said Mr Beluncle. "I remember I was Henry's age. It is what people used to do in those days. It was very wrong."

"Aye," said old Mrs Beluncle, "it's what made a man of you. At your age a great boy like you was ought to have known better. The whippings he gave Constance too and she never writes. I'd never bring up children the way Ethel does, she knows no better, it is how she was brought up. On the streets, I've no doubt, like miners' little children."

Old Mrs Beluncle closed her eyes. She could see the long street of her village with the geese on the green; and she could hear her mother saying, "Close the gate, close the doors, the miners are coming to drink and fight and starve their children. Keep decent people indoors."

"Loosen, loosen the laces properly, I've often told you," said Mr Beluncle to George, while his mother went on.

"Pull it right through. Not like that.

"Don't be stupid," pleaded Mr Beluncle.

"Aye," said the grandmother. "That George was always the backward one, I ne'er took to him, I ne'er took to him when he was a baby. Lazy, sinful hands he's got and I ne'er liked a sulky face."

"Pull," said Mr Beluncle sadly. "I didn't say pull my foot off. By the heel. If I've told you once I've told you a thousand times."

Ethel came into the room with a plate for the table.

"Ease the sock for me, old girl," pleaded Mr Beluncle.

"Aye," wailed the grandmother agreeably, "I lay many

a pair of stockings he's pulled off elsewhere. Aye, elsewhere," she said.

"Where's Henry?" pleaded Mr Beluncle, out of his deep sadness.

"In," said Ethel.

"How long?" said Mr Beluncle.

"You speak to him. I don't know. I don't watch my children. I don't whip them. I don't spy. I don't ask questions," said Ethel.

She coloured with that obstinacy of hers which told him what was true or what was untrue this evening would depend, for her, on moods not yet formed.

"I've had," she said, nodding to the grandmother, "a bad day with her."

The grandmother did not hear this but knew she was being talked about.

"Homework in the kitchen. Dad!" said George. "A man called Penrose offered me a job."

"You've what?"

"Fred sort of took me to a man. I've got to see him nine o'clock tomorrow."

"What man? What job?"

"Penrose," said George eagerly. "I don't know what it is."

"You're offered a job; you don't know what it is. Who asked Fred to do this? I didn't ask Fred to get you a job. What were you doing over at Hetley?"

"Seeing Fred," said George. "I asked him."

"*You* did," exclaimed Mr Beluncle, with jealousy. "Oh! Your own father isn't good enough for you, you have to go to Fred. What do you think Fred will think of me? Fred will say, 'Why doesn't his father get a job for him. There must be something wrong with this boy.' Some boys would be glad to ask their father first. I would have thought that I knew more about the business world than Fred."

"You haven't done anything," said George.

"Ten months this boy has been hanging round the house waiting for you," said Ethel, laying the table.

"As if I had nothing else to do but what this boy ought

to do for himself. I did at his age. I didn't hang crying round my father," he said.

"He whipped you out of the place—if that story is true," said Ethel.

"I often wish I'd listened to my father," said Mr Beluncle. "You go to this Mr Penrose, my boy. Go and see him, do. You think he's superior to your father, you think he can do better for you than your father, you think he loves you more, thinks more of you and your future—you go. Do."

Mr Beluncle closed his eyes and lay back in his chair. He had seen a miracle, an actual miracle, the work of God; and he came back to things like this.

He took a long, deep breath. An extraordinary passion rose and fell and wrestled in him. He had the sensation that George was a part of his body, a part that was being ripped away, leaving a terrible red and unjust wound; he felt that his heart was being torn out; he saw, with terror, the bad things that could happen to his son. But above all, he felt that he was stretched out on a rock in the middle of middle age, and that his mother, his wife, his children and the other woman, Mrs Truslove, and her sister, were taking pieces of flesh off him, picking him to the bone. And it was that cripple, of all people, and not himself, who had experienced the miracle. He opened his eyes and considered the room where the table was now laid and Leslie, the youngest, came in. He went over to the armchair, opposite to Mr Beluncle, sat down and put up his foot.

"Eth," Leslie said. "George! I'm tired. I've had a heavy day. Take my boots off. Loosen the laces. No, don't pull like that, you'll have my foot off. . . ."

Mr Beluncle gazed and listened with amazement.

"Here have I been doing my homework and you sit there. Grandma's dying of hunger. She's only eaten a cow today."

Mr Beluncle's body suddenly heaved with laughter. He got up with a roar of laughter and hysterical tears came to his cheeks. He saw the boy nimbly slip out of the chair to the far end of the table, which he accidentally kicked.

"Another pound off when we sell," Leslie said.

A wonderful optimism and good nature suddenly rose in the Beluncles.

"Tell us the love story in *The Windsor*," said Leslie, sitting next to his grandmother at the table. "They put me next to you to keep you quiet. Does," he now shouted in the old lady's ear, "does she wait for Sir John to come back from the Crimean War or does she marry the gamekeeper?"

The old lady sighed.

"Eh, she was true to him," she sighed. And was about to go on, but Leslie stopped her.

"Not like some, no doubt?" enquired Leslie, looking at each member of the family.

"She didn't have a baby?" said Leslie.

"A beautiful bracelet he gave her," said the old lady, mishearing.

"See?" said Leslie to his family. "Traps the man by getting in the family way and he steals his mother's jewellery."

George and Henry lowered their eyes. Mr Beluncle took his table napkin out of his collar, and went scarlet, then violet in the attempt to choke back his laughter, which however spread from chin to chin and then to his swelling neck. Only Mrs Beluncle did not laugh.

"Not in front of me, Leslie," she said prudishly, "with that talk."

"No," said Mr Beluncle, collecting himself, "not in front of your mother."

Leslie lowered his eyes.

"Somebody ought to tell grandma how life began. She'll only pick it up from me," Leslie murmured.

"Enough of that," said Mr Beluncle, suddenly at last quietening his family. Mr Beluncle sat forward in his chair with his legs apart, put four pieces of sugar in his coffee and stirred it. His shrewd and restless eyes inspected the ceiling of this room.

"This place, Ethel," he said, nodding at the ceiling and the walls and lifting the cup to his heavy lips as he did so, "this place will fetch its price. I should say"—he screwed up one eye—"it will fetch two thousand pounds."

"Oh," groaned Mrs Beluncle.

"Two thousand—even two thousand two hundred," said Mr Beluncle kindly.

"Five," said Leslie.

"Seven-fifty," said Henry.

"Why don't we sell, then?" said Mrs Beluncle.

"Don't be silly," said Mr Beluncle, putting his cup down with annoyance. "The house doesn't belong to us. I was thinking of what the landlord would get for it."

"Oh, what does that matter?" said Mrs Beluncle gaily. "Sell all the same. We could sell this sideboard; sell this carpet, I'm sick of it. The fire-irons."

Excited, she stood up:

"Sell my dress," she cried. "Look at these shoes." She kicked them off. "Fifteen shillings. They pinch. I'll be glad to get rid of them."

Mrs Beluncle sat down again and rocked with laughter and spread her fingers over her face.

"All those suits," she cried.

"And the piano," she said.

"Sell me," muttered Henry morbidly.

"Pay me back the ten shillings you borrowed from me that Christmas when I was twelve. You said you would," said George dreamily, for this was an incident in his life to which he often returned. His father and he would travel back on the road of his love to that meeting-place where they would be united and a wrong put right.

"Sell grandma," said Leslie.

"Leslie!" warned Mr Beluncle.

"Not that you would get much," Leslie said. "She's mortgaged."

They turned nervously to look at the grandmother. On a sofa which had belonged to her house she sat with her magazine in her lap, stretched like a little girl, asleep.

The laughter that had started suddenly stopped. They all studied Leslie with the incredulity of those who hear the truth spoken.

"You go too far," said Mr Beluncle. "It's time you were in bed."

"Yes, it is," said Mrs Beluncle.

"While it's still there, yes, I will," said Leslie, getting up. "Good night, dad. Good night, mum. Good night," he said to the grandmother.

When he had gone Ethel Beluncle said gravely:

"It is wicked how we carry on. God will punish us."

XXXIX

When her magazine fell to the floor, the grandmother woke up and Ethel took her up to her bed. Very quickly the old lady walked and up the stairs scampered with the precise energy of old age.

Before Mrs Beluncle left, she made signals with her eyes to her husband. She indicated Henry.

"George," she said, "it is time for you too."

The boys noticed her unconvincing voice and glanced at each other for help. They both got up for common protection and went to the door.

"Just one moment, Henry," said Mr Beluncle.

The two youths looked with amused, anxious and different love into each other's eyes. George dawdled at the door, longing for the privilege that was to be his brother's: the privilege of being alone in the room with his father and hear his father rage. To George it seemed a misfortune that his brother, who would wilfully and bitterly misunderstand what was going to be said to him shortly, should have a "blowing up" wasted on him; how deeply George envied Henry the trouble he was shortly going to experience.

"Treachery," George murmured sympathetically to Henry at the door, using a word Henry often used, and speaking it only for this reason; for George wished to experience treachery too. Reluctantly, he shut the door on the scene and went upstairs to his bedroom.

Mr Beluncle stood humbly in the wonder of his own life. He leaned to smell the roses in the bowl on the table.

"I want to talk to you," said Mr Beluncle, resting his arms on the table.

Henry sat down at the other end of the table. He quickly decided upon what objects in the room to look, while his father talked. The hands of the clock showed the curls of his father's grey hair, a coloured drawing of two comic red-nosed Scotsmen with whisky bottles was to the right of his shoulders. To the left was a small beaten-bronze letter-rack which had been put to one side of the mantelpiece because, as Mr Beluncle said in a kind of terror, "That space is empty." If he could concentrate on these, looking at every inch of them, Henry thought he might be able to save himself from the so easily overwhelming gravity of his father's voice that would go to his bowels and unman him.

Mr Beluncle joined his white hands and said:

"I wish to talk to you and I don't want you to get the idea that what I am going to say is unkind, because it isn't meant unkindly. . . ."

"No," said Henry's small hard voice. He was staring at the clock hands.

"I only think of your good because you're my son and it's natural for a father to think of the good of his children; it's no good saying he doesn't know better, he does. You may think you know a lot, but you haven't the experience, that's the point. An ounce of experience is worth a pound of theory. A man came to me today and wanted my opinion. I told him, 'You can have it, but I don't give my experience away and it will cost you ten pounds,' so you see I'm not talking through my hat, I'm *giving* you what many people would have to pay for. . . ."

Mr Beluncle had not intended to digress on to this last point, but once his tongue got going he couldn't resist an anecdote and had in fact travelled back to some time in his own youth when in the Commercial Room of the North-Eastern, Leeds, he heard some old traveller say it; and in re-telling it, Mr Beluncle was not so much making a shrewd hard point as showing his life to his son.

"Did he pay it?" said Henry, hoping to deflect the discussion, for he was still safe. His eyes had followed every detail of the carving on the top of the clock and had now moved to the letter-rack.

"I was just illustrating my point," said Mr Beluncle. "And don't try to take me up."

"No, father," said Henry steadily, for he had gained a point. It was far easier for him to withstand the sarcasm or angers of his father than his affection.

"I've noticed that about you. You try and take me up," said Mr Beluncle. "You try to be clever, but let me tell you this, I wish I'd taken my father's advice. Not a day of my life passes, but I wish to heaven I'd followed what he said, not that we depend on others, you've got to live your own life, if you make a mess of it that's your affair, it's no good coming to me and saying, 'Father, I wish I had done as you said.' It will be too late."

Mr Beluncle won back his lost point there. It was by the use of the word "father" and putting the words into his son's mouth.

The red-nosed Scotsmen in their comic picture, and the Scottie in his tartan ribbon beside it, gleamed. What (they seemed to ask) have you got against us? And they reproached Henry as a creature alien to the normal currents of sale-ability: something out of nature, an unnatural son, a jealous brother, a coward in love. They could see he was weakening. Henry's uneasy eyes looked at his father's face.

This was Henry's last defence: to study his father's face. To see the slightly sunburned forehead and the rind-like cheeks, as some kind of cratered moon; to think of all the train journeys it had done, the cigars it had smoked, the telephone calls it had taken, the goods it had sold, the rows it had had with customers, the laughs it had given in hired cars, the amount of industrial smoke the nostrils had breathed, the commercial anecdotes the ears had heard, the food the mouth had eaten, the hymns it had sung. The face became larger, the face of a city, smelling of trains, theatres, chapels and smoke rooms, warehouses and urinals; and it was as if, flying in an aeroplane over London or Birmingham, or some huge city, he looked down and the city was his father's face.

"You are still seeing that girl, aren't you?" said Mr Beluncle, in that sudden manner which startled and confused his customers. Henry's fantasy was unavailing and it vanished. But he had been prepared.

"What girl?" he said, but not defiantly. He simply wished his father to say the name of Mary Phibbs, for if he spoke the name then surely the love he felt would come unawares to his father's lips.

"Mary Phibbs," said his father, sharply. "You know what girl I mean." And to Henry's horror, when his father spoke the name, the opposite thing had happened; she was half destroyed, reduced to nothing or to the ordinary run of female creatures.

"You are seeing her?" repeated his father, following his advantage.

"Yes," said Henry, from his store of coolness.

"After I asked you not to. After you promised."

"I didn't promise. You said, I . . ." Henry's voice trembled. He was in danger. He had been about to have the folly of saying, "One is obliged to agree with you. A promise forced is not a promise freely given." But then he would have to admit his physical fear. Mr Beluncle swept on, bringing his hand to the table, preparing to hit the table if he were provoked enough, and as it lay there the hand, easily, softly clenched.

"You deceived me. That is to say, you think you deceive me. But you don't. I know what people are doing. You think I go round the factory and don't know what people are doing?"

"No," murmured Henry. And he could hear the voice of Mary Phibbs fading as it said, "This is where you must stand up to him. If you love me as you say." Mr Beluncle saw the weakness of his son's position and the strength of his own and spoke lightly, but on this subject he could not conceal a personal disgust.

"You think you are in love," Mr Beluncle said.

"You have been in love?" said Henry.

"Of course I have. Dozens of times," laughed Mr Beluncle, but he remembered to check his laugh, "before I met your mother.

"It doesn't matter what I've been," said Mr Beluncle. "I don't want you to see that girl any more. It's against my wish and you will see one day that I am right."

"Why?" said Henry, but his voice was giving. He had lost the power to say more than one word.

"Why?" asked Mr Beluncle, greatly astonished at being questioned.

But, good God, my boy, don't you know there has been a miracle, he wanted to say. We were never like other people, but now we are quite extraordinary. Anything may happen. All the things we want, we can now have. This is your chance: to want only the most advantageous things.

"Yes," said Henry, falsely encouraged. "What harm . . .?" But, suddenly, as always happened, he was lost. His trembling voice crumbled on the words. The tears, long held back, now sprang from his eyes, and before he could raise his hand, they were rolling in huge drops down his ashamed and angry cheeks, running into his mouth, while sobs, like creatures that had suddenly rushed into him and taken possession of his body, broke out and shook him with their grotesque antics. His struggles only finished the wreck of his stand. He was helpless, ugly, gulping, choking, trembling, incapable of speech and he saw Mary far away, left, lost, forgotten, betrayed.

Mr Beluncle took his arms from the table and, sitting back, let his hands lie in his lap. He had glanced at his watch as he moved them. He had won. He was satisfied. He regarded the face of his son with pity. He had had enough to do, in his time, with his wife's tears, with Mrs Truslove's tears. "Here I am trying to save him from marriage," he said to himself. "I try to save him and he cries."

"I want you to get on. I want you to have an important position. I want you to get a better position than me," said Mr Beluncle, suddenly pitying himself. "And one day you'll find the right girl, not this girl, some other, the right one. We may move into a bigger house, a better one, larger perhaps, perhaps *Marbella*, or in the country. I saw one advertised today. It had kennels, and if we do that one day, if we can get a place further out—for I do want to be further out, you can't breathe in this place—I hope you'll find a girl. Some nice girl, who'd be friends with me too, whose arm I could take, and who would talk with me, who'd appreciate me and I could say, 'Jolly nice. Jolly good. This is Henry's wife. Jolly good.' That's the sort of girl I want—I want you to have, I don't say with money, don't misunderstand me, money isn't everything. In fact, money is nothing, nothing at all. We want ideas not money; I don't mean," Mr Beluncle dreamed, "if there was money I would say No—I wouldn't; it's a bond. You don't love a person less because they have money, you can say it adds to the love. You might be glad to have a wife who could put money into my business."

And at this Mr Beluncle raised his right hand and tapped fast with its spread fingers on the table.

Henry tried several times to speak. His sobs had stopped and now he was cold, angry and hard in defeat. His mouth was dry and burning, rage drying him up, and his head had a band of pain across his forehead.

Mr Beluncle went on:

"You are young. You are my son, my child," he said. "And that is how I wish you to be. I do not want you to think you are growing up. I do not want," he said with sudden emphasis, going, indeed, pale in the skin when he said this, "you to think of yourself as a man; there are youths you see everywhere at the street corners who think they are grown up and are very knowing, perhaps they do know things which you don't know, I don't want you to know them. In a sense it makes me feel old and I am not old, and I don't feel old."

Struck by his contradiction Mr Beluncle said:

"I don't feel old. I feel young," and he looked accusingly at his son. "But when I'm old, though you know as well as

I do," he said with anger, "that there is no such thing as old age—what is time? Has anyone seen it? Can you see time? Of course you can't. When that comes, I may want you to carry on the business."

Without reflecting, without fearing or considering, Henry said:

"I don't want to stay in the business."

But after he said it, his heart began to beat heavily and fast.

"What?" said Mr Beluncle, waking up from his dream.

"I don't want to stay in the business. I want to go abroad. I want to learn foreign languages. I . . ."

It was Mr Beluncle's turn to be shaken by emotion. He became as pale as his son had been when their talk began and, for a reason he could not understand, he could feel tears rising in his breast, for that is how they seemed to come; from his whole body. But Mr Beluncle easily mastered his emotion; and, just as his son's voice had become cold and hard, so his own became hard too.

"Pardon me," said Mr Beluncle coldly. "Pardon me. I think there has been a misunderstanding. It was my impression that you invited yourself into the firm and not that the firm invited you. You don't imagine that we wanted you there: I know many that would go down on their bended knees to work with me. Mr Chilly cried. He cried in my office."

"Oh, I'm not the only one," Henry laughed wryly.

"I do not mean," said Mr Beluncle, "when I say he cried, that he actually cried. A considerable sum was involved. That's the point. And remember this: we don't want you, the business doesn't want you. You are not so important that it can't go on without you. Conceit is your trouble, but beware. God doesn't want us, we want Him. Go, go—and don't mind me. But I can't imagine what Mrs Truslove will say. It is hardly polite to her."

Ethel Beluncle's voice was heard calling from the top of the stairs.

"Come on, you two," she said, in an artificial and playful voice. "What are you talking about?"

Mr Beluncle stopped. He was glad to escape from his son.

He wished to be in the room alone with him no longer. He saw to his astonishment that the boy had grown up; the love affair was nothing, but this new claim to go away, to be different, to have some entirely different interest in life, was serious. Mr Beluncle for the first time saw in his son a will.

He gaped with total incomprehension at the frail, tired-eyed, pasty and pretty-lipped boy who rejected him and who —for it amounted to that—told him that his life work had no interest for him whatever.

XL

Mrs Beluncle was standing on the landing waiting for them, with her shoes off and her skirt undone and her hair down. She gave her son a sharp but airy look as he came up and coldly kissed her.

"Whatever is the matter with you?" she said ironically.

"Nothing," he said, and went to his room.

In his own room, Mr Beluncle stood in his shirt sleeves while his wife undressed. She stepped out of her clothes and left them in circles all over the floor. She enjoyed, he suspected, making his room untidy and she liked to sit naked and pleased with her smallness in it, in order to annoy him. This bedroom of his own, like his office, was a way of getting away from her. He stood defeated in his shirt sleeves.

"I thought," he said, "—it was a dream—my son would be glad to work with me. Proud even. But no!"

And raising his chin to the mirror, he took a brush and angrily brushed his wounded head. And then he put on various lotions with which he treated his thick hair, for undressing was as long a process with Mr Beluncle as dressing was, a careful criticism of the clothes he had favoured on that day. A button, a collar, a sock, might have been unworthy.

"Why did you go on at him the way you did about that girl?" said Mrs Beluncle. "You were young once. You were always after girls, that girl in the cash at Beedles now. . . ."

"I wasn't," said Mr Beluncle truthfully. "I had other things to think of."

"You were unnatural," said Mrs Beluncle. For it had been her despair in her young days with him she had had no one to be jealous of except his mother, and jealousy was everything to her. "It would have been better if you had. Why didn't you let him alone? What did you want to talk to him like that for?"

"But," said Mr Beluncle, with surprise, "it was you who told me to, this evening. You said, 'He's still seeing that girl, you ought to speak to him.' . . ."

"A woman," said Mrs Beluncle, with spirit, "doesn't like to see a girl after her son."

"I wish you wouldn't drop hairpins all over the carpet, old girl," said Mr Beluncle. "They might get into my feet. And do put a little something on," he said. "It's not nice, you'll catch cold. . . ."

"You are a hard man, you were brought up unnaturally—look at the way you've treated Mrs Truslove," she said, for seeing her husband defeated she could not resist taking the side of the conqueror.

"But you *said*," protested Mr Beluncle, who was baffled by the changes in his wife's mind, "you said . . ."

"Oh, I say," said Mrs Beluncle. "And I think too. But I don't go about breaking people's hearts."

She began crawling on her bare knees picking up the hairpins.

"You only go for him because you've got something on your conscience," she said. "The way you accuse others, it's as plain as a pikestaff what you've been up to."

But as she said this Mrs Beluncle narrowed her eyes and fiercely resolved to speak severely to her son for attacking and upsetting his father as he had done. His father was not like other men (she was going to tell Henry) and that was just as well. He thought he was God; look at the men who don't think they are God, what a lot they are—who would touch them? They are nothing. They have got only themselves.

XLI

Henry lay awake most of the night. Anger and grief came down upon him out of the darkness of the room as, a hundred times, he went over the scene with his father. He seemed to have been brought to a precipice in the night; in the morning he would be over the edge of it. For he could see Mary no more. He loathed his own cowardice, his failure to speak, the betrayal of his nature and his will. And yet as the impossibility of seeing Mary any more became clearer, so there grew a determination to see her, to descend into deeper places of secrecy. He yielded, yet he would never really yield. He lay in the first destroying rage of his life. The next day, pale, unspeaking, sick, burned up and ill, he went giddily to his father's factory. His head throbbed, the muscles of his face were stiff with hatred of the world, which seemed to go on around him, distantly and mechanically, as if he were deaf and a wall of glass stood between him and every other person. The traffic in the street, the machines in the factory, seemed soundless. As for his father and himself— they passed each other without speaking much. He read scorn in Mr Beluncle's insulting expression. But that common look of Mr Beluncle covered the intensity of his concern for the miracle and a sternly hushed determination not to mention it. After a couple of hours at his factory Mr Beluncle went down to Hetley to see Mrs Truslove again.

XLII

"You must be quiet," Mrs Truslove said to her sister. "You must rest."

"I have been resting all my life," said Miss Dykes. "I must walk. I must go out. Soon I shall run. That is what I'm longing to do. I want to open the door and run all the way to the grocer's. People will see me running. Are you afraid of people seeing me? I believe you are. You wish I was still a cripple."

"No," said Mrs Truslove. "I don't. Don't be childish. How could I wish that?"

"It is you who are ill. You ought to rest," said Miss Dykes, with a counter-attack of new authority.

When Mr Beluncle came she said to him harshly:

"I shall dance. I shall dance with you."

Mr Beluncle shuddered. Miss Dykes shuddered too.

Lady Roads came and tenderly sat with her arm on Miss Dykes's shoulder.

"When can I testify?" Miss Dykes said. "When can I go to church and give thanks? My heart is longing to pour out the gratitude I feel. When can I go? This week?"

"I should wait," said Lady Roads.

"I'm impatient," said Miss Dykes. "I know I am."

"We will let you go soon," said Lady Roads.

She looked sadly at Miss Dykes. They were all, in their hearts, afraid of her.

She will turn on me, Lady Roads was thinking. It was always happening: the people she helped always turned on her and denounced her. The more the goodness of God was manifest the greater evil seemed to grow. Lady Roads sighed: the miracle would be one more trial of her faith.

"It is fatal," a voice inside her said, "to succeed." And again:

"I have given birth to a monster. I have done evil."

Lady Roads had never doubted her religion, but now, half the day, she found herself denying it.

"I have cast out the devil from this woman and it has entered into my soul." This was one feeling and she clung to it; for there was another far more horrifying:

"I have put a devil, the devil of life, into this woman."

She had not "played straight" about the miracle; for having begged everyone to keep silence about it as much as possible, in Miss Dyke's interest, Lady Roads had gone off and talked about it herself recklessly. Now, she reflected, she was punished: though words of love eloquently came out of

254

her, instinctively she felt a physical disgust before the woman. It was a disgust that had come to life in the early days of her marriage, a horror that the flesh—the flesh of all things—should be made whole.

XLIII

Miss Dykes could stand and she could walk a little way slowly with help from her sister's or Mrs Johnson's arm. Her thin back was curved and her head leaned forward and her eyes peered at a place two yards ahead of her, as she stepped. She made a continuous small progress. The act of walking made her tremble and she exhausted herself by talking about it all the time; as she heard very poorly in one ear and did not catch quickly what people said, her walks seemed to others like a precarious stepping over words. The archness of Miss Dykes's voice had given place to hoarseness and stridency; her mouth seemed to have lengthened or she drew back her lips with more strain than she used to show when she was ill. Absorbed in her chrysalis change like some ingenious moth, she had forgotten her interest in her clothes and she had been obliged to put aside her elegant shoes for a pair of boots that would hold her weak ankles.

In her crippled state Miss Dykes had had the firm and settled look of the invalid, had sat in her chair as if it were a little throne or a small royal carriage, boldly announcing that the misfortune did not affect her, impatient of sympathy, sensitive to those who were repelled. She had always been able to detect these people and would get Mrs Johnson to wheel her to them at once. Then, her conversation had been aggressive and she had used her war language. She had felt herself to be at an advantage and had prided herself on observing people more closely than they observed her. In general, she had had respect and, among young people, sympathy and fear. A girl like Mary Phibbs loved her. Miss Dykes's strongest feelings were for women.

Towards men Miss Dykes had been false and hostile. Her eyes mocked, her voice hardened; she sought the male vanity, to injure it. She tried to punish them for being unable to see in her a sexual object. She had been quick to notice the attraction of men to other women.

But, above all, in her chair, Miss Dykes had been secure. Now her security had gone and some of its health too. Her yellowish skin had reddened at the cheekbones and brought out a number of small feverish marks or irregularities in the skin. She now looked ill; or, at any rate, thinner and haunted, consumed by the spiritual power which had visited her. She seemed to be inhabited.

At last, Lady Roads gave in. She told Miss Dykes she could go to church.

"You are to take a taxi," she said to Miss Dykes. "It will be tomorrow."

When the day came Miss Dykes was breathless with her arrangements. She was going to sit at the back of the hall with Lady Roads, who would not be reading the lesson on that evening, and on the other side of her were to be her sister and Mrs Johnson.

Mrs Truslove listened many times to this arrangement. Two hours before the meeting, Mrs Truslove said:

"Judy, you are not to mind, but I do not think I shall come."

"Oh, Linda, please," begged the cripple.

"It is against my conscience," said Mrs Truslove.

A sharp quarrel broke out between the sisters. Miss Dykes pleaded, but Mrs Truslove did not change her mind.

"You are hard," said Miss Dykes.

"I have always respected your beliefs," said Mrs Truslove. "You must respect mine."

"But it is the Truth," said Miss Dykes.

"There is no answer to that, is there?" said Mrs Truslove. "I am being kind really. It would spoil it for you if I were there. You can speak more freely. I'm going out with Mr Cummings and his wife tonight. I did not arrange it, but it's just happened."

"Oh," said Miss Dykes quickly, with her old malice. "It was Mr and Mrs Beluncle, now it is Mr and Mrs Cummings."

"Yes," said Mrs Truslove. "But I am older. I am worth a great deal more than I used to be. You are going to be well and I shall really be free!"

"You are going to leave me," said Miss Dykes.

"You," smiled Mrs Truslove, "are going to be leaving me. Isn't that it?"

XLIV

Miss Dykes spoke at the meeting of the Boystone Branch of Mrs Parkinson's Group. It was a long time before she could get away from the people who gathered round her afterwards. Many kissed her when she left. Only Miss Wix and Mr Phibbs remained out of the crowd after they had spoken to her. The humble Miss More had not been able to shake her hand. It was she who went outside to stand by the taxi to open the door for her. The last cinema queue was moving into the Royal when at last Miss Dykes came out slowly, shining with her happiness, on Mrs Johnson's arm.

"Oh," cried Miss Dykes, at the sight of the crowd oozing into the Royal. "If I could take them in my arms!" Gazing at the crowd she did not notice Miss More in the darkness. Miss More had opened the door, but in her obscurity was too slow to close it when Miss Dykes got into the taxi; the driver pushed her away and closed the door himself.

The taxi drove through the avenues of Boystone and Miss Dykes sat forward on the seat smiling at the dark empty streets.

"The silence!" she said. "The beautiful darkness. I shall wander about all night. I never thought of the nights before."

Mrs Johnson did not answer.

"When I go courting," said Miss Dykes, teasing Mrs Johnson.

"Oh yes, I'm going courting. Don't think I'm not."

Mrs Johnson dabbed her eyes with the back of her hand and then tapped on the window of the cab.

"Opposite the pillar-box," she said to the driver.

The taxi stopped outside their house and Mrs Johnson leaned forward, putting her arm across Miss Dykes to open the door. As she did this, she suddenly put her hand to her neck and gave a cry. There was a rushing sound like hail falling as a shower of small gravel fell on the windscreen and bonnet of the cab.

"It hit me. A stone," said Mrs Johnson.

They got out of the cab and the driver got down too. He looked at the cab and then went a few yards down the road into the dark.

"That wasn't boys," he said. "It came from the corner."

"Get into the house," said Mrs Johnson, and she forgot to watch Miss Dykes go painfully in. Mrs Johnson stood with the taxi driver. She was holding her neck and trying to pay him at the same time. She was trembling.

"Quick," she said.

She was glad to see a spear of light from the open door marking the path down to the gate and she hurried towards the house. At the first step her foot touched something soft and earthy on the path: it was an uprooted plant. She looked beyond it. There was another and another. All the plants in the small garden had been torn up. They were thrown on the path.

Anger came into Mrs Johnson's heart. She walked all over the small lawn to see what else had been done to the little garden she loved. "Oh, another! Another! Oh, they've been into the garden. Oh, my poor garden," she cried. She was in tears. She got to the thick hedge separating the garden from the house next door. Suddenly she stepped back. She gave a cry and could not move. The body of a man could be seen in the fan of light cast by the door, lying face downwards, close under the hedge. In the light he looked like a soft length of old sacking. She had nearly trodden on him.

"Here," she called out, not knowing whether to make her voice soft or loud.

With a scramble and a thump, the man got heavily to his feet and faced Mrs Johnson. His teeth were showing like a rabbit's in fright and he had one arm raised; his eyes seemed to dig into her face like a pair of light chisels. He was panting and Mrs Johnson felt his breath. Down came the arm clumsily, a clod of earth flew out of it. There was the sound of glass breaking as the clod went into Mrs Truslove's front window, and the man muddled through a gap into the next garden gasping as he went, before Mrs Johnson moved.

"A man! Help!" Mrs Johnson choked.

The sound of his breath, grunting, like some animal's, made her sick.

There were lights in many of the houses of the street, but no window or door opened. There was no sound from the house next door.

"Help!" shouted Mrs Johnson. She saw the stumbling blur of the man go through two gardens and into the street until he was lost.

There was no sound even from her own house.

Four minutes went by before an upper window was opened in a house many doors down the street and a lazy voice called out:

"What is it?"

Then other doors and windows opened.

Slowly a group of neighbours got together and some took advantage of the opportunity of seeing into Mrs Truslove's house. They came foolishly to consider the broken window. Miss Dykes had been upstairs at the back and heard nothing. Mrs Johnson was a quiet, simple woman, but now she was talking violently. It was a long time before she calmed down. Miss Dykes, exhausted by her evening, was nevertheless hard and collected. She was not disturbed. She sternly treated this as an occasion to show herself to the astonished neighbours.

Mrs Johnson swept up the glass and got Miss Dykes to go to bed. Then Mrs Johnson moved out of the kitchen and sat in the sitting-room, guarding the hole in the window and waiting for Mrs Truslove to come home.

Mrs Johnson was too upset to read, to sew or to do anything. She sat listening to every sound, feeling the insinuating cold air from the broken window on her shoulder. She had seen the man's face and his grey hair. He was old, stupid and frightened. It recalled to her the face of Granger, Vogg's old man.

It *was* Vogg's old man. He got into the mews and waddled through the next street.

"I done it. I bore the Witness," he was breathing the words out hard, like steam. He was quietly screaming it to a ship at Southampton where Vogg was.

Mrs Johnson, with her brown dress, her earthy skin, her round brown eyes, and still short of breath, sat sizzling without thought a teapot on the hob. She knew what had happened; knew it obscurely in a way impossible for her to express.

The attack had begun. You couldn't do what you liked (Mrs Johnson knew), in Hetley. And Hetley was not this new suburban place, barely forty years old; Hetley was the old Hetley, the conquered region of small urban cottages, old shops, like Vogg's, pubs buried down side streets. It was Last's the greengrocer's, where the dwarf worked, it was Vogg's Gospel Hall in Princes Road, the back-gardens filled with colonies of sheds and, in themselves, like small villages behind the houses. The old Hetley was conquered, built over, grubbed up by the new commercial life, but like inextinguishable weed it still came through.

Mrs Johnson herself was old Hetley: she knew without having to articulate the matter to herself, what old Hetley thought. There was no private life among the inhabitants; there were no secrets among them. Everything was known, everything was said aloud with a slow dispassionate rancour. The thieving families were known, the immoral families, the fighters, the drunks, the hypocrites, the heroes. A woman could kill a newborn child, a man could beat his wife twice a week, there could be adultery,

fornication; all these things were known. And knowing them, Hetley was satisfied and wished to do nothing more about it. On Saturdays and Sundays, this old population put on its carefully kept and stiffish clothes as villagers do, and sat in the public-houses or the gospel halls in their groups, no one alone. They sat in the twos and threes in which they lived, as if they were groups of human beings cut inseparably from the same piece of wood or riveted together, publicly, fondly exposing the frailties, the fantasies, the wounds of their families.

The old Hetley (Mrs Johnson knew) plundered the new Hetley. What the old Hetley hated in the new Hetley was its suburban attempt at perfection and privacy. People who went in for privacy were trying to rise in the world, to cut themselves off. The Dykeses were an example of this. Postman's daughters and already, shutting themselves off, seeking other society, taking up with a new religion from London, the Dykeses had broken their ties and were claiming to be better than their neighbours. This had been the cause of Vogg's envious dislike of them. His religion, growing fast in the old Hetley, drew upon this population, fed upon its belief—when it saw the new life growing around it—in calamity impending for all except themselves.

Mrs Johnson had seen the old man's face. She had seen the stones fly, she had seen the plants pulled up and she knew these were the classical moves of aggression in old Hetley. The war had started. Ruled though she was by her love of the Dykeses, she could not conceal from herself her share in the common mind of her people. Old Hetley had always hated the sick to get better. They came back in dribs and drabs from Boystone hospital on visiting days, loudly stopping in the streets to announce the outrages they had heard of there. The dead left all night in the wards, the wrong girl operated on and dying of it, the nurses who mixed the prescriptions, the operations in public view without anæsthetics: old Hetley spread the muttered slander of its folklore in the corners of pubs, in the buses and the trams.

The old Hetley that would not stand for doctors would,

Mrs Johnson knew, never stand for miracles. It would fight, in the end, by its own peculiar methods, for its cardinal belief in calamity.

Mrs Johnson had been at the doctor's. She had been telling him for the twentieth time of the wickedness of Vogg.

"But," said the doctor, vainly trying to find out exactly what had happened when she had found Vogg and Miss Dykes together: he had been told, though at different times, of robbery, attack, even—well, not quite rape, but something called "insulting her", which he took to be sexual exposure.

"But," said the doctor, "you must be glad Miss Dykes can walk."

Mrs Johnson pulled her bag on to her lap and her soft simple face hardened and became an unpleasant liver-like colour.

"Well, no, to be fair and square, doctor, no, I am not. That's the truth. It's no good telling you a lie. I'd sooner her crippled for life than that wickedness, it's upset me."

"But it may have been the work of prayer and God," said the doctor gently. "You ought to be glad whatever the reason. I've seen four or five cases in my life and I'm always glad."

Mrs Johnson looked suspiciously at him.

"No," she said, with the hardness of a sentimental heart. "I shan't ever be that. She was contented as she was, as happy as a child; if she had something to complain of, I can understand it, but no, she never said. Waited on hand and foot. I did my best. It was always Mrs Johnson this and Mrs Johnson that. I don't want thanks for what I did, I did it willingly, I was a mother to her, the poor thing," Mrs Johnson cried. "I pushed her about like a baby." And Mrs Johnson showed him her two large, now unused, hands helplessly. "I hardly know how to walk without that chair. And now to be turned on. It's 'I'm all right now, Mrs Johnson, I can manage myself. I'm not a cripple.' Doctor, it hurts, it cuts me to the heart."

It was the chair Mrs Johnson loved. To see it empty, emptied her body.

"If I'd known when I pushed her to that church twice a

week and sat there with her, that this is what would happen, I'd never have gone," she said. "After all I did for them."

Mrs Johnson saw years of work wasted. She had loved sitting in the meeting-hall of the Purification. She had loved listening to the accounts of illness at their mid-week meeting. She had enjoyed above all these the peace of a "good sit down", resting her big working legs and her heavy arms. There, during the reading of the lesson, she had day-dreamed of the things she liked most to dream about: polishing the floor of the hall, for example, dusting the chairs, giving it all a "good old spring clean". Not cramped any more by a small place, she would let herself go there on a large scale, and by the end of the service she would feel the exhilaration of one who has done a notable piece of work. There had grown in her mind the pleasurable feeling that Mrs Parkinson's Group owed her an ever-growing debt of gratitude. Now she would be required no longer.

As she sat by the broken window in Mrs Truslove's house and saw the curtain move in the draught, Mrs Johnson could not conceal from herself a rising sense that justice was beginning: Hetley was attacking.

Mrs Johnson got up from her chair and went to bed. She did not wait for Mrs Truslove to come home. In the morning when she carried in the sisters' breakfast she did not speak. After breakfast she cleared away the things and Mrs Truslove said to her:

"What happened last night, Mrs Johnson?"

A roar of conversation came from Mrs Johnson. She was, she said, giving her notice. Things were not right. To be left alone in a house, with men breaking into it, tearing up her garden, she was not going to stay.

"It was not the same when Mr Beluncle used to come," she said. It was her final sentence. "When things change," she said, "it is time to go."

She had never complained, she said, when Mr Beluncle came, night after night, sitting there till all hours, though people talked. It was not her business why Mr Beluncle came and why he stayed—but she had nothing on her conscience.

Mrs Johnson left the room and the sisters looked in silence at the closed door.

For Mrs Johnson, as Vogg had so often prophesied in his tracts which she had always read, the world had come to an end.

Mrs Johnson went out to a sister's in Hetley, came back for her bags, which were already packed, and went. They saw her only once again in the crowd at the Hetley bus-stop, where the decisive incident happened. There was always a crowd on the five o'clock bus and a rush to get on it.

"Isn't it wonderful?" Miss Dykes was saying to anyone who would listen in the crowd. "This is the first time in my life I have ever been on a bus."

"Ssh," whispered Mrs Truslove, "you know you were told not to draw attention. Mrs Johnson is here. I've just seen her."

"Where?" said Miss Dykes.

But the green bus drew up, they were pushed by the crowd towards the door. Mrs Truslove saw Mrs Johnson's head and shoulders, getting nearer to them in the crowd, and Mrs Truslove looked down to help her sister. As she did so, among the pushing legs of the people, she saw the foot of a large woman step out, hook it for a second upon her sister's shin and immediately Miss Dykes had lost her balance and fell to the ground as the crowd gave to one side. Who had done this, Mrs Truslove could not tell. Mrs Johnson, who had been behind them, was now pushing ahead on the step of the bus.

This was the incident that brought Mrs Truslove to her decision. Her sister was sent away to stay with Lady Roads.

XLV

"How is Miss Dykes?" Mrs Beluncle said to her husband.

"I must tell her," thought Mr Beluncle. "I hope it will not be as bad as I fear."

"Something very extraordinary has happened," he said. "In a way wonderful."

Mr Beluncle saw his wife's solicitude go. It was going to be as bad as he feared; his wife would be unable to tolerate anything good happening to the Truslove household. He said coldly:

"Miss Dykes can walk."

Mrs Beluncle stepped back and crouched with fear: her husband had gone mad. Mr Beluncle explained to her with wounding simplicity.

"Shut the door," he said, first of all. "I don't want those boys to hear." Then he explained. Mrs Beluncle listened and asked no questions, and so encouraged, Mr Beluncle elaborated the story. The day of miracles had not passed. This should convince the sceptical and so on.

"Her poor sister," murmured Mrs Beluncle. She was being sorry for Mrs Truslove.

"Poor? Why d'you say poor?" And Mr Beluncle, embellishing the subject, drew a picture of Mrs Truslove helpless with gratitude, on the point of conversion, after all these years. Now Mrs Truslove would be less difficult.

Mrs Beluncle continued to listen.

"When did it happen?" she asked.

"Well, just lately, a week or so back."

"Oh, I thought you meant yesterday," said Mrs Beluncle.

"I think it must have been, let me see . . ." began Mr Beluncle.

"When you told me she was ill?" said Mrs Beluncle, sharpening.

"Yes," said Mr Beluncle. "That's it. Not ill, let me correct you there, I did not say ill, I said she was going through a crisis. . . ."

Mrs Beluncle was sitting on the edge of the chair. She picked up a poker from the fireplace and doodled on the tiles of the hearth with it. There was no fire, but this was a habit of hers and Mr Beluncle read it with apprehension.

"Liar," said Mrs Beluncle suddenly, putting the poker down. "I don't believe you. Saying she's ill, when she's walking, saying she's walking! That's what you've been doing the past fortnight. Having it all over, all nice and sweet and cosy with dear Mrs Truslove all to yourself and don't tell your wife, you liar.

"Ha! Ha!" laughed Mrs Beluncle. "Miracles! Walking! Don't tell me. Down there helping Miss Dykes to walk, holding her hand—whose hand? I wonder. I don't wonder. I know. Why didn't you tell me?"

"I . . ." began Mr Beluncle.

"You fool, telling me that woman walks. Walks! Lies down, I bet. What a religion."

Mrs Beluncle had not made one of her larger scenes for two months. She now gathered together all the costumes, dialogues and properties of her temper and was presently going over vivid incidents in her married life, accusing her husband of adultery, sometimes with Mrs Truslove, sometimes with Mrs Parkinson. Mr Beluncle sat, occasionally saying a word, but Mrs Beluncle snatched the word away like a hurricane and shouted on. Very soon her hair became loose; then tears were pouring down her face; after that she began to pull her blouse off saying that she was going to run naked from the house and call the police. Mr Beluncle got up and she threw the poker.

Henry and George and Leslie were listening outside the room. The grandmother had gone to bed. When they heard the poker hit the sideboard, Henry opened the door and went into the room.

"Shut up!" he said. "I can't read."

Mr and Mrs Beluncle both rounded on Henry.

"How dare you say 'Shut up' to your mother," said Mr Beluncle.

"You encourage your own children to insult me," screamed Mrs Beluncle.

George listened admiringly for more items of rage. Leslie smiled in his elderly way.

"I am going to bed if anyone wants me," he said.

The two parents continued the attack on George and Henry and then returned to the attack upon each other.

The holes of daylight closed up between the trees outside the window and the quarrel went on into the night.

Mrs Beluncle went to bed at last, locking herself in her room. Slowly she calmed down. She had, she felt, expressed important truths: that she was not going to have God on Mrs Truslove's side against her; it was bad enough to have Him on her husband's side. One more miracle and they would be penniless, begging on the streets, in the bankruptcy court, in prison.

"I shall leave in the morning and take my children with me," she sobbed. She had been saying this for years and had not noticed that the cry was now meaningless. Her children were almost grown up.

Mr Beluncle was appalled by this scene. Large portions of it were not new and he had them by heart, and once or twice with a kind of exhilaration he had spoken some of her well-known lines for her, to remind her, in one of her pauses. He was used to being appalled; what disturbed him was that he had not, perhaps, correctly judged the consequences of the miracle. Some of the things his wife had said seemed dangerously right.

The large scene was followed by smaller ones in the next few days and these gradually became reasonable conversations. Having injured her husband as much as she knew how to do, Mrs Beluncle softened and took his side, treating him as an invalid.

"Your poor father," she said to George, "must not be worried. He has a lot on his mind. You are not to ask him about a job. He'll be lucky if he has a job himself."

XLVI

Henry Beluncle had not seen Mary Phibbs for two weeks.

He felt when his father came into the room totally possessed by him, physically and spiritually, so that what he

K

intended to say he could no longer find words for; his very thoughts were forgotten and he found himself saying what his father wanted him to say.

One day at the office Mr Chilly asked Henry to dine in his rooms near Connaught Square.

Mr Beluncle said lightly:

"I am sure I have been misinformed, Chilly. My son tells me that you have asked him to have lunch with you."

"Oh yes, sir, you have, sir, didn't I make it clear, sir—dinner, sir."

"The evening!" exclaimed Mr Beluncle.

"At half past seven, sir," said Mr Chilly.

"You surprise me," said Mr Beluncle.

"Do I, sir? I like your son, very promising boy," said Mr Chilly. "Full of ideas."

"Very few right ideas, Chilly. Peculiar ideas about his father, Chilly. Imagines he knows better than his father. No sense of gratitude. . . ."

"Oh surely, sir . . ."

"Do I know my son, or do you?" said Mr Beluncle. "Imagines himself in love."

"Rather!" said Mr Chilly cheerfully. "It's the age. When isn't it?"

"What!" said Mr Beluncle. "You take it as natural a boy that age, hoping to make a position in the world, always telling his family what a brain he has got, what a mind—though he knows or ought to know, there is only One Mind—should have time to go out to dinner in the evening and to be in love. You, I am sure, were not in love."

"I am a queer case, sir," said Mr Chilly austerely.

Mr Chilly had moments of austerity.

"No, I never heard of such a thing. But why do you ask me?" said Mr Beluncle.

"Henry seemed to suggest that it might be polite," said Mr Chilly.

"The first I heard of that boy being polite," said Mr Beluncle. "Gratitude is what he lacks. A sense of obligation. Did he mention obligations to you?"

"No, sir, I'm afraid we didn't get on to that, I mean . . ." said Mr Chilly.

"I thought not," said Mr Beluncle. "It's the last thing he thinks of."

Mr Beluncle sent for his son.

"I hear you have been pushing yourself on to Mr Chilly," said Mr Beluncle coldly. "Mr Chilly is here to learn the business. He pays me a considerable sum to learn it. It will have to be very considerable before I finish teaching him; he has a long way to go. I do not know whether he realises it, but I consider the distance very great. While you waste his time discussing social engagements with him (and when I say his time I mean mine), though time is an erroneous concept as you know: tide and time wait for no man, not even for Mr Chilly. Why did you ask Mr Chilly to ask you to dinner?"

"I didn't."

"But you must have. Why on earth should he ask you? Mr Chilly has his own life. It is different from our life. Where does he live? Near Connaught Square, you say, well, what is fine about that? I lived near Connaught Square once, there's no point in going there. If you want to see Connaught Square, surely the natural thing is to ask your father. I never hear of you asking me to dinner."

Mr Beluncle smiled waggishly. Henry laughed.

"I could not afford it," he laughed.

Mr Beluncle became stern.

"Afford it? Of course you can't. I can't. I can't afford to go to dine with Mr Chilly. I just can't afford the time, the thought. I am too busy when I finish my work here thinking of what Mrs Parkinson has taught us. You have heard of this wonderful thing that has happened to Miss Dykes and you talk of dining with Mr Chilly! There are things in you past my comprehension, Henry. You don't feel that the teachings of Mrs Parkinson are the most important things in life. You don't feel you have a debt to your mother, that your place is with her in the evenings. And to your brothers. To your home. Oh no, your home is not good enough for you. You take it for granted."

"Can I go to Mr Chilly's tonight?"

"I thought I had made it clear," snapped Mr Beluncle, who was going down to Mrs Truslove's house that evening. "You do what you like. You are free. Free as the air."

"In that case I shall go," said Henry coldly.

Father and son glared at each other.

"What? In those clothes? In that suit?" enquired Mr Beluncle. "Don't you know what society is like?"

"It isn't society."

Mr Chilly came gaily in.

"Well, is that settled?" he said cheerfully.

"We should like to come and dine with you one evening," said Mr Beluncle amiably. "Not tonight. I have an engagement. I think this boy feels . . ."

"Yes, I am coming tonight," said Henry.

Mr Beluncle became pale. When Mr Chilly had gone Mr Beluncle said:

"I don't want to speak to you. You have deliberately gone against my wishes. You have made your bed, you lie on it. You will probably break your mother's heart. You know how ill and tired she has been."

At half past seven Henry arrived at Mr Chilly's rooms. He stood in a pleasant ground-floor front room gazing at Mr Chilly's books and at an incomprehensible modern picture.

"My dear!" said Mr Chilly, taking both his hands. "I am so glad. You don't know what you have done for me. You have saved me."

Mr Beluncle had saved Mr Chilly earlier.

"You have saved me from a girl. My cousin, Miss Roads," he said.

"Yes," said Mr Chilly, still holding his hands and leaning back to gaze at Henry distantly, as if getting him into perspective, and then dropping into his offensive third-person address.

"It understands girls, I am sure, better than I. Now sit down and I will give it a glass of sherry and I will tell it *all* about the beautiful bitch who is coming in a minute. Will it like her, I wonder? Will it fall? No, it is innocent."

Henry was unable to speak.

"It has resisted Miss Vanner," Mr Chilly said. "But for how long?"

"I can't bear her," said Henry.

"No more can I," said Mr Chilly. "But how nearly, how dreadfully nearly one slithers, Henry. You are not calling me Everard. I asked you to."

"Yes . . . Everard," Henry murmured.

"Now I want to ask you a lot of questions," said Mr Chilly very briskly. "Miss Roads—well, she's for you if you like. Will you like? One can't tell. But, Henry—something much more important. Your Aunt Constance. My dear, there's a woman. You see I speak frankly. I mean I'm hiding nothing. Handsome, voluptuous—horrifying really, Henry, you don't mind my talking about your Aunt Constance like that?"

"I haven't seen her since I was seven. She lives abroad."

"Oh no, you're wrong, Henry. She lives here. In London I mean. Oh yes, how curious you don't know her. She likes you. She spoke of you. I took her home the other evening."

"She's my wicked aunt," said Henry.

"Oh, but you ought to see her," said Mr Chilly. "She's full of interesting information. Now, you mustn't tell anyone I said so, but I am just a little bit put out by you."

"By me?"

"By all of you. The Beluncles. Aunt Constance has the idea that I am going to lose all my money. What d'you think?"

The feather-headed Mr Chilly looked suddenly severe and dangerous.

Henry thought: Good heavens, how I have misjudged Mr Chilly. What is he up to?

"I mean," said Mr Chilly, "Aunt Constance says that Beluncles are going up the spout."

Henry could not answer, and in any case, before he could Mr Chilly said:

"There now. I don't think it loves its father very much and I have made it worse, I oughtn't to have mentioned it. Let us forget about it. Let us think about Miss Roads. She would do for you. D'you know, I believe I'm shocking you."

"No you are not."

"Charming, that sulky expression. I am shocking. I'm behaving badly. You will hate me in a moment. No one loves me. I don't believe your father does any more. The way he speaks now. I notice it. I mean," said Mr Chilly suddenly, "it would be a mistake to become a director, don't you think, if the firm is rocky?"

"I didn't know the firm was rocky," said Henry. "It's always been a worry. Father is extravagant. I . . ."

"Rocky, I'm afraid, is the word," said Mr Chilly, with a touch of annoyance in his smile. And then his austere manner went and he said, "My dear, I'm awful. I knew it was rocky when I came in. I always fall for rockiness—and then your father's personality. I wonder if you are going to have personality? Aunt Constance has got it, too, you know. There's something terrible about Aunt Constance that gets me."

"We're always told she's a bad lot. I expect she's better than we are."

"Oh no!" exclaimed Mr Chilly. "She's as black as she's painted; that's the fascinating thing."

Henry was alarmed by Mr Chilly.

"Now let me tell you about Celia Roads," he said. But he did not have time to tell Henry very much. The bell was rung and presently Miss Roads was shown into the room. She was a straight, dark girl of twenty-five, with thin bare arms, a little hairy, and cold weak hands and a hard educated voice in her throat. She lifted her upper lip and her eyes had a brilliant moment of anger when she saw Henry.

"I thought," she said coldly to Mr Chilly, "we were going to be alone. How nice."

"Henry works with me. He is almost my boss," said Mr Chilly, taking her coat. "And, my dear, you'll have everything to talk about: Mrs Parkinson, my dear." And Mr Chilly wagged a finger.

The girl looked ironically at Henry.

"Are you anything to do with the Parkinson Group?"

"My father is. I . . ." said Henry.

"We're going to have a hell of a dinner if you are," said the rude Miss Roads.

It was a difficult evening. Miss Roads was not pleased with Mr Chilly and Mr Chilly was not pleased with her. She shot pellets of bread across the table and laughed loudly. She was a girl who appeared to live between public-houses and a lot of furnished rooms, among young men who were in debt, who were turned out by landladies, who dossed down on the floor of her rooms, who sold her things; at the same time she appeared to travel abroad and to be snobbish about her family connections. She snubbed Henry.

A glass of wine buzzed in Henry's head. A desire to have personality filled him. He suddenly could not stop talking about the customers in the furniture trade. He informed her that there was a slump in the price of the best woods, that labour was difficult, that several well-known shops were bankrupt. He went on to the system of invoicing. He pointed out to Miss Roads that what passed for mahogany was *not* always mahogany but Chippendale was always Chippendale, you could tell it.

A small kink appeared between Mr Chilly's fair eyebrows. He listened, with a wistful desire for instruction, to Henry.

Miss Roads argued about a set of Chippendale chairs her mother had been left and then sulked because Mr Chilly waved his weak hand at her and said:

"Listen to this. This is interesting. Henry really *knows*."

Henry realised that he was having personality.

Miss Roads was not pretty but her yellow-brown eyes burned in her pale face, and the face was alive, fine and nervous. Her voice jarred on him, but that he began to find attractive.

And then, he admired Mr Chilly's rooms and thought that was how he would like to live. He brooded upon the story of Aunt Constance. Another mystery in his squalid family. He coloured with shame at the thought of Mr Chilly meeting Aunt Constance, who was always drunk. He coloured at the thought of what Mr Chilly must be thinking of his father. He coloured most at the thought of what Mr Chilly must think of himself. And suddenly he began to hate Mr Chilly.

Miss Roads began to make conversation about going. She asked about Henry's trains. Could it be that she was trying to get him to go, while Mr Chilly was trying to get him to stay? Henry felt that his personality must stay.

"My dear," whispered Mr Chilly, when she was out of the room, "protect me. Stay. Isn't she too irresistible? My dear, you must stay and make a hit."

And then a peculiar expression came on to Mr Chilly's face, a sad, lumpish, pondering, despairing expression. Quite clearly, it said to Henry Beluncle: "It's quite hopeless. You have not made a hit. Not even with me, my dear. You are too curious altogether. It will be years before you are presentable."

And the serious look of one saying "Goodbye" came on to Mr Chilly's face, followed by his convenient look of folly.

Henry thought of Miss Roads all the way home in the train. If he saw her again he would fall in love with her, on the general principle that if he saw a girl twice it would be inevitable for him. It was a kind of fatal arrangement he had with himself. He saw, in his mind, the room, the books, the incomprehensible picture. To be as old as Mr Chilly, have one's hair a little receding, not growing thick on the forehead like his own! Henry stood up in the empty compartment of the night train, and, taking his pocket knife out, began to saw off a few pieces of hair in front at the parting in order to gain a little on the sluggish pace of experience.

The front door of his house was opened by Mr Beluncle.

"Ten o'clock," said Mr Beluncle. "How dare you come reeling into your home at this hour. Who the devil do you think you are, keeping me up? Get out of my sight before I lose my temper, before I say something I regret—before I break your back. Is that your idea of the religion of love, your mother worried to death?"

XLVII

Henry was a hero to his brothers.

"What time?" said George.

"Ten o'clock," said Henry.

"Did he use language?" said George eagerly.

"Yes," said Henry.

"Abominable," Leslie said dryly.

Two days later Henry was walking to the station and had reached the rusting chestnuts where the park began. He was thinking of Celia Roads. She has a head (he thought of her attractions), a quick tongue, she talks fast, she contradicts, she has a fur coat; she doesn't like me, she is at war with her mother, she is unhappy, Mr Chilly is frightened of her. She was discontented in that lovely room. She talked of being in Italy. Fancy leaving a home which had Chippendale chairs in it. How do you ever meet people like that again?

He looked up. Mary Phibbs in the dark blue frock she wore in her shop was coming towards him. She had never come so near to his house before and, at any moment, his father might be overtaking them if he had the whim of catching the same train.

Mary was not walking in her slow, heavy, shy way, turning her head to the gardens or the wall, pretending not to see him. She was rushing and at the sight of him she ran towards him. Henry turned anxiously. He would have been glad to have run away.

"Where have you been?" she said. "What has happened? Why haven't you come to the house? I waited for you all Monday, all Tuesday. I've been so worried, I haven't slept."

She put her arm on his. Her arm was not light and soft any more, but was heavy and pulled with all the power of her anxiety. Her small eyes looked into his.

"Trouble at home. That's all," he said. "I couldn't come."

She had both hands on his arm. She was giving herself to him as she walked and her mouth opened with a small twist of pain that was in itself beautiful.

"I am going to the station with you. You haven't stopped loving me? Is it what I said about not going to church? About losing your faith?"

"No," said Henry. "Trouble at home. The usual thing, but worse now."

"I can't believe it," she said. "I told Sis and she said I was a fool, she was so cross with me. 'You're in love with a boy, not a church,' she said. I was silly. Forgive me. When you didn't come, I cried. I shall get told off for coming this morning. Sis said I wasn't to. I got up early and I didn't have breakfast. Mother said, 'What has got into our Mary's head?' but I said nothing." Mary chattered complacently, imperiously, startled by herself, her eyes sparkling and alive. "Oh," she said, pressing her nails into his arm, "I thought I had lost you. Why didn't you write, even? If I had known. But not to see you, not to have a word!"

"I have had a terrible row about us," Henry said.

"Oh," she said softly. "I am so sorry." She stopped. "It is terrible for you to suffer. My boy," she said. "Kiss me. If we have each other."

He had never felt the power of her heart until then, her unpractised hands had never held him as they held him now. Her waist was now soft and he could feel the weight not of her love alone but of love itself, as he awkwardly kissed her.

"Oh, I have got you," she said. "I thought I had lost you."

He looked anxiously up the path and across the park. They walked on, talking of what they could do and how they could meet for longer times, openly, not in this secrecy, and Henry, feeling her leg bump heavily against him as he walked, longed for this too.

"I have thought of you every night," he said.

"I have too," she said. And she said, "I wanted you to be with me."

"I do too," he said.

"I mean," she said quietly, "when I was thinking of you. Last night terribly. It was wicked, wasn't it? I'm often wicked."

Henry sat in his train. The train passed two or three

stations before he noticed where he was. At the fourth
the freshness of the sunlight was dimmed by a film of smoke
that gives to central London the aching light of an eclipse.

The torture began. The sight of love in her face for the
first time, the knowledge that she was not a girl, but a
woman, the sudden strength of her womanhood in her hands,
the awkwardness of open desire in her mouth, showed him
that, whatever his feeling for her was, it was not a love like
hers. The pride, so flattered by her, now turned against her;
she was pursuing him, she was asking from him, she was
demanding him. She had gone over to the enemy, for by her
innocent action, she had shown him that his father was right.
A terrible revelation came to him: I do not love her.

He got out of the train and walked the few hundred yards
to the Bulux offices. It was a wretched neighbourhood. There
was the vast hospital where already the sick were out on
their balconies, the nurses passing like white-winged birds,
the cars of the doctors turning in. There were the warehouses
with their cold doorways and their warm ones, and the sunlight on the railway arches opposite to them. The worn pave-
ments, which, in this labouring part of the city, seemed thinner
and softer in their dirtiness than they were in the wealthier
parts, frequently were broken by the cobbles of side streets
and alleys; and out of the long fog-yellow tunnels of the
arches, leading to the river, came the sudden, brassy, thrash
of vans. As he passed by others going to work in these warehouses, Henry wished there was someone to whom he could
speak. He was astonished that no one looked at him or spoke
to him, for he was surely as conspicuous in his guilt as a man
walking with a rope round his neck.

At lunch-time he walked to the middle of London Bridge
and looked at the brown river between the wharves. Rows
of men and women leaned here during the lunch hour
and the seagulls flew over them. One minute Henry was
smiling with pleasure at the memory of the love in Mary's
face; then the pleasure sickened with offence at the pursuit.
He did not notice the people leaning beside him.

Presently he heard a woman's voice saying:

"Wake up. We are stand-offish, aren't we?"

He saw Miss Vanner beside him.

"Looking at the boats? Thinking of going to sea? I've been talking to you for ages." She looked at him shrewdly.

"I am sorry," he said, "I did not notice you."

"Oh, I don't mind," she said, in an offended tone. "You're superior, aren't you?"

"No," he said. He was blushing. "I didn't notice you."

"Are you miserable?" she said kindly, leaning on the parapet with him. "You looked as though you were going to throw yourself in."

"No," said Henry.

"Had a row with your girl-friend?"

"No," said Henry loudly.

"Oh," she laughed. "Caught you, you dark horse. You've got one. When are you going for your holiday? Are you going with her?"

"Good Lord, no," said Henry indignantly.

"Poor girl," she said, laughing at him.

"I'm going with my boy," she said. "We always go together. Well, what is wrong with that?"

Henry said there was nothing wrong. Her face was near to his and she said sympathetically:

"I shall be glad when Mrs Truslove is back, your father's nerves! Has he been at you again?"

"No," said Henry.

"Oh well, if you don't want to talk, don't. But don't be shut up in your pride. I suppose you'll be a partner one day."

"Oh no," said Henry earnestly.

"No?" Miss Vanner gaped.

"I'm leaving when I can."

"What are you going to do?" she said, amazed.

"I'm going abroad," he said.

Miss Vanner studied his face and gave a genial glance of unbelief at his clothes.

"You're right," she said. "What does your girl-friend say to that? I wouldn't let my boy go abroad. Out of sight, out of mind. It's funny," she said, as they straightened and walked away from the bridge, "running into you like that. You're peculiar. I should go mad if you and Mr C. were away together. You're not familiar, like the others, neither is he. Not familiar. I like a man to be stand-offish. My boy'd have something to say if he saw me walking with you. I saw you there standing wrapped up in your thoughts, quite sad, that's why I spoke. Quite romantic, wasn't it?"

Henry laughed to avoid answering.

"I know what you're thinking," she said.

"What?"

"I know," she said. "I know what you're thinking all the time."

"What d'you mean?"

"I'll tell you some time. You're thinking about me. Don't get hot and eager, will you? You know what is the matter with you? You're too pious. I was going to ask you a question."

But Miss Vanner would not reveal her question. It was concerned with what he was thinking, she said, and she knew what he was thinking, it was in his face. One day, she said, perhaps. She pulled her blouse down at the waist and looked at him with sudden offence. And she widened the distance between them as they walked the last fifty yards.

"Mr Chilly," she said, "has manners. I mean, if you conduct a conversation with him, you enjoy his full attention. And he gives you his confidence. Not that I prefer older men."

They arrived at the whitened doorstep of Bulux Ltd. and Miss Vanner stopped and beckoned Henry back a few yards to be out of earshot, she said, of any Nosy Parker inside.

"Here," she challenged. "You say you're leaving?"

"Yes."

"Is it true that this place is going up the spout?"

"What d'you mean?" said Henry.

"Oh well, you wouldn't tell if you knew," she said. "But there are plenty of rumours in the office. Mrs Truslove's leaving, isn't she? Chilly isn't here this morning. He put money in. There's a rumour going round—your aunt's been in and Chilly went to see her about re-organising the firm.

He's got money. Only your father doesn't want it. Chilly's away. Or is he? I don't know."

"I never heard anything," said Henry. "When was my aunt here?"

Miss Vanner said: "You're close."

They walked on: "Poor Mr Cook, at his age, where will he get a job?" she accused.

"Oh God," thought Henry, "am I to be made responsible for that too?" Henry sat at his desk.

"I do not love her. I do not love her," Henry was saying to himself. "It was terrible seeing her."

And then he changed to the other side.

"When you say you do not love her you are simply being bullied into thinking so by your father."

New voices came into the dispute: his brother's, Mr Phibbs's, Mrs Truslove's, Mr Chilly's. They became so loud, egging him on, holding him back, accusing him of treachery, praising him for clear-sightedness, arguing all over the page of figures under his hand, that by the middle of the afternoon, the sounds of the office became blurred, as if the floor and the walls were made of felt. Then a glass window came down between him and the clerks. He could see their lips move and watch them walk but they made hardly a sound. Miss Vanner thrashed her typewriter and no noise came from it. "Dear Sir, We are in receipt," he heard Mr Cook say. And Mr Cook kept on saying it. Henry got down from his stool smiling sadly at the doomed foolery of Mr Cook and was going to laugh out loud with him. He was going to say:

"That's good: *we* are in receipt. Not *you*. Not Mr Cook." But he changed his mind. His ears roared. Henry rushed out of the office to the lavatory and was sick and his head seemed to be breaking up into streets and buildings and rooms. He came out shuddering with cold and Miss Vanner saw him coming back along the passage.

"Are you all right?" Miss Vanner asked.

Henry smiled. His last impression was of a loud roar and of her red mouth wide open as he fell to the floor, which rang as though he had hit iron.

XLVIII

She was standing as a rule when he saw her, behind three or four tiers of fancy cakes at Lippard's, so that he generally saw no more than her head and shoulders. She was a dyed blonde of forty-five, with dark, irritated eyes, a double chin, heavily made-up and pale and she had a small mouth that seemed to be shaping the words "Pardon me". She wore heavy spectacles. It was a pleasure, Mr Beluncle found, to watch her. She was the manageress. She kept her eyes on the girls. She bullied the men who came up with trays of cakes from the kitchens, in a surly way, not saying very much. She could do three or four things at once and still appreciate Mr Beluncle's bantering conversation as he sat on the stool on the other side of the counter drinking coffee and eating cakes. When she came from behind the cakes, she was seen to be a heavy woman with a light step. She reminded him of a trimmer and cleaned-up version of his sister Constance— Constance as she could have been. He admired her because —except for the hair—she looked like himself.

Mr Beluncle used to come in for a cup of coffee on Tuesdays and Thursdays.

"What's biting you?" he used to say perkily,

or

"Put it all on today, haven't you?" nodding to her jewellery

or

"What's the matter with the coffee?"

The manageress played up to Mr Beluncle's role of the difficult customer, who was always cheerful, always pretending to complain.

After this, he got on to "old times".

"What happened to that woman who used to be upstairs?"

or

"I remember this place before they opened up at the back."

They were now old acquaintances. For a long time the manageress had thought he was one of those dangerous

middle-aged men who can always bring a car round the
corner and "run you down to Brighton", "a good sport". He
was not. She sighed. "Good sports" were dropping out of her
life. Resignation, melancholy and long-faced thoughts came
to her when she saw Mr Beluncle; he was respectable. He
was what she had missed. He belonged to the large class of
jovial, paternal arm-squeezing middle-aged fathers of family
who wanted sympathy. She relapsed into that: her figure had
gone—"if you want to know"—her voice sagged, she wanted
sympathy too. A common physical desuetude and tiredness
drew them together, the consolation of wagging their tongues
about their lives to someone who knew nothing of their lives.
They knew the cards to play: Mr Beluncle had always liked
manageresses; he knew the compliments they liked. She—
her name was Mrs Robinson—had always liked a manager.
Their meetings were a kind of suicide pact in which their
voices and their autobiographies died together over the
counter twice a week.

"Freedom at last, after twenty years' hard labour, as you
might call it," said Mr Beluncle gaily. Mrs Truslove was still
away.

"I'm surprised they let *you* out," said the manageress.

Mr Beluncle knew all about her. It was the usual story:
the ageing mother, the husband killed in the 1914 War, the
understanding "friend" who had "gone away". Mrs Robinson patently wanted a man. Mr Beluncle saw this. He did
not want to be the man; but he liked being the kind of man
who knew that women like Mrs Robinson wanted a man. It
made him not a "real sport", but "sporty". He chaffed her
(as he called it) and in a serious voice said what kept him so
spry and on top of the world was the Purification.

Mrs Robinson forgot her girls and customers for two or
three minutes and listened, with the greedy gloom of one
reading the crimes in a Sunday newspaper, to his stories of
the miracles of the Purification.

A touch of religion always worked wonders in the trade,
Mr Beluncle thought, when he went away. People liked it
better than a drink. "It brings out private life; once a man

shows his hand, you can do business. There's not a man or woman in England who isn't calling out for God."

Mr Beluncle had no business with Mrs Robinson; all the same he believed business is what a man should always be doing and he regarded his relations with her as a business affair. Who knew? It might become so.

The manageress knew all about Mr Beluncle. He told her everything.

"It's a terrible thing having a partner. But she's been away two months. The difference! I can breathe now. I can see how I was held back, but now I can fill my lungs."

It was the wrong thing in life, he said, how people try to hold you back. That was one thing he had learned, he would never hold his own children back as he was held back when he was young. His father to begin with. Then his sister. He had married young and he would not say a word against his wife, but—well, you sometimes wanted to breathe. His partner again—well, if her husband hadn't died, it would have been a different story.

"What we all need is release," said Mr Beluncle. "Freedom. If you're down, give yourself a surprise. Surprise yourself."

Mr Beluncle talked about his tomb one day. Mrs Robinson became very interested in this subject. If he died, Mr Beluncle said, he would like a simple funeral, no flowers, no show. Mrs Robinson said this was her notion too. She recalled the funerals of two kings. Mr Beluncle let the interruption go and resumed the account of his funeral.

He wanted to be buried in his native town, Mr Beluncle said, in a simple country churchyard. A plain stone, he said. And on it, he said, some simple words, such as an epigram, or should he say epitaph?

"My son Henry, he would tell me. He's quick to take his father up," he said.

"Epitaph," said Mrs Robinson. "What would you have on it?"

"Reminds me of the story of the man and his wife," said Mr Beluncle. He told Mrs Robinson this story. She had heard it dozens of times in her life; that was a funereal bond in itself: "If there's room we'll meet in Heaven," repeated Mr Beluncle. "Eh? Jolly good.

"No," said Mr Beluncle, "I haven't much use for the usual run. Too much old theology in them. I've always liked something out of the common. I'd like something that would make people stop and think 'Ah, that fellow *thought*. He was a surprising man.'"

That, said Mrs Robinson, come to think of it, would make a good epitaph. "He was a surprising man."

"I am," said Mr Beluncle.

That day when he went out, Mr Beluncle said curtly: "You start surprising yourself."

He went away feeling he was full of surprises.

Mrs Robinson saw that Mr Beluncle was a serious person. She liked a man who moralised. She was impressed by the account of his funeral. She often thought, she said, on later Tuesdays and Thursdays, of what he had said about surprising herself. She had often thought, for example, she said, of starting up on her own in a little place. Mr Beluncle pointed out that that required capital. Mrs Robinson said she had capital. Mr Beluncle quoted a few figures. Mrs Robinson said she had four hundred pounds.

Mr Beluncle clipped advertisements of shops for sale out of the newspapers and handed them to Mrs Robinson. It turned out that Mrs Robinson was being cautious. She leaned one day on the counter, resting her bosom there, and staring at him shrewdly through her spectacles and going hot under her make-up, she confided that she had nearer a thousand pounds.

Mr Beluncle put on his glasses when she said this. They leaned together in a sensual trance of self-interest, looking through their heavy windows at each other.

"You be careful what you do with it," said Mr Beluncle.

"You're telling me," said Mrs Robinson, with a sharp nod.

They nodded curtly to each other, deeply bound by the confidence, when he picked up his bowler hat and went out.

"Fancy a woman like that having a thousand pounds,"

said Mr Beluncle to his wife. "The world is a wonderful place."

Mr Beluncle increased his visits to the teashop. It was not always possible to talk very much to her, but he could watch her. Or rather he watched her thousand pounds, walking about in high-heeled shoes and in black, creaking satin. He shook hands with her now. If he met her walking across the shop he would give her a surprise; quietly he would take her by the elbow. It was fat and cool, like a soft chin. He looked at her bosom and thought of the thousand pounds it contained. It seemed to give out a warmth. Mr Beluncle refrained from speaking of the thousand pounds. He had sensations of enormous, light-headed innocence.

When Mr Beluncle talked of his partner whose husband had died, Mrs Robinson talked of her husband who had been killed. Mr Beluncle talked of his friend, Mrs Truslove, who was "away". Mrs Robinson talked of the "friend" who had "gone away". A new significance inflected these old stories. Confessing to him that her £400 was really £1,000 had enlarged her interest in Mr Beluncle. She had often said: "In this trade you see a lot of people all the time and yet you see no one."

In telling Mr Beluncle she had £1,000 she had relieved herself of a burden, unveiled her beauty to him in all its importance and helplessness.

Mr Beluncle was disturbed by this change. He heard that she liked the cinema, but she had no one to go with. Wednesday night, she said, she was always free; but, she said, Wednesday came round week after week, and she did nothing. Wednesday was a good night because her mother went out. From a woman of forty-five this seemed momentous. At that age, her eyes clearly said, one does not shilly-shally.

The look in the eyes of the manageress became large, brown, still and brooding. She attended to an occasional customer, she called her girls, she spoke into the speaking-tube to the kitchen, she ordered the men to carry trays of cakes out to the van; but in between these things, she would come for a moment back to Mr Beluncle, lean on the counter and talk to him in a low voice.

The words she said were desultory and commonplace. "Four pounds ten at Evans's," or "If you get a woman in they charge you," or "I go home and mother says 'Your nerves!'," but the mutter gave these words a deeper meaning. He could feel her breath sometimes, and she half smiled. "Well," she said, "you can't always sit with the same person, can you?" The sea, she said, on a day like this, it's a pity some nice man wasn't driving her to the sea. "They're all married, I suppose," she said.

Mr Beluncle walked away in temptation. He knew his manageresses. They liked their money and then, of course, they got afraid; and when they were afraid, if a man happened to be there—well, Mr Beluncle went over cases he knew. He knew Mrs Robinson was afraid. He knew she was on the point of wondering if he was going to happen to be there. A sudden blaze of lust, as if he had walked towards a fire, branched in all his veins. He had a blatant lust for the £1,000 of Mrs Robinson: it would help to buy *Marbella*.

Or rather, he found himself walking in a vision. If he had been his sister Constance and if Mrs Robinson had been a Mr Robinson, Mr Beluncle knew exactly what would have happened. Constance would have been in bed with Mr Robinson in no time and would have collected the £1,000. As he walked away into Piccadilly, Mr Beluncle felt himself becoming Constance. It terrified him. Mrs Truslove was away, and he had become quite a different man since her departure. He had breathed. He left his home in the morning and, for the first time, he breathed all day long until he returned home to rest and get ready for the great breathings of the day to come. He could do, he thought, tilting his bowler hat in a shop mirror, and defying his face there, exactly what he liked.

It had never occurred to him in his life before to do such a thing, perhaps because he knew other men did it: but now the temptation was plain. Mrs Robinson was asking him to be her lover. He had only to go to bed with her and she would be asking him for a safe investment for her £1,000.

For the first time in his married life, at the age of fifty, Mr Beluncle felt the demand of lust. He was horrified.

A vegetation of fantasy, tropical and violent, sprouted in Mr Beluncle's mind. It grew a huge mushroom growth of dreams at night. By day he made these dreams as orgiastic as possible. He daubed on the colour of temptation; he daubed it thickly.

He knew what he was doing. He was pretending to be afraid of his lust; but what he was afraid of, what he was trying to paint out with the heavy colours of his fantasy, was something very different. To feel lust was nothing; but what it had revealed, like lightning playing along a landscape at night, was the outline of his life: "This is what I have always been doing: getting money out of women."

That deathly piece of self-knowledge: that he and Constance, whom he thought so wicked, were exactly alike.

Mr Beluncle went home. His first words when he stood in the hall of his house were :

"How is Henry? Has he been up today?"

"He was up for an hour but I made him go back. I wish you'd get the doctor to him," Ethel said.

"Now, now!" said Mr Beluncle.

Mr Beluncle went straight up to his son's room.

"Please don't shout at him," begged Mrs Beluncle, on the stairs.

"Shout? I don't shout! He's my son as well as yours," said Mr Beluncle, with jealousy.

"I mean, don't argue about Mrs Parkinson with him," said Ethel.

"I don't argue," said Mr Beluncle.

"Well, whatever it is," pleaded Ethel.

Since Henry had collapsed at the office and had lain in bed gaunt with fever, Mr Beluncle had gone to his room at once when he came home every evening. He arrived there with his hat still on his head and his umbrella in his hand, pushing past his wife, standing embarrassed by the sight of his son. Mr Beluncle did not know what to say. He smiled. Then he said, "Hello, old chap." Then he murmured "Excuse me" very politely, and respectfully took off his hat. He had told Mrs Robinson how his son had been taken ill. Every time he went to the tea shop she asked him, "How is your son?" "He is very ill," Mr Beluncle said.

Mr Beluncle took a deep breath; he could feel passion like an anthem in his blood. He felt passion for his wife, passion for his son and knew their passion too.

Mr Beluncle talked to Henry about his day and Mrs Beluncle stood there, blinking, nervous, watching her husband, ready to stop him if he talked about the Purification.

"I don't know what your mother's worrying about," Mr Beluncle said. It was a way of saying that he loved his son as much as Ethel did. Henry knew this. With the langour of the ill he regarded with detachment the curious bidding of their love. He thought it extraordinary that he could rely on the love of his father.

"I thought you were going to get up today," Mr Beluncle teased.

"I did for an hour," Henry said, "then I came back."

"Back to bed?" said Mr Beluncle incredulously.

"You can see he's in bed," snapped Ethel. "He's ill. Can't you use your eyes? The boy's ill, very ill. He needs a doctor. He's as weak as a rat."

"All right, all right. I know," Mr Beluncle said.

"Leave it," he wanted to say, "to *my* passion. I can do anything."

"You must get better quickly," said Mr Beluncle, "if you're going to France."

"France?" said Henry.

"Yes, France, France. Parlez-vous français," said Mr Beluncle gaily.

"When am I going to France?" said Henry, leaning up on his elbow.

My God, thought Mr Beluncle, he *is* ill. Look at his thin cheeks.

"Get better. I want you to go to France. I suppose you've got money."

"Twenty pounds," said Henry.

"That's not enough. We shall have to see what your old father can do," said Mr Beluncle.

Henry frowned.

"You're not going to send him to France," said Ethel.

"Listen to your mother," laughed Mr Beluncle. "Finest experience in the world. Six months, a year in France."

Henry looked unbelievingly at his father and reluctantly, cautiously, enquiringly smiled.

"Look at him," said Mr Beluncle. "He's well already."

Mr Beluncle went downstairs. The decision had come to him in the train: lust had seized his son. This was no new thought to Mr Beluncle; but before, he had fought the love affair of his son on general grounds. Now he could see the true nature of the violent temptation Henry must have had. No wonder this love affair was at the bottom of his illness. The boy was in terrible temptation. Useless to forbid him. One must fight beside him. Send him away, give him his real desire.

"Henry must be saved," Mr Beluncle said, "from ever going to that tea shop again.

"I should say," Mr Beluncle corrected himself, "bookshop—where Miss Phibbs is."

The next day Mr Beluncle left his office in the afternoon, took a taxi, and again was in the West End. The dream came with him. Since he had woken up in the morning it had been round his arms and legs and his head like invisible strands of wool, and it would not have been surprising if someone had stopped him and said, "Excuse me, look what you are dragging after you."

He could not exactly remember the dream; he was beginning to wonder whether the woman had been Mary Phibbs. But he was totally certain that she was *not* Mrs Robinson and his main impression was that a decision had been made.

He got out of the taxi in Piccadilly and walked towards the

tea shop. He was not a man to run away from anything.
He looked at the window and between two large boxes of
chocolates he found a gap in the partition. Through that he
could see the crowd having tea in the shop, the men sitting
up at the counter, and the golden cap of Mrs Robinson's
hair. She was giving a twist to a paper bag, taking some
money and calling and pointing to one of her girls in her
commanding way.

He waited. He waited for the electric shock of lust. There
was no shock at all.

Mr Beluncle raised his chin. He had known there would
not be one. He marched away with the joy of a Marine
Band. His heart trumpeted with delight. He had conquered.
He was free.

"I was mad," said Mr Beluncle.

What a potentiality for evil had revealed itself; now it
was a potentiality for the good. After the cold mad wave,
the spicy breeze, the warm and generous sea. Mr Beluncle
felt himself swept along. Now for the good life, now for the
Kingdom, now for fidelity.

Fidelity to Mrs Truslove, of course. He had never been
tempted by infidelity to his wife; she had no money. But the
money of Mrs Robinson had tempted him to be unfaithful
to the money of Mrs Truslove. Here he was, a man who had
turned down an openly proferred crime. He owed it to
Mrs Truslove to make restitution.

EPILOGUE

"I want to speak to Mr Beluncle."

Mr Chilly heard Mrs Truslove's voice on the telephone.

"Mr Beluncle is out," said Mr Chilly. "I am most awfully
sorry. If there is anything I can do, but no, you want to
speak to him, oh dear. Where is he? In the West End. Yes,
he's at the showroom. Well, we've had such a rush, please
don't worry about it. He has put me in charge here and he's

gone straight there. How, if I may enquire, how is your dear sister? Oh, I'm sorry. Oh, **how** worrying for you."

"I can't get away from here," Mrs Truslove said. "Yes, the sea is nice. I have brought her here. No, he can't telephone to me. There is no telephone in the house. I asked him for the letters. I have had nothing for a fortnight. . . ."

"Oh, don't worry, Mrs Truslove. Please don't get anything on your mind. I am sure you have enough as it is. I will tell Mr Beluncle. I did tell him. He's been so busy with the buil . . . Oh dear, I oughtn't to have said anything. Oh dear, my tongue. Nothing, nothing, just a little—nothing. Wait a minute, here *is* Mr Beluncle. Oh no, I'm sorry, I thought it was Mr Beluncle.

"My dear," said Mr Chilly, ringing off and speaking to Miss Vanner, "I'm awful. Help me."

Miss Vanner struggled.

"If I can be of any value in rendering assistance," she wished to say, but Mr Chilly paralysed her word-making faculty.

"What?" was all she could say.

"Oh, Miss Vanner," said Mr Chilly, "you are charm itself. I nearly did it. I nearly told her Mr Beluncle's surprise."

Miss Vanner could not express it in this way but what she wished to say was that she understood he was querying in confidence whether by nearly happening to mention the word "builders" on the phone, Mr Chilly had evinced a lack of diplomacy.

"You mean," said Miss Vanner, "she's rumbled you."

"My dear Miss Vanner," said Mr Chilly, "that is my horrid dread.

"But you know, Miss Vanner," said Mr Chilly, "I have had a terrible thought. You can't imagine what is going on in my mind. Or can you? You know what I think it was, Miss Vanner, made me say 'builders' on that horrible thing."

And Mr Chilly pointed to the telephone lying in its coil of wires.

"The unconscious, my dear," said Mr Chilly, nodding

severely at her. "I mean, my dear, it does seem peculiar, don't you think, Mr Beluncle hasn't *told* her he's moving the whole office to the West End. I mean, after all, she is a director. I mean, when you're married, your husband will think it *odd* when he comes home in the evening to find you've moved next door."

Mr Chilly stared at her.

"Or not?" said Mr Chilly.

"Oh, I do wish Henry were here," sighed Mr Chilly. "I have such haunting doubts."

"Yes," said Miss Vanner, giving up the struggle with her vocabulary and made angry by Mr Chilly's longing for Henry.

"Where's the money coming from? Who's got the dibs? Someone's," said Miss Vanner, making a very ugly mouth, "a sucker. A girl can see a lot. More than some."

Another day and Mr Beluncle telephoned. The partitions were down, he said.

"The partitions," said Mr Chilly to Miss Vanner, ringing off, "are down."

Miss Vanner's eyes were frightened when she looked at the eyes of Mr Chilly.

At the end of the week, another call from Mr Beluncle.

"The painting has begun," Mr Chilly said.

He sat down and seemed to hang a weak hand for her to gaze at. She put her own hand on the desk.

"Off white," he said. His voice appeared to come from a crypt.

Miss Vanner's eyes widened with increasing fear at the information of Mr Chilly.

"In a week we shall expect to have the Turkey carpet fitted," said Mr Chilly.

A day slid by, a night closed down upon Mrs Truslove and her sister in a room looking on to the sea at Bexhill, a new day came and Mr Chilly put down the telephone and said to Miss Vanner:

"What furniture would you suggest? I mean, I am sure you are always thinking of your——" He paused. (Was Mr

Chilly ill? Why did a hiss come so often into his voice?)
"Of your *nest*," hissed Mr Chilly.

"We've got our three-piece. It's at mother's," said Miss
Vanner rapidly, taken off her guard.

"I mean," said Mr Chilly, "suppose you were moving
your offices to the West End at a time when owing to world
conditions, the possibility of a general *conflagration* . . ." (Mr
Chilly tipped his eyes back and Miss Vanner filled hers to
bursting.) "I mean, trade was ebbing, in fact, had ebbed;
and—just a moment—owing to the unforeseen absence of
your partner due to an unfortunate family illness, you had
been unable to deal with one or two letters with a rather
legal turn of phrase . . ."

"Don't," said Miss Vanner, putting both hands to her
hair. "Don't! I shall scream."

"I mean, would you choose real Chippendale?" said Mr
Chilly. "At the price? I mean—it's a question, isn't it? I
begin to ask myself where does God get all this stuff from?"

Miss Vanner narrowed her eyes:

"Mr Beluncle's barmy, he's nuts," she said.

"That's what worries me!" exclaimed Mr Chilly. "You
have put your finger on it, you delightful girl—*is* he barmy?
Or is he . . . well, d'you see what I mean?"

The telephone rang again.

"It's Mrs Truslove!" said Mr Chilly, putting his hand
over the mouthpiece. "Oh God! I can't *bear* this kind of
thing. I shall die. I know I shall say something. . . ."

"Hullo, Mrs Truslove. Good morning. My dear, no reply
from the showroom? There was. He wasn't *there*? Oh, but
he must be. Yes, I am quite sure. They can't have cut the
telephone. I mean, he must have been at the back in the
Board Room."

Mr Chilly clapped his hand to the mouthpiece.

"Damn!" he said. "Did you hear that? I said it. What
shall I do? I couldn't say lavatory, could I?

"Hullo, Mrs Truslove," said Mr Chilly. "How is your
sister this morning? Oh, I'm so sorry, how worrying. What
does the doctor say? Oh, my dear Mrs Truslove. . . ."

Mr Beluncle stepped back from the builders' ladders and boards to let the man and boy who had laid the Turkey carpet go by. Alone now, he went into the room at the back which they had left.

He had been thinking of something unpleasant; well, not unpleasant, but about human nature. It rather shocked him. He had been stopped in the street that morning by Miss Wix.

"I want to speak to you, Mr Beluncle," she said.

"Conversation is free," Mr Beluncle had said.

"About your son," she said. "Your son has broken that poor girl's heart. You know I am referring to Mary Phibbs."

"I am not aware," Mr Beluncle had begun. He told Miss Wix a number of things he was not aware of. She was wheeling a bicycle. He did not object to her wheeling a bicycle, but one would have thought that a prominent member of the Church of the Last Purification would have been able, after all these years, to have "cleared her thought of what was holding her back" and to have had a car. A small point, he thought, but significant.

But that was not the unpleasant thing. There was a split in Mrs Parkinson's Group. Lady Roads had gone too far, Miss Wix said. To make the lame to walk was good—but not if, like Lady Roads, you did it by the wicked power of animal magnetism and personality which could be summed up in two words: Rome and Witchcraft.

A terrible thing human nature, Mr Beluncle had been thinking. Miss Wix and forty members (Mr Phibbs, of course, among them) had marched out of the Boystone Church. They were meeting over Dorman's Restaurant.

But now the hammering had stopped in the showroom and the men had gone, he dismissed the matter from his mind.

He opened the door and looked at the room. It was excellent. The walls were painted pale green. Heavy cream curtains hung over the two frosted windows. He switched on the lights and drew the curtains and the light brought richness to the Turkey carpet, the huge table, and brought out the winy lustre of the Chippendale chairs. Four clocks—he had not yet decided which one to buy; he really wanted all of them—chattered on the mantelpiece. He picked up a small shaving from the carpet and looked, with his insulting look, at the perfect place. It was the Board Room. His first Board Room and he was fifty years of age.

How (he had asked himself at the end of that unnerving period of his life, less than six weeks gone, when God had helped him to master the terrible temptation of Mrs Robinson in the teashop)—how could he use the great energy which the rejection of sin had left him with? Surely by some spectacular affirmation. Surely by showing Mrs Truslove that he was absolutely faithful to her; surely by offering her concrete evidence of his years of devotion and gratitude.

What were Mrs Truslove and himself? They were directors of a company. What do directors do? They run the company. What is the object of running a company? To make money. How do you make money? By expansion, surely. How does a business expand? What is the sign of expansion? Acquiring new directors. What is needed for new directors? A Board Room. Mr Beluncle had hit upon the fatal deficiency of Bulux Ltd. It had a factory. It had a small showroom in the West End; but it had never had a Board Room. It was buried in a slum. The whole floor in the West End was vacant. Unmistakably the Voice had spoken to him.

Mr Beluncle put the chairs round the table. He saw the crowded scene, the blotters, the blank sheets of paper, himself at the end, rising from his chair.

"Gentlemen," he was saying.

The telephone rang in the front part of the building. He let it ring. But it rang and rang. In irritation he went back across the disorganised rooms outside where the general offices were going to be and he answered. Mr Chilly, never good on the telephone, was speaking.

"Good evening, sir. I am sorry to trouble you, sir. I hope I do not disturb, sir. It's a telegram, sir."

"All right, sir. Read it, sir," said Mr Beluncle, irritated to the point of mockery.

"It is from Mrs Truslove, sir," the voice of Mr Chilly said.

"It was sent—my dear" (Mr Chilly was talking to Miss Vanner), "what does it say at the top?"

Mr Beluncle said, "There is no need to bother about the top. The top of a telegram is nothing. What does it say at the bottom, that's the point."

"At the bottom, sir, of course. I think," said Mr Chilly, "I will get Miss Vanner, sir, to read it, sir. She is standing beside me now. Miss Vanner . . ."

Miss Vanner read a telegram sent off at 4.15 from Bexhill:

Judy died this afternoon. Tuberculosis. Truslove.

Mr Beluncle went back to the Board Room where he had left his hat. He was out of breath and the smell of paint made him feel sick. He drew back the curtains and let air and the noise of the traffic into the room. Even that did not annul the gritty, pointless chatter of the clocks which gossiped forward into featureless years to come where no miracles occurred. Mr Beluncle sat down.

He could guess what was going to happen now. He could foresee exactly the state of mind of Mrs Truslove after this. He could hear what his wife would say. To have died at this moment!

"I thought when I heard it," Mr Beluncle said, "it was going to be mother."

Mr Beluncle shut the window and sat down at the end of the Board Room table and closed his eyes to pray.

"I deny it," he began. "It hasn't happened. I absolutely deny this seeming occurrence. It's a mistake, a dream and—by the way, I'll give you a thought there, where is the dream when you wake up?"

Mr Beluncle opened his eyes. He recognised that in his deep fear he was not praying and that, even worse, he was giving no thought for the grief of Mrs Truslove. What she must have suffered! The stress she must have lived under!

"She won't want this," he said, looking round at the Board Room. "She'll want," he said, surprised by his own power of intuition, "a change."

There came to him the sound of voices, men clearing their

throats, settling into chairs. The Board Room was filling up, and, presently, giving a tap on the table, Mr Beluncle rose and began again:

"Gentlemen . . ."

It was a simple, moving speech. He told the meeting how he had worked for years with the inestimable aid of Mrs Truslove, and how now the time to retire had come. The negotiations just concluded, he said, had been successful. One or two members might think, had indeed suggested, that the purchase price put on the Company was high. (A voice: "It ought to be higher.") Well, he would describe it as not unsatisfactory. He only wished . . .

But here the spokesman of the buyers rose up. No price could really be too high, he said, for a concern once owned by Mr Beluncle and, for years, subsidised by the infinite resources of the Divine Mind. In his own speech Mr Beluncle had spoken of his gratitude to Mrs Truslove and of her need for a rest; but Mr Beluncle must not forget himself. Mr Beluncle needed a rest. A long rest. A voyage abroad, per- haps. Yes, Mr Beluncle ought to go abroad. He had worked; he had made a modest fortune; he had showered benefits on his partner; surely it was his turn now. And let him not con- fine himself to the South Coast towns. There was the Riviera, there was the Taj Mahal, there was the Nile; and (the speaker added, he would give them a thought there) the point about infinity is that it really is infinite, only we in our benighted belief in money . . .

Mr Beluncle woke up.

It was the first but it was also the last function to be held by a director of Bulux Ltd. in that room.

At the factory, Mr Chilly was saying to Miss Vanner:

"What is a writ? I mean, one reads of them, of course, one hears of them, but what does it look like?"

Miss Vanner's face became transfigured with importance and fear. She was carried without thought into one of her few successful interchanges with Mr Chilly.

"I have never been in receipt of such a document," she said. "Oh, don't say we . . ."

Mr Chilly stopped her from wrecking her perfect sentence:

"My dear," he said, "do you know, I rather think we shall have one all to ourselves—tomorrow. We shall see."

"Oh, Mr Chilly, what a dreadful thing. Poor Mrs Truslove. Her sister—like that," cried Miss Vanner.

"I fancy it will be from Mrs Truslove," said Mr Chilly.

Miss Vanner opened her mouth, but no sound came from it.

"Now, my pet," said Mr Chilly, putting his arm round her, for she was going to the door. "No, my dear," he said. "Not all over the office. No spreading of the sad news. If you would get your coat and hat, if you would like to toddle with me to some little place—I feel much has been going on which I have not understood and you with your inside knowledge—Henry, you know, never knew a thing. I might have put my money into a mission for all that boy could tell me."

"One sec. and I'll be outside—round the corner," said Miss Vanner fiercely. "My God! A mission, you're right!"

"Or a poem?" said Mr Chilly, detaining her. "Hiawatha's bankruptcy. You shall hear how . . ."

Miss Vanner's mouth stiffened with doubt—even now, just when all her inside knowledge was ready to flow, there was something dubious in Mr Chilly. Was he getting at her? Or was he—oh, but of course, that was what it was: he was a gentleman, he was concealing his feelings, "hiding his ruin," she was able to quote, "behind the gambler's impassive mask."

Miss Vanner fetched her coat.

READING GROUP GUIDE

1. "For Pritchett," writes Darin Strauss in his introduction, "radical religion (and the rejection of it) was a means to examine hypocrisy, self-discovery, the influence of one's parents, the price of nonconformity, and the warped vanity of the outcast." Discuss.

2. How would you describe Philip Beluncle's marriage to Ethel, and how does this compare with the oddly intimate relationship he shares with his business partner, Mrs. Truslove?

3. "I am in the middle of the family," thinks George. "I am going to be the bad son; perhaps that will attract their attention." How would you describe the distinctive roles that Henry, George, and Leslie Beluncle serve in the Beluncle family? How do they relate to their parents and grandmother?

4. According to the writer and scholar John Bayley, "Pritchett had a delicate sense of the way people live inside clichés." Can you find evidence of this in *Mr. Beluncle*? Which charac-

ters seem based on stereotypes, and is Pritchett successful in turning them into unique and compelling individuals?

5. "If there is one thing I am proud to say of myself," says Mr. Beluncle, "it is that money has never governed my life. Money has never entered my calculations. I have seen the hell it creates, the lives it wrecks." Is Mr. Beluncle's self-assessment accurate? How does money, or the lack thereof, serve as a recurring theme in the novel?

6. Describe the miracle that Mrs. Dykes experiences. What, or who, do you think is responsible for it? How does it change her, and what impact does it have on Mrs. Truslove, Mr. Beluncle, and the community as a whole?

7. "What the old Hetley hated in the new Hetley was its suburban attempt at perfection and privacy," writes Pritchett. "People who went in for privacy were trying to rise in the world, to cut themselves off. The Dykeses were an example of this. Postman's daughters and already, shutting themselves off, seeking other society, taking up with a new religion from London, the Dykeses had broken their ties and were claiming to be better than their neighbors." What do you think of Pritchett's depiction of upward mobility in mid-twentieth-century Britain? Which characters have the highest social standing, and who is on the bottom of this social hierarchy? Where does the Beluncle family fit in?

8. What is your impression of Pritchett's depiction of love, courtship, and marriage as depicted in this novel? How does he portray motherhood and the relationships between mothers and sons?

9. According to John Bayley, V. S. Pritchett, in concluding his fictional narratives, "leaves a plurality of existences to run on apart, after they have come together for the duration of his story." After reading the epilogue, what do you suppose will happen to the principal characters in *Mr. Beluncle*?

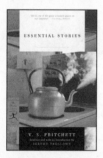

MODERN LIBRARY IS ONLINE AT
WWW.MODERNLIBRARY.COM

MODERN LIBRARY ONLINE IS YOUR GUIDE
TO CLASSIC LITERATURE ON THE WEB

THE MODERN LIBRARY E-NEWSLETTER

Our free e-mail newsletter is sent to subscribers, and features sample chapters, interviews with and essays by our authors, upcoming books, special promotions, announcements, and news.

To subscribe to the Modern Library e-newsletter, send a blank e-mail to: **sub_modernlibrary@info.randomhouse.com** or visit **www.modernlibrary.com**

THE MODERN LIBRARY WEBSITE

Check out the Modern Library website at
www.modernlibrary.com for:

- The Modern Library e-newsletter
- A list of our current and upcoming titles and series
- Reading Group Guides and exclusive author spotlights
- Special features with information on the classics and other paperback series
- Excerpts from new releases and other titles
- A list of our e-books and information on where to buy them
- The Modern Library Editorial Board's 100 Best Novels and 100 Best Nonfiction Books of the Twentieth Century written in the English language
- News and announcements

Questions? E-mail us at **modernlibrary@randomhouse.com**
For questions about examination or desk copies, please visit
the Random House Academic Resources site at
www.randomhouse.com/academic